I, JUDAS

This Book Is Dedicated to
Our Late Editor and Friend,
Lee Barker,
Whose Idea It Was

FOREWORD

WHEN THE CHRISTIAN ROMAN EMPEROR Justinian destroyed the great and famous library in Alexandria—which contained much of the wisdom of the world—in A.D. 500, very few of the mighty books survived, and very few of the priceless parchments written by sages. Thus humanity has been forever denied access to the gathered learning, erudition, knowledge, science, literature, poetry, and enlightenment of ages previous to Christ—and all in the name of "preserving the purity of Christianity from the corruption of pagan writings." So said the new Christian convert, Justinian, with edifying virtue.

However, a small portion was saved from the fire, either by accident or by the action of a few quiet men who loved wisdom. Among these men was one Christian Egyptian monk, Iberias, a very learned man of an ancient Alexandrian family. He had found a partly charred manuscript, on durable Egyptian parchment, among the ruins of the awesome library, and he concealed it under his robes and took it back to his cave in the Valley of the Kings, the burial place of the Pharaohs. There, by concealed candlelight or by the light of a smoking oil lamp, he read the manuscript, which was written in highly polished Greek with some extrapolations in erudite Latin, and he understood that this book had not been written by some crude, partly literate scribe, but by a gentleman of education.

He discovered that the manuscript was really a long diary of a man's agonized hegira through life, and that the man's name was Judas Iscariot, and it was explained by the writer that Judas was the son of a rich and powerful Pharisee Jew family who lived in Jerusalem but who also possessed a small palace in Alexandria and another in Cairo. (His actual name was Judah-bar-Simon. He was also the son of Leah-bas-Ezekiel, daughter of Ezekiel-bar-Jacob, whose uncle was a member of the Jewish Supreme Court in Jerusalem—the Sanhedrin.)

The monk Iberias was astounded as he read the manuscript to discover that Judas Iscariot was not the impoverished thief depicted by tradition and by revolted writers, but a rich young man in his own right who had abandoned his devoted family and his wealth to espouse voluntary poverty—in order to follow one he truly believed was the Messiah of the ages, Joshua-bar-Joseph, a Nazarene born in Bethlehem of a virgin named Miriam-bas-Jochan, whose mother was one humble Hannah of Nazareth. (Later, Joshua was called Jesus by the Romans and Christos by the Greeks.)

Because Iberias was a prudent man, fearful of denunciation as a heretic, and a man of learning himself who feared the ignorant, he hid the manuscript carefully, for he was fascinated by the terrible story written on the parchment. He often found himself in tears when meditating on it. He knew he dared not reveal the manuscript to his brethren, who firmly believed that Judas was a thief and a betrayer who had sought thirty pieces of silver in his greed. (Acceptance of thirty pieces of silver was mandatory under the laws of the Sanhedrin, for it indicated that the betrayer had revealed his knowledge in good faith—a refusal of the silver assured the judges that the betrayer had lied.) So the puzzling fact in the Bible, that Judas threw away the thirty pieces of silver a little later—he who was supposed to have rendered up his Lord for gain—was explained in the manuscript.

There were a few intellectuals among Iberias' brethren, men he trusted, and so he let them read the manuscript in secret. On his deathbed he conveyed the document to a beloved younger monk, and for centuries it was kept hidden in monasteries, to be read by other trusted men. It was taken all over Asia, and Europe and Africa, to be studied with reverence by a very few who were also terrified of the new arrogant and ruthless ecclesiastics rising from recently pagan societies who believed that all past wisdom and learning and writing were accursed by God (whose authors were doubtlessly in hell with all the countless multitudes born before the Christ). The truly Christian and enlightened lived in fear of these new ecclesiastics who interpreted Christianity individually and in accordance with their own bias, even if often they engaged in conflict with the Holy Father, the Pope. (The history of the Church teems with accounts of these conflicts.)

The manuscript finally came into the hands of a notable German family, lateral descendants of a bishop, and they kept the manuscript hidden for fear of confiscation and destruction. When the German family fell under the suspicious scrutiny of the Nazis, they were forced to flee to Portugal, leaving all their possessions behind, including the manuscript. These were seized by the Nazis. But a German officer who secretly loathed Hitler and feared for his country stole the manuscript and bid it himself, knowing that if the Nazis found it it would be destroyed as "the work of a Jew" which therefore had no verity and no value.

The manuscript has just been revealed by a member of that German family to whom it was returned. It has been carefully translated. And the reader may judge its quality for himself. But that Judas Iscariot was the son of a rich and famous Pharisee family, and himself heir to a fortune, is clearly beyond dispute.

I, JUDAS

CHAPTER ONE

JUDAS

HOW CAN ANY JEW REST while the invader still stalks his land!

My own heart is aflame.

How long, O Lord, are we to bear this tyranny? How long shall the hand of the oppressor grind us into the dust and girdle our head with thorns? I grieve for the dead but more for the living who die a thousand deaths every day. Where is our ancient pride, where the Joshuas and Davids and Maccabees who subdued adversaries as hateful as Rome?

The city is appalled, but no hand is raised against the despot, nay, not even an outcry, so craven have we become. There are only dark mutterings by the great unwashed, the humble peasants and shopkeepers, the Amharetzin, whom no decent Pharisee or Sadducee would so much as spit at.

What matters that these dead are Galileans? They are still blood of our blood, soul of our soul, worshipping the same God. They were defenseless, unarmed, unsuspecting. Some huddled over their young, others threw themselves between the soldiers and their wives and sisters. The Romans spared nobody, young or old. There was no resistance. How does one resist in God's own place of worship?

The bodies, grotesquely sprawled on the cobbled pavement, were strewn not only over the Court of Gentiles, but even into the Court of Israel, where some had scurried for refuge.

The massacre occurred only that morning, and many of the bodies were still warm. The Levites who toiled in the Temple were carting away the corpses and ministering to the wounded. The moans assailed my ears, and I gritted my teeth. Shaking my fist, I looked up from the littered courtyard to the Fortress Antonia and saw the red-cloaked myrmidons of Rome idly chatting. What is Jewish sorrow to these pagans? I saw a tall, commanding figure, his hairless dome of a scalp gleaming in the sun, looking down on the hell below. I could almost see the smile on the thin cruel lips. Pontius Pilate, the Procurator of Judea, was enjoying his day.

Walking rapidly, to put the melancholy scene behind me, I passed through the Court of Israel, into the Court of Women, and finally the Court of Priests. I turned past the Temple guards and moved into an antechamber, where a guard let me through at mention of my name.

My summons had come from Joseph Caiaphas, High Priest by virtue of his marriage to the daughter of a High Priest. Though I had little in common with these collaborators of Rome, I responded at once, out of curiosity if nothing more.

I paused before a gilded door. In a moment it was flung open by a Levite attendant. A man considerably shorter than myself was standing at a window, looking out on the courtyard below.

"A pretty sight, is it not?" I said.

He faced me without any warmth or seeming interest. "Come, let us talk," he said coldly. I ignored the proffered chair and we stood staring at each other, the High Priest with a faintly ironic gleam in his dark eyes.

"I have a mission for you, Judas-bar-Simon," he said finally.

I regarded him mistrustfully. "What does a Sadducee friend of the Romans want with me?"

He had lost some of his customary aplomb, and one had only to look out the window to understand why.

"Normally," he said defensively, "the Romans allow us to manage our own affairs."

"Of course," I said. "On the holiest of holidays, the Day of Atonement, the High Priest must beg the Romans for the sacred vestments with which he performs his office. And this is independence!"

The color rushed to his cheeks. "We must learn to live with Rome. The rest of the world does. We have our own courts, administer our own religion, and collect our own taxes."

"Yes," I said, "and we bury our own dead."

A ripple of impatience ruffled that haughty face.

"We have privileges. This is the only province which need not serve in the armies of the Emperor. But if we Judeans do not maintain the peace, the Romans will maintain it for us. Yes"—he shut me off with a wave of the hand—"yes, just as they do today."

His high-bridged nose wrinkled in disdain. “I warned the Galileans, knowing the temper of Pilate, but they only smiled in that idiotic way of theirs.” His voice rose angrily as if by their imprudence they had created a problem that justified the fate that had overtaken them.

“What business was it of theirs that Pilate took the money from the Temple treasury to build his aqueduct from the Bethlehem Pool to his fortress when the pools outside the city ran dry?”

“Solomon’s Pool is sacred to all Jews for its healing waters, and so this was no provincial matter.”

Caiaphas laughed harshly. “Pilate mistook them for Judeans. Naturally, he couldn’t tell one Jew from the other.”

“The Galileans have courage.”

“This is no time for courage,” he said darkly.

“You speak to one whose namesake drove the invaders into the seas.”

“The Romans are not Syrians, and there is no Judas Maccabee on the horizon.”

I ignored his Hellenized version of Judah, for so they did with every name, even the Messiah. “There is one greater than the Maccabees who will restore Israel to its ancient glories,” I said.

He sneered. “I have known a dozen Messiases. They sprout like the winter wheat, these false prophets, and harvest only trouble for the nation.”

How could he mock what all Israel was pining for? “Isaiah told us where to look for him, and when.”

“He said that we would not know him when he came.”

“The Sadducees have no faith in the Prophets,” I said.

He had recovered some of his aplomb by now.

“We have an interest in the Messias, but we must be sure of him.”

“Without faith how can you be sure? ‘And so he came and we knew him not.’ But he will be known, as he leads Israel in triumph over all nations.”

His eyes held a glint of curiosity. “How will you know him?”

“He shall have been born in Bethlehem, of the House of David. His mother shall be a virgin, and though a King in bearing and tradition, he shall ride meekly into Jerusalem on an ass.”

Caiaphas shook his head in mock despair.

“This drivel is for the poor and the shiftless, the Amharetzin and their ilk. Who can take the son of Simon of Kerioth seriously when he speaks like a shopkeeper?”

"I am not my father's son in all things. I am a Zealot, and care not who knows it."

"Speak not so freely," said Caiaphas, lowering his voice, as if fearful even to be seen with somebody of this party.

"We are zealous for Israel, zealous for the Messiah, and zealous against Rome," I said, enjoying myself thoroughly. "Is there any crime in this?"

He motioned significantly toward the window. "What crime was there in that?"

"To demonstrate is one thing, to talk another. The Romans understand the importance of action. For this reason they rule the Greeks, who call them uncultured, and the Jews, who think them barbarians. Give the Caesars their blood money, rattle no sabers, and you may talk day and night."

My nerves were still taut from what I had observed in the courtyard, and I was drawn irresistibly to the window once more.

"Pilate will pay dearly for this one day," I cried.

"Remember, they are only Galileans, and, as our fathers said"—his voice contained that familiar sneer—"what good comes out of Galilee?"

"Anyone who opposes Rome is my friend."

"Waste no tears on these clods. They are not of any tribe, but mere converts, who speak only the language of Syrian Aram, and that not well."

"I care not about their Aramaic tongue. They suffer because they are Jews like us."

"Like us?" The heavy eyelids, blackened with kohl, widened sardonically.

"What have Sadducees and Pharisees to do with Galileans?"

The gulf I felt was not that great. "Someday they will stand side by side with the Zealots, from Dan to Beersheba."

Caiaphas gave me a pitying glance. "And how will this be accomplished?"

"The Messiah will lead us."

"What makes you so sure that he even lives?"

"There was a Sibylline prophecy told to Herod the Great on his deathbed that his line would be superseded by a newborn King of Kings. Before he expired Herod ordered the execution of every male under two years in Judea. This massacre of the innocents was in the reign of Caesar Augustus thirty years ago. And that child should now be ready for his ministry."

Caiaphas shook his head incredulously. "Even so, what assurance do you have the child survives?"

"The Prophets tell us that the child was spirited off to Egypt by his parents and raised there till it was safe to return."

We stood looking at each other, with thinly veiled hostility, I wondering why he had summoned me, and he, no doubt, thinking the same. The silence was broken by a rustling at the door. Two men slipped quietly into the chamber. I would have known them anywhere.

"We have come from Pilate," said the older man, whom all of Israel would have known from his gray forked beard and tall conical hat. "For once he realizes he has acted hastily."

This was not the Pilate I had observed in his tower, but I saw no point in arguing the matter.

"Peace unto you, O Annas," I said, barely touching his hand.

His companion came forward and offered me an embrace.

"And how," said the teacher Gamaliel, "does it go with the son of my dear Simon?"

"My father would be surprised," I said stiffly, "to find his Gamaliel in this company on so dark a day for Israel."

"Judah, Judah," he cried, "one day your impulsive nature will do you great harm. Is it any sin for the young to listen to the gray beards?"

Though short and slight, the Rabbi Gamaliel radiated a grandeur beyond even his position as head of the Sanhedrin. He had an air of openness, but there was a glint of steel under that easy exterior. Annas showed him a certain deference in overlooking my remark.

"You are here because of the Reb Gamaliel," he said coldly. "He feels the fruit does not fall far from the tree."

I was not to be led off by flattery. "It is unlawful for the tribes to have anything to do with another nation. And the Sadducees dine and wine their Roman friends, and do their bidding in all things. We call ourselves Jews and our capital cities are Caesarea and Tiberias. We worship in Hellenized synagogues, and are governed by a Hellenized Sanhedrin. Small wonder that the Pharisees have greater respect from the people as interpreters of the Torah."

Annas' face grew grim. "You were not summoned to lecture the rulers of your state."

"What rulers and what state?" I cried. "If not for the peasants I see in the streets, I would think I was in Rome."

Annas turned with a sardonic smile to my old mentor. The Pharisee leader spoke to me gently.

"Pharisees and Sadducees," he said, "must keep a common cause if we are to survive long enough to greet the Messiah promised by the prophet Daniel."

"That time is already here. Even the Romans know of the coming of the King of Kings."

"They have already found their divinity," said Annas drily. He flipped a Roman shekel out of his purse, and held the inscription to the light. "Caesar Augustus, son of the God."

I whipped out a coin, a Jewish silver shekel, which I held up in plain view. On one side it said clearly: "Jerusalem the Holy." On the other were three lilies, and the legend: "I shall be as the dew unto Israel. He shall grow as the Lily."

Annas managed a bleak smile. "Do we have three Messiases to deal with?"

"I know not the meaning of this trinity. But he shall come and the people shall adore him."

Caiaphas had not spoken for some time. He turned querulously now, appealing to the others. "How can this hothead be trusted with so delicate a mission?"

"We can use some of that fire, properly transmuted," said Gamaliel with a tolerant smile.

He rested his hand on my shoulder. "We share the same desire," he said softly, "that same burning excitement over the prospect of the Messiah. The whole land is eagerly awaiting him. Some say he is already here, others that he will be shortly."

"It cannot be too soon."

"It has been too soon," Annas put in wryly. "Judas the Galilean called himself the Messias and two thousand Jews died for his folly. The Romans make short work of revolutionaries."

"True," acknowledged Gamaliel, "there are the false prophets, but one day there will be that one."

Annas gave him a speculative glance. "Our law stipulates that any presumed Messias must be examined by a Council of the Sanhedrin. Otherwise, he has no standing and is to be prosecuted as an impostor or worse. Better for one to die than a nation to perish."

"The High Priest is right," said Gamaliel. "The Romans are not ones to brook uprisings. The Galilean summoned five thousand to arms under the Maccabean banner: 'To God alone belongs dominion.' The bands attacked the legions, and drove the tax collectors out For a spell, they savored the sweet smell of victory. But the long arm of Rome brought reinforcements from Parthia and Syria, and the broadsword triumphed as usual. The Galilean's forces were hunted down like animals in the mountains and caves.

The leaders were nailed to the cross. Others were carted off to the slave markets and the galleys. This lesson the Romans repeat every so often. Let us not provide them a new opportunity."

The conversation suddenly struck me as amusing. "We sit here and chatter about things we all know and Pontius Pilate does as he pleases."

"Pilate," said Annas, "is no ordinary governor. In the thirty provinces of the Empire, only one procurator is permitted the company of his wife abroad."

"And of what moment is that?"

"Some say Claudia Procula is the natural daughter of Julia, Augustus' daughter and late wife of the Emperor Tiberius. This marriage to a Roman knight is a mark of the high favor in which Pilate is held in Rome."

"He is no more than a glorified tax collector," said I, "and would topple in a moment if there was a rising."

"You speak too boldly," chided Annas. "Nothing would suit Pilate better than a full-scale revolt. It would give him the opportunity to show Rome, by ruthlessly putting down the revolt, how valuable he might be elsewhere."

Gamaliel broke in soothingly. "We have nothing to fear from Pilate so long as we are discreet."

"Pilate takes pleasure in mocking us. He set the tone of his government on his arrival, flaunting in our faces the effigies of the Emperor in contradiction of our law. He gave in only when the protesters dared him to cut them to pieces."

"Yes, he gave in," said Gamaliel, "but he does what his ambitious master Sejanus, the new favorite, would have him do. All one has to do is look out the window."

All I knew of Tiberius' first minister came from the grapevine. As chief of the palace guard he had gained the confidence of a doddering Emperor by stealthily carrying out his darkest designs. He was as great an enemy of the Jews as Haman, having banished all Jews, except for Roman citizens, from Rome itself. And Pilate was his man.

"Pilate was dispatched to rid Israel of its customs," I said. "I have that from the younger Agrippa, Herod Antipas' brother-in-law, but it is apparent in any case. Pilate not only marched into Jerusalem flying the colors of the Twelfth Legion but put the figure of a Roman eagle over the gates of the Temple. He broods in his palace at Caesarea, and comes to the Fortress Antonia only when he means mischief to Judeans."

"The Romans," said Caiaphas, "care not how anybody worships so long as there is no resistance to their authority."

"They are very much aware that too much freedom here sows dangerous ideas in the remaining provinces."

Caiaphas gave me a sly glance. "There are other ways of conquering a people. The Romans are as much Hellenized as we."

"Agreed, and that is the danger."

"Yes, Judas." He accented the second syllable of my name.

I felt the blood rush to my face. "I call myself Judah, my Hebrew name, but cannot help what others do."

He continued to eye me sardonically. "I admire your flowered tunic of fine linen. I have seen no finer in Athens or Rome."

"What difference what we wear? It is our hearts that count."

"You, Judas, or should. I say Judah"—he smiled mockingly—"mentioned the subversion of our customs. So they call the Messiah the Messias and the Anointed, the Christ. Is this what you object to?"

Two could play the same game. "Now I hear they are considering a ban against circumcision, through the device of forbidding mutilation."

Caiaphas' eyes narrowed. "They will not interfere with Jewish worship so long as the people remain orderly and pay their taxes."

"It would surely be a scandal if the sons of the pious were not circumcised into the covenant of Abraham the customary eight days after birth."

"This is only talk. It gives Pilate pleasure to bait the Judeans."

"If the rite were proscribed," I said, "it would mean a considerable loss to the Temple."

His face quickly clouded. "The hierarchy is concerned with more basic things than money. First and foremost, we must keep Israel one."

Whatever happened in Rome was soon common gossip in Jerusalem, borne on ready tongues of the collaborators.

"There is some strange tie between Sejanus and Pilate," said Gamaliel thoughtfully, his eyes squinting into the late-afternoon sunlight. "After the convenient death of Germanicus, the next in line, Pilate, married royally and was made a Roman knight."

A thoughtful look crept into Annas' cunning face. "He was rewarded with one hand, and with the other sent to an obscure province."

"It is whispered," said Caiaphas, "that Tiberius' friend Calpurnius Piso had a potion put in Germanicus' wine."

Annas' crafty eyes lit up. "Yes, and Pilate was the instrument."

I found this petty intrigue tiresome. "But what has this to do with Israel?"

"We contend with a restless, ambitious functionary, frustrated by his exile."

"And with it all," put in Gamaliel, "he is backed to the hilt by Sejanus, who keeps him here."

I shrugged disdainfully.

"The renegade prince Agrippa told me in Rome that Sejanus would ride high for a while, then go the way of all palace favorites. The Emperor who cheerfully disposed of his own nephew will not hesitate to cut down a lesser rival."

Both Annas and Caiaphas seemed impressed by my remark, and even Gamaliel looked at me with new eyes.

"You are indeed your father's son," said Annas, with an approving glance. "We must hope for the winds of change."

I saw no distinctions between Romans. "Our great friends Pompey, Marcus Crassus, and Cassius invaded the Holy of Holies, desecrated the Ark of the Covenant, and stripped the sanctuary of its golden doors and altars. And you speak of Roman friendship."

"Their depredations have not gone unanswered." He gave that silky smile I mistrusted so much. "Think how these three died, violently, in alien lands, mocked by their enemies. The Holy One looks over the Chosen in his own way."

I shook my head vigorously. "Judah Maccabee demonstrated that God helps those who help themselves. Not until his armies conquered the Syrain hosts did God's light shine once more on Israel."

"The Lord rode with the Hasmoneans on that day," said the Reb Gamaliel, "just as he did with Joshua outside the walls of Jericho."

"Then the Lord must have approved the Maccabeans shedding blood on the Sabbath. For until the Maccabeans' revocation of the Sabbath laws, the Chosen preferred to be massacred in their homes and caves rather than defend themselves."

Annas and Caiaphas raised their eyebrows. "The Sabbath belongs to God. Anything else is blasphemy."

I made short work of such hypocrisy. "In the Temple, on Hanukkah, we celebrate the Hasmonean liberation of Israel, even though for only a hundred years. And the High Priests take sacrificial offerings, celebrating this rededication of the defiled Temple, regardless of the desecration of the Sabbath which made this holiday possible."

There was an awkward silence, which Gamaliel sought to smooth over. "The Sabbath is sacred to all Jews, Sadducees and Pharisees alike."

"Of whom there are ten thousand in a land of a million souls."

"We keep the law of Moses," said Gamaliel, "the people follow."

Suddenly, above the conversation, came the piercing trumpets summoning the faithful to prayer, and the ecstatic response of the Temple thousands crying: "Hear, O Israel, the Lord our God, the Lord is One."

The three dignitaries paused long enough to make their obeisance to the God of Abraham, Isaac, and Jacob. As they prayed, I looked out the window, letting my eyes roam from the courtyard, where the dead and injured were still being carried away, to the turrets of the Fortress Antonia, which rose high above the Temple walls.

"What does Pilate say of these murders in the Temple itself?"

Annas shrugged. "The Romans are a law unto themselves. They would lay waste to all Israel if it suited them."

"The tetrarch Herod will surely protest the death of his Galileans."

Gamaliel clucked his tongue. "Tiberius no longer listens. He enjoys the baths in Capri with his pubescent bedfellows. Sejanus rules unmolested."

"Why else," put in Caiaphas impatiently, "did Pilate attack these Galileans? He knew he could do so with impunity."

"The Romans have only three thousand troops in all of Palestine," I pointed out, "and these are nearly all mercenaries, led by only a handful of Roman centurions."

"The roads would soon be clogged with Roman troops from Syria and Egypt."

"The Zealots have no fear of Rome."

Annas favored me with his most syrupy smile. "We, for our part, are surprised at your company."

"I am only surprised," I replied, "that all of Israel hasn't rallied to the Maccabean party."

Gamaliel shook his head sadly. "Violence only begets violence, of which the Romans are past masters."

"So be it. With the help of the Messiah, the nation shall be delivered. But while Roman soldiers man these ramparts there is no freedom."

Annas stroked his long beard thoughtfully. "But first you must find the Messias. Is that not correct?"

"We will know him by his works." My voice rose with emotion, as always, when I thought of our deliverer. "'How beautiful he is,' say the Prophets, 'the Messiah King who shall arise from the House of Judah. He will gird up his loins and advance to do battle with his enemies and many kings shall be slain!'"

The Reb Gamaliel looked startled. "I see a different Messiah, born out of God's love for his people, and hating no man. He is the Prince of Peace, the Wise Counselor foreseen by the prophet Isaiah and so many others."

He recited softly from a half-forgotten psalm. "He will call the holy people together in justice. He will govern the sanctified tribes. No iniquity shall be allowed in them. And no wicked man shall remain in their midst. For God has made him strong in the spirit of holiness and rich in the shining gift of wisdom. How happy are they who shall live in this day, to see Israel rejoicing in the Assembly of the people."

It was an innocuous homily.

"I see him as he must be to accomplish that for which he has come," I retorted.

Gamaliel gave me a piercing glance. "Has it occurred to you, Judah-bar-Simon, that the Messiah you visualize is not sent to restore Israel to any temporal glory, but to redeem us from our sins? Is he not the Righteous One promised by Jeremiah?"

"It is all very clear that he comes to deliver Israel from foreign domination. As foretold by the prophet Daniel, he will make an end to our suffering as a nation."

Gamaliel smiled wanly. "There is no greater prophet in Israel than Moses, for only he was permitted to see the face of the Lord. And in his promise of a Messiah he speaks of no warrior king." The Reb's eyes lifted heavenward and became dewy with emotion. "This was Moses' promise to the twelve tribes in the desert: 'The Lord thy God will raise up unto thee a prophet from the midst of thee, of thy brethren, like unto me.'"

"Did not Moses deliver his people from the Pharaohs?"

The Reb gave a small sigh. "Think as you will, Judah-bar-Simon, you cannot alter God's plan one iota."

I strove to curb my impatience. Were these old men so blind they could not see the truth, or so afraid to face reality, lest they be compelled to make a move that would risk their precious hides?

Annas sucked in his breath impatiently.

"He is all things to all people, this Messias, and for the sake of Israel we must put to rest all these rumors agitating our people."

His cold eyes dwelt for a moment on his son-in-law. At his nod, Caiaphas turned to me uncertainly.

"The elders," he said grudgingly, "have decided to entrust you with a very critical mission."

I smiled incredulously. "Why, in all Judea, would the Temple choose a rebel like me for any mission?"

"Just because you are that man you speak of," said the Reb Gamaliel. "The Pharisees and the Sadducees can agree, as you see, but the Zealots are irreconcilable."

"We have nothing to do with either party. We stand for an independent Israel, free of burdensome masters of any stripe. And we have no sympathy for the fawning minions of Rome."

Annas and his son-in-law, looking daggers, were about to turn on their heels, but Gamaliel stayed them with a detaining hand. His brown eyes probed deeply into mine, and he spoke more in sorrow than in anger.

"You do your father an injustice, Judah-bar-Simon. For he thought, as we do, that Israel must not be torn apart by warring factions if it is to survive."

For a moment a shadow darkened my thoughts.

"What has my father to do with this?"

"If he were alive, he would instill in you a sense of the tradition in your family since David's time. You are of this royal lineage, as you know."

"Why else do I speak of deliverance, with one of my own as Master, not some grasping monster in Rome?"

Even though the room was bare, and the doors closed, the High Priests' eyes darted about nervously. "Caution, young man," Caiaphas cried, "there is some talk that even the Romans hearken to. Guard your tongue. Their Emperor is their God, and they will not have him blasphemed by such as we."

"Such as we indeed."

I had turned away angrily, when Annas' voice caught me at the door. "And if I would commission you to find this leader you speak of?"

I retraced my steps slowly.

"I would tell you that you are not the High Priest, nor the father of five High Priests, and that the river Jordan flows upstream."

Annas permitted himself a ghost of a smile. "Listen closely. There is a man who calls himself a prophet, who lives like an animal in the Wilderness, with a camel skin for a robe and a loincloth for a tunic."

I had moved insensibly closer.

"And what is he called?"

"The Baptist, because he purges men of their sins in the river Jordan."

"And so our forefathers, too, used water for their purification ceremony."

"He baptizes differently."

"Who is this Baptist?"

"An Essene, we understand, a fanatical leader of a fanatical sect from the monastery at Qamram by the Dead Sea."

I regarded the three men solemnly. "You must have some reason for wishing to know more about him."

"There are reports that he heals the sick and comforts the poor with tales of a happy land beyond."

I felt a tingle of expectation.

"And what, pray, is wrong with that?"

"If he were to limit himself to these harmless exercises, nothing. But he preaches that Jews should deny tribute to Rome, and drive out the tax collectors. This will not sit well with Pilate."

"Or with the Temple treasury."

I knew there must be more, for why else would they summon an outsider like myself?

He hesitated for only a moment, saying with a grimace: "His followers look on him as the true Messias."

My intuition had served me well. "And is that not what all Israel is seeking?"

Annas shook his head grimly. "The nation must not suffer for the misdeeds of one man."

"Do you seek a Messiah or a martyr?" I said in a voice harsh even to my ears.

Gamaliel's hand stroked his untrimmed gray beard. "In this sad land of ours, Judah-bar-Simon, he could be both." He sighed wearily. "Who knows what our future is?"

I found myself strangely troubled by the lack of resolve on the part of this spiritual leader of the Pharisees.

"If he should be the Messiah, are we to disown him? Why then my mission?"

"At least," said Annas, "we will be able to watch him and come to a decision in due time."

My curiosity had been piqued by the little I had heard. "Of what lineage is he?"

"The same as your own." Annas' thin lips formed a sardonic smile. "There must be ten thousand like this in Jerusalem alone, born of the House of David."

"Born in Bethlehem near an ox and a donkey?"

He clucked his tongue impatiently. "I have no time for guessing games. The Sanhedrin's Council of Five will decide, if and when a decision must be made."

"Where is this man now?"

"In the Wilderness, south of Jericho. He baptizes at the ford at Bethabara, on both sides of the Jordan."

"In Perea as well?"

"So they say."

"Then he comes under the jurisdiction of Herod Antipas, as well as the Temple."

Annas waved his arms airily. "It is all one. Herod rules Perea and Galilee at the sufferance of the Romans. His kinsman Agrippa has been supplanted by Sejanus and can no longer help him."

I had a gnawing curiosity about this man the Sanhedrin was so concerned about. "By sacred prophecy this man should be born of a virgin."

The High Priest gave me a pitying glance. "How could a man born of a woman be born of a virgin?"

Gamaliel was standing with an amused smile on his lips, as if enjoying this duel between his former pupil and the supreme head of the Jewish theocracy.

"The Pharisees," said I, hoping to woo Gamaliel to my side, "believe in the angels of God and the resurrection of man. There is not one life but many. It is quite possible for the Prophets, even Moses, to be reborn if the God who made heaven and earth in six days so wills it."

Annas was not impressed. "The Sadducees hold there is only one life, and it is of the flesh."

Believing in reincarnation, from my Pharisee days, I was not easily put off. "Who were this man's parents?"

Annas threw up his arms in disgust. "Is there no end to your questions?"

A pleased Gamaliel interposed helpfully: "The father was one Zacharias, a teacher in the Temple, a true son of Judah, and"—with a twinkle in his eyes—"a Pharisee, to be sure."

"And the mother?"

"She was one Elizabeth, also a Judean."

"And this was their only child?"

"Yes, it was thought she was barren, and could have no children, for she was long after the age when women normally bear. But, lo and behold, as with Abraham and Sarah in olden days, she gave birth wondrously to this boy. It was in the time of Herod the Great. To escape the wrath of this despot who slew three of his own sons in a frenzy of suspicion, the couple fled Jerusalem with their son. He was called John, the God-given, for only through God's will, in their belief, could he have been born."

I marveled that my old teacher, so absentminded at times, should be so familiar with the child's birth.

He laughed. "Zacharias had more reason to be grateful than most fathers, and therefore was more inclined to be talkative."

The canny Gamaliel had read my hesitation correctly.

"None knows, of course, by what agency this child was conceived?"

"It is not a question one asks a teacher in the Temple."

"Could it have been a virgin birth?"

"But Elizabeth was surely no virgin."

"But could not the spirit have been planted in Elizabeth's womb by the power of God?"

Caiaphas snorted his ridicule. "You must be mad."

"Why call me mad?" I said. "Did not God make the first man?"

"You make no sense," cut in Annas coldly.

"That is because you Sadducees do not believe in continuing life. But if it is God's will for a child to be born of a virgin, what need has he of man? Is he not the creator of Adam, before whom there was no man?"

Gamaliel clapped his hands together in his pleasure.

"Your father would be proud of you this day."

Annas stirred in his chair.

"It grows late," he said, "and it is best we conclude this business. Can you begin your commission at once?"

"In two days," I said. "Time enough to wind up my affairs."

He sat down at a desk, and his quill raced over a sheet of the thinnest parchment. "Take this, it will serve as your credentials. But I suggest it be used only in unforeseen situations."

I looked at it quickly before slipping it inside my tunic. I, Judah-bar-Simon, of a noble Judean family, was an agent of the Sanhedrin. It was enough to give one a nightmare, but it gave me my opportunity to seek out the Messiah wherever he was.

"You will report back to us from time to time, but tell no man. For yours is a most delicate mission. Dress plainly, be as nondescript as possible. Watch and listen, say nothing. Observe not only this Baptist, but his followers, and the temper of the crowds. You have it within your power to perform a great service for the nation."

I would have been impressed had I not known him for a coldblooded, rapacious cynic.

"My only allegiance is to Israel."

"Good," said he, rubbing his thin hands together, "we shall have no trouble then."

"To whom do I report?"

"The same that must review the actions of any claiming to be the Messias."

"But the Messiah is sent by God. How can a Council judge God's work?"

"We judge what is best for Israel."

I saw the trap readily enough. "Whatever I find you can negate."

"Your role is that of fact finder. On the basis of what is found, we will make our decision."

Not for a moment was I simple enough to believe this. Still, if John the Baptist was the Messiah, if he were the God-sent Deliverer of our people, I would be the first to know it. If not, the search would turn elsewhere.

The High Priests had walked off to one side and Gamaliel was about to embrace me when, suddenly, there was a hue and cry from the court below. We ran to the windows. The massacre, incredibly, was being resumed. In the vast Court of Gentiles some of the wounded had managed to get to their feet and were advancing, unarmed, against Roman troops emerging from their fortress via a subterranean tunnel. The Romans attacked with cudgels and the flat of their broadswords, cutting down the battered pilgrims as if they were wheat.

"Pilate," I cried, "must have his last drop of Jewish blood."

The others had turned away shaken, save for Annas. He seemed almost pleased. "Pilate owes us this day," he said softly.

My own feelings about the Galileans were mixed. They were certainly not our equals before the law, few being of the twelve tribes, but they were still Jews capable of bearing arms, and the aqueduct against which they had demonstrated was certainly a classic example of Roman tyranny.

An expression of disgust had turned down the corners of Annas' fish-like mouth as the slaughter continued. "What fools these Galileans be."

"Heroes, not fools," said I, "brave men who need only to be armed to show how vulnerable Rome is."

"You, Judas, are a greater fool than I thought. Do you think we would tolerate the Romans if there was any other way?"

"Spartacus was only a slave, yet with an army of slaves at his back, he kept the Roman legions at bay for three years."

Annas gave a contemptuous grunt. "And where are Spartacus and the rest?"

"They were defeated only because they lacked the purpose of free-born men."

"You talk like a child. The Romans would make short work of us. We are important to them, but not for ourselves. Israel is but an insignificant speck on their maps, but in all our insignificance we are the passageway for the great caravans that ply daily from their storehouses in Egypt to Damascus, supplying their military. For this reason they tolerate us, but once let the peace be broken and we shall feel the iron heel that crushed Carthage into the dirt. Beware, Judas, you trifle with a sleeping giant."

CHAPTER TWO

THE TEMPLE

I WAS APPALLED BY THE HAVOC wreaked by the Roman soldiers. Even more disconcerting, not a helping hand had been raised in a Temple city of fifteen thousand shopkeepers and seven thousand religious functionaries. Was Israel so craven that it would not fight, or was only a leader needed to fan the flame of revolt? I threaded my way nervously through the throng of worshippers, which appeared to take courage with the carting away the last bodies. I tried to think positively, sorting out my thoughts, to best take advantage of the opportunity that had been given me. I remembered enough of my Pharisee upbringing to know that God had a way of thrusting a man's footsteps on the path marked by destiny. This meeting was indeed a stroke of fortune, even though it required a semblance of cooperation with the Sadducees and the Sanhedrin they clearly dominated. It also posed a problem or two. Obviously, the Messiah meant different things to different people. Could he be both a Warrior King and a Prince of Peace? Hopefully he could be anything, for was he not sent of God?

I winced at the stains where the bodies had fallen, the crimson mercifully fading under the feet of the milling crowd. I recalled that somewhere the prophecy stated that the Promised One would first purge the Temple, and surely not a moment too soon. This was more a marketplace than a place of worship, defiled not by the heathen, as in the Maccabeans' time, but by the very priests chosen to consecrate it to God. To every Jew the Temple represented not only his oneness with God but the political integrity of the nation. Essentially, we were a theocracy, founded with God's blessing, with every aim and aspiration modeled by prior allegiance to that God.

"God chose us," said Gamaliel, "so we have no choice but to choose him."

Where was that wrathful God now? Certainly the Temple was not his habitat. Perhaps the Romans were the instruments of his vengeance and these sins must be washed from the body of the nation before the liberator would come. As I wended my way, I wondered how the Temple could have been so ignobly prostituted and demeaned. Everywhere there was a stall or a shop, more than three thousand in all, arranged by commodity for the shoppers' convenience. There was one area for ironware and kitchen utensils, another for wool and clothing, livestock, bread and grain, fresh fruits and vegetables. Even alcoholic beverages had their place, and from their manner these merchants seemed to have liberally sampled their own wares.

I saw the vendors haggling over their goods and marveled at God's patience. Was it not plain who the culprits were? Without the sanction of Annas and Caiaphas, this desecration would not have existed, for there was no stall, however small, that did not pay its tithe to the High Priests of Israel. The Levites hovered about the stalls to sanctify the foods as pure, but as far as I could see, this food was no different from the unsanctified, except a mite costlier because of the rite performed over it. How the God of Israel must frown in his abode in the sky. Was it any wonder he was sending his Messiah, this wonderful leader whom the prophet called the Elect of God?

"In him dwells the spirit of wisdom and the spirit of enlightenment, the spirit of knowledge and of strength, and the spirit of those who have fallen asleep in justice. He will judge all nations, punishing those who have oppressed the just. At his coming, the dead will rest again, heaven and earth will be transformed, and the just become heavenly angels, will abide with him through life everlasting."

But even now, amid the rankest materialism, there was heartening evidence of the common man's devotion to the augury of the Messiah. It all became bearable, even the red-cloaked soldiers sneering in the great square, when the faithful considered their nearness to the Promise. The smell of the animals became sweet then as the pilgrims paid their tribute to Jehovah. Only a few feet away I could hear a pilgrim as he kneeled in prayer while the sacrificial lamb he had just purchased was led to slaughter. There was a break in his voice as he beat his breast and cried:

"Blessed be Israel, unto that day the Promised One delivers us from our enemies."

Not to some tarnished Israel would the Messiah come but to a land of milk and honey, cleansed by proper penitence before the Lord.

I took a while getting through the Court of Gentiles, for this was the teeming center of public activity. It was as much a crossroads of the Empire as Damascus and Alexandria. For here the people of the world forgathered, and the cosmopolitan and sophisticated rubbed elbows with the Scribes and Talmudic scholars, the legatees of those whose eyes had dimmed over Holy Scripture long before the wolf cubs had climbed out of the Tiber marshes.

My eyes rested for a moment on the elegant beauty of the Portico of Solomon. Its Greek columns were laid out in three spacious aisles so that the rabbis could sit comfortably in the shade and discourse leisurely on the Talmud. Their pupils were legion, for during the holidays, of which there seemed no end, the pilgrims descended on the Temple by the tens of thousands. On the slopes of the Mount of Olives and Mount Scopus, I could see the tents covering every available patch of ground. How wonderful if, instead of pilgrims, these were warriors, and instead of walking sticks there were swords. I saw still other pilgrims, wandering for weeks from the profaned cities of the Diaspora, sinking to their knees and reverently planting their lips on the rough stone. Their shrill cries sent a surge of excitement through me. "If I forget thee, O Jerusalem, let my right hand forget her cunning. If I do not remember thee, let my tongue cleave to the roof of my mouth."

They stood and wept unashamedly, and secretly I wept with them for the lost glories of Solomon and Saul. And yet the Herodian Temple was twice Solomon's and infinitely more grand. Huge walls had been flung against the hills to support the four courts rising on successive plateaus to the Sanctuary. After forty-six years, Herod's Temple was not yet finished, and priests trained as masons still toiled in chambers forbidden to the laity. But outside, the money changers cheerfully rattled their coins, and the pilgrims swarmed over one another to obtain their sacrificial offerings. Priests occupying booths vied with the merchants, selling tokens to be converted into goats, calves, sheep, birds, even oxen. Doves, normally a few pennies, cost twentyfold during the holidays, and the regulars bitterly protested this legalized larceny.

"Robbers," a middle-aged man shouted to a one-eyed vendor.

"Sir," the thief replied, "is it not worth anything that your wife bear you a son?"

He held up a dove which squirmed to get away.

"With the blood of this beautiful love bird, she will become fertile enough to bear twins."

The pilgrim gave him a jaundiced look. "Six months ago a dove like this cost but a few pennies, and there was still no child."

It was no wonder that the reformists inveighed against the Temple. How did one find God amid all this grubbiness and confusion?

Every so often the silver trumpet signaled a sacrificial offering. From their mournful looks, the animals seemed to know they were about to become inspirations to the faithful. My nostrils were assailed by the stench of frightened animals. The noise was deafening, the screams of the vendors drowning out even the braying of the donkeys. I hated every minute spent threading through the clamorous throng, watching the haggling and bickering, the money changers taking their usurious five percent for converting the unholy Roman coinage into holy Jewish shekels, good for any rug or robe, bird or beast.

I was in no mood to tarry, brushing aside the badgering mendicants, who like the others, paid the priests for the privilege of begging inside the Temple walls. The merchants were as bad, jumping out of their stalls at passersby. Had I seen anything I wanted, I still would not have bought it, so incensed was I by this mockery of worship. And so I was thoroughly upset when a rude fellow threw himself in front of me, blocking my passage. I moved aside, and he moved with me. There was a smile on the dirty, hook-nosed face and a filthy, grimy hand thrust a bottle of horrible-smelling Syrian whiskey under my nose.

The leering face drew close to mine.

"This nectar for a prince," cried this rough fellow with the pocked countenance of a sponge.

"What manner of Jew are you?" I asked.

"I am a Samaritan, sir."

"You are not permitted in the Temple then," I said, drawing away as if he were a leper.

"But I am a good Samaritan," said he. "My ancestors were of the twelve tribes of Israel, returning to the land of their fathers after the prophet Daniel made his peace with the Babylonians and the Persians ended our time of slavery."

"You speak falsely. No true son of Israel has counted himself a slave since the prophet Moses led his people out of bondage in Egypt. Even in Babylon our fathers kept their customs and spoke their minds."

"We Samaritans are as good Jews as any," he said in his wheedling voice, "and our temple on Mount Geritzim, in a place blessed once by Moses, is equal to your own temple in splendor." He winked slyly. "And besides, we have only one whale's mouth to feed, not six or seven, like some."

I noticed that the Roman seal on the whiskey was broken.

"If the tax collectors see that broken seal, my man, you'll be flogged within an inch of your miserable life."

Without taking offense, he rummaged around for a moment in his filthy bag.

"I see from the fringe of your cloak, sir, that you are a pious Pharisee, and a Scribe at least, who knows something of the law."

There was something about the fellow's persistence that stirred my curiosity. When he straightened up I could see that he was of a good height, and his shoulders were strong and supple under the rough brown muslin. He had shaken off his cringing manner and blandly showed me a tunic of silk with the initial "M" plainly embroidered in Hebrew rather than the ordinary Aramaic.

"Why do you show me this?" I demanded.

He drew up close, his foul breath reeking of garlic, causing me to take a backward step. After looking around at the shoppers preoccupied with their own errands, he leaned forward and touched the inside of my sleeve.

"The letter stitched inside your cuff," he whispered, "there are a hundred like it in this court at this moment, waiting only a leader to avenge the massacre."

As a shopper approached he quickly resumed his servile manner; but as the man passed, he nodded his head toward a truncated column at one end of the court. "I heard the soldiers laugh," he muttered between his teeth, "as they dropped the column on the heads of the Galileans, crushing a score or more to death."

I studied this odd figure of a man for a long moment, realizing that it was no stroke of chance that he had singled me out.

"How do you know I am not a Roman spy?"

He laughed, showing his yellow teeth. "Not with that face. Only a Pharisee could have that constant look of smelling something bad. The upturned nose and arched eyebrows are more of a badge than the striped sleeve of this haughty sect."

"You know my name?"

He nodded slyly. "We wait for a leader."

"I am not he." He had drawn me off to a corner and kept digging new wares out of heaping baskets.

He held up a white silk robe, similar in quality to that worn by Annas and his son-in-law. "How do you like this garment?" He laughed over a hoarse whisper. "Tonight, in the Garden of Gethsemane, in the great room of the olive presses, the Maccabeans will gather."

Abruptly, his manner changed again and he began to gesture wildly, berating me rudely at the same time. "Why I wasted my time with such as you," he cried, jamming his goods back into his baskets.

I was about to respond angrily when I caught his eye and looked back over my shoulder. A Levite with the red badge of a Temple collector had been nosing through the adjacent stall. His eyes ran over my cloak, dwelling for a moment on the striped blue sleeve, and he gave me a respectful nod. He was less circumspect with the merchant. "Your licenses," he demanded.

With much grumbling, the man fished out the required documents for each commodity offered for sale. The collector perused them carefully, and then, like all petty officials, anxious for the last word, left with the injunction: "Don't let me see you annoying anybody with proper business in this Temple, or it will go bad for you."

The merchant followed the retreating figure with a sour eye. "They are worse than the Romans, these lackeys who do Rome's bidding."

In spite of myself, I started, for this ugly-visaged, crude, coarse stranger had echoed almost to the letter my own thoughts about the High Priest and his cohorts.

"What name do you go by?"

"Joshua-bar-Abbas."

"And the watchword is what?"

"You do well to ask, for without it you could not approach the Garden of Gethsemane." He lowered his head. "Simon," said he, "Simon the Zealot."

I didn't give him a second look, but went on my way, oblivious to the hawking cries of the merchants. How many of these, I wondered, were, like Joshua-bar-Abbas, part of the underground resistance against Rome? It was a stirring thought, and for a change I did not bridle as a pair of helmeted soldiers swaggered noisily by with their broadswords clanking on the cobblestones and two shameless daughters of Israel on their arms.

Soon I was out of the Temple and in the city I loved. I never ceased to thrill as I wandered these familiar streets. In the Upper City, near the

Temple, dwelt the aristocracy, enjoying the purified air at rarefied altitudes of more than twenty-five hundred feet. The new quarter stretched ahead of me, past the Sheep Gate and the wall paralleling the Valley of Kedron. I passed the Dung Gate, beyond which a trickling stream ran with its stench of urine and offal through the gutters, and where the lepers, forbidden the city, clustered together in their misery hoping for a miraculous cure in the holy water of the pool. On the far side of the Kedron, at the foot of the Mount of Olives, were a collection of storehouses for the hides of the sacrificed animals. I held my nose passing the Dung Gate, for all the garbage of Jerusalem was carried out here and flung into the Kedron Valley. Just outside the walls I saw the beggars poking for food through the stinking debris piled up in the dingy alleys behind the warehouses. The Kedron's brook was tinged with the blood of the sacrificial animals, and I stopped for a moment to observe the racing stream.

"Someday," said a strange voice, "this stream shall run red with a different blood."

I turned and saw two hazy figures in the gathering darkness. Though the cool of evening had not yet set in, I felt a chill down my spine. And then quickly I shook off my uneasiness. How had the voices carried so clearly? I must surely have imagined it.

The streets were quiet before the evening meal. And looking at the rows of yellowish stone houses, jammed together except for the spacious Roman homes and the palaces of Jewish dignitaries, I recalled the saying that a man could walk for miles over the expanse of these flat, earth-covered roofs.

Quickly I left the quarter, with its unsavory odors, and soon burst upon a rich residential area ablaze with the bloom of red poppies, soft blue lavender, and lilies of the valley. Farther along I came on beds of cumin and sharp peppermint, intoxicating ginger and nutmeg, branches of saffron, oleander, and cypress, all adorning the gardens of the rich. Their sweet fragrance made one forget the hideous running sores of the grotesque lepers with their lion-shaped faces, and the ragged beggars with their grimy hands out for alms. On some mounds rising above the limestone homes, I spotted the aromatic helboh and lebonah, ground and dried into incense for the Temple services. Would that the spirit of Israel were as fruitful as its land.

I must have walked for hours, for my mind was seething with the new life I was about to begin. Where it would take me I had no way of knowing. But I did know I was about to meet my savior, the Messiah of Israel, of that there was no doubt! For even as a boy, listening to the muted discourse of my father and his friends, I knew that I was born to serve him one day. That was my destiny, and there was no denying it. Did not the book of our fathers say that the Philistine struggled against his stars to no avail? We could choose our way, to be sure, but it was a way already marked out for us. The elders had set me on the path, and the Promised One beckoned, yet, as Isaiah said, I knew him not. But the instant my eyes fell on him the curtain would be drawn. He was my Master, and I would die for him if need be.

The Baptist, they said, was an Essene. I had pictured the Savior as somebody not quite as austere. Still, with all my disapproval of the High Priests. I knew the Reb Gamaliel was right in saying that Jews had to unite in the common cause. We were already a nation divided, making it unnecessary for the Romans to implement their policy of Divide and Conquer. Still walking briskly, I took stock of the differing groups and their philosophies. The Pharisees felt that fate dictated all matters and that nothing could happen to man which was not governed by this fate. But unlike the Greeks, who considered the character of the individual the determining factor, the Pharisees believed this fate was not a mindless force, any more than the movement of the planets or the rhythm of the seasons. It was all God's design, and as we drew closer to the designer, understanding him as we grew to understand ourselves, so did we comprehend his purpose.

I was intrigued by this philosophy, but it seemed the highest indulgence of the ego to believe that God was interested in the trivial course of each and every life. What was it to God that I was betrothed to Rachel-bas-Nathan and was bored to distraction? I am sure very little. Why else were there prophets if God spoke to all? Surely, he would not have selected a Chosen People if the Gentiles were as dear to him.

The Essenes had no love for the Sadducees, for the Temple hierarchy denied divine intercession in the affairs of man, holding every man free to choose his own course. They had no concern with morality, saying that God was not moved by the sins of humanity, and so, said the Essenes, it was easy to see why the Sadducees behaved as they did. They paid a grudg ing respect to the Pharisees for a fanaticism which they could appreciate if not agree with. Like the Pharisees, as well, they accepted the message of the Prophets as part of the gospel. The Sadducees cynically accepted only the five books of Scripture till Moses' time, excluding even the prophets who foresaw the Messiah. For their authority they fell back on the Scribes, who had worked hand in glove with them from the Babylonian Captivity four hundred years before. There was a saying in Jerusalem that when a Sadducee ate, a Scribe belched for him. I liked neither the Scribes' cynicism nor their sophistication, for they made a syllogism of everything, including the tyranny of Rome.

I was so lost in thought that I did not remember passing the Roman Forum and Theater, which patriotic Jews shunned like a roasted pig. But after a while, passing Herod's palace, I came to my father's house. From the street it did not appear expansive, for wise Jews concealed their wealth from the hungry wolf. But as I unlocked the gate, and walked through an open corridor, I emerged into an atrium which overflowed with an abundance of cypress, palms, and karob trees, gathered about a cluster of marble fountains. My dear father, God bless him, had been Hellenized in his later years and cultivated a taste for Greco-Roman statuary.

"Take the best of every culture," said he, "and use it to your advantage."

I paused at the door. I had already gone over my excuses to Rachel and my mother. We had planned to dine with friends, but my mind was drawn like a magnet to the Garden of Gethsemane. The Zealots from all of Palestine and their sympathizers as well would be on hand, for Pilate's show of might had precipitated a crisis of action. It would not do for Rome to think us all cowards.

My mother was first to greet me. There were anxious lines in her worn face as she took my hand and lightly kissed my cheek. "You are home so seldom these days," she sighed in reproach.

Over her shoulder, I saw the lovely face of my betrothed. "Rachel," I cried, "you grow in beauty every day."

She flushed prettily and her hazel eyes brightened.

"How would you know, Judah, when you are here so seldom?"

"You question my work?" I asked more harshly than I intended. "How would we live if not for my father's estates?"

My mother gave me a sidelong glance. "Simon the Cyrene was here earlier."

"Oh, that pleasure-monger," I said carelessly, "what new disaster does he report?"

The Cyrene, so styled because of his, hedonistic philosophy, bad been my father's overseer for years, and continued after his death to serve me.

"He worries," she said, "that he so seldom sees you."

"It is a cheerless trip to Kerioth, and he can as easily bring his problems to Jerusalem."

Rachel pouted, her upturned nose in the air.

"I am becoming an old maid, and you do not even notice."

"I know," I laughed, "and you almost sixteen."

"And you an old man of almost thirty."

"Not quite. Please don't age me before my time."

My mother smiled mirthlessly. "I am afraid that I am the one feeling the years."

The servants brought refreshments into the library, my favorite room, where my father and I had argued history into the small hours of the night.

I sipped slowly from a fine Syrian wine.

"I cannot sup with you, Mother, as much as I had hoped to."

Her voice trembled a little. "But, Judah, you cannot disappoint your guests. They will be expecting your announcement."

"What announcement, Mother?"

The cup slipped out of Rachel's hand and smashed on the tile floor.

"He does not even remember," she cried.

"You were to announce your wedding date."

I sighed with regret. "I cannot be here tonight, Mother. I am sorry, Rachel."

Rachel appeared stricken. Her bosom heaved with emotion and she fought off tears. "If you do not want me, say so, Judah. I know that I am only a poor relative, an object of charity since my parents died."

My mother reached for her hand. "You are my own child, the daughter I never had."

I found the situation embarrassing.

"I must meet later with the Reb Gamaliel. He has tidings to discuss."

"And when did you see him?"

"Only today," I replied truthfully, "but there were others about. You know what a friend he is, and how he wants to further my career."

She frowned. "Is not your father's fortune ample for us all?"

"I cannot help it, I must be there tonight." I resented having to lie when no excuse should have been necessary. "Why do you not tell them the date in my place?"

My mother had a pained expression. "But you, Judah, are the head of the house."

As always, when unfairly pressed, I lost my composure. "Then allow me to be the head of the house."

My dear, kind, sweet mother rose from the couch and took. Rachel by the hand. "Come, child, we must see to the supper. The guests must not be disappointed."

There she was, as usual, forcing me to feel guilty.

"I want to marry Rachel," I said.

My mother spoke without turning her head. "And will you be as mysterious with her about your movements?"

I moved to kiss Rachel but she tossed her head, tumbling her magnificent auburn hair about her shoulders. I had never seen her more beautiful and I felt a sudden yearning for the slim, taut body so voluptuously silhouetted under the gossamer gown.

"Come, Rachel," repeated my mother. "Judah has business elsewhere."

Women were unreasonable, forever immersed in their own little desires, not once even thinking of the needs of the nation. As for God, what was he to them but a word? They stood upstairs in the synagogue, frowning over the sacred scrolls to steal a look at their menfolk praying so solemnly below. They cared nothing for the Messiah. It mattered little to them whether he appeared or not. Give them their daubs and their oils, to paint and glorify face and body, and they were blissfully occupied. I could not be concerned with this frivolousness when whispers of the Messiah were in the air, carried to every part of the land by the prayers of his people.

"Deliver us, O Deliverer, for we are yours."

Supperless, but too excited to care, I proceeded by foot for Gethsemane. Taking the shortest route across the city, I passed through the public concourse separating the Temple from the Fortress, and emerged by the Golden Gate into the gardens and groves which ascended into the mountains. It was a shadowy night, the moon flitting in and out of the silver clouds, and by the dim light I could make out three crosses with a figure straining from each beam. They were not dead yet, for I could hear their moans. They had been hung upside down, as was customary with brigands caught in a murderous act. From their cries I knew they would dangle till morning before the Roman soldiers broke their legs and put them out of their misery.

I would have given them a little wine, if I had it, and some comfort, if I had the time. But these bodies hung on trees all over Judea, filling travelers with fear. The Romans didn't believe in prisons. They were a waste of time and money. "Why feed a dead horse?" Pilate asked.

The Garden of Gethsemane, with its gnarled old olive trees and abandoned warehouses, had always fascinated me. It had such a deserted air that I shivered at times in passing. It gave me the uneasy feeling of having been there before. I suppose if one believed in reincarnation it was quite possible that some half-forgotten memory of another lifetime lingered in the storehouse of the mind. However, while my Pharisee schooling allowed me to ruminate on the idea of continuing life, this was the only life I was sure of. If this life didn't count, how could any other?

Lost in these thoughts, I was startled by a dark figure jumping out from behind a clump of trees.

"Give the word," a rough voice challenged. I felt the flat of a sword against my chest and instinctively drew back.

"Simon the Zealot."

"Pass, Judah-bar-Simon. You are late."

By the light of the moon, straining my eyes, I made out the sharp features of a Syrian Jew. "They call me Cestus, for I am the cord that ties the dissident patriots together."

His face had a strength and determination, even in that murky light, that I found reassuring.

"You are the last," he said, "but I must stay until I am relieved." He drew his hand across the blade of his sword. "It will go ill with any trespasser."

I followed the path he indicated. Three times I was challenged before I reached the abandoned warehouse, ringed with armed sentries. I was searched at the door and a dagger removed from my tunic.

"I am a Zealot," I said angrily.

"We are all Zealots," the sentry said, "and the rules are the same for all, even for Simon Zelotes."

"What if the Romans were to break into the meeting?"

He smiled. "We have a man behind each tree. The movement is growing, brother. The time approaches."

"Good man." I clapped his shoulder. "This is the talk I would hear."

He passed me into the building. It was brighter than I would have expected. The light came from small lamps which, from the odor, were burning the black tar scooped from the soil of Persia and the Sinai. My entrance occasioned no interest. Not a head turned. There were possibly a hundred people sitting around on the floor of the spacious room, listening to a man of imposing presence. From his slurred speech it was plain that he was a Galilean. But he spoke with the assurance of one from the tribes of Israel. And in truth there were some in Galilee of the seed of Abraham, whose fathers had resettled there after the Maccabeans had driven off the Syrians and Aramites who would not be circumcised.

He, too, had been in Rome and was appalled by the corruption, the preoccupation with vice, and the rampant homosexuality. "The ruling class has grown soft with luxury. They diddle in their baths all day, playing with their little nymphets, and allowing ambitious upstarts, such as the grasping Sejanus, to handle the affairs of state. The lower class have become mobs and have lost the desire for work. In Judea there is a saying that a father who does not teach his son a trade teaches him to be a thief. But in Rome they idle all day, robbing and fornicating in their shiftlessness, supported by the largesse of a timorous government which keeps their minds busy with games and their bodies inert with free grain and meat."

The floor was so thick with people that it took me a little while to find a place in the front. The speaker's eyes rested on me for a moment, and I detected a smile. But how could that be? I had never seen this brawny giant of a man before. But then, suddenly, the robe he wore became the cuirass of a Temple guard, and recognition dawned. Of course I had seen him before. He was the Levite who earlier in the day had threatened the whiskey-monger. No wonder they knew me. They were everywhere.

I soon learned his name, for a man, vaguely familiar, with the face of a hawk and the mane of a lion, stood up boldly and said: "Simon Zelotes, I respect you as the leader of the Zealots and agree that this is not the Rome of the Republic, but it is still Rome. Anyone who thinks it will crunch like a rotten apple at the first bite will hang upside down for his mistake."

I would hardly have known this man, his dress and bearing were so changed. But his name soon confirmed who he was and the game they had played between them for my benefit.

"Well said, Joshua-bar-Abbas," replied Simon Zelotes, "but rest assured there will be no half-hearted assault on the Empire. Nothing of importance will be done until the time is ripe. But we can prepare ourselves for that time, establishing arsenals at every ambush point on the Empire lifeline from Egypt to Syria."

Joshua-bar-Abbas looked at him doubtfully.

"With all respect to you, Simon Zelotes, and to myself, we need a leader to inflame the people and stir their imagination."

"True," said Simon, "and that can only be one man."

There was a quickened awareness in the crowd, and shouts of "Hosanna, hosanna, to the Messiah, the Deliverer of Israel."

I felt a surge of excitement in finding others who felt as I did. But still I disagreed, for I had seen in Rome the sullen faces of a slave population that outnumbered their masters, and I knew that the right spark would start the conflagration that would consume this evil whore.

Not all there were Zealots; some were simply sincere patriots concerned about an Israel straying from its fathers. An old man stood up, and I recognized him with surprise. This was Nicodemus, a liberal Pharisee like Gamaliel, whom some considered the richest man in Israel. He was no Zealot and made no pretense of it. “My only interest,” said he in a slow but resolute voice, “is that Israel survive as the land of the Chosen. I walk the streets of Jerusalem and am dismayed to see how things change. Our young men are becoming Romanized. They dress like Romans, and strut like Romans. They enter the gymnasiums, patronize the arenas, and dream of becoming Roman citizens. Some have had themselves uncircumcised because the Romans find this custom offensive. Our daughters fraternize with the conquerors and intermarry, leaving their traditional worship. It is a sad state of affairs.”

“And how,” asked Simon, “would you turn this about without violence?” It was well known that Nicodemus counseled caution in all matters for fear of Roman reprisals.

“I am an old man,” said Nicodemus, “and I have seen much of life. I, too, have seen a decline in the Roman character which can only lead to their ruination.”

“And how,” asked the fiery Joshua-bar-Abbas, “do we know at what point the character of a people weakens? It is not like a man who deteriorates through his thoughts and actions before your very eyes.”

“When they give over to government,” said Nicodemus, “those duties which they should be pleased to perform themselves. When they are told they will be fed and sheltered even when they won’t work, when they are promised security from the cradle to the grave, when they are told the state will take over the supervision of their children and say what schooling they should receive and where. When they are told all these things and supinely accept them.”

Joshua-bar-Abbas shook his head fiercely. “I have not an old man’s patience.”

“Give it time,” urged Nicodemus. “We cannot consider our fate without considering Rome’s. In this Rome there is no Cato the Censor, no Marcellus who put his own son to death to preserve the principle of duty first to the state. There is only a corrupting greed that I have seen with my own eyes. Greed for power and for the luxuries it brings, for fine homes and furnishings, for great estates and licentious sport with wine and women. All the seeds of decay are there. The citizens of the greatest power on earth have come to prefer idleness and games to work. Rome will fall of itself to the first positive idea that comes along. I promise you that."

Nicodemus believed that socio-economics ultimately determined the fate of nations. "There is a decline in the Roman family that bodes ill for Roman vitality. Only the baseborn and slaves indulge in large families, which they know the state will support. The middle and upper classes so often do not marry and make a business of abortion. Soon there will be nobody to support the hordes who are born slave and stay slave, happy to be fed and entertained, and occasionally to fill their pockets with excursions into dark alleys, preying on the very people who support them."

Joshua-bar-Abbas was not impressed.

"All that Nicodemus says may be correct, but we cannot wait for Rome to complete its decline. By that time the change will be so great in Israel that our sons and daughters will be Roman and declining as well."

There was some laughter at this sally, and even Nicodemus smiled good-naturedly. "I counsel patience for the sake of us all. First let the Messiah arrive and decide how Israel shall be saved."

The meeting was not going well. Many were beginning to look around restlessly. I rose to my feet.

"May I say a few words?"

Simon Zelotes held out his arms. "Here is a young man," said he, "who could live in luxury but who has cast his lot with us. Speak, Judah."

I had never spoken publicly before, but my mind was clear and precise. I could pick out faces in the crowd and sense their quickened interest. I wasted no words.

"In the beginning," I said, "the Maccabeans were a handful, fewer than we. But they had purpose and faith. 'Many,' observed Judah the Maccabean, 'can be overpowered by the few. Victory does not depend on numbers. Strength comes from heaven alone.'"

I could see Nicodemus' long face break into the semblance of a smile. But Cestus stood stolidly, his arms folded, and the younger Zealots sat quietly.

"The Maccabeans were not a warrior people. They were farmers like many of you. They tended sheep and goats and cattle, minded their pigeons and tilled their fields. They were a peaceful but also a freedom-loving people. The Jews in that time would not do anything on the Sabbath. Antiochus and his Syrian Greeks rejoiced in their holiness and celebrated their Sabbath by massacring them by the thousands in their caves. Only when ordered to worship idols did the Jews finally resist."

My voice rose. "But when they were ready, a leader came in answer to their prayers."

I had the audience in my hand now.

"Mattathias the Hasmonean was rich in sons. John and Simon, Judah, Eleazar, and Jonathan. They banded together with friends and neighbors, attacking when the enemy least expected. They harried him constantly, raiding his caravans, pillaging his arsenals, picking off stragglers. They fought not only on the Sabbath but on the Day of Atonement, and every other day as well. In a pitched battle, on the plains of Emmaus, the mercenary army of the Syrians fled at the first assault. Their heart was not in the fight. With each victory, the Maccabees"—I held up my sleeve to show the emblem—"the Hammerers of the Lord, gained new followers. But they were still outnumbered. At Elasa, Judah, facing a vastly superior force, told his tiny band: 'It is not hard to die, if one dies for freedom.' And he was right.

"In the end, Judah retook Jerusalem with an army of a hundred twenty thousand soldiers, enough to liberate any people." My eyes traveled over the silent crowd. "And it shall be done now as it was then. God has not abandoned us. He will send us the Messiah, and our enemies will be as chaff before him."

This was what the crowd wanted to hear, and they reacted warmly, voicing their approbation as though every success of the Maccabeans were mine. It was nice to know that one could so easily stir others by appealing to their desires.

But not all were so easily swayed. Nicodemus' long face appeared to have grown longer.

"The Romans," he said drily, "would hardly agree to the description of themselves as chaff."

Knowing I had the crowd with me, I rejoined boldly: "Does Nicodemus imply that the Messiah sent by God will not have power to deliver Israel from any adversary?"

He stroked his chin thoughtfully, not the least abashed.

"First we must know he is the Messiah, and then he must know it as well."

"Of course he will know it. How else can he lead us?"

"True, but he may march to a beat different from ours."

Offended by what they considered nit-picking, the younger Zealots began stamping with their feet and shouting: "Down with the unbeliever."

Nicodemus' eyes flashed. "I am a believer," he said quietly, "or I would not be here. I stand for any cause that will prepare the way for the Deliverer of our people. And I will support any cause that I believe in."

This last, of course, was a telling blow, for money was badly needed to support the projected uprising, and Nicodemus, the wealthiest merchant in Palestine, was not one to be sneezed at.

Joshua-bar-Abbas held up his hand. "Nicodemus, as a friend of freedom, is entitled to his say."

I saw a flaw in Nicodemus' argument. "In the slave population lie the seeds of many revolts. They outnumber their Roman masters by far, and would likely join any uprising."

He did not agree. "They have no spirit, or they would have risen long before. These are not the gladiators who fought with Spartacus up and down Italy, but household parasites so long provided for that they no longer care for anything but free food and shelter. You will have to look elsewhere for support. It will not come from the mean-spirited."

In my heart I knew he spoke the truth.

"Then it will come from the brave in heart," I responded in ringing tones, "from those who lead the legions against enemies they do not hate, from taxpayers who wince under every crushing new demand, from fighters everywhere for the cause of freedom. Nobody loves the tyrant, nay, not even the Romans. What happened to Julius Caesar could happen to lesser than he."

"For every fallen Caesar, ten will rise," said Nicodemus.

"But they will not be sent by God and have God's unlimited power. Does not the Scripture say that when he comes all nations will make obeisance to him? Does Nicodemus question the Prophets? Certainly, he is not a materialistic Sadducee blinded by his wealth into thinking there is nothing before and after."

"The Zealots and the Pharisees have no quarrel, except in the matter of zeal. You know that, Judah, for there was no more distinguished Pharisee and patriot than your father."

"I know that the time has come to resist. It has been two hundred years since the Maccabeans gave us freedom, and a hundred years since the Romans took it away. A hundred years of Rome is enough, I say, enough of Tiberius, who would rid us of our customs, enough of Sejanus, who hates Jews because they speak for freedom, enough of Pontius Pilate, who would make of Israel a footstool for his own petty ambitions. I say to God, dear Lord, reveal to us the Promised One, and we your loyal servants will do the rest."

Again I showed the hidden emblem. "Let us look to the day," I shouted, "when this stands not only for the Maccabeans but for the New Deliverer, the Messiah, who is already here and waiting. This I know, for the time is ripe, and this the whole world will one day know."

I sat down amid deafening applause. Even the grim Cestus found cause to smile. As for Nicodemus, what did it matter that he frowned and seemed troubled? He was an old man, and the old forever counsel patience, when it is impatience, the refusal to accept the inevitable, that brings about the miraculous changes that give life its flavor. I would rather die a thousand deaths than live one life a slave.

With one speech I suddenly found myself a leader among the Zealots. Previously, I had not made any significant contribution, listening as others talked and planned.

Cestus and Joshua-bar-Abbas now wrung my hand.

"You have given us a splendid idea," said Cestus with a grin that split his ferocious face.

"I am gratified," said I, looking my pleasure.

"Until we are strong enough to take the field, we shall do as the Maccabeans. We shall loot their arsenals and ambush their caravans until the Romans no longer brag that their highways are as safe as the Forum at noon."

I remembered what Annas had said about the lifeline of the Empire from Alexandria to Damascus.

"They will not take this lying down."

Cestus had been joined by the Idumean Dysmas, a sentry Just relieved of duty.

"By the time they know their adversary we will have an armed force, fully supplied, stronger than anything they can bring against us." He laughed mirthlessly. "They already have their hands full with the barbarians in Germany, the tree climbing Britons, and the Parthians."

"And what of a leader? Without the Messiah there is no hope for a general uprising. All wait for the Deliverer and will not be delivered without him."

Bar-Abbas chuckled in his scraggly beard.

"If we do not find a Messiah, we will manufacture one."

CHAPTER THREE

THE BAPTIST

I KNEW HIM at once.

He was standing knee deep in the muddy waters of the Jordan, his hand on a young man whose dark head was bowed in resignation.

"Repent, and be cured," he cried in a voice that carried beyond the shore.

The youth, with an effort, lifted up an arm, and it was withered, the fingers cramped and deformed.

The Baptist, it could have been no other, passed his hand briefly over the afflicted arm. "Pray to the Father, who can do all things, even to moving mountains." His voice held a vibration which seemed to send out a current of energy. I could feel it where I stood, and so did the youth. "I feel the heat," he cried.

"You are open," said John, "that is well."

I had never witnessed a healing and had no faith in them. How could anybody heal that which defied the finest physicians? It seemed a silly superstition, but the mind did wondrous things. Believing something was often the next step to the thing itself. How many swore they had seen Simon the Magician grow wings and fly, and yet he was only a conjurer duping the gullible?

But with my own eyes now I witnessed a miracle. It could have been nothing else. The arm had been paralyzed, and now, incredibly, the shriveled skin began to smooth and the muscles took shape.

"In the name of the Lord God," boomed the Baptist, "Azriel, the son of Hammon, is made whole." The young man uttered a cry of jubilation, raising his restored arm for all to see. A sound that began as a murmur grew to a crescendo. The lame, the halt, and the blind in the marveling throng fell to their knees and shouted: "Hosanna!"

"He must surely be the Messiah," said an old woman with a cane. "Only the Anointed of God can do these things."

The Baptist seemed unmoved by the crowd. He stood the youth straight in the water, cupped his own hand in the swirling river, and doused the youth's bare head with the water.

"Love God and be purified," he said. His eyes were directed at the young man. Nobody else existed for him in that moment. "I baptize you Isaiah, which means the salvation of the Lord, after the prophet whose words are about to unfold."

The youth kneeled in prayer, the river coming almost to his shoulders, and in this posture raised his head in supplication.

The Baptist's eyes gleamed. "He is well pleased in you, Isaiah, rise and know that you are purged of sin and in your new virtue are ready to know the Lord."

The youth stepped forward in gratitude to embrace his benefactor. But the Baptist quickly stepped back, and the nearby Essenes cried out in horror."

"He would rob him of his power. He must not be touched when he communicates with God."

As I wondered how this could be, the Baptist waded back to shore. His sharp blue eyes roved over the multitude, seeming to see everything and everyone in those few moments. He had captured the throng but for a few sneers and crooked smiles. There were always the cynical. I had seen Pharisees and Sadducees in the crowd, and even some publicans, tax collectors, recognizable by their badges of office and the wide berth given them by the people. All feared these toadies of Rome who squeezed from the workers whatever the priests had left them.

I was surprised to see a number of rabbis, bearded and black-robed, with skullcaps and, bound to their arms, small leather boxes, phylacteries, which they kept touching while repeating from the scroll it contained:

"Hear, O Israel, the Lord our God, the Lord is One."

There were even some of my own people there from the surrounding Wilderness, bleak, gaunt-looking hunters and woodsmen. I knew well these people of the Wilderness. It was a harsh, forbidding land, but it was my land, for my people had lived in nearby Kerioth for ages. Here Simon, the last of the Maccabees, made his stand in the chalk mountains near Jericho where the gray slopes are cut by a dark gorge rushing headlong into the Jordan. Here eagles swooped overhead and jackals slaked their thirst where the river wound like a serpent across the glittering sands. It was a land where the Temple and its problems seemed a distant nightmare until I took time to sort out the different elements I saw here.

By and large the motley assembly was made up of the Amharetzin, who, with the native astuteness of the common man, had fallen out of traditional observances of the law because of their disdain for the commercialism of the Temple. They were chiefly menials, employed in carrying off the garbage and sewage, or artisans engaged in carpentry, smithing, or fishing and farming. They worked in the shops and the bazaars, toiling with their hands, for they had no head for learning. Seldom were they in any of the honorable professions such as law, medicine, or teaching.

They were readily identifiable by their rough dress and manner. I even recognized a few, such as Adam the Tanner, who kept his leather shop on the Street of the Tanners in the Holy City. He was a heavyset man with a grainy face that resembled his own hides. His eyes were small and squinted out on the world with the suspicion so typical of his breed. His companions were as loutish as he, drinking cheap wine from gourds they kept dangling at their sides and talking crudely in loud voices.

Not for the Sanhedrin, but to satisfy my own curiosity, I wandered among them, thinking they might be easy converts to the revolution, for he with little to lose had more reason to chance what he had.

With my hood over my eyes, Adam did not recognize me, though I had frequently patronized his shop, for his leather articles, such as bucklers and cuirasses, were eminently suitable for the troops we would eventually field. Mopping the wine from his beard with the back of his hand, he watched my approach with narrowed eyes.

"What brings you here, Adam?" I asked, enjoying his start at the mention of his name.

If possible, his eyes became even more mistrustful. He looked about uncertainly, as if seeking assurance from his companions.

"How do you say my name?" He advanced on me menacingly.

"It is a well-known name," I said, relishing my little game.

His reddish face, the wide nostrils flaring, breathed into mine a revolting smell. I drew back involuntarily, the intermingling odor of sour wine and stale garlic almost causing me to retch.

His beady black eyes gleamed malevolently. "I knew it," he cried triumphantly, "the mucker's a spy. Look how he's got himself all covered up." He thrust out a ham of an arm to snatch back my hood, but I coolly stepped aside. How coarse these creatures were, but useful, as bar-Abbas had pointed out For what was needed in any battle was not the wise and the thoughtful, but the unwary who would follow their leader to the death, like sheep if need be, without too much counting the cost or the cause.

"Keep back, fool," I cried in a voice that rang with greater authority than I intended.

Despite all his bravado, he fell back a pace.

"I know that voice," he said.

"Just as I know your name and face."

I lifted my hood for a moment, and his eyes widened.

Immediately, his manner became subservient, even craven, for such was the mettle of these fellows.

"What do you here, sir, and in disguise?" he asked in a humble tone.

"That was my question, begging the disguise of course, for I would know you anywhere"—my eyes lightly took in his companions—"by the noble company you keep."

The unruly crowd was now pressing us before it, and so before we were separated I quickly suggested a meeting, as I was eager to know more about the temper of the people.

He beamed with pride.

"It will be an honor, sir."

He leered, with one eye closed. "And how is my merchandise holding up?" His voice dropped to a whisper. "You must be outfitting an army."

I gave him a severe look. "You were not to utter a word, on penalty of instant retribution."

His manner quickly became servile again. "Only to you who already know it, so there is no harm in it, is there, sir?"

Before I could say anything more, we were cut off by the surging mob.

The Baptist, with his remarkable charisma, quieted them with an outstretched arm. In the ensuing stillness a tall man with a youthful face stepped forward, encouraged by his neighbors. He had the slurring tone of the Galilean, and I wondered what he was doing so far from home. He carried a quill over his ear, and I thought that he might be a Scribe, but he was a scrivener of a different order.

He inquired in a voice strangely without guile:

"Master, is it enough to be baptized to become pure?"

His query touched off a ripple of laughter, quickly silenced by the Baptist's frown.

He looked the young man in the eye.

"You, Levi, though a publican, will be found worthy in the eyes of the Lord. But it is your destiny to be cleansed by one greater than I."

Levi's disappointment was apparent.

"Since you know my name, never having known me, how can there be one greater?"

"In time your mission will become clear."

The Baptist's growing fame had drawn pilgrims from all over the land. They were eager for miracles. "Baptize us, Master, baptize and heal. Heal, heal, heal."

They crowded about him in their zeal, clutching at what little clothing he wore, but were flung back by a determined ring of his own followers.

His eyes searched the crowd. Some, chiefly the Amharetzin, were sparsely clad, barefoot and in rags. Others were in elegant robes, with tunics of silken gold and silver slippers. His piercing glance seemed to probe beyond the fine raiment, and many grew uncomfortable under his gaze. In this mood, his powerful voice burst on them like a clap of thunder. "Who," he cried, "has warned you to flee from the wrath to come?"

The uneasiness settled over the crowd like a cloud, and I was minded of the chiding of the prophet Jeremiah. Could he indeed be Jeremiah reborn, as some thought, or Elijah, the trumpeter of glad tidings, as others rumored? Whatever, or whoever, he held the crowd prisoner.

"Repent like young Isaiah, and be not pious before the multitude. Bring fruits worthy of repentance, and say not smugly within yourselves, as do the Sadducees and Pharisees, we have Abraham the patriarch to our Father. For I say unto this generation of vipers that God is able of these stones about you to raise up many children unto Abraham. There is nothing sacred about the twelve tribes not sacred before God. The High Priests forbid the Samaritans, the Idumeans, and yea, the Essenes, to worship in the Lord's Temple in the God-given City. So I say unto you that this Temple is no longer the Temple of the Holy One, but of the vipers who serve the God of Herod and Rome."

The skies trembled with the applause of the disinherited, the selfsame Amharetzin, while the dark looks of some indicated they might be Pharisees or Sadducees. It was small wonder the High Priests wanted a report on the Baptist. He was never more devastating than in attacking their stewardship. "As we all know," he declaimed, "two families dispute the miter of the priesthood, those of Annas and Boetus, who has long been out of power because of the fecundity of Annas' loins. But the dried-up

Annas has run out of sons, and now has only sons-in-law to collect tribute from Jews scattered around the world. For if they tithe not, the Lord God of Israel will not welcome them to worship."

The Essenes and the Amharetzin laughed uproariously, for his voice was heavy with sarcasm. "The Talmudic scholars have a saying: 'Woe is me for the house of Boetus because of its measures. Woe is me for the house of Annas and the hissing of the vipers. They are the High Priests, their sons are the treasurers, their sons-in-law the officers of the Temple, and their servants belabor the people with staves.'"

As he went on in this vein, I quietly took stock of him. He was tall, taller than me, and his gauntness added to the impression of height. His arms were thin yet corded with muscles, and with the fanatical gleam of his fiery eyes he seemed to exude boundless energy. A camel-hair tunic fell to his hips, and he was spared nakedness by the flimsiest of loincloths. From what I had heard, his wants were simple. He ate but a few figs and dates a day, a little bread, honey and locusts, and once a week a morsel of lamb or fish. He was an Essene, and so a celibate. But in his intense single-mindedness, I am sure he never gave it a second thought. His was a world of ideas. His Essenes, like himself, came from the monastic center of Qamram on the Dead Sea. They were of a grim and forbidding nature. Fierce and wild-looking as their Master, they vehemently registered their approbation whenever he attacked a familiar target. They held themselves scholars and devoted their lives to interpreting the law. Except for their devotion to the Baptist, they appeared to have withdrawn from the mainstream of life. They seemed to regard everybody with suspicion. I was glad of the hooded cloak which veiled my eyes, for it hid my contempt for their senseless rigidity. They owned no property, employed no servants, not even at harvest. They would neither eat nor drink on the Sabbath, nor even empty their bowels on this day of rest. They would not take an oath because they believed in speaking only the absolute truth and thus saw no reason for reaffirmation. They offered no animal sacrifices, saying it was enough to keep the covenant of Abraham, and so were excluded from the Temple in Jerusalem. Annas and Caiaphas had no use for Jews who did not swell their coffers, just as the Baptist had no stomach for the Temple hypocrites. Since his father was a Temple priest, it seemed odd that he should take so opposing a course. However, he was little different in this respect from me, for none was higher in the Temple councils than my father. Yet, even with my passionate desire for freedom, I could never become a monk like the Baptist.

They said that the Baptist had superhuman powers. He could walk endlessly through the hot desert and over the frosty mountaintops, going without food for days and not requiring water like other men. He could talk for hours without tiring, and it was his practice, from time to time, to single someone out of the crowd, nearly always the physically afflicted. It was no wonder some thought him the Messiah, for he truly seemed sent of God. With all his fire and passion and the spell in which he held his audience, I could easily see in him another Judah Maccabee, ready to spring out against the tyrant. He was the embodiment of everything I hoped for. And he fitted the prophecy, even to being born a Judean close to the time predicted for the birth of the King of Kings.

He moved his arms eloquently as he spoke, and I could visualize that strident voice and those compelling arms summoning Israel to battle. His power was manifested in his remarkable healing abilities. It didn't matter who the person or what ailed him. He would merely touch him, piercing him with a hypnotic stare, and the healing would be accomplished. Sometimes there was a mental problem, and he would drive out the devil from the demented one.

"Why do you wonder so?" he asked the marveling throng. "You believe in Elijah, who healed whoever came to him, so why question whoever is sent by the same?"

His healings gave him credibility; otherwise he might have seemed just another street-corner orator. Still, I sensed in him a presence so ethereal that it seemed not of this world but a tenuous link to the God he invoked with such passion.

He seemed to work himself up by degrees, artfully connecting the Temple to the Roman authority.

"Worse than the Romans," he cried, "are the Romanizers, and none is worse than Herod Antipas, a true son of the godless Herod, called the Great. The Great One raised monuments to his Roman friends. He built the Fortress Antonia, from which Rome watches over the Temple, and brazenly dedicated it to the triumvir Mark Anthony, despised even by the Romans as a dissolute rake. This evil king constructed forums, theaters, circuses, public baths, all in the Hellenic-Roman manner, and prided himself on being more Greek than Jew. Even while building a Temple for God in Jerusalem, he set up statues of Augustus for Jewish worship. He looted the graves of David and Solomon and created the great Mediterranean city of Caesarea for the conquerors. And there the plotting Pilate sits today when not in the Antonia overseeing the massacre of pilgrims."

There was a sharp intake of breath among the throng. Some faces grew hard with anger and some eyes grew moist. For all Israel understood that this senseless slaying was a thrust against them. The Baptist's voice rose emotionally. "These were Galileans who died, but what protest did the son of Herod make? Herod Antipas was busy with other matters, reveling in his palace in Perea with the adultress he calls wife. What was the law of Moses to this wicked man who stole his brother's wife? Like the Romans he lives for the flesh, but he is worse than the Romans. They are pagans and know no better, while he fancies himself a ruler of the Jews and mouths the law. And still we pay tribute to both."

The Baptist raised his eyes to the skies, and I saw them take on a radiant light. "Beware, you sinners, for one comes who will purge the wicked of their Godlessness. He is closer than any dream."

I could tell from their faces that the crowd was stunned.

This oblique reference to another was unexpected and disconcerting. Did we have to look still further when our search had seemed finally over? My only fear had been that his polemics against taxes would bring Pilate and Herod and their minions down on his head. And now we were confronted with fresh uncertainties. Was he only another Jeremiah, scolding, when the time had come for action? But he did have the faculty of moving his listeners. He spoke not directly of revolution, yet he planted the dissension which is the partner to insurrection. He was not as simple as he seemed. But like a true prophet, he spoke sometimes in roundabout terms meaningful only to those familiar with the law. What Roman, what heathen, could understand as he shouted out: "And now also the axe is laid unto the root of the trees. Therefore every tree which fails to bring forth good fruit is hewn down, and cast into the fire."

Levi the Publican was as astounded as I was. He raised a hand to inquire: "Then the law of Moses, which gives preference to the twelve tribes of Israel, is subject to alteration by mere man?"

The Baptist shook his head slowly. "I baptize all who repent with water, but that soon will no longer suffice. For he who comes after me is mightier than I. He shall baptize with the Holy Ghost, and with fire."

It seemed incredible. For if there was one mightier than the Baptist, he was a mighty prophet indeed.

"It is no virtue alone to be baptized," he continued, "wherever there is water and someone thinking to be made holy. But without a true wish for salvation the immersion is useless. And so we baptize only those of an age truly to repent.

"For as the prophet Ezekiel said: 'I will sprinkle clean water on you, and you shall be cleansed from all your filthiness, and from all your idols will I cleanse you as well.' But that is not enough. There is no salvation in being cleansed, not even of Ezekiel, but in being reborn. And that comes not through me, but through the one of whom I speak."

I could sense the crowd's restlessness whenever he mentioned another than himself. Some had come a long way, braving the deserts and the mountains, for a glimpse of the new Elijah. Surely they did not want to hear that they had made the journey in vain.

The Essenes, of course, closed their ears to his self-deprecation.

"Master, Master," they cried, "no man of woman born is greater than you."

He smiled, and I realized then, seeing his face shine like the sun, that his features were usually set in a scowl.

He had spoken for hours, neither eating, drinking, nor stopping for the ordinary ablutions. He held perfect communication with the assembly, remarkably responding to even unspoken questions.

"I will heal no more today," said he, reflecting my own wonder as to when he would repeat the miracle. "But there will be many healed by their own faith as well."

His healing had convinced even a number of soldiers in the gathering of his special power. They had been alternately yawning and frowning until young Isaiah's arm was made as new. They questioned the boy and rubbed their hands over his arm. If the healthy arm were not enough, the boy's own enthusiasm should have sufficed. There was no doubting his radiance. He was truly reborn.

I had observed the soldiers with some uneasiness. They were obviously not of Rome, for they wore a leather headdress instead of the metal helmet known from the Judean Wilderness to the Northern Islands. Moreover, they had not the Roman's galling cockiness which made the Judeans less than nothing in their own land.

But these troops, by the look of them sent by Herod, now seemed as fascinated as the rest by the Baptist. One soldier, most likely a Samaritan mercenary, seemed pleased by the rebuke to the tribal aristocracy. "What then shall we soldiers do, who must do the bidding of our masters?"

"I care not what your masters say. Do violence to no man, neither accuse any falsely, and be content with your wages."

On one hand he advocated sedition, on the other he advised them to be good soldiers. Herod would indeed be baffled by this enigma.

Encouraged by his response to the soldiers, a well-dressed man, a rich merchant, judging from his purple cloak, raised his hand.

"I am of the illustrious House of Benjamin . . ."

The Baptist cut him short. "Again I say to the seed of Abraham, there is no promise of a continuing covenant without salvation, and salvation comes not arbitrarily to the people of the promise."

"Is there no salvation for this son of Abraham because he is of Abraham?"

"Not because he is of Abraham any more than because he is not of Abraham."

"Then what brings salvation for such as I?" The words were humble, but not so the demeanor.

The Baptist's voice held a cutting edge. "If you would truly repent, take off your fine cloak and give it your neighbor who has none."

"Then," smiled the merchant, "he would have a cloak and I would have none."

"The Lord," said the Baptist, "notes what is given and what is received."

"Is it better to give?"

"Who asks unless he has never given?"

The blood came to the already florid face. The merchant quickly slipped off his cloak and held it disdainfully in the air. No groping hands reached for it, and with a shrug he finally put it back over his shoulders.

A bemused look came to the Baptist's eyes. "They know you, merchant, better than you know yourself."

The man seemed to shrink within himself, and slunk away, the Baptist's words following after him:

"If you have meat and your neighbor has none, impart that also to him."

The Sadducees and Pharisees had pressed into the front rows, and from their expressions they were preparing to challenge the Baptist. There was a smugness about these Temple birds that I found sickening. One rabbi, whose hauteur pronounced him a Sadducee, perched himself squarely in front. The Essenes moved swiftly to displace him, but a wave of the Baptist's hand restrained them.

"Let the Sadducee speak." he said with a gleam in his eyes. "I have no need to see his badge to know who sent him."

The Sadducee, a small, dark man with a crooked back, gazed blandly at the Baptist.

"You speak with such authority," said he in silken tones. "Are you then the Promised One, the Messias of Israel?"

"I have already spoken of him who comes to deliver us from evil. Stay and meet him as well."

My ears perked up.

"And when does he come?" In my eagerness, I forgot my anonymity.

He gave me a keen, searching look. "You will know him when he comes and he will know you."

A tingle went up my spine.

The Sadducee's mullet eyes tarried with me a moment, then returned to the Baptist.

"You are right, sir, in calling me a Sadducee. My name is Sadoc, of the same family who founded our party and kept the code of Moses alive in the Babylonian Captivity."

The Baptist seemed to enjoy the colloquy. "And now you sit, like your fathers, in the Great Sanhedrin and pass judgment on the Promised One."

Sadoc, to give him his due, did not appear daunted.

"You say well to disavow yourself as the Messias. For all know that a son born to man cannot be the Anointed. It is well known that you are the son of the Pharisee Zacharias and of Elizabeth, Judeans both, and so of the twelve tribes."

A murmur rose among the Essenes, to quickly subside at a look from the Baptist.

"The Sadducee," he said, "does me honor to know my lineage."

A brawny giant who had assisted the Baptist at the river rose to his full stature and roared his disapproval.

"You, Master, are the prophet Elijah, returned to lead Israel to freedom."

The Baptist shook his head. "As I have said, I am the forerunner, the voice of one crying in the wilderness, to make straight the way of the Lord."

Ahiram the Giant, meaning a brother of height, was not so easily turned away. With a scornful glance for the twisted little Sadducee, he quickly interposed: "But, Master, all know that you were born to Elizabeth long after it is given to women to bear children. So surely, as of old, it was God's gift, and for this reason you were called Jochanan or John, the God-given?"

The Essenes clapped their hands in a wild chorus of approval, but the Baptist only smiled indulgently, as if at so many children. Sadoc's face had set in grim lines. He had the look of the Inquisitor about him. I feared him even more than the scheming Annas, for his humped back was a *yetzahara*, an affliction from birth, and could well have filled him with hate, prompting him to prove himself superior to the normal man. A *yetzahara* had put the devil in more than one man.

I knew Sadoc by repute. He was considered second only to Annas in wiliness and guile, a true son of the rival Boetus hierarchy, which traditionally made the Temple its private preserve.

He spoke now with elaborate courtesy, as the serpent may have addressed the rabbit he was contemplating for supper.

"And may I ask when we can expect this dignitary greater than you?"

The Baptist had taken Sadoc's measure.

"Stay and see, O messenger of the All-Highest, and perhaps it will be sooner than you think."

"A prophet should have no trouble foretelling this event."

The Baptist suddenly lost patience with this game of cat and mouse.

"Is it a healing of body or mind that you seek, Master Sadoc?"

Sadoc's calm left him, and his voice trembled in suppressed fury.

"I see your future, prophet, better than you do mine."

There was a hush now, and the Essenes edged closer to the bristling Sadoc, only to be stayed again by the Baptist.

"I know my future, Sadoc, as I know the future of Israel. Sing no sad songs for me, for I walk with the Lord and fear no evil."

His voice rose powerfully, singing out triumphantly, as he made a hymn of the words of the prophet Isaiah.

"We ask where he is," he trumpeted to the sky, "and Isaiah has told us where to look, if we have eyes to see and ears to hear, and a heart to feel."

"'For unto us,' said he, 'a child is born, unto us a son is given, and the government shall be upon his shoulder, and his name shall be called Wonderful, Counselor, the mighty God, the everlasting Father, the Prince of Peace.'"

How many times had I thrilled over these words and prayed the prophecy would be fulfilled in my lifetime? How many times had I tried to picture him as I studied the Prophets? My heart rejoiced now with the realization that a prophet as great as Isaiah was heralding the glorification of Israel. It had never before seemed so imminent.

"And there shall come forth a rod out of the stem of Jesse, and a branch shall grow out of his roots." And the spirit of the Lord would rest upon him, the spirit of wisdom and understanding. He would be a true leader, no mealy-mouthed merchant of platitudes, counseling patience in the face of oppression. And as a true son of David, for a slingshot he would carry a sword.

"With righteousness," the Baptist went on, "shall he judge the poor, and reprove with equity for the meek of the earth: and he shall smite the earth with the rod of his mouth, and with the breath of his lips shall he slay the wicked."

Only a few in the crowd seemed displeased. "No, no," they shouted, "it is you, Master. You are the Promised One who shall free us from the oppressor."

He shook his head.

"I speak of another, far greater than I, whose shoes I am not fit to tie. I am of this earth, he of the Kingdom of Heaven."

The protests grew stronger. "Say not so, for you heal the ailing with a touch of the hand and drive the devil out of the deranged with soft-spoken words. Who else could do as much?"

I liked his fierceness. Yet when he spoke of the Lamb of God his voice became gentle and his eyes softened.

The Lamb of God offered hope. The tithes to the Temple would be abolished, as would the dietary laws governing impure and pure food. Unfair taxes would be eliminated. The nation would be restored. And the Romans had better look to their laurels. For had not the psalmist promised:

"He will break his enemies with a rod of iron and dash them in pieces like a potter's vessel."

Always in prophecy he was called a "rod" or "branch" from the Hebrew *nazar*. Perhaps there was a clue here, to be revealed with his coming. Jeremiah said the branch was out of David; Zechariah, more specifically, that his name would be the branch. Would that I had the Baptist's trust in these prophecies, for, however boldly I spoke, I had some misgivings at times.

At these prophecies, the Baptist's face glowed with an inner light. So might he have looked when he saw the face of the Lord.

"He shall feed his flock like a shepherd. He shall gather the lambs with his arm, and carry them in his bosom, and shall gently lead those that are with young."

John had the mettle of a great leader, but he was obviously not assertive enough for the militant. I sensed this in the attitude of some whom I knew as Zealots. Indeed, looking about just then, I noticed the apparent inseparables Cestus and Dysmas standing stony-faced next to some Essenes who had raised aloft a banner with the sign of the fish. I knew enough of astrology to know this betokened the new Piscean Age, ending the Arian Age, which was symbolized by the ram's horn and its call to sacred worship. Had not Isaiah warned against this mischievous quackery of the Babylonian soothsayers? The zodiac suited Babylon or Rome better than it did a prophet of Israel.

The two Zealots had a question for the Baptist. And he apparently divined as much, for he turned to them with a nod.

Cestus' curiosity took the same lines as my own.

"This Messiah you speak of, will he gain Israel freedom from Rome?"

The Baptist smiled enigmatically. "He will liberate us from every tyranny, including the tyranny of death."

This was not quite what a Zealot wanted to hear.

"How can there be no death?" said Cestus, with a faint smile of disbelief.

Obviously the Baptist had evaded the question.

"We speak of Rome," said Cestus, "not some vague, indefinable tyrant hidden in the clouds."

"All will make obeisance to him who comes," the Baptist said mildly, "and none shall bow lower than Rome."

An air of excitement raced through the crowd, for the Baptist spoke with a quiet conviction more impressive than any oratory.

I saw the surly Sadoc busily taking notes and, to my surprise, the publican Levi scribbling on a scroll.

Sadoc's eyes held a malicious gleam. "Rome will be pleased to note that one man will manage its overthrow."

"That, Sadoc, was not what I said. You would do well to listen."

As the two Zealots melted into the crowd, I realized that in the great multitude fanning out from the riverbank there was a cross section of Israel.

I stood near John, watching the faces in the crowd, and I saw the untrimmed beards and the striped blue shawls of three Pharisees who stared at the Baptist with hard, unyielding eyes. The foremost of the three was a Pestle Pharisee. In his unctuous piety he appeared to lean forward like a pestle in a mortar.

"Rabbi," said he, using the common term for teacher, "tell us how you know of this man who comes."

A smile illuminated the Baptist's face.

"In the mountains of Moab I had a vision. In this vision I saw an angel of the Lord, and he proclaimed in a voice such as I had never heard before the fulfillment of the prophecy so disturbing to our elders in the past. 'I the Lord have called thee in righteousness, and will hold thine hand, and will keep thee, and give thee for a covenant of the people, for a light of the Gentiles.'"

The Pharisee's eyes clouded with wrath.

"What has our Messiah to do with the Gentiles?"

The Baptist's voice was faintly mocking. "You do not accept the Promised One, and yet you challenge the conditions of his coming?"

He closed his eyes. "Is your name not Eleazar, and do you not sit in the Sanhedrin?"

The Pharisee appeared stunned, but he quickly recovered.

"I have been pointed out to you. My father, Nathan, was associated with your father in the Temple."

The Baptist's eyes remained closed. "I never saw you until today, and I shall never see you after you leave here, but the Lord God will mark what you do one day. You and your brethren."

Eleazar looked about uneasily, then said with a show of assurance, "No new prophets arise in Israel."

"One greater even than Moses shall come, and you will know him not."

Eleazar fell back on a crabbed interpretation of the law. "It is forbidden the sons of Abraham to hold familiar intercourse with the Gentiles."

The Baptist slowly opened his eyes. "Why," he said, "do you keep this news from the High Priests, who dally every day with Rome?"

Although the thought of a Messiah to the Gentiles appeared preposterous, I joined in the general laughter. Eleazar, however, was not easily put off.

"Then this Messiah you speak of would dissolve God's covenant of exclusivity with the Chosen of Israel and consider the Romans with the same favor as he would his own people?"

John saw the trap. "I had a vision," he repeated with a touch of irony, "in which an angel mentioned the sacred words of Isaiah, describing as a light to the Gentiles the one yet to come. Do you question the prophet all Pharisees profess to adore?"

As a new gale of laughter swept the assembly, the Pharisee darted a murderous look at the Baptist. "You speak as if the angel were addressing this message to you."

John shook his head slowly. "Listen well, for I am indeed the voice of him that cries in the wilderness, to make straight in the desert a highway for our Deliverer."

The Pharisee's face reddened.

"And when, pray," said he in a rasping voice, "can we count this Messiah in our midst?"

"Look and you shall see. Listen and you shall hear. He shall be everywhere. O Zion, that brings good tidings. Get thee up into the high mountains. O Jerusalem, that brings good tidings, lift up your voice with strength. Lift it up, be not afraid, say unto the cities of Judah, behold your God."

The Zealots had listened impatiently.

"The Hammerer taught Israel that God listens to those who fight for what they hold dear."

"And what, Dysmas, do you consider dear?"

Again the uncanny use of a name confounded the individual.

"How do you call me thus? You have never seen me before."

For the first time there was a hint of compassion in the Baptist's smile. "I have seen you many times," he said softly, "would that I hadn't."

"You seek to intimidate me."

"On the contrary, I find you blessed for the way you shall one day enter the Kingdom of God."

Dysmas sputtered for a moment, then fell silent and looked about uneasily. Could this be a premonition?

There was a compelling openness about John. He was an Essene but not a captive to that philosophy, though he lived monklike, in the Essene tradition of neither mating nor procreating. But he was sophisticated enough to know that not all could be Essenes or in time there would be nobody to preach to and nobody to save.

It had been a long day, and the Baptist had promised an early start in the morning. And so as the multitude went off to their camps I found myself wondering what I could report to the High Priests that Sadoc and Eleazar would not already tell them. But at least I was at the hub of things, and could fan out from there, exploring the popular mood, a prime factor in any revolution. In this wise I hastened to my appointment with Adam the Tanner and the Amharetzin, thinking to find out how they had reacted to the Baptist and his promise of another.

They were sitting in a small circle, about a dozen of them, their rough faces even rougher in the shadowy light of the campfire. The tanner rose to greet me, making a low bow so exaggerated that I regarded him suspiciously. Was this clod making fun of his betters?

He called off the names around the circle, and each nodded blankly: Simon, Noah, David, Solomon, Abraham, Isaac, Jacob, Joseph, and so forth, great names for garbage collectors, draymen, and the like. But without such as these, there could be no rebellion and no freedom. It was important, since there were so many of them, that our cause become theirs, for the Zealots were a leadership corps, an officer bank, nothing more. Strong arms and backs were needed.

I preferred to stand and look down at them, feeling a certain advantage in this stance. My eyes surveyed the circle slowly, then returned to Adam the Tanner, who was doing his best to look intelligent. I saw no point in beating around the bush. They were either with us, or not. Still, it did no harm to flatter them.

"I am pleased," I said, "by the many Amharetzin I have seen here. I did not know the plain people were so religious."

For some obscure reason, my remarks touched off a ripple of laughter.

"They mean no offense," said Adam, "but it is not religion they seek."

"Why else would they visit the Baptist?"

"We came for a Messiah, but he says we came for nothing."

"Then why do you stay? Knock out your fire and leave, it will go on without you."

"Because there is still hope for the morrow, And that is all we Amharetzin have. We do not have the fine homes of the aristocracy and the Romans, the lavish foods and wines, the alluring women whom only wealth can provide. We live in simple hovels, and we see nothing better in sight. For the freedom you speak of does not mean the same thing to us. It matters little whether the Sanhedrin or the Fortress Antonia rules, for our lot will be the same. But with the Messiah there will be a new day, for do not the Prophets say that he comes to help the oppressed and the meek?"

I could hardly restrain a smile. Meek indeed. He gave himself more airs than the High Priests.

"But you have no feeling that the Messiah is a religious leader, so how will he help you?"

"Not in the religion of the Temple, but he will still be of God. For without God he is not the Messiah and would be no more powerful than others who came with fine promises and brought only ruin to their followers."

There had been so many false prophets that it would have been idle to ask whom he meant.

"So if it is not freedom you seek, what is it you want?" A very wise man, I think it was Gamaliel, had once told me that he judged people not by what they said or even did, but by what they wanted.

Adam looked morosely over his company of clods. And then, suddenly, his eyes flashed. "We want freedom from fear," he cried. "We want to know there is some purpose to these miserable lives we lead, and that when we die, having not truly lived, we do not step off the brink of some precipice into a bottomless abyss of unknown terror."

I was momentarily taken aback, for how did a lout like this come by these thoughts?

He read my surprise correctly. "We, too, are people, sir, who have the same secret cravings for assurance as the rich and the mighty."

"Is it not enough," I said, 'to know the God of Israel watches over the children of the covenant?"

This statement, for some reason, inspired another ripple of laughter. The woodcutter, Solomon, a sly rogue with a single yellow fang, gave a malevolent chuckle. "He may watch over you, sir, but we are not so sure about the likes of us."

"His eye marks the fall of the smallest sparrow."

There was a gust of laughter, and two or three of the clods doubled over in merriment.

"Sparrows," cried Solomon, "have fine feathers compared to us. The aristocrats, I suppose, are peacocks."

I looked at him in disgust.

"You are drunk," I cried.

Solomon wiped his evil mouth with a grimy hand. "What other way can we woo oblivion? For life, kind sir, is not the same for the rich as the humble."

"Yes," said the tanner, "common sense tells us that our lives lead but to a pauper's grave. For some this comes sooner than others. The carcass is laid in the cold earth, and in a few days, Adam the Tanner is not even a cherished memory. None cared that he was born, and none shall care that he dies."

Solomon brought a large mug to his mouth. "I'll drink to that, for one and all." He lofted the vessel over his head. "And to you, too, kind sir, I wish you a hearty burial as well."

My disgust turned to loathing. No wonder some Pharisees considered it a good deed to knife an Amharetzin on sight, or at least cast their spittle on his face.

"What would the Messiah want with such as you?" I said with contempt. "I came to see what kind of men you are, and I find drunkards who make no sense."

Adam the Tanner stood up.

"We are not drunken sots," he said. "We have a few drinks and have some fun, for otherwise we would cry out in self-pity in our misery and fear. We cannot believe in the God of Annas and Caiaphas, for no man can buy the true God with petty sacrifices of animals and money." He touched my hand. "Forgive us our sport, for we mean no harm and only laugh in truth at ourselves."

I was impressed by his apology and accepted it in good grace. He had a surprising dignity at times for a tanner.

"So you are ready to do the bidding of the Messiah?"

"If he is the Messiah," said the tanner, "we are ready to sit at his feet and listen."

I gave them an appraising look. They were as ugly a band of cutthroats as ever I saw.

"Would you take up arms in his behalf?"

They looked back at me silently.

"Why then look for a Messiah if you will not follow him?"

"By what he does we will know him for what he is," said the tanner.

"You cannot put your own construction on his aims. If he is the Messiah, he is the Deliverer and so must deliver us against our enemy."

Adam looked at me roguishly.

"And who might that be?"

I gestured impatiently. "The Romans of course. You know that as well as I."

His slightly mocking expression did not change. "We have more than one enemy."

"And so do the Zealots, the Temple priests who traffic with the Romans, and Rome itself, the greatest predator of all. Does not your blood rise when you see your women dallying with the red-cloaked soldiers in the streets and taverns of Jerusalem?"

Adam smirked. "Our women don't go off with the Romans. We take care of them, don't we, mates?"

This touched off another gale of laughter.

"If laughter is your response to fear," I said, "you people must live in constant terror."

Adam's red-flecked eyes instantly became solemn. "We do, sir, for we have no education and do not understand the actions of the planets upon this earth." He lowered his voice to a confidential whisper. "We understand on good authority that we are coming to an end of the world, with the finish of the Age of Aries and the onset of Pisces."

I had no stomach for astrology, pure rubbish with which the illiterate amused themselves.

"Is this why the Baptist's followers carry aloft the sign of the twin fishes?"

"It is an evil portent, for in this sign, they say, with the death of the Emperor Tiberius the very heavens will be rent, and the earth broken, and fire and flood will sweep the world as in Noah's time."

"Don't you know," I snorted, "that Tiberius is a divinity, just as Augustus was before him, and divinities live forever?"

"It is no laughing matter," said the tanner, "for Tiberius could die suddenly and violently at any time, from what is known of the wicked Sejanus."

"If you, a tanner in Jerusalem, are aware of these conspiracies, then certainly the Emperor knows of them as well."

He held out his arms in a gesture of helplessness. "The eagle is not always mindful of the hawk."

"And what," I asked, "has the Messiah to do with all this?"

He thought for a moment. "If he is the one, he will bring us God's word, and that is all we ask."

"And this is all you require to offset your fears."

He held up a dirty finger and blew his foul breath into my face.

"Is it not true, sir, that God created heaven and earth, and so can dispose of it as he likes?"

His companions had looked up with evil grins.

"I do not know what God proposes."

"True." There was a gleam in the bloodshot eyes. "But the Messiah will know, for he will be our King, and there is nothing that God knows that will not be passed on to him."

"And if this paragon, who speaks for God, speaks then of war against Rome, what have you?"

I could see him wiggling for a reply.

"Whatever," he said softly, "that God wills."

I had the feeling they were as pleased to see me go as I was to leave. Nevertheless, it was time well spent, for I knew that these people could not be counted on in any uprising unless it was behind a Messiah of their own choosing.

I elected to spend the night among the Essenes and not seek out the Zealots or Pharisees, for anonymity suited me at this time. I wanted only to observe and bide my time. The Baptist had indicated the Promised One would arrive soon. How soon was that?

And so, in my pilgrim's habit, I sought out the Baptist as he rested after the evening meal in his hillside camp overlooking the Jordan. His phalanx of Essenes predictably tried to block me off, but he waved them aside.

"Speak to me, Judah," he said.

He laughed at my surprise. "Know you not, Judah, that you cannot hide anything from the eyes of God?"

"Then you call yourself God?"

"I speak for God at this time, as you shall at another."

He looked at me with eyes that seemed to hold a certain sorrow.

"Why speak you like this?"

"So that you will know that you are an instrument of divine will."

I responded to a sudden impulse.

"Would you cleanse me of sin?"

He shook his head. "That is not for me, but another."

"But you baptized all who were penitent before God."

"I baptize only in water, and you, Judah, shall be baptized in fire and blood."

My heart leaped at the thought, for what could this be but the baptismal of battle?

"Shall the Messiah then come and lead Israel in triumph over Rome?"

His eyes glowed with a faraway look. "Such a triumph, Judah, as you would never fancy in your fondest dreams. For he shall preside at the seat of their Empire, and they shall humble themselves in his name."

My heart sang with joy, for there was no doubt that he was a prophet and spoke with a prophet's vision.

"And how soon will he be here?"

His disciples, including the giant Ahiram, had been staring balefully at me, but he again wagged them away.

The sun had just cast its purple shadow over the mountain wilderness.

"Before another sunset he will come. That I promise."

CHAPTER FOUR

JESUS

A SOLITARY FIGURE CAME SLOWLY over the rise. His arms were swinging evenly, and he moved with a determined stride. There was a handful of pilgrims on the highway from Jericho, but the lone wanderer cut across the desert sands and scrub and headed in a beeline for the ford where the Baptist stood waiting, his eyes on the horizon.

A murmur spread through the crowd, and even as I felt my own pulse leap I wondered why we were all so sure that it was he.

I had struck up a conversation with Levi the Publican, who seemed well acquainted with whatever went on in camp.

"If this man is the Messiah," I said, "then it surely cannot be John."

His eyes, like mine, were straining after the approaching figure.

"It is not John. Isaiah told us what to expect. He will be as gentle as a lamb and as brave as a lion."

I laughed. "I can hardly picture the Baptist as a lamb."

"Not in speech at any rate," Levi agreed.

I had reservations about Levi. He had impressed the Baptist, but whatever there was in his character that had made him a servant of Rome was still there.

"Why do you wait?" I asked.

He gave me a cool look. "For the same reason as yourself."

"A tax collector for Rome hardly qualifies for the reception committee for the Son of David."

"You did not mark well what the Baptist said."

"He who is not for us is against us."

A curtain dropped suddenly over his eyes. "I hoped to make you my friend, but you speak like a Zealot."

"And you still smack of Rome."

"If that were true I would not be here."

I acknowledged grudgingly that there was something in what he said. "But Sadoc is also here, is he not?"

His tone became more conciliatory. "We both live with the same hope. Let us not quarrel."

The oncoming man looked neither to right nor to left. As he drew closer I could see that he was plainly clad in an old robe and hood. He walked barefoot, carrying his sandals in his hand. I could see the heavy yellow dust in his clothing and hair, for his hood had fallen back on his shoulders.

John had advanced a little distance ahead of the rest to be the first to greet the stranger. As he saw John his stride quickened and he seemed to radiate light.

As his features now came into alignment I was aware of Levi's sharp intake of breath, even as I felt a shock wave of my own. Isaiah had said he would not be comely, but he was beyond comeliness, for his beauty was not of his features. There was an aura almost like a halo that seemed to envelop him and herald his imminence. It dazzled me to look directly into his eyes. Their blueness held my own like a magnet, and I could not have moved at that moment to save my soul.

It is difficult to do him justice, for even when I mention how tall he is, and how beautifully formed in his coarse robe, I have not described his presence. His steady blue gaze was encompassing, not seeming to vary a shade in expression, nor did the sharp planes of his golden brown face soften for a moment. And yet there was an indescribable impression of sternness, compassion, love, and resolve without any effort on his part. His face seemed to soften only as he leaned forward and kissed John.

They stood off for a moment, regarding each other quietly.

John's face had an ethereal look, as if, confronted by a vision, he took on some of its quality.

"Behold," he cried, "the Lamb of God, who shall take away the sins of the world. For as he walked toward me I saw the spirit descending from heaven like a bird, and it dwelt in him. And so was I told that this would be he that came after me but would take precedence because he baptized with the Holy Ghost while I baptized with water."

"You knew me not until then," said the stranger, "but I have heard of you often and so knew your works."

"I know only that you should be made manifest to Israel and that your ministry would endure long after Rome is gone."

Suddenly, as they kept gazing at one another, a glint came into the Baptist's eyes and his stern face broke into a smile.

"I know who men say you are and am honored that we are of the same blood on this earth."

"Yes," said the stranger, "I am Judean like you, bred from birth in the same tradition, and born like you to fulfill the ancient prophecy."

For a moment a shadow crossed the Baptist's face. He spoke in a low voice. "We must make haste, for the time grows short."

"There will be enough time for what I do."

The Baptist's voice throbbed with emotion. "Did you know it would be me?" It almost seemed as if he wanted some assurance of his mission.

"My mother," said the stranger, "spoke of you, and so I knew what to expect."

His voice had a surprising resonance and was soothing at the same time. It was the voice of one born to lead.

"And my mother," said the Baptist, "regaled me with stories of your birth."

"Yet," said the stranger, "you will be present at my birth."

"For that I was born," said the Baptist simply.

"I come at the right time," the stranger said.

"True," said the Baptist, "a year ago I would not have been ready. A year from now, it would be too late."

He looked at the visitor with concern. "But you have come a long way and hunger."

"I thirst for the living water with which you redeem Israel."

A shiver ran down my spine. Who could this be but the Messiah?

"It has been written," I whispered, "that the nation must first repent before the Messiah makes himself known."

"I know," said Levi. "That is why so many have offered themselves for baptism. For it is well known that the sins of only one may curse the nation."

"Just as the sins of the father may afflict the children."

The stranger's quick eye picked us out, and I flushed to the roots of my hair. I was sure he had heard everything. But he smiled with his eyes, and I felt an impulse to kneel and kiss his hand.

I could see that he had a similar impact on others. I had thought that John would overshadow him, as he did all men. But I now understood what he meant when he said he was not fit to tie his shoes. For when he smiled one did not notice what other men were like, or even that they were there; it was as though a sorcerer had cast us in his spell. With a thumping heart I realized I had met the Master with whose life mine would be joined.

All Israel would do his bidding, of that I was sure. All he had to do was say the word and Jews of every persuasion would rally behind him. He was clearly irresistible.

I could hardly wait for him to speak.

Yet when John, his eyes afire, was about to introduce him to the multitude, the stranger stayed him with a graceful motion.

"Do first what you must do," said he. "And I will do as much."

John bowed slightly. "As you will."

They walked side by side to the riverbank, drawing the people after them. The stranger, still barefoot, stepped into the water. Though only slightly taller than the Baptist he seemed to tower over him. The muddy Jordan swirled about their legs. All the others had kneeled before the Baptist but he stood erect, gazing on skies that matched the blue of his eyes.

The Essenes watched with mixed feelings. But there was no doubt where Sadoc and the Pharisees stood. From their expressions, they felt the whole scene had been prearranged. And so it had, but not as these sterile scholars of arid ritualism thought. Cestus and Dysmas, as usual, stood shoulder to shoulder, skeptically waiting. And they were joined this day by Joshua-bar-Abbas and Simon Zelotes.

The Baptist dipped his hand into the water and, with a look of reverence, crossed himself in a gesture I had never before seen. There was a faraway look, the look of a visionary, in his eyes and even in the tilt of his head. "I do not of myself baptize the Son of Man," he said in a flaming voice. "For he is greater than I and will do greater works. For what I do on earth, he shall do in heaven."

They stood facing each other, unmindful of the multitude.

"It is more fit," said the Baptist, "that you baptize me. For you are sent of God, and there is none on this earth with superior knowledge of God's ways."

The Master put his hand on John's shoulder. "You, John, have been sent to prepare the way. And you herald my ministry, not in heaven but on earth. None that baptizes on earth has more authority than you. For this you were given to Zacharias and Elizabeth late in life. And you are my own kinsman in the flesh as in the spirit. Of you my Father said: 'Behold I send unto you Elijah the prophet before the coming of the great and terrible day of the Lord.'"

John was still not satisfied. "I have need to be baptized of you, and you come to me?"

"It is as I have said," the Master rejoined.

"But you are without sin, and I baptize for purification as in the olden days, and for the remission of sin."

"You baptize me so that the sins of the nation be washed away before I reveal myself to Israel."

There it was. Even as I wondered why he had waited, he had declared himself. My heart was filled with joy. Looking at Levi, I saw something of my own exaltation. Dysmas and Cestus still had a look of reserve, as did Joshua-bar-Abbas and Simon Zelotes. The Pharisees and the Sadducees gnashed their teeth in horror of this blasphemy.

Again John's hand dipped into the Jordan. "I baptize in water only," said he, his eyes never leaving the Master's, "but you baptize in the Holy Spirit."

The Master, with an embrace, let it be understood that he in no way demeaned the prophet who had filled the faithful with hope in recent months.

"I am of the earth and speak of the earth, and he sent from heaven is above all."

The Master looked at him with eyes of love.

"And so shall I continue. But how beautiful upon the mountains are the feet of him that bringeth good tidings, and that saith unto Zion, thy God reigneth."

The Baptist still hesitated. "As I decrease, you must increase. For salvation comes through you."

"And you," said the Master, "are the voice in the Wilderness, the messenger clearing the path to Judgment."

The Baptist turned to his followers, many of them dispirited by their leader's submission to the stranger. "Bear me witness that I said I am not the Messiah, but that I am sent before him."

"But," said the brawny giant Ahiram, "God sent you first for a reason."

"Not to establish my precedence but my role. He ranks ahead of me because he existed before me."

I saw a malicious smile darken Sadoc's countenance. For with all these allusions, the stranger would have lived before Elijah, centuries ago.

John cared little what other men thought. "Repent," he cried into the crowd, "for the Kingdom of Heaven is at hand."

"And you," said the Master, "make straight in this desert a highway to that heaven."

A glow came to the Baptist's face. "Would the Son of Man baptize him who cried alone in the Wilderness?"

"As you will, but first sprinkle me with the water you have made holy with your faith."

"That I will do. For a man can receive nothing except it be given him from heaven. He who has the bride is the bridegroom, but the friend of the bridegroom, who stands near him, rejoices greatly because of the bridegroom's voice. This my joy is therefore fulfilled."

The Baptist plainly spoke not only to the Master but to the multitude.

"Since he is greater, I baptize him through the prophet who said how we would find the Son of Man, and how he would find us."

Looking at Levi and the others, I saw a reflection of my own emotions in their faces. For all Jews knew that the Son of Man was the Anointed, the Messiah or Christ, promised by the prophet Ezekiel.

How well we knew the words of the prophet.

"And he said unto me, Son of Man, stand upon thy feet, and I will speak unto thee."

The Master's head was lifted to the heavens, and in the immense depths of his eyes I could see the endless ages of time.

Not even Ezekiel could have spelled out his own words with greater fervor.

"And the spirit entered into me when he spoke unto me and set me upon my feet. And he said unto me, 'Son of Man, I send thee to the children of Israel, to a rebellious nation that hath rebelled against me. For they are impudent children and stiffhearted. I do send thee unto them, and thou shalt say unto them, Thus saith the Lord God. And they, whether they will hear, or whether they will forbear, yet shall know that there hath been a prophet among them.'"

The Master inclined his head, as if to indicate that all surely knew this prophet was John.

As a Judean of the twelve tribes, I exulted that the ceremony now unfolding was a fulfillment of all that had been written.

"And thou, Son of Man," said John with unaccustomed tenderness, "be not afraid of them neither be afraid of their words, though briers and thorns be with thee, and thou dost dwell among scorpions. Be not afraid of their words, nor be dismayed at their looks, though they be a rebellious house. And thou shalt speak my words unto them, whether they will hear, or whether they will forbear; for they are most rebellious. But thou, Son of Man, hear what I say unto thee: Be not thou rebellious like that rebellious house, but open thy mouth, and eat that I give thee."

The Baptist again dipped his hand into the Jordan and gently put his hand to the Master's forehead.

"Son of Man, I have made thee a watchman unto the House of Israel. If thou warn the righteous man that the righteous sin not, and he doth not sin, he shall surely live, because he is warned. Also thou hast delivered thy soul." His voice rose. "Son of Man, lift up thine eyes toward the north. Seest thou what they do? Even the great abominations that the House of Israel committeth there?"

I stole a look at the carping Sadoc, for all knew the Holy Temple was meant. His face flushed and he gave the two in the water a poisonous look. But they were oblivious to such as he, for clearly the Divine Spirit had passed between them. And they were in a realm apart.

The Baptist's eyes had closed, but when he opened them I saw the tears. He had a distant look, and his voice, too, seemed far off, as though peering beyond the veil of time, for the message was still Ezekiel's. "And he brought me to the door of the court. And he said unto me, Go in, and behold the wicked abominations that they do here. So I went in and saw, and beheld every form of creeping things, and all the idols of the House of Israel, portrayed upon the wall round about. And there stood before them seventy men of the ancients of the House of Israel, and he said unto me, Son of Man, hast thou seen what the ancients of the House of Israel do in the dark, every man in the chambers of his imagery? For they say, The Lord seeth us not; the Lord hath forsaken the earth."

It was clear that the Sanhedrin's body of seventy was meant, but what had these venal men to do with the Son of Man? The Messiah was not their concern, but the Council's.

For the Baptist, none existed but the man whose hand rested on his shoulder, and he intoned in a voice suddenly tinged with sorrow: "And when I looked, behold, a hand was sent unto me. And there was written therein lamentations and mourning and woe. For, behold, Son of Man, they shall put bands upon thee, and shall bind thee with them."

I looked to see how the Master took these foreboding words of Ezekiel, but he only inclined his head slightly, and then peered over the Baptist's head into the crowd.

"Whatever my Father wills," he said, "I accept in his name."

The Baptist appeared to be listening to a distant voice. Abruptly he held up his hand and said with a throb in his throat: "I hear the voice of the psalmist. And he tells who we have here today, and whom he serves." He would have fallen to his knees, but the Master stayed him. Almost engulfed with emotion, he sang out the psalm until it echoed over the heads of the people.

"I will declare the decree. The Lord hath said unto me, Thou art my son. This day have I begotten thee." He bowed low before the Master, and his voice rang out: "You are indeed my son with whom I am well pleased."

I had been ready for the Messiah, the Deliverer, the Prince of Peace, but not this. The Son of God. He himself must then be a deity. It was a stultifying thought, and I could tell from the stunned silence that even the most enthusiastic were thrown into confusion. Did not our schema, wrapped inside every phylactery, remind Israel that the Lord God was one, indivisible, and that there were none before him? We could accept the Messiah, for whom all Israel was waiting, but a Son? Was he then a God as well?

But this crisis was soon resolved by the Master himself. "I come to you," said he, "on the wings of the prophet Isaiah, who tells Israel: 'Behold my servant, whom I uphold, mine elect, in whom my soul delighteth. I have put my spirit upon him.'"

The Baptist was in no mood to retreat.

"You are the embodiment of Israel and will fulfill the covenant God made with his people."

And what could that be but that God, through Israel, would triumph over all nations?

My heart sang with joy. He would find us worthy. We were ready to do battle, and with him we would win. For truly he was God-sent for one like John to be subordinate. John's smoldering eyes appeared to demolish the doubters. And in his fiery style he lashed out once again. "Behold, I will send my messenger, and he shall prepare the way before me. And the Lord, whom you seek, shall suddenly come to his temple, even the messenger of the covenant, whom you delight in. And who shall stand when he appears? For he is like a refiner's fire and like fullers' soap. And he shall sit as a refiner and purifier of silver, and he shall purify the sons of Levi, and purge them as gold and silver, that they may make unto the Lord an offering of righteousness."

Surely this meant that the Master, whose name we did not even know, would launch an assault on the Temple before moving against the tyrant who kept these false priests in power.

I searched the Master's face for a clue.

"I will do what I am sent to do," he said quietly.

"It will come after I am gone," said John.

The Master's eyes were like the dew and I recalled with a start the inscription on the Jewish shekel: "I shall be as the dew unto Israel."

A look of resolution came over the Baptist's face. "I do now what I was sent to do. In the name of God the Father, and the Holy Ghost, I sprinkle you, Joshua-bar-Joseph, with the living water. Hereafter, because your mission will extend into every nation, you will be known in many tongues as Jesus the Christ, the savior of the world, Anointed of the Lord. Through you shall salvation come for the peoples of the earth."

I detected a barely perceptible change in that serene figure whose name we had just heard. His face paled and his hand shook. His eyes closed for an instant. And then I realized that whatever he was to God, he was human as well and could suffer like the rest. I was glad, for I had no faith in Gods who walked like men. Rome was full of them. Better, I thought, looking at him reverently, a man who walked like a God.

The Baptist had knelt now, like so many had unto him. And the man Jesus dipped his hand in the Jordan and lightly touched the Baptist's head.

"In the name of the Father, I prepare the way for you, John, once Jochanan-bar-Zacharias, into the Kingdom of Heaven. You have served God well, messenger of Israel."

He rubbed his palms together to dry them. "No more shall these hands baptize, for no greater than he shall hereafter baptize, though many others shall baptize in my name."

They came out of the water together, John's head bowed, the Master, as I would know him, making ready to address the expectant crowd. His eyes roamed over the assemblage, taking note of the least stir. The two had been speaking Aramaic between them, with occasionally a word of Greek. But he now spoke in Hebrew, as if to stress that his ministry was first to his own people.

His voice was deep and musical and pitched effortlessly to whatever range or place he wished his words to carry. About his broad shoulders he had now thrown a plain prayer shawl, free of the stripes which reflected the separateness of the Pharisees from the rest of the religious community.

There was nothing of the fanatic or the ascetic about him. Indeed, as he looked about him and saw the long faces of the Essenes, a gleam almost of mischief came to the azure blue eyes.

He searched the sky. He appeared to be listening.

"I have not come before," said he finally, "because Israel was not ready. None would have believed, and though many will scoff, some will believe. And these will carry the message of another kingdom, greater than this, to the Chosen of Israel, so that one day the world will be aware of God's salvation.

"Israel is again in the hands of the Philistines, but this, too, shall pass. For the greatest enemy is not the enemy without, but the enemy within: your own wavering loyalty to God, the commandments, and the emissary sent from heaven unto you."

From the gasps on all sides I could tell that he had stirred in the multitude a sense of wonder. Who was this stranger, vouched for only by John, who was now talking so boldly of descending from heaven?

He had spoken for only moments, but I already knew that his was not to be an easy ministry. He had come to shock the people out of their complacency. This was evident in his every word. There were no sacred sheep in his flock. For with one breath, he now chided both the Pharisees and the Essenes, who made such a show of their piety.

"Piety without joy, faith without cheer, duty without pleasure, prayer without delight—these do not please the Lord God."

Some dour countenances took on the purplish color of their fringed shawls, and even the Baptist seemed struck silent.

But he was not at all disconcerted, for he went ahead almost as if speaking of a new faith. "I have not come to put new patches on old garments. And the ways I have chosen are my own. Has not God said, justice do I demand of you and not the blood of sacrifices? I have not come to call the righteous to repentance, but the sinners. And not alone by mortification and fasting shall man serve the Lord. I say unto you that you shall come close to him only in joy. For the good man, like the good tree, gives forth good and not evil. Beware of too much righteousness, for they that fast overmuch are sicker than the sick in body."

Sadoc's beady eyes looked triumphant.

"You say you come from heaven?"

Jesus looked at him calmly. "No man shall ascend to heaven unless he comes from there."

I understood of course that he was speaking of reincarnation, but not for a moment would any Sadducee grant this concept.

"And you call yourself the Messiah?"

The hint of a smile played on the Master's lips.

"You say that, Sadoc."

Sadoc was visibly taken aback.

Like John, Jesus obviously had the gift of divination, for how else could he name a man he had never seen before?

"You have accomplices in the crowd," cried Sadoc in his frustration.

"Many I trust," said the Master, serenely moving his eyes over the throng.

"You call yourself the Son of God?"

Jesus shook his head good-naturedly. "John was reciting from Scripture."

Sadoc's look said the impostor would not get off so easily. "He applied it to you, and you accepted it as much."

"We are all children of God, Sadoc, even you."

Again, Sadoc seemed to be getting the worst of it. But he drove on relentlessly.

"If you are the promised Deliverer, from what will you deliver us?"

"From hatefulness and hypocrisy," the Master replied.

The Baptist seemed restive under this attack on Jesus, but there was no stopping the Sadducee.

"Should we not know more about you before we acclaim you our leader?" he said in his silkiest voice.

"Ask what you like."

"Who are your parents, that you should be born in heaven?"

"My Father is in heaven."

"Have you no parents on this planet, or did you appear in a cloud one rainy day?"

"My earthly father was Joseph, a poor carpenter of Nazareth, dead these many years, and my mother, Mary, a sainted angel if there ever was one." How clear it all was now, the rod of Jesse, the *nazar*, the Nazarene.

Sadoc sensed that the people were troubled about the newcomer's antecedents.

"But the Messiah," he said with an air of triumph, "was to be born in Bethlehem of a virgin of the royal House of David."

Jesus smiled. "Many have been born so, without being the Messiah."

"You deny being a Nazarene?"

"I deny nothing, now or ever. Only God knows what I am, for by his will alone am I here."

He was being evasive, but I could hardly blame him in the circumstances.

"In the five books of Moses," said Sadoc, a malevolent gleam in his eye, "the Lord God warned his people: 'If there arise among you a prophet, or a dreamer of dreams, and he shall speak of other gods, thou shalt surely kill him. Thine hand shall be the first upon him to put him to death, and afterwards the hand of all the people.'"

Jesus gave him a placid look.

"I lead no man from God, only to him, just as Moses led the people of Israel out of bondage in Egypt to the Promised Land."

Sadoc laughed in his glee. "You make yourself the equal of Moses?"

"I do nothing of myself, only with my Father's help."

Sadoc had been biding his time. "Then, Almighty Prophet, with the connivance of your father, save this small child, if you can."

It was a cruel thing to do. Looking behind him, the Sadducee brought forward a mother and child. The child was clinging to the woman and sobbing in fright. She could have been no more than seven or eight years old. Her body quivered, and I could see that she still shook after she ceased weeping. She suffered from the palsy, an incurable ailment.

"Cure this child, if you are sent of God."

A frown clouded the Master's face, and I could see his fingers clench and unclench.

"God's work is not a spectacle for the curious."

Sadoc rubbed his hands together in his exuberance.

"So it is only talk."

I saw a momentary indecision, and then a light seemed to emanate from Jesus' eyes.

"The Lord loves little children, for they have not yet learned the wicked ways of the world and so, in their innocence, are dearer to him than any."

"You will not talk your way out of this one," cried a jubilant Sadoc, drawing so near Jesus that the Baptist stepped into his path.

Jesus moved forward coolly and gently touched the child.

Sadoc was about to scoff further when the shouts of the people drowned him out. "It is a miracle," they cried. "The child is healed."

The quivering had indeed stopped, and the child, her arms about her mother, was crying: "Mother, I felt warm, and then the pain left me. I am well."

Where Jesus had placed his hand on the child's neck, the skin had turned red. Presumably a healing energy had flowed out of him into the child.

"It is a trick," cried Sadoc. "The man is a magician and practices black magic like the Chaldeans."

Jesus gave him a scornful glance. "And if the child had not been healed, what then? I tell you, Sadoc, you have much to answer for in cynically abusing one of God's children." He lifted up the mother, who had fallen at his feet. "Rise and go with your child, knowing that God took notice of this day."

Jesus then mingled with the people. Their watchful reserve had melted away with the remarkable healing, which did more than any words to convince them that this man was indeed sent by God.

Levi and Simon Zelotes pressed through the throng to kiss his hand. Others clamored for healings, but he appeared not to notice. I held back, not knowing how to behave in his presence. But after a while his eyes fell upon me and his head inclined slightly, as if encouraging me to come forward. I saluted him, bending to the ground.

"You are indeed the Son of God," I said in a voice hoarse with emotion.

He stood off and gave me a sad smile, as if he knew something that I didn't know. Before I could speak his eyes swiftly took in Levi and Simon, and the Zealots, Cestus and Dysmas, who still hung back, still unsure, apparently, that he was the leader they were looking for.

His sad gaze returned to me.

"I will be at the campfire tonight. Join me there if you will."

The crowd still looked on him expectantly, save for the glowering Sadducees and Pharisees, who wisely kept their own counsel, judging correctly that the throng had swung over to him.

"Ask what you like," said he, "and my Father shall hear you. For he is everywhere, in the very trees and flowers, in the skies and the earth, and in you yourselves, when you permit it by good thoughts and actions."

Again there was a clamor by the ailing. "Help us, help us," they cried, holding up their canes and pushing forward their withered limbs and raddled faces.

He held up a restraining arm. "I come not as a physician to the body, but to the spirit. There the illness begins."

Since he could heal, I wondered why he did not heal all who needed it.

"You have been put on earth," he said, as if divining my thoughts, "to meet the challenges of life, learning in time, with faith in God, to behave in such a way as to establish yourselves as worthy companions of the Lord."

This in no way stilled the shouts of the sick, preoccupied with themselves, as they were.

"Think not of self, but of others," he said, "and your thinking will free you of the chains of the flesh. Your Father knows what you need before you ask. So pray to him, but use not vain repetitions as the heathen do. They think to be heard because they pray loudly and often. But in this way they stress weakness, not faith, which should be strong and sure."

The multitude did not understand. For the cry went up: "Tell us, Master, how we should pray."

"Not with words alone, but with the spirit."

"But what are these words?"

"If it were but words, the ailing could say them and be cured."

They still clamored for the magic words.

"Pray then in this manner, repeating each word after me, knowing that what you ask of God will be answered."

His eyes were raised as he spoke, and a responding murmur came from the crowd.

"Our Father, which art in Heaven, Hallowed be thy name.

"Thy kingdom come. Thy will be done in earth, as it is in heaven.

"Give us this day our daily bread.

"And forgive us our debts, as we forgive our debtors.

"And lead us not into temptation, but deliver us from evil: For thine is the kingdom, and the power, and the glory, forever."

I could sense a letdown in the crowd, which was clearly disappointed that the prayer wrought no miracle. And he realized it as well, for he now exhorted them.

"Let your light so shine before men that they may see your good works, and glorify your Father which is in heaven. Unless your righteousness shall exceed the righteousness of the Sadducees and Pharisees, you shall in no event enter into this Kingdom of Heaven I speak of."

From their faces it was quite evident that the crowd had expected more.

"You ask of others," said Jesus, "ask first of yourself. Blame not others for that which you do or don't do, for the errors of omission are often more reprehensible than those of commission."

The irrepressible Sadoc had edged himself into the forefront of the assembly.

"You mention My Father, Your Father, Our Father—exactly whose Father do you speak of?"

Jesus smiled. "Well said, Sadoc, for he is the Father of all who heed his voice. And before you report to the High Priests let me say that I have not come to destroy the law, or the Prophets, but to fulfill that said of old."

Sadoc's face gave him away.

"I speak only for myself," he blustered.

"But you account to others. Account fairly then, for you must account to one greater than I."

He did not speak like a Galilean, for most spoke only Aramaic, and that with a slur that was almost a lisp. His Hebrew was better than mine, and his Greek was flawless. Where had he studied that he should be letter perfect in these languages?

I thought, observing him closely, that he was in his early thirties, perhaps a few years older than me, but only months younger than his cousin the Baptist, from what I had overheard. Yet he seemed ageless, of any time or place.

He had drawn away from Sadoc now, and had asked Levi, like myself, to join him later. And so after our evening meal of flat cakes and goat's milk, with high expectations we proceeded up the hillside to the great campfire which served as John's headquarters. Several others were already there, speaking informally with the Master, who was reclining comfortably on the grass while a young man of great beauty anointed his feet with oil.

From their speech I took these men to be Galileans. One, standing tall and majestic, was called Andrew. The other, a hulking figure with a low forehead and a slack jaw, was his brother Simon. I disliked him at sight; he seemed to dominate the conversation, and yet added little to it. The young man, certainly no more than twenty, they called John, and with him was his brother James. They were the sons of the boatbuilder Zebedee, a prosperous man by Galilean standards. I gathered from the conversation that they had come to Bethabara to be baptized by John and had been surprised by the appearance of their fellow Galilean.

Simon-bar-Jonah was happiest when he was talking. He discussed this first meeting with Jesus with any who would listen. "Andrew and I were fishing on the Galilean Sea and kept bringing back empty nets all day long. A stranger on the shore called for us to drop the nets from the other side of the boat, but we saw no point to it, since others had been fishing there without any luck. But when he insisted, we did as he suggested, and lo and behold, we had the biggest catch of fish ever, so great indeed that it tore the nets, so that the fish escaped."

He did not realize how ridiculous he sounded.

"So," Levi whispered maliciously, "he was impressed by the Master because he helped him with his fishing."

The others I was more familiar with, the Zealots, Cestus and Dysmas, Joshua-bar-Abbas, and Simon Zelotes, a Galilean also, but more strident in speech and action because of his political persuasion. The Baptist stood over Jesus, with his disciples Ahiram and Abner. He seemed bemused by the younger John's ministration of the Master, performed with such loving care.

The Master did not appear to be listening, yet he would add an ironic touch to the conversation every now and then. When Cestus and Dysmas mentioned that the Messiah of Israel could prove himself only by liberating his people, Jesus smiled, saying: "And if he be the Messiah, the Deliverer that Israel seeks, need he take his instructions from any but he who sent him?"

Cestus and Dysmas frowned, for they had been answered, without receiving the answer they sought.

"It is not enough," said Cestus, "for one to say he is the Messiah."

"True," said Jesus, "nor that others say it as well."

The two leaders of the Zealot party now interceded. Joshua-bar-Abbas was considered something of a military expert, having served with the Roman legions in Egypt for a while, and Simon Zelotes was the religious authority, for he had combed through the Torah, the books of Moses and the Prophets, and could recite from them whatever was expedient to his cause.

"The Torah," said Zelotes, "proclaims that the Messiah shall reign as the King of Kings over all nations."

"And how else," put in bar-Abbas quickly, "can this rule be accomplished than through the destruction of the Romans?"

Jesus' blue eyes twinkled.

"There is more than one way of conquering an adversary."

"And which is that?"

"With love, by turning the other cheek when he smites you."

The Zealots looked at him incredulously.

"Turn the other cheek," bellowed bar-Abbas, "and the Romans will have your head."

"Nonetheless," said he, "in Rome itself they shall bow before the one god."

Young John had now finished anointing Jesus and turned inquiringly to the Baptist. The Baptist shook his head impatiently, as if to quash the notion that he might so pamper himself.

Jesus took the alabaster box from John's hand and kneeled before the Baptist.

"As you have ennobled me before the Father, let me honor you this day."

The Baptist would have drawn away, but something in Jesus' glance held him.

"Only I, John, can anoint you for the journey you make."

The Baptist submissively lowered his shoulders, and the Master, carefully, lovingly, anointed the bare feet that looked as if they had never known sandals.

"I anoint you with the Holy Spirit, John, for after tonight I shall not see you on this earth."

The Baptist's eyes glowed with a deep flame.

"I have done what I came to do, I am ready."

They stood together and embraced, Jesus holding him as if he would keep him by his side always.

With a sigh, he finally released him.

John drew his two disciples to him. "I go to Salim, there to baptize in Judea for the last time, and then into Perea, where the wicked Herod and his whore Herodias pollute the air. From there, only the Lord knows whence."

We watched as he stalked off, his camel-hair skin fluttering in the night wind.

"There," said Jesus, "goes a prophet than whom there is none greater, for he has yielded himself up to his own prophecy."

The Zealots viewed his departure with a rueful eye, for with the exception of Zelotes, the Baptist was more their idea of a Messiah than he who told them to turn their cheek.

"There," said I, the words slipping out, "goes a fighter for freedom."

"Some speak of freedom," said Jesus, "and make themselves a prisoner of this freedom."

Cestus looked at him doubtfully.

"This seems a fine phrase to me."

"Often people do not act, but react, losing the freedom of action which wells up naturally from their own souls."

"You mean," I suggested, "that in rebelling against tyranny we lose our freedom?"

Jesus smiled. "You speak of tyranny, but this passion for freedom is an even greater tyranny. It governs mind and body and sets an erratic course which takes you anywhere."

"Then should we bend our backs to the lash, and bid the Romans scourge us and then nail us to a cross for the infamy of wishing to be free?"

"Think not so much of freedom for itself, but free yourself from this yoke of freedom you have fastened around your neck."

"Then how, Master, do we find freedom?"

"In existing for others we exist for God, and in God we find this elusive freedom."

Cestus shook his head slowly. "We exist for Israel and the Messiah who delivers Israel from her captors."

"So say you, but not God," said the Master, and there was a great sorrow in his voice.

CHAPTER FIVE

THE ZEALOTS

AN AIR OF TENSION SETTLED over the campfire. Levi nudged me in the ribs. "Have you ever seen a more disreputable trio?" he said for my ears alone. Indeed, there was a fierceness about the Zealots that boded ill for any who crossed them on a dark night.

Bar-Abbas, with his hooked nose and rough stubble of a beard, looked like some predatory bird poised over its prey. Cestus and Dysmas were like wild-eyed hawks, ready to take wing against any adversary at any time. They would give a good account of themselves in any battle.

The Zealots, including Simon Zelotes, looked to bar-Abbas for the initiative.

"How," asked bar-Abbas, "can a carpenter from Galilee lead Israel against the mightiest army in history?"

The Galileans bridled at his tone, and I took offense myself.

"The Maccabean was but a shepherd," I put in quickly.

"I know," bar-Abbas rejoined, "and David slew Goliath with a slingshot. But slingshots won't do against Rome."

Jesus had been staring quietly into the fire, not appearing to listen. With a glance, he cut off any reply from his indignant supporters. He spoke mildly, still gazing into the flames.

"Let me give you a parable, from the prophet Daniel, who saved himself and his people in captivity by correctly interpreting the dream of the Babylonian King Nebuchadnezzar. The king had been frightened by a most terrible image. The head was of fine gold, the breast and arms of silver, and the belly and thighs of brass. Then came stalwart legs of iron, but with the feet set in clay.

"None of the wise men of Babylon could translate this dream, but to Daniel came a vision through the Lord. And this vision he told the King. 'Together with your kingdom, you are this head of gold. But after you shall rise another kingdom, of silver, the Medes, inferior to you. There shall be still another kingdom, of brass, that of the Greek Alexander, which shall rule the earth. The fourth kingdom shall be strong as iron, insofar as iron breaks into pieces and subdues all things. But as the feet were partly iron, and partly clay, so the kingdom shall be partly strong and partly broken.'"

He paused for a moment, musing into the fire, and we knew then he spoke of Rome, for what kingdom but Rome was mightier than the Grecian conquerors of Darius the Mede?

"And the iron and clay shall mingle themselves with the seed of men, but they shall not cleave one to another, even as iron is not mixed with clay."

Again Levi whispered in my ear. "He speaks of the disunity of this Roman Empire, which will not weld into one, no matter how many Emperors and legions there are."

There was more.

"And in the days of these kings," the voice soared, "shall the God of heaven set up a kingdom, which shall never be destroyed. And the kingdom shall not be left to other people, but it shall break in pieces and consume all these kingdoms, and it shall stand forever."

There was a silence for a moment, and then Simon-bar-Jonah, the brother of Andrew, interposed with his usual obtuseness:

"But, Master, if these kingdoms be consumed how can they continue?"

The Master gave him a fond smile. "You, Simon, are my weather vane, for by your response I know how the common man receives the message I impart."

While Simon's rough-hewn face showed his bewilderment, his brother Andrew said gently:

"We know what kingdom he speaks of."

Jesus' eyes swept over the company. "You, Andrew, shall be my first disciple. As the oldest you shall advise the others. And you, Simon-bar-Jonah, shall be second, though you become first in many things."

The two Galileans smiled in their simple pleasure.

"Thank you, Master," they breathed.

"Thank me not, for the road will be rough and tortuous, and the rewards not of this earth."

"We will follow you anywhere," said simple Simon.

Jesus' face clouded for a moment. "And so you shall, though little you know what you say."

I longed more than any to be his disciple.

"And how many disciples will there be, Master?" It was the first time I had spoken to him directly and my heart thumped wildly against my breast.

"There will be twelve at first, Judah, representing not only each tribe of Israel but a cross-section of humanity, reflected in the universal zodiac. Our own sign is Pisces, the sign of the fish, for it depiots not only the conflict of two opposing forces, good and evil, swimming against each other, but the new age of worship."

"It is also your birth sign," said Andrew, speaking as one who knew him from boyhood.

I came forward with Levi. "We would serve with Andrew and Simon," I said.

"And so you shall, but first know that many are called but few are chosen."

I was dimly conscious of the disapproving glances of the Zealots, save for Zelotes, who seemed as eager to join as I was. But then, like Levi, he was a Galilean, and they had a provincial pride in regarding the Messiah as their own.

Cestus and Dysmas had stepped forward as well. "We would be disciples," said the Syrian, "if we could be sure that you were really the savior of Israel."

"If you are not now sure," replied Jesus, "then you will never be sure, for God demands faith of his children."

"Is it not just," argued Cestus, "that the Messiah prove himself before we risk all by following him?"

"You risk more by not following him," said Jesus enigmatically. "But follow and see for yourselves."

"You think little of Israel's freedom," said Dysmas dourly.

"I think of nothing else, but it is not your freedom."

I had listened enough. "Did you not hear him say that his kingdom would consume Rome, and last forever?"

The Zealots were not convinced.

"I have never seen a Roman slain by a barrage of words," said bar-Abbas.

Jesus seemed unmoved by the criticism. And yet, earlier, he had reacted strongly to Sadoc's attack. His next words quickly explained the distinction.

"They speak from a love of Israel; let them be."

He now appeared to withdraw within himself, and Andrew signaled that the meeting was over.

The Zealots went off to their own camp, telling me to join them the next day. "Remember," bar-Abbas grumbled under his breath, "you have thrown in with us for better or worse."

I sighed inwardly. Here I was, ostensibly an agent for the Sanhedrin, a Zealot committed to the revolution against Rome, and a would-be disciple of the Messiah of Israel. God forbid that any of these loyalties should get out of joint.

"I will be there," I said.

Jesus' eyes followed them down the hillside until their forms merged into the darkness.

"The Prophets sing of God," he said almost wearily, "but your friends march to their own tune."

I got up the courage to ask: "Is it wrong to be rid of the oppressor who keeps his foot on our necks?"

"It is not wrong, Judah, and I would that Israel were as free as in the days of David and Solomon. But now the Lord asks more of us."

"How can we do more than spread his word through all lands?"

"And how would you accomplish that?"

"The Prophets say that the Messiah shall deliver us from the enemy and make Israel triumphant over seventy nations." I hesitated lest I seem overbold. "If we do not accept the Prophets, then what hope is there in Israel for the Messiah?"

"Ask better what hope is there in the world, for the same God that created Israel, Judah, likewise created all in heaven and earth."

The Galileans had been listening, their mouths agape.

"In other words," said a frowning Levi, "there is no distinction between Jew and Gentile."

"I did not quite say that, for we differ in the Torah and what we hold dear."

"But are we not the Chosen People?"

"God chose us because we chose him. But we have not always kept the faith, and the Temple is no longer a fit place for him to dwell."

"Are we any better," I asked, "for the Romans sitting astride their ramparts, casting their offal into our Temple, and massacring our friends from Galilee?"

Andrew quickly interceded. "You speak too sharply, sir. Mind your tongue."

Jesus waved him aside. "He speaks well who speaks for Israel." His eyes moved over the Galileans and I saw them mist with emotion. "If it were not for my friends, Judah-bar-Simon, I would not be here tonight, for their massacre was the sign I waited for, the sign that not only Israel but Rome itself needed saving. Yes, Judah, I knew these pilgrims well."

A shiver went down my spine.

"Yes, Judah, as I shall know you, and Pontius Pilate."

That night, Jesus took Simon-bar-Jonah and young John, and climbed into the mountains of Moab, where the prophets Moses and Elijah had kept their vigil before him.

"I go to wrestle with the devil," he said.

"And where is this devil?" said Andrew.

"He is the devil within me, which bends my ears to the cries of the oppressed of Rome, to the stricken Galileans, and to all slain for their faith in Israel."

What kind of a devil was it, I wondered, that he blamed for saving his own people? But I dared not say more after that rebuke from the soft-spoken Andrew.

He embraced his Galileans, and they kissed his cheek, bidding him peace on his journey.

"I have come far from Nazareth in three days," said he, "and I go to find how much further I must go."

He turned to me. "Embrace me if you like, Judah, for you are as dear to me as the rest."

I fought back tears of joy, and kissed him lightly, sending my heart on his way.

"Meet me in Cana, Judah," he said. "I will be there in a month."

I could think of little but him as I sat the next day with a committee of Zealots, presided over by Joshua-bar-Abbas. They seemed so commonplace even with all the fire shooting off their tongues.

"We cannot wait for him to decide which way he blows," said bar-Abbas. "It is time to arm, and to begin our war of attrition. Small but strong bands shall attack the remote garrisons and take over their arsenals. Other bands, sweeping out of the desert on swift camels, will harass the caravans, depriving the enemy of his supplies. We shall wreak this havoc, growing stronger each day, until, like the Maccabeans, we shall have a force to match any that Rome can pit against us."

I looked to see how all this was received by Simon Zelotes. For this valiant fighter, who had served with Judah the Galilean in his ill-starred revolt, was so staunch a Zealot that none could question his patriotism. Only he, like a Roman hero of old had won a surname in battle.

His gaunt face reflected the gravity of the moment. "I believe in him." he said slowly. "I believe be is the Messiah, sent by God to deliver his people, and I believe that he feels the oppression of Rome as strongly as any of you. When he spoke of the massacre of the Galileans he was almost overcome with grief. In the mountains he will commune with the Prophets and so define his mission."

"Perhaps he already has communed many times," said Cestus with a sneer.

Zelotes looked at him coldly.

"What does that mean?"

"It means that he could draw his own image from the composite pictured in Scripture."

Simon's eyes grew even sterner. "You speak like a Sadoc or an Eleazar, mincing little men with mincing little minds and no soul."

Cestus had the grace to flush. "Our lives are the stake. We cannot depend on the lackadaisical. Is that not so, Judah?"

I liked not the way he looked at me.

"I agree, but as has been said, only the Messiah can unite the nation behind him. The Judeans follow one, the Galileans another the Samaritans still another. But all, good Jews or bad, tribed or tribeless, will rally behind the Deliverer sent by God. Of that you may be sure."

Zelotes clapped his hands. "Wise words from an aristocrat." His eyes clashed with bar-Abbas over the scanty midday meal. "I believe we should hold off and give him a chance to declare himself. We have little to lose waiting a few months. By that time we may have help from Nicodemus, if he becomes convinced of the Messiah."

"Delays, delays, and delays," cried Cestus and Dysmas in unison. "Rome was not won like this."

"Rome," said Simon drily, "took twenty years to destroy Carthage."

"We do not have twenty years," said bar-Abbas. "Our skins will be hanging from crosses long before that if we are unsuccessful."

"Let us not quarrel among ourselves," said Simon, "but let us review our resources for the day we can bring them to bear behind the leader."

"He is no John the Baptist," cried Dysmas. "He would never lead armies into battle."

"It is only necessary," said Simon, "that he advocate revolution, and all Israel will rise." His voice took on a tinge of irony. "You, bar-Abbas, can lead those armies. How many troops do you command as of now?"

Bar-Abbas' grin gave his beaked face an evil look. "I command a thousand Idumeans, Pereans, Samaritans, not a true Israelite in the lot."

"And I two thousand seasoned veterans of other fights," said Simon proudly, "but with the Messiah's blessing that two thousand would be multiplied twenty-fold."

"It would do no harm," said bar-Abbas in a wheedling tone, "to forage on the countryside, for if this were done discreetly, with a minimum of killing, it would be thought the work of robbers and brigands, no more."

Simon laughed until his whole body shook. "And how far off would they be, bar-Abbas?"

"I like not your humor," growled bar-Abbas, but when the rest, including Cestus and Dysmas, joined in the joke, he laughed as well, holding his sides.

"I agree," said Simon. "Raid the caravans, but nothing more, no garrison attacks and no ambushes of small details of soldiers until the time is ripe."

"Agreed." Bar-Abbas held out a horny hand, and we shook hands all around.

My mind was already made up. I would follow Jesus to Cana, in Galilee, to Jerusalem, even to Rome if need be. The Romans had not heard the last of him, nor the Temple priests, nor any others who stood between Israel and its God. How could any question that he was the Messiah? He filled the description in every way, and his familiarity with the Prophets, particularly Isaiah and Ezekiel, revealed an exciting awareness of his own destiny.

My path was clear. I could not love him and another. I would be honest with Rachel, which I had not been before, and not so candid with the Sanhedrin and the High Priests. For as long as it behooved them to employ me, it served me to appear in their employ. Dissembling with the dissemblers in no way disturbed my conscience. Jesus had said: "Do unto others as you would be done by." But he surely could not have been speaking of the High Priests. What did they know of honesty but to pervert it to their own ends?

The Zealots had decided that Simon Zelotes and I should attach ourselves to the Messiah and be the watchdogs for the party. I quickly acquiesced, for that was my wish in any case. As a Galilean who had already fought in one rebellion, Simon had a special interest in a leader sprung from his soil.

"But he is a Judean," I had argued, "of the royal House of David."

"But his heart is in Galilee," Simon countered. "I saw it in his eyes. It was only to fulfill the prophecy that his parents contrived to have him born in Bethlehem."

"They had little to do with it," I said. "It just happened that way."

"Nothing just happens. Jesus can tell you that. We are mere puppets, responding to the will of the Lord."

Simon ran deeper than I thought.

"Then why do we struggle so, if all is planned?"

He laughed mirthlessly. "Because we do not know God's will until we have already committed ourselves to a course and learn too late what it is."

I thought for a moment.

"Does anybody then know God's will?"

"Some say that the learned rabbis and priests know from their studies of Scripture."

"Would Jesus then know?"

"If he is the Messiah, which I believe then none would know better than he, unless it is God himself."

"Then why, does he go into the mountains and meditate on his mission? Is it not clear to him from its onset?"

Simon Zelotes sighed. "Perhaps there are two sides the heavenly, in which God's will is plain, and the earthly in which he is but human like the rest and must find his own way."

"All I know," said I, with ringing tones, "is that the world has never known his like before."

"We will know more," said Simon, "after our sojourn in Galilee. He does not speak lightly. He means for us to be in Cana for a very good reason. He does nothing without reason. I know this because I know men."

I regarded him curiously. "How well do you know yourself?"

He hunched his powerful shoulders. "As well as I know you, Judah-bar-Simon."

"And what do you know of me?" I was annoyed that he should judge me so hastily.

"You are overly moved by emotion and do not always think things out before acting."

"You could say that of anybody."

"You speak much of God and the Messiah, but it is Rome that bothers you, Judah."

I looked at him in surprise. "Doesn't Rome bother you?"

"Yes, but I make no pretensions. I do not speak of God and Israel like you. Rome oppresses Israel, and that is enough for me. It is not wholly a religious question. If the Messiah helps unite the country, fine, but if there is no Messiah, then we go it alone."

"It will not come alone, for without the Messiah there can be no fulfillment of Israel's triumph."

He chuckled in his scraggly beard. "You treat God and the Messiah as if Israel were their only concern."

His words gave me a start, for had not Jesus said fundamentally the same thing?

"He said he would triumph over Rome, and I believe him."

"And if not, what then?"

"All he need do is declare himself, the rest will follow."

He gave me a long look. "You put into him what you want."

"I put in nothing that is not there, waiting to be wakened at the proper moment."

"Have it your own way," he chuckled. "But I am a realist and see things as they are."

"Is it for this reason you work in the Temple?"

He mimicked the arrogant voice of a Temple guard. "The devil you know, Judah, is safer than the devil you don't know." Then he added enigmatically: "Joshua-bar-Abbas watches the Temple, and I watch him."

It was time for us to separate for the present. We embraced perfunctorily and promised to meet in Cana.

"Meanwhile," he said with a curious smile, "think over your own motives, Judah."

There was nothing to think about except my immediate problem. I had thought of postponing the inevitable but knew it would be best to get it done with, and so not be constantly plagued by Rachel's reproachful eyes.

As I had surmised, it was an unpleasant affair. She laid her empty head on my shoulder and cried. I felt the swell of her breast against my own chest, her bosom heaving in rhythm to her sobbing. I moved a hand to comfort her. She took my hand and kissed it, pressing her lips down hard. And then as I sought to stop this unseemly behavior, she transferred her lips to my mouth, kissing me in such a way that I forgot my earlier resolves. She did not wait for my trembling fingers to loosen her blouse or her robe, and so transpired the last thing I had wanted to happen. In all the time I had known Rachel, not once had I trespassed on her virtue by look or act. And now as I gazed at her, purring in my arms on my father's couch, I felt a stirring of guilt. She looked up and pouted, her child's mind not once grasping what was running through my own. "Do you love me?" she murmured.

A pang of remorse was quickly succeeded by annoyance and then a start of revulsion. Why should this insignificant chit of a girl complicate plans of such grandeur that she could not begin to fathom their importance?

"I am sorry, truly sorry," I said.

She stopped my lips playfully with her fingers.

"There is nothing to be sorry about. We shall just be married sooner than we planned."

"Married?" I sat up straight in one convulsive movement. "But I have just told you why we cannot be married."

She tittered like a child. "But that was before . . . You have made a woman of me now. And if you do not marry me you will have made me an adulteress, for that is the law of Israel."

I looked at her in horror. "You tricked me," I cried.

"Not so, Judah, I love you."

I found her more revolting than I would have believed possible.

"I shall not marry you." I rapidly disengaged myself and got to my feet, slipping on my robe in the semi-darkness.

She stood up and pressed her breasts against me.

"Don't you understand? Never, never, never, shall I marry you, or anyone else."

She shrank back in disbelief. "I don't believe you. You are my own cousin. You could not do this thing."

"It is done," I said, stalking out of the room.

My mother's attitude was no help. I had never seen her so severe and uncompromising. "The wedding," she said, "will take place as planned, on a Wednesday, as is the custom of our people."

I looked at her with a sinking heart, and then my confidence returned. "I am the head of this house," I said, "and I make the announcements. This is one announcement that shall never be made."

She did not relent. "Then, as head of the house, you have doubly sinned, betraying not only your betrothed but a guest in your house."

"She is not without sin," I said.

Scorn sharpened her tongue. "You accuse a fifteen-year-old child of sin, you, a man almost thirty, of some experience of the world. Yet you blame her. For shame."

I had refused to have Rachel at the meeting, for I did not want to hurt her further.

"Tell her," I said, "that I will settle any amount of money on her, enough to give her a home of her own and to keep her for the rest of her life."

"And will you give her back her virginity?"

I felt the same annoyance now with my mother that I had felt with Rachel. "What is so wonderful about this virginity?"

"Don't be a fool, Judah. You know she cannot find a husband with this stain on her character."

She was looking at me accusingly. But instead of being contrite, I had the feeling of being trapped.

"She need not be lonely," I said. "She can live here with you as your companion. You love her as a daughter. I will deed you this house. I will have no need for a place in Jerusalem hereafter, for I will be traveling."

There was no glint of interest in her eyes.

"Is this your last word on the subject?"

"I shall not change my mind. I shall never marry."

Her voice was so cold that it filled me with foreboding. "Good," she said, "for better the line should stop with you than there should be a son of your blood."

"Mother," I cried, reaching for her hand.

She drew away with a gesture of disgust. "Do not call me mother, for you are no longer my son."

My eyes widened incredulously. "All this for Rachel?"

She shook her head. "You have behaved abominably. You have violated a sacred trust, Judah. Your father would turn in his grave if he knew."

"You will think better of me in time."

"I never want to see you again. We shall leave this house in the morning, Rachel and I. We want nothing of yours."

"Please, Mother, you would fill me with guilt."

"You can still repent."

So that's what it was, a trick to make me relent.

"I have nothing to repent."

"You have betrayed an innocent child."

"You make too much of it. None will know."

"God will know. Is that not enough?"

I had no recourse but the truth.

"She threw herself at me," I cried.

She drew back horrified.

"You do not even play the part of the gentleman."

"I am sorry, Mother. Is that not enough? I will make whatever amends I can. But I will never marry."

She looked as if she were seeing me for the first time.

"You think only of yourself, Judah. You are not to be trusted."

"Every man has a right to make his own bed."

She bent her gray head for a moment to hide her tears, then brushed me aside as I tried to take her hand.

"I can never forgive you, Judas," she cried, using the Greek version of my name for the first time, as if to indicate the gulf that had come between us. "You have dishonored your father's name."

I could think of nothing to say, but with it all I still felt a sense of relief that Rachel was out of my life.

She walked slowly to the door and stopped a moment. "I never thought I would turn my back on my only son, but with all your fine talk, Judah, you have no care for right or wrong. You serve only your own whims. And I warn you"—I thought I detected a break in her voice—"you shall one day suffer for the suffering you cause others through your self-indulgence."

The door closed and she was gone.

I went to my chambers and meditated. It was all a bluff; she would not leave the home she loved so much, with all its tender memories, for so slight a reason.

I slept late, and upon awakening I could tell immediately from the servants' frozen silence that something was amiss. "Your mother left in the night with your betrothed," they said in hushed tones. I could feel the accusation in their voices.

I decided that I would not spend another night in the house. It was hers, and she would come back after a while, grateful that I had turned the place over to her. She had often said she wanted to die near my father. I gave the keys to the chamberlain with instructions that he keep the house open for my mother's return. "Send somebody to bring her back. Go to Kerioth, her family's home, and there she will be."

It would all work out. My mother would get over her pique, and Rachel would marry in time, given the proper dowry. She was a comely girl, but not overly bright. She would do well to marry somebody her own age.

First things came first, in any case. I had my report to deliver, and I had to stay alert, to say no more than they already knew while saying enough to keep Gamaliel's confidence, at least. As I passed again from the Court of Gentiles into the Court of Israel, I shrugged at the sign warning

Gentiles that they entered under pain of death. What a joke, for the Roman officials went wherever they liked, asking permission of nobody.

The three were waiting in the same chamber as before.

As Gamaliel embraced me, inquiring, as usual, about my mother, Caiaphas nervously tapped the floor with his foot.

"Let us hear the man," he cried.

Gamaliel gave him a cool stare. "It will keep," he said shortly.

I saw Annas' warning glance. It would not do to offend Gamaliel and the Pharisee party.

Annas sat in a comfortable chair, his hands calmly folded in his lap.

"Do we have a Messias to report?" he asked with a bland expression.

"What does Sadoc tell you?" I replied boldly.

"You answer a question with a question."

"I am not blind. Both the Baptist and the one after him"—I was reluctant to speak his name before the High Priests—"were interrogated by Sadducees and Pharisees alike. It made me wonder at my commission."

"You tell us nothing," growled Caiaphas.

"What can I tell you that the others haven't?"

"Tell us of your impression, man," Caiaphas barked. "That was your assignment."

I had no intention of giving them any information that would bring the Master before the Sanhedrin.

"I saw nothing to convince me that either man was the Messiah. Neither claimed this role for himself."

"Did not the Baptist salute the other as the Deliverer sent by God?"

"Even so, this would be only his opinion."

"But it was an opinion," said Annas, "that influenced the crowd."

"Not the Essenes," I countered. "They gave the Baptist precedence over the other."

Annas looked at me closely. "Does this other not have a name?"

"He is called Joshua-bar-Joseph."

"Was he not baptized as Jesus, and called the Anointed? Come, man, we are not fools. Why do you dally?"

I sighed heavily. "But again, this is only the Baptist speaking. Joshua-bar-Joseph claimed nothing for himself."

"Only that he was the Son of God."

"But he said we were all God's children."

Gamaliel interceded gently. "What of the crowd, Judah, how did they take it, all in all?"

"They were confused. Some had come, as I did, to determine whether the Baptist was the Messiah, only to find to their dismay that it was a mantle he would not wear."

Gamaliel's brow had furrowed in thought. "Joshua-bar-Joseph. The name is familiar, but it is not possible. It was so long ago. It cannot be the same."

I had no time to think of what he said, for Annas' eyes bored into mine. "What of your friends, the Zealots? Were they out in numbers?"

I had learned that a half-truth could be an ally in the art of dissembling. "A few were present, but they did not seem impressed by Joshua-bar-Joseph."

"What manner of a man is he?" asked Gamaliel, with an interest he made no effort to disguise.

I hesitated, but only for a moment. "He is a simple man, a Galilean, from Nazareth, a woodworker whose father schooled him in his trade."

Gamaliel nodded approvingly. "A very good custom, for work is the anodyne of the masses, and he who does not work becomes a trouble to himself and the state."

Caiaphas' foot was tapping again.

"Where is this Joshua or Jesus now? He seems to have disappeared into thin air."

"You seem more concerned with him than the Baptist."

"The Baptist is embarking for Perea. Herod will soon gobble him up."

I tried not to show my surprise. "How do you know of his movements?"

"As you said," Caiaphas rejoined carelessly, "you are not our only observer."

"I do not seem to be of much use," I said, not caring at this point whether I was retained or turned loose. There was little I could gain from them, except for that single slip, if such it was, revealing an agent in the ranks of the Baptist. There had been a dozen at the campfire when he disclosed his plans, but he could have discussed it with others. My mind ran over the company. The Zealots, Simon, bar-Abbas, Cestus, Dysmas, the Baptist himself, his two disciples, Jesus, the Galileans, Andrew and Simon-bar-Jonah, James and John, and me.

How could it be any of them? But then who would suspect that a grimy whiskey-monger was the stormy petrel of the revolutionary party?

Annas interrupted my reverie.

"These are parlous times for Israel. It is essential that we give Pilate no provocation."

"He needs none," I said, "only his natural detestation for a people different from himself."

"We must keep an eye on this Jesus. He is more dangerous than the other."

Gamaliel gave him a shrewd glance. "Why do you say that?"

"Fanatics we can deal with. They thrive on emotion, and that soon spends itself. But this one deals in reason, and is mild and moderate. He wears better."

"He wishes only to bring salvation to Israel," I said casually.

"You see," said Annas, "already he has a champion in Judah-bar-Simon. He must be a fine talker."

"He performed a miracle of healing."

"We have many healers in Israel and yet the sick throng to the shrines outside the Temple and throughout the land."

I gave vent to my frustration.

"If he were the Messiah, would he not supplant the High Priests as the principal servant of the Lord?"

Annas eyed Gamaliel speculatively before he spoke. "The High Priests have survived a dozen Messiases."

Gamaliel's eyes kindled.

"If he is the Messiah, he will not hurt his homeland. For then he will be a true son of Israel."

Plainly he was different things to different people.

"You will give us another report," said Annas.

I shrugged. "Where would you have me look?"

Annas tweaked his thin nose. "Where you know him to be."

I would have quit the whole matter, there and then, but that it gave me a means of knowing what his adversaries were up to.

"I will do what I can," I said, which was surely no lie.

Caiaphas had watched me malignantly. "We need somebody to watch the watcher."

"You already have that," I rejoined sharply.

His sallow face clouded with hostility. "I say let us move against this Jesus and be done with it."

"With what would you charge him," Gamaliel asked sweetly, "that he urges us to repent of our sins and believe in the one God?"

"Give him enough rope," said Annas, "and he will hang himself."

"And Israel with him," muttered Caiaphas.

I was becoming increasingly aware of the underlying friction between the Nasi head of the Sanhedrin and the High Priests.

"The Sadducees," I said along these lines, "resist even the thought of the Messiah, while the Pharisees welcome the prospect but question only his identity."

Gamaliel gave me an approving smile. "Well said, son of a great Pharisee. Your father would be proud of you."

Hardly, I thought wryly, his praise only serving to recall my mother's bitter words.

The meeting had left me vaguely troubled. I allowed my mind to drift, blocking out my conscious thoughts; for the unconscious mind, I found, was a better guide at times. And then it came to me: I had been sent to scout the Baptist, and yet there was no longer any interest in him, and no surprise that a stranger should supersede him. They were curiously well informed.

On the way out I peered into an anteroom where the sacred shewbread was kept for the priests, and marveled at the doors and tables and candelabra of solid gold. There was a king's ransom in this room alone, amassed by the sweat of thousands of pilgrims who faithfully paid their tithes in the hope of gaining salvation.

In the Court of Gentiles my steps took me past the whiskey stalls and I saw my beak-nosed friend still boldly hawking his wares. He spotted me at almost the same time.

"You have much business here," he said with a leer.

"No more than yourself."

He rubbed his dirty hands together. "Well said." Then, looking around furtively, satisfied that nobody was in earshot, Joshua-bar-Abbas said in a hoarse undertone: "Good work, keep them guessing, but tell them nothing."

"I have nothing to tell." I said, "any more than you do. I assume that all our discussions are confidential."

"You assume correctly." He pointed dramatically to the high mound barely visible over the west wall of the Temple. "Otherwise"—he laughed without mirth—"we will all be hanging upside down on a tree of Calvary."

"That may come," I said pointedly, "if we do not hold our tongues." My eyes traveled around the marketplace, from the moneychangers rattling their coins to the bickering and haggling over merchandise that obviously had little value except for souvenir considerations.

Bar-Abbas' crafty face was covered with concern.

"What is it, Judah? Are you ill?"

"I was only thinking."

He drew closer, and his evil breath turned my stomach. He played his part well.

"They must have been sour thoughts."

"I was thinking about what you said about manufacturing a Messiah."

"But we have one, Judah. You think so yourself."

I studied him closely.

"Do you think so?"

He drew in some air and then let it out, laughing.

"As long as the people think so, what else does it matter?"

CHAPTER SIX

THE MIRACLE WORKER

THE MASTER'S FAME had already preceded him. Only fifty had been invited to the wedding, but some two hundred had turned out, ostensibly to honor the bride and bridegroom, but in truth for a glimpse of the prophet who had come out of Galilee.

Simon Zelotes and I had to fight our way into the house. It was a little more elaborate than the usual clay hut with a thatched roof, for the father of the bride, Ephraim-bar-Anaim, was the wealthiest fishmonger in all of Galilee.

I saw Andrew and Simon as I came in. They were conversing with two men I had not seen before, of about my age, or perhaps a year or two younger. The two brothers hailed us as old friends. We paused for a moment, looking vainly for the Master, then walked over to greet his first disciples.

I was in for a surprise.

"These two," said Simon, indicating the strangers, "bring the disciples to six."

Philip and Nathaniel were ordinary-looking men, nondescriptly dressed. I saw no distinguishing features. They came from Bethsaida, like Simon and Andrew, and were also fishermen. Nathaniel had become converted through Jesus' visualizing him under a fig tree long before he had actually seen him. This flash of clairvoyance had completely won him over. It reminded me of Simon-bar-Jonah's fish story. On what slim premises these simple Galileans turned over their lives to God.

"And who are the other disciples?" I asked with a twinge.

"John and his brother James. They were called the day Jesus came down from the mountain."

My eyes continued to roam over the crowd, searching for the man whose charisma had drawn me to this dreary land.

Andrew quietly put himself at our disposal. He pointed to a long table laden with rich foods of all kinds, fit rather more for the home of the High Priest or some Judean dignitary than for a Galilean fishmonger. I savored the variety of meats and game, fowl and stuffed fish, all flavored in the Jewish style with onion sauce, and a sparkling red wine which was excellent for Galilee.

“Is it proper to take refreshments before the festivities?” I inquired.

“Many guests have come a long way, and so it was thought the better part of hospitality to minister to their wants so they could join in the gladness without fretting about groaning stomachs and parched throats.”

The proud father was a kinsman of Andrew, accounting perhaps for the presence of the Master.

“And where is he?” I asked, still craning my neck.

“In the atrium, with his mother and brothers.”

“His brothers?” Somehow he had seemed a man without family.

“Joseph, Simon, Jude, and James are really his cousins, but Jesus’ father looked to their welfare when their own father died.”

“And his mother?”

“Mary is one of the wonders of our time. She looks no older than he, they would easily be taken for brother and sister.”

“There is then some resemblance?”

“Not in features, but perhaps in the radiance of their smiles. But judge for yourself.”

A young-looking woman of an almost ethereal loveliness had come through the door and appeared to be looking for someone. She was dressed in a simple white gown that fell to her feet and wore a plain gold band around her swanlike throat. Her hair had an auburn tint and was curled back on her neck as befitted a matron. Her eyes were dark and piercing, yet with a gentleness that permeated her entire countenance.

She moved gracefully, appearing almost to glide in our direction.

“Have you seen him?” she asked.

There seemed almost a conspiracy to avoid his name, as if such familiarity was a presumption, even by his own mother.

“Is there a problem?” Andrew asked.

“Because of the unexpected guests, Ephraim is embarrassed by a lack of wine.”

I wondered how this could be Jesus' concern. He seldom imbibed himself and certainly carried no wine with him. But maybe the disciples had brought some as a gift. This was not uncommon.

Andrew showed her the greatest deference. "Let me take you to him," he said, motioning for me to follow.

We threaded our way through the throng, everybody giving way before the solemn majesty of Andrew. I did not see Jesus at first, for a knot of people blocked him from view.

"Wherever you see a crowd," murmured Andrew, "there is the Master at the center of it."

He was half reclining on a couch, telling a story, when Andrew caught his eye.

He looked past Andrew at his mother, and a smile wreathed his face. She came to him and kissed him lightly on the forehead.

He rose to his feet and embraced her. "Woman," he said fondly, "what have I to do with you at this time?"

I thought his greeting a little harsh, but it was softened by his smile. And then I remembered that in Galilee "woman" was used as a term of affection.

"They have no wine," she said, as if that explained everything.

As I wondered why she bothered him with this irrelevant detail, he looked through the doorway at the milling crowd. "You do right to come to me, since my presence is surely the reason for the overflow of guests and the resulting shortage of wine."

Ephraim had overheard the conversation and, as a good host, protested that Jesus should not disturb himself about such a trifle. "You, sir, are our honored guest."

Jesus waved his objections aside.

"Summon your servants," he said in a commanding tone.

When the servants came running, Jesus inquired how many stone waterpots were available for the ritual of purification, an important part of the wedding ceremony.

After some hesitation, they replied: "There are six in number, each containing some eight gallons."

"Now fill these pots with water and show them to me."

Again they hesitated, looking uncertainly to their master.

Before the master could so much as nod, Jesus' mother said quietly: "Whatever he tells you, do exactly as he says."

Jesus trailed after them into the room where the pots were kept.

"Now fill these pots to the brim," he ordered.

He made an airy motion of his hands and whispered under his breath, so softly that nobody could distinguish his words.

"Now," he said, "take your pitchers and draw out the contents and take them to the governor of the wedding feast, and let him give them out to the guests."

My eyes widened as I saw the red sparkling liquid flow into the clay pitchers. The servants seemed almost terrified by the transformation they had witnessed, while our host turned the color of alabaster. But I saw only a pleased smile on Mary's face, and Andrew's only concern was that Jesus may have taxed himself with this chore.

"Would you rest more?" he inquired.

"Now is the bride and bridegroom's time, Andrew. My time has not yet come."

We preceded Jesus into a large room where the ceremony was to be performed. I was still overcome by a confused feeling of unreality and was more curious about the wine than the couple to be wed.

I noticed the governor of the feast, a hearty man with a red face, handing out goblets of the sparkling fluid to the eager guests.

"Blessed be the creator of the fruit of these trees," they cried, and I was again filled with wonder, for this was the toast delivered only when the wine was unadulterated by water. Had they detected water in it, the toast would have been: "Blessed be the author of the fruit of the vine."

Ephraim, shaking his head incredulously, helped himself to several heaping beakers of the liquid, as though to drown his wonder at what had transpired before his eyes. I drew a beaker myself and sipped slowly from the wine. It was exquisite, with a bouquet such as I had never known before. And so with the others I drank to the couple, thinking at the same time how unworthy they were to be the central figures of such an occasion.

The bridegroom, a callow youth with a pimply face, hovered over his bride, a dulcet-eyed goose, who was trying to look demure while quivering with delight at the prospect of what soon awaited her. She was another Rachel, to be sure.

The governor of the feast proposed a toast to the precious pair. And then, sipping from his cup he turned to the smiling Ephraim with a gratified look. "At the beginning of a feast," he said, "the host usually brings out his best wine. And then after the guests have drunk awhile, and are not able to distinguish the good from the bad he commonly brings out the worst wine, considering that none will be able to tell the difference. But you, Ephraim have saved the best wine until now."

Simon Zelotes' eyes were as wide as mine.

"He must surely be the Messiah." he whispered reverently.

It was now time for the wedding to proceed. Oddly, the wine had been served in clear, uncolored vessels, as was traditional with water, and from containers left uncovered. Ephraim, as his name betokened was of the tribe of Ephraim, and kept the law, at least in honoring his virgin daughter.

Jesus appeared to enjoy the ceremony.

The local rabbi, with his little skullcap, mouthed the traditional words of union unto death. Then the ritual vase was broken, signifying the beginning of a new life together. The most solemn oaths of fidelity were exchanged under the shadow of the bridal veil. There was much kissing and embracing and the usual letting of tears and then the bride, with great aplomb, was triumphantly carried from the house in a chair and through the street into the nearby house Ephraim had given the couple for a dowry.

"Hosanna, hosanna," the crowd cried good-naturedly. None seemed more radiant than Ephraim, not even the beaming newlyweds trying to hide their lascivious smiles behind a façade of innocence. I smiled to myself. How happy Ephraim must be. It was indeed worth all he had given and more to lose a daughter.

At the same time I understood why Jesus had summoned us to Cana. Whatever doubts I may have entertained were washed away with the wine.

"I see it now," I told Andrew. "John at Bethabara baptized with water, but Jesus baptizes with a living water that is the wine of life."

Andrew smiled. "Whatever he wills is the living water by which man is purified. The atmosphere holds no secrets from him. For through his Father in heaven he understands the laws of all creation, which have been universal since the first man."

We tarried after the wedding, Jesus wishing to exchange a few words with the friends who had come to acknowledge a prophet in his own country. For the most part they were bluff, open-faced Galileans, unmistakable by their speech. I had been relieved to see no Pharisees or Sadducees in the party. And then, with a start, my eyes alighted on the familiar face of a pious Pharisee, whom I knew as a friend of my father. They had served together on the Sanhedrin, and with Gamaliel and Nicodemus were the nucleus of the liberal party which dreamed of Israel's redemption with the coming of the Messiah.

He was standing in a dark corner of the room, his eyes riveted on the Master. There was a tender look in his long saturnine face, and the large dark eyes were soft and liquid in their wistful melancholy. I knew Jesus had nothing to fear as I marked his expression. I could see the same yearning in his eyes that I felt in my own heart. Still, it gave me pause that a prominent member of the Sanhedrin should have taken the trouble to ferret out the Master's whereabouts and followed him to this abode.

Bowing low, I addressed him with the deference due a distinguished elder of Israel not of the Sadducee persuasion.

"Joseph of Arimathea, what brings you to this humble dwelling?"

His eyes flickered with annoyance and then cleared somewhat as he recognized me.

"I am not here in any official capacity and do not wish it known."

"As you will, sir."

"And what do you do here?"

I nodded to the small circle surrounding the Master. "I follow him."

"You do well," said Joseph of Arimathea, "for he is the light of Israel and the hope of the world."

We had moved off from the crowd and stood alone. "I speak frankly to you, not only because you are Simon's son but because I know of your interest through the Reb Gamaliel. Know whom you follow, and listen not to idle talk."

"I do know," I said. "I have seen him heal the sick and change the living water to wine."

He waved his hand in a gesture of dismissal. "That is nothing. What is important is that he is sent by God in fulfillment of ancient prophecy. I dreamed of him before he was born, and in this vision God revealed to me that I should not die until he proved himself."

"And now you have seen him?"

He smiled benignly. "Oh, I first saw him in the manger in Bethlehem when I followed the glorious star that foretold his birth. And this was not all, for with my own eyes I saw the two humble beasts of burden that symbolized his birth." He held up a finger, and his voice became low and mysterious. "The ox knoweth his owner and the ass his master's crib. Even these animals seemed to know they were parties to a great occasion."

What a thrill it was to meet someone who knew him so well. The questions tripped off my tongue.

"But was none there to assist in the birth?"

"Her husband, Joseph, helped, but God allowed the child to be born painlessly."

"But why," I asked. "were they in the manger?"

"Such was the prophecy of the ox and ass," he said, "but ostensibly there was no room in the inn for many had come to register for the census in the place of their birth."

"And so Joseph, too was a Judean?"

"Of the House of David, as was Mary."

"Were there no others there?"

"The three wise men, being astrologers acquainted with the peculiar conjunction heralding his birth, had also followed the glorious star, arriving soon after me. But they did not tarry long, for they were fearful that Herod the Great would find them out and destroy the child that prophecy said would grow up and become the King of Kings."

Caspar, Melchior, and Balthazar had looked into the makeshift crib and satisfied themselves that this was the Promised Child foreshadowed in Scripture. And Caspar, kneeling in prayer, had solemnly murmured: "There shall come a star out of Jacob and a scepter shall arise out of Israel."

Joseph of Arimathea had befriended the couple. He brought them food and comfort and went with them to the Temple in Jerusalem on the eighth day, when the infant was inducted into his faith with the sacrifice of the doves.

Tears had come into the old man's eyes. "I myself held the infant in my arms and assisted in the ceremony. And I blessed the Lord for this great privilege, praying that he would now let his humble servant depart in peace, for my eyes had seen the salvation which he had prepared before the face of all people." He sighed. "But a voice told me that my mission was not yet complete, not until I had once again witnessed his birth."

I looked at the old man with some misgivings. Had I been listening to a doddering old fool long past his prime?

He smiled sardonically. "Have you never heard voices, Judah-bar-Simon?"

"I shook my head and then with a start remembered the voice telling of the Kedron running red with the blood of man.

"Yes," I said soberly, "I have heard voices."

There had been still another unexpected visitor on that momentous occasion, Anna, the seeress from Jericho of whom but little was known. She was a toothless hag with a wicked leer, and her presence made even Joseph of Arimathea uncomfortable.

Only Mary did not wince as Anna took the tiny babe in her horny hands and peered into that innocent face.

"He is the one," she cackled. "I give testimony to this before the forces of darkness and light, for there shall be both before the end. There shall be no greater King in Israel than he, but his kingdom shall be universal, and he shall not reign till he is gone."

Only Mary seemed to understand, for she nodded, then closed her eyes as if to put the thought out of her mind.

Joseph of Arimathea made a move as if to drive off the woman, but Mary stayed him with a gentle motion.

"And how long shall I have him?" she asked quietly.

The old hag's face wrinkled in thought. "He shall be with you until a new tyrant rules in Israel, one who shall be remembered only because of this child." Her face softened and became almost beautiful in the transformation.

"Blessed are you, Mary, for you shall be at the beginning and the end, and know both for what they are."

More than any other, this Anna intrigued me. For she seemed to intimate great things though some was clearly witch talk.

"What did she mean by his reign not beginning till he was gone?"

Joseph of Arimathea gave an impatient shrug. "I had no time for witches. It was enough that the child was born."

He had not yet told me why he was here at Cana.

"I came to see his mother," he said. "We have a great bond and comfort one another."

"And will you talk to him before you leave?"

"It is not necessary. He sees me here and knows that I am devoted to his family. I will be there, too, when he is ready, as you shall yourself, Judah."

I looked at him sharply. "What do you know of my mission?"

"Only what he knows."

It was vexing to be constantly confronted with these little enigmas, but Joseph of Arimathea had turned away and, with a wave of his hand, disappeared through the door.

Again, I had more than an inkling that the Pharisee command was intrigued by Jesus and was praying that Israel's quest for the Messiah be fulfilled in this carpenter from Galilee. Gamaliel, Nicodemus, Joseph of Arimathea, all good and holy men with influence in the Sanhedrin, presaged strong support if it came to a vote. But how did one vote for a

Messiah? It was an absurdity that only the Sadducees would compound to curry favor with Rome.

The meeting with Joseph had turned my mind back to the time when this great merchant had visited our home as though it were his own. My father would put aside whatever he was doing when this pious Jew came to pay his respects. Seldom did they talk business, except to speak of the grinding weight of the taxes.

"We pay for Rome's bread and circuses," I remembered my father saying, "for those too shiftless to do an honest day's work."

"Yes," replied Joseph, "they keep the masses anesthetized with chariot races and gladiators and free corn, but one day they will demand more."

But mostly they sat and talked of other matters. It was from the lips of Joseph that I first heard of the Messiah.

My father listened closely, but I could tell he was not convinced.

"You will not know him when he appears," said Joseph, recalling the Prophets.

"With that I agree," said my father good-naturedly.

"I have seen him with my own eyes. His mother was young, but fourteen and a virgin. His adoptive father, Joseph, was a simple Galilean carpenter. But both were of the House of David as the Prophets foretold."

My father playfully ran his hand through my hair.

"And so is my six-year-old Judah. Would you call him the Anointed One?"

"The wise men knew him, for they had the glad tidings from God's own angels, as well as the stars. They were without doubt, scorn, or fear. So all wise men approach their God."

"So then where is he, this Messiah of yours?" my father teased. "This son of a virgin."

"He would be only twelve now, preparing himself for the ministry that will one day shake the world."

"What world do you speak of, Joseph of Arimathea?"

Even though I was not old enough to have any idea of the immensity of the Empire, his answer sent a thrill through me.

"The Roman world, dear friend. His coming shall rock the Empire to its very foundations."

With all this talk of visions and voices, prophecies and premonitions, it was not surprising that a Messiah should materialize in the minds of men. And public acceptance, as bar-Abbas had intimated, was perhaps even more important than the actuality.

Jesus' public career had hardly begun, yet adoring crowds mysteriously appeared wherever he went. Stories of his transformation of water into wine could be counted on to spread like wildfire and add to his luster. As I watched the wedding guests thronging about him, anxious to touch or hear him, I was never surer that he was the Promised One.

"One word from him," I said, "and the people would take arms against Rome."

Andrew regarded me solemnly. "Is this why you follow him?"

"Is it not reason enough?"

"It is not our reason."

"Is it not enough that he is the Messiah?"

"We do not presume to tell the messenger his mission."

"Nor do I, but is it wrong to assume that the Deliverer of Israel must deliver her?"

We had been edging through the room to the couch where he half reclined.

Simon-bar-Jonah and the other disciples hovered about him protectively, allowing nobody to touch him.

"Each contact draws on his universal energy," whispered Andrew.

I considered for a moment. "Is this how he heals and enriches the water?"

"He does it all with God's help."

"But something still takes place in him, and in the atmosphere; there is a connection of some kind, for these wonders to materialize."

Jesus had looked up at our approach.

"Ah, here is our friend Judah. Come with us to Bethsaida and there shall our company be completed."

I envied his closeness with his disciples and again felt a longing to be one. But it could only be at his call, that I knew. "I will follow you anywhere," I said.

He had turned to Andrew. "See that Judah has lodgings in Bethsaida. We have much to do, and so little time."

He rose easily, and the crowd parted to let him through. Many bowed in reverence, and an excited murmur trailed after him as he moved into the street, where a few peasants raised the cry "Hail to the Son of David." And others, first looking about carefully, added to this cry: "Hail to the King of Israel."

He frowned, and no wonder, for who knew where the spies of Rome or the Sanhedrin lurked?

I looked at Andrew to see how he took this tribute. "I am not the only one who sees him as our Deliverer," I said.

"True," he replied, "but we who follow him do so only because we believe in him. This you and Simon Zelotes must be ready to accept."

"Simon Zelotes?"

"Yes, he represents an important faction of the people."

Bethsaida was no more than I expected, another bleak Galilean fishing village with country clods in evidence wherever we went. The most prosperous citizens were Jonah, the father of Andrew and Simon, and Zebedee, the father of James and John. They owned not only several fishing boats in concert but a market for fresh fish and a fish-drying plant. The whole settlement smelled of fish, but these hearty creatures with their red faces and great bodies did not even seem aware of the odor.

Andrew had arranged for Simon Zelotes, Levi the Publican, and me to stay for the few days at the Zebedee household, and I must admit that they were a warm, generous family, though young John seemed to have taken a dislike to me for no reason at all. After the brothers had come down from the mountain with Simon-bar-Jonah, they had been called as disciples, baptized by Simon, who had been baptized along with Andrew by the Baptist but a short time before.

Though all were fishermen they would cast no more nets in the Gennesaret Sea, which was popularly called the Galilean Sea. Over the dinner table, laden with a dozen varieties of fish and green vegetables, the handsome John, almost too good-looking for a youth, happily regaled us with Simon's confusion at being told by Jesus that he was now a fisher of men.

"Do you mean," the wide-eyed Simon had asked, "that I can no longer cast a net with my father?"

"Only if there is a man in it," Jesus had replied with a smile.

More seriously, John described how the Zebedees had fished all day with their crew without taking anything in their nets until Jesus, speaking from the shore, had directed them to a certain spot where the waves formed a crest.

"There you will find more fish than you can handle."

"But we have fished there before, and our nets came back empty."

"Fish there again," cried Jesus.

John laughed boyishly as he recalled Simon-bar-Jonah's amazement at the full nets they pulled back, so strained with the weight of the catch that the cords tore and the fish slid back into the sea.

"It certainly made a believer of Simon-bar-Jonah," he said.

The story was an old one to me. "You were on the mountain quite a while," I said, changing the subject.

"A few days," said John noncommittally, "and then Jesus spent some time healing the sick and the infirm on his way from the Wilderness to his home in Nazareth."

As I had surmised, Andrew had handled the arrangements for the stopover in Cana.

My curiosity about the excursion into Moab had been heightened by John's evasiveness, which led me to believe that something momentous must surely have transpired.

"Was the journey into the mountain anything like Moses' experience on Sinai?" I asked as casually as I could.

John and his brother exchanged glances. "There is nothing we can say about it," said James.

For a moment I felt excluded, and then with a shrug I dismissed the matter as of no account.

The next day we were to meet with Jesus at Jonah's house. "It will be good to talk to a man without secrets," I said.

This was the occasion for Salome, the wife of Zebedee, to say with some waspishness: "And why does not Jesus stay here, is our home not good enough for him after all these years?"

The good-natured Zebedee responded with a smile. "Now, Mother, he has his reasons. The mother of Simon-bar-Jonah's wife is sick with a fever, and Jesus went to heal her."

"And she is healed?"

"But of course," Zebedee said. "He merely touched her hand and the fever left her, and she arose and made their dinner, she felt so relieved."

He had then healed a host of others whom Andrew had arranged to be there, one of whom had attacked him before he could cast the devil out of him. The crusts and sores had fallen from another, a leper normally forbidden in the community, when Jesus passed his hand over the disfigured face.

Levi the Publican had listened with a wondering look. "All this has been done," he said, "to fulfill that spoken by Isaiah: 'He took away our infirmities and lay bare our sickness.'"

Salome looked up with a chuckle. "You are not saying that this village boy is the Messiah? How absurd."

Her sons chided her with their eyes. "All right," she said, "I know his mother had a vision, but many mothers have visions about their children. That establishes nothing."

"You will come to him on bended knee one day, Mother, and be happy to acknowledge that he is sent by God. I only wish that I could tell you what James and I saw on that mountain."

"All right, John." She kissed his forehead. "I fear that I feel only a mother's resentment that my two sons give up their home and their right to a family of their own to follow the uncertain path of a leader who takes them God only knows where."

I had held my question for a while. "How is it that Simon-bar-Jonah is a disciple, since the disciples must have neither wife nor child?"

"That is a good question," put in Salome. "But Simon, like Andrew, leaves his wife and a child to be supported by old Jonah and his wife. You would think that he would pick only on single men."

John and James protested together. "But, Mother," said John, "each disciple stands for something special that Jesus sees in him."

She snorted. "I am a Galilean born and bred, but since when does this remote region hold a monopoly on geniuses in Israel? Argue not this matter with any Judean you meet on the road."

In spite of ourselves, we all laughed together, and the tension was eased.

"Go now," she said, "and meet with your Savior. And bid him repair the bench he once made for this house. One of its legs fell off. I hope this has no great significance, for I understand he tells parables on less ground than this."

Zebedee shook his head wearily, and then his voice rose so that we understood why he was called the Thunderer. "Woman, hold your tongue. Your sons go to serve God. Any fool can tell that Jesus is no ordinary man, even if he did nothing but walk through this community without raising a hand to heal the sick or bless the whole."

She closed her eyes. "All right," she said with a sigh. "I bid a tearless goodbye to the children of my womb."

I knew not what to expect when we marched silently into Jonah's house and were led by a servant into an upstairs room. We were greeted quietly by Andrew and Simon-bar-Jonah, who was variously known as Peter since his own baptism by John. Jesus sat in the center on a large cushion, his piercing eyes sending a welcome to us all.

"I have summoned each of you for a reason that may not become apparent until your last breath. And then you shall know eternity, for you are the Chosen of God. Remember this well, however spitefully the world considers you: that for judgment came I into this world that they who see not may see, and those who see may become blind in their blindness."

His words fell swiftly like the strokes of a sword.

"Six of you have already been blessed with the living water, and now the six remaining shall be sprinkled with the water of a new life, by Simon-bar-Jonah and Andrew, for I baptize not after John."

I could see the others were excited as I was. Their faces were pale, but there was a look of exaltation in their eyes.

"First," said Jesus, dropping his hand into the water, "let me bless the Holy Spirit which makes you as one with God, with hearts hungering to help humanity."

I felt myself tremble, thinking now how unworthy I was. Thoughts of Rachel and my mother, mingled with memories of my childhood, of Joseph of Arimathea, Nicodemus, Joshua-bar-Abbas, Cestus and Dysmas, Annas and Caiaphas, Gamaliel, all came crashing together in my head.

Andrew beckoned Levi forward, and Simon-bar-Jonah, with a grandeur I would not have expected, sprinkled him lightly with water. Yet Jesus, though he did not baptize, still dominated the ceremony.

"Levi the Publican," said Jesus, "I name you Matthew. I took you from your office, and you are indeed, as this name indicates, a gift of the Lord. Your name shall be coupled with mine as long as God's name is remembered, for you shall be our chronicler."

Simon Zelotes was next, and as he received the water, Jesus said solemnly: "A proud son of Galilee, and a patriot as well, who speaks for the Zealots in their struggle to rid the homeland of the invader. Be as great a warrior, now, Simon, for an even greater cause."

Even as I wondered what cause could be greater, his eyes looked fondly on the two sturdy Galileans who were obviously twins. "James and Jude," he called, "sons of Mary of Alpheus, who stand as a constant reminder that no family ties are as meaningful as those consecrated in God. You who were my cousins are joined now by a bond dearer than blood."

The next was Didymus, whom he called Thomas, which also signified a twin. "You shall attain glory for leaving your doubts, and your own twin, for a doubtful cause. And though your doubts return, your faith shall redeem you."

"Judah!" I jumped at his call. "A proud Judean of a proud house. You shall sit on my right, and in the unaccountable ways of the Lord you shall serve in your own way to establish the living truth of life everlasting.

"Whenever the name Jesus Christ is mentioned, yours shall be added almost in the same breath. For though you are the twelfth to be named, your fame shall not be least. You shall be our treasurer, and guard the purse strings, for only a Judean versed in his father's estates can manage our affairs well enough to keep flesh and spirit together while we minister to the poor."

His eyes held mine, and his dear face softened for a moment.

"You, Judas, shall make your first excursion into the countryside with Matthew, who was Levi. and you shall carry my word and heal in my name. Remember that your power comes from the Father through his Son. For all things are delivered to me of my Father. And no man knows who the Son truly is but the Father, nor who the Father is but the Son, and he to whom the Son will reveal him."

I had no sense of his power coming through me. How could I make the leper whole, or make steady the hand afflicted with palsy?

He seemed to have read my mind.

"I say this to the Twelve, all of whom I love equally, that with faith in the Father you can do what the Son has shown you to do."

I felt almost naked in my helplessness.

"How do we support ourselves?"

"Spoken like a true believer." He had a sardonic smile. "Ask the birds and the butterflies, the lilies in the fields, which neither toil nor spin. God takes care of them, as he will you. Forsake not so much your worldly goods as your worldly thoughts, go forth like the deputies of the Lord, for that you are, and embrace the world with the love of God in your hearts."

Matthew, too, was confused.

"And when begins my assignment to record this ministry for those who follow?"

"It has already begun, for your mind is already teeming with the words heard here today, and the activities at Bethabara and Cana, and even on the mountain, where you were not."

Matthew still hesitated. "May I go anywhere and ask what I like about your mission from God?"

"Yes, even to Nazareth."

In nearly everything, Jesus showed an awareness of his Judean heritage. Just as Moses appointed twelve tribal chieftains, so Jesus chose twelve whom he called Apostles.

"As Apostle means one sent," he said, "you are sent from me."

We were also disciples, pledged to his teachings, but our apostolic authority rested in the intimacy we shared as his family.

"Henceforth I call you not servants, for the servant has no idea what his master is about. I shall call you my friends, for everything I have of my

Father I shall pass on to you. You shall bring forth sweet and bitter fruit, and whatsoever you ask of the Father in my name he shall grant you."

Each Apostle was authorized to name five disciples, Jesus himself selecting the rest, until there were seventy in all. Moses had named as many, and this number ruled the affairs of the Sanhedrin.

In choosing this number did Jesus challenge the authority of the Temple elders?

He smiled, "Our whole ministry, Judah, is a challenge to what the Temple does."

Some of my brethren found me contentious, but as Jesus looked around at these pacific faces, he said with a reassuring twinkle: "I come not to bring peace but to stir up the established order."

Simon-bar-Jonah, as usual, held up his hand.

"And how shall this be done, Master?"

"With the truth, for the truth is God's revelation, and it does not vary from King David's time to this. Do you not remember David saying to Solomon: 'Keep the charge of the Lord thy God, to walk in his ways, to keep his statutes, and his commandments, and his judgments, and his testimony, that you may prosper in all that you do'?"

There were smiles of satisfaction among these simple Galileans. For as they felt themselves moving in the footsteps of Abraham and Moses, they felt comfortably reassured. Except for Zelotes there was not a revolutionary in the lot.

Jesus had not finished. "And David spoke that day of the promise made by the Lord. 'If your children walk before me in truth with all their heart and with all their soul, there shall not fail you a man on the throne of Israel.'"

"Are you he whom your father David mentioned?" I asked.

"I am he," he said, smiling, "whom the Heavenly Father mentioned."

Philip reflected the general bewilderment.

"Master, show us the Father, and we shall be satisfied."

"If you believe not in what I do, how can you believe in what Moses did?"

Matthew, whom I still thought of as Levi, obviously took his role of chronicler with great seriousness, for he was already scribbling on thin sheets of parchment, with a ruffled brow.

"If you come only to redeem Israel by the law of Moses, Master, how does your mission differ from Elijah's, who banished false Gods from Israel?"

The Master sighed. "I do not come to change a tittle of God's law. God cares not what man eats, nor on what platter it is served, as long as that man serves Him by loving his neighbor and himself."

I was not sure I had heard correctly. "Is this not a form of egomania, condemned even by the Greeks in their fable of the beautiful youth Narcissus, who fell in love with his own image and died of unrequited love?"

"To love oneself, as God would have it, one must first esteem his own being. He must be honest in all things, treat others as he would be treated, and be true to himself. Without self-respect, he cannot command the respect of others. Nor will his head rest easy on his pillow."

Matthew was still not satisfied. "But are not the books of Moses supreme in Israel for all time?"

"In matters where God's voice is plain."

"How does one know God's voice from the interpreter's?"

Jesus smiled. "You see, I have made a good choice. His gospel will be preached even in Rome one day, and will be favored of the Jews, even as John's word will strike a chord with the Gentiles."

John blushed at being singled out.

"Tell them, John, what you saw on the mountain. This shall be an answer to Matthew and the rest."

"But, sir," said Simon-bar-Jonah, "you enjoined us to relate this vision to no man."

"True," said Jesus, "but I keep nothing from any of you, for the knowledge shall be helpful in doing God's work. What John and James and Simon-bar-Jonah were privileged to know then, all of you are now privileged to know."

John stood up, and his fair face, with its perfectly chiseled features, seemed to glow from within.

"It was an exhilarating day," said John, "the mountain air was crisp and clear, and there was not a cloud in the sky. I looked at Simon and James, and could see them breathing deeply, savoring the freshness as if it were wine. Then my eyes traveled to the Master, and I saw him in a white light, and his face shone as the sun. He appeared to be conversing with two figures cloaked radiantly in the light, speaking as if they were Moses and Elijah. Simon-bar-Jonah suggested we make a tabernacle of branches of palm leaves for each of the prophets who appeared with the Master. But even as Simon spoke, a bright cloud loomed out of the blue sky and cast Moses and Elijah in its shadow, so that they were no longer to be seen or heard. A voice full of majesty then rolled out of the cloud and said: 'I have sent you my beloved son, in whom I am well pleased. Listen to him.'"

At this heaven-borne voice, the disciples fell on their faces, afraid to peer into the cloud, for only Moses and Elijah had seen God's countenance and lived. But Jesus reached down and touched them. "Arise, and be not afraid, for there is no harm in your Father," he said.

As they came down from the mountain, the disciples looked apprehensively over their shoulders and spoke not of the voice but of Moses and Elijah.

"Why, Master," asked a tremulous Peter, "were these two overshadowed by a bright cloud, while the light remained with you?"

Jesus' eyes held an ironic glint.

"You have answered your own question, Simon-bar-Jonah. The others faded into the past, while the Son of Man gave forth new light."

"Does your word then take precedence over theirs?"

"Did you not hear the voice say: 'Listen to him'?"

Their minds were still not clear. "But has it not been said that before the Son arrives Elijah shall come first?"

"He would not have been seen had he not already come," Jesus replied.

And they understood that he referred to John the Baptist, who had borne Elijah's spirit in his flesh.

There was a hush as John finished his recital, only Matthew's scratching quill marring the silence.

I found it important that the extent of his mission be defined.

"If God is infinite, then is not the Son infinite as well?"

Jesus' eyes held my own.

"So long as he does God's will."

"Then what is the full meaning of God's removing the light from the prophets who were sent to free Israel?"

Jesus' eyes moved slowly around the room.

"God's light is no longer for Israel alone. There is a new prophet and a new day."

CHAPTER SEVEN

THE VIRGIN MOTHER

SHE DID NOT WONDER why we were there, but quietly put forward flat cakes of barley bread, some honey, and wine.

"My son is not home," she said in a voice as clear as a bell.

"I know, for we come from Bethsaida."

"Yes, he stays with the sons of Jonah and their families."

She was completely without guile or artifice. She sat with her hands folded before her, her dark eyes looking out with tranquillity on the world.

"You must be proud to be his mother," I said rather lamely.

"Does he send you to me?" she inquired.

"No, but I would know more about him."

"He has no secrets."

"It is about his birth," said I in confusion. "Joseph of Arimathea has told me some things, but I would know more."

Her eyes peered into mine, and I felt, for a moment, as though my very soul was bared.

"As you will," said she. "None can harm him except God be willing."

"I would defend him to the death. I adore him."

She gave me a mystifying smile, and I saw compassion in her eyes.

"What is it you would know?"

"I cannot understand why a husband would take a wife about to give birth on so arduous a journey. It is not what the midwives would prescribe."

"My husband had his reasons."

"But it was surely not for the census, since only adult males were commanded to enroll in the place of their birth." Her eyes never left mine.

"I went because God willed it."

"So that he could be born in Bethlehem?"

She nodded, and again I marveled at the dewy freshness of her countenance, so like a girl's, so like a virgin's, in fact.

"He was born where it was intended he be born."

Could it be possible, in the realm of human affairs, that the mighty Caesar Augustus, ruler of the world, had issued his census-taking order as an unwitting, unbelieving instrument of a God whose ways were so often obscure? It was a mind-boggling thought.

"You knew then"—I hesitated—"whom you were carrying?"

I thought I detected an impish light in her eyes, but she replied with her wonted serenity.

"Both Joseph and I knew, for we were given a vision through the angels of the Lord."

Never having had a vision myself, I questioned the visions of others. But Matthew was not so skeptical. Or else, like many chroniclers, he was unwilling to dig too deeply Jest he spoil a good story. With soft words, he encouraged the mother to describe the vision however she remembered it.

She smiled. "How does one forget a visit from the Lord?"

It had occurred in the evening, after she had put away the dishes. Joseph, to whom she was betrothed, was reading from the Psalms by the flickering light of a lamp. She suddenly felt a little drowsy and sat down to clear her head.

At first she thought it a dream. She looked over to Joseph and could see his lips moving as he read. So it was certainly no dream. The vision was in white, and there was a halo around its head. It looked like she had thought a vision should look, ethereal and pure, with a clear voice and a pristine authority almost divine in its regality.

"Mary, daughter of David," it said, "you are blessed among women, for you have found favor with God, and you shall bring forth a son who shall be called Joshua (that shall become Jesus), meaning the savior of the Lord. He shall be called the Son of the Highest, and the Lord God shall prepare for him the throne of his father David. And he shall reign over the House of Jacob forever, and of his kingdom there shall be no limit, even unto the Gentiles shall he prevail."

She was no more than fourteen when she saw this spirit and was greatly troubled. For though she had been aware, with most of Israel, of the national yearning for a Messiah, she had not for a moment associated it with herself.

She had inquired of the apparition (for what else could it be?): "How shall I be with child, when I have never known a man?"

"With God," came the reply, "all things are possible. The Holy Spirit shall descend upon you, and you shall bear a son of God, just as Adam, before whom there was no other man, was conceived of the Holy Spirit."

Overwhelmed by her experience, she could only murmur: "Let God's will prevail within me. I shall be proud to be the handmaiden of the Lord."

She was cautioned to tell none but Joseph and then only when it became necessary. He was much her senior, espousing her after the death of her parents so that he could take her into his mother's home without causing idle tongues to wag.

I had heard whispers that the older Joseph had married her only after she was large with child. But as I looked at this saintly figure, I knew this to be false. Nevertheless, I needed to know more, to refute the attacks bound to come from the Temple.

Matthew now deferred to my questioning.

"Was Joseph then his real father?" I asked.

"He was all the father he knew from birth."

"Then he was not born like other men?"

"He has never been like other men."

She was amused by my clumsiness.

"We were only betrothed at the time. But in accordance with sacred custom, he respected my virtue, for he was a kindly man."

I was so jarred at this thought that I barely heard Matthew inquire:

"Was it not difficult for a simple man to place credence in a vision he had never encountered?"

"Joseph," replied Mary, "was no ordinary man. But"—a shadow clouded her face—"it was only natural that he should question me." He had not chided her, but because of his mother he was sending her away to avoid scandal. Her belongings had been gathered and she was to leave in the morning for the home of her kinswoman near Jerusalem.

But that night, Joseph, too, had a vision in a dream.

"Joseph, son of David," the angel said, "fear not to take Mary, the daughter of Abraham, as your wife. For that child which has been conceived is of the Holy Spirit."

On rising from his slumber, Joseph announced that they would be married and raise the child together. For he, too, was honored that God had chosen him for his design.

At this time, though Mary knew it not, her kinswoman, Elizabeth, the wife of the priest Zacharias, was also with a child which appeared to have been conceived of God's will, though not of God. For both were long beyond the age when people normally hoped for children. Indeed, Zacharias was so old that he would not even listen to the angel who brought him these tidings.

"He was standing at the Temple altar, burning incense," Mary recalled, "when the angel Gabriel appeared and announced to him that Elizabeth would give birth to a child who would prepare the people for another sent of God."

Zacharias calmly turned his back on the angel and proceeded with his religious duties.

How droll, but how typical for a priest to put his incense above the messenger of the Lord.

"He had seen the angel of the Lord," I said, laughing, "but was more impressed with his ritual."

"For his lack of faith," she continued, "Zacharias was told he would be struck dumb until he recognized the truth. When he went to summon the people to their devotions, he found he could not speak." But he still did not believe, for the day of visions, the Temple felt, had ceased with the Prophets of old. It was a dead God they worshipped.

Taking Elizabeth, Zacharias returned to their country home outside Jericho, not far from the Essene monastery at Qamram.

Before her own child became noticeable, Mary yielded to an impulse to see her cousin. She found the house desolate. Zacharias, still mute, was moping about with a long face, and Elizabeth, who had so long thought herself barren, was too embarrassed to leave the house.

Mary tried to lift the older woman's spirits. "Take heart," she said, "that you have been chosen by God to bring glad tidings to Israel."

Elizabeth was still depressed.

"What would the Lord want of an old woman like me?"

"Have faith," she replied, "for Zacharias' affliction is itself evidence of God's hand."

She then confided her own secret.

Elizabeth was more confused than ever. "How can all this be?" she cried.

Mary had meditated long over her situation.

"God," she had decided, "can conceive whatever he will, for neither heaven nor earth holds any secrets from him who is responsible for every form of life."

As Mary affectionately embraced her Elizabeth felt a stirring in her own womb, and a voice told her she was filled with the Holy Spirit.

In an ecstasy of belief, she accepted now what had been so troubling before. "Blessed are you among woman," said she, kissing Mary, "and blessed is the fruit of your womb." Calmly she received her son's own subordination to Mary's unborn child.

It was difficult, observing this angelic mother, not to be impressed. And vet why would God look for his Messiah in the humble whose lineage was their only pride?

"God." said Mary, "has a way of putting down the mighty from their seats of power and exalting those of low degree. He fills the hungry and barren with good things and sends the rich away empty. For, in the end, all inequity is resolved."

It seemed to me that if everything was God's will there was little meaning in bending our efforts toward any goal.

She smiled. "We ask for strength, and God gives us difficulties, which make us strong. We pray for courage and God gives us danger, which makes us aware. We ask for favors, and God gives us challenges, which make us grow." Her eyes glowed with an inner radiance. "And blessed is the prophet who sees all this, and gives us hope."

Mary stayed with Elizabeth for three months, until the child was born. She had fondled it lovingly, knowing that this infant, six months senior to her own, would be his forerunner. The elderly couple had planned to call the boy Zacharias, meaning remembrance of the Lord, after the father, but Elizabeth suddenly insisted that he be called John. Zacharias' relatives were dumfounded, since there were none by this name in their line.

"Why," they asked suspiciously, "would you name him John?"

She looked significantly at the mute Zacharias.

"John signifies one who speaks for the Lord."

They asked Zacharias how he would name the boy. He quickly scrawled: "Let his name be John." And then he opened his mouth, and read the name after them, speaking for the first time in nine months.

As his family marveled, Zacharias got down on his knees and asked God for forgiveness for not recognizing that he had been favored with a vision from the Lord.

During the ceremony of circumcision, he held the baby in his arms. Although but eight days old, the infant appeared to look out on the world with wise old eyes. And he, the descendant of Aaron, who had denied the first vision now appeared to have another. For his eyes gleamed with a holy light and he peered off into the distance.

"This child," he said in a voice filled with emotion, "shall be called the Prophet of the Highest and shall go before the face of the Lord to prepare his way. He will give light to them that sit in darkness and in the shadow of death will guide their feet into the way of peace."

And so it had all come to pass.

As she sat, childlike, her fair brow composed, it was hard to believe that all this had happened thirty years ago and more. Joseph was gone now, dead some ten years, and so were the others, but she lived on gloriously in the destiny of her son.

"He has raised up a horn of salvation for us in the house of his servant David, saying that we should be saved from our enemies, and from the hand of all who hate us. That we should remember the promise he gave our father Abraham, that he would grant unto us one who would deliver us out of the hands of our enemies so that we might serve him without fear all the days of our life."

We regarded her silently, struck by the dignity with which she recalled God's promise to Israel.

"And is he the one?" I asked finally.

"That is for God to say."

"But how will we know unless he delivers us from our enemies?"

Her eyes drilled into mine.

"But who can say who that enemy is?"

"We have no enemy greater than Rome. All know there will be no peace in Israel while this enemy remains."

"Our worst enemy is within us. There is no peace outside us, unless first found inside."

The interview had gone on some time, and Matthew was concerned that she might be tired.

"I have so few visitors," she said, "I am happy for this opportunity."

His birth still intrigued me, for it was coupled with so many of the prophecies from olden times.

On that day there had been many visitors: the three astrologers, with their frankincense and myrrh; the simple shepherds who left their flocks to follow the star of Israel; Joseph of Arimathea, still loyal to mother and child, and Anna, the toothless soothsayer. Were there any others?

I saw the secret sorrow in her eyes. Her voice trembled for a moment as she flew back over the years. "There was a man Simeon, not a prophet by any means, but a simple man with a vision."

Matthew and I exchanged glances. It seemed odd that so many had visions concerning the birth. Did coming events indeed cast their shadow before them, so that the Lord's wishes would be known?

She did not know what vision had come to Simeon, except that he murmured gratefully that he could die happy now that he had seen the Messiah promised of God.

"Who was this Simeon?" I wondered. She shook her head. "I knew him no more than I knew the seeress Anna or Joseph of Arimathea." Yet she had not been surprised when the old man appeared and sank down on his knees before the newborn babe.

She closed her eyes as she recalled that day in the manger. "He took the child from me in its swaddling clothes, and he looked to the heavens, saying in a voice full of fire: 'Behold, this child is set for the fall and rising again of many in Israel, and for a sign which shall be spoken against.'"

Levi (whom I must now call Matthew) interposed: "And this sign, what was its nature?"

"The sign of the cross, which his disciples shall treasure until the advent of another age and his return."

I frowned. "What is this return you speak of?"

"Our time is short indeed, if he does not deliver us from the grave."

I could see from Matthew's face that he was as puzzled as I was.

"Was there anything more?" he asked.

She hesitated, then said with a tiny shiver: "Simeon said that a spear would pierce my own soul at the given time."

"Why the soul?" I asked. "Spears and swords have no effect on things of the spirit."

She spoke with ineffable patience. "I gathered that it would be a soul-stirring event."

"And the nature of this event?"

"We must wait and see. For God's will may change."

There was a hint of tears in her eyes, and Matthew said gently: "You would prefer he was like any other?"

"I have learned to share him, which is as he wants. Andrew told him one day that his family was waiting." Her laugh was like a bell. "He spoke up: 'Who are my mother and brothers? Whoever does the work of the Father, that is my brother and sister and my mother.'"

"You did not mind?"

"I understood the point he made. For he was born, not for one family, but for all."

"He did not see you that day?"

"Oh, yes, he promptly came out, but he seizes on every situation to make a lesson of it, so men will better know God's purpose."

"And in this case it was brotherly love?"

"That all who love God are his children."

She had put away a well-worn scroll as we came in, and now she picked it up and turned to one of its psalms. "May I read?" she asked.

Her voice was soft and melodious, like the call of the birds at daybreak.

"I will make him my firstborn, higher than the kings of the earth.

"My mercy will I keep for him for evermore, and my covenant shall stand fast with him.

"His seed also will I make to endure forever, and his throne as the days of the heaven."

It was gratifying to see her pride. For she and Joseph had built their lives around Jesus, Mary because she believed in her vision, and Joseph because he believed in Mary. They fled to Egypt when Herod the Great's search for the child extended from Judea into Galilee and were but a few hours ahead of Herod's men when their boat sailed out of Joppa for Alexandria.

They had friends in Alexandria, and living in the Jewish quarter was almost like being in Jerusalem. "We had our own temples, our own worship, languages, and customs. The Jews of the Dispersal were happy to see us, and all they could talk of was the Messiah. They had heard rumors that a new prince was born in Bethlehem who would one day deliver Israel from the alien yoke, and they were anxious for the day of liberation, so they could return to Israel free men."

It seemed odd that so many would prefer Egypt to their own land.

"But was not Egypt under Roman rule as well?" Matthew asked.

She smiled. "Yes, but the Jews of Alexandria were transients with no sense of being Egyptian, and so it mattered little to them whether they paid their taxes to Rome or the Pharaohs."

In Alexandria, with a larger Jewish population than even Jerusalem, Jesus grew up almost as though he were in Israel. He was a prodigy, amazing not only his parents but the rabbinical community. At four he knew Hebrew, and by six, Greek and Latin. He spent his days poring over the Talmud and the Torah, and memorized the Psalms of David and the Songs of Solomon.

Daily, he went to the famous Alexandrian library, which had assembled more books on history, philosophy, and the occult than all the libraries of the world combined. He enjoyed going by himself, and Mary indulged his whim, for he seemed mature and wise even then. Sometimes she would find him in earnest discourse with the scholars and rabbis.

"They would talk about the Messiah," said she, "and he would nod gravely at their descriptions from the Prophets."

"None will know him when he comes," she overheard him say once, "for a prophet has no honor in his own country, nor among his own people."

They regarded him respectfully as he explained. "They will all want something of him that he was not sent of God to bring. The sick will demand to be healed, the poor will ask riches, and the rich would take their riches with them." Even as a lad of eight he knew what it was to sigh. "And all desire to be liberated from Rome and be freed of taxation."

"If the Messiah is not for the liberation of Israel," said one scholar, "then we have been deceived all these years by Isaiah, Ezekiel, Zechariah, and Jeremiah." His voice held just a trace of gentle irony.

The boy was not in the least disconcerted. "Salvation for Israel lies not in things of this earth but in knowing the way to eternal life."

The Zealots scoffed at the idea of a Messiah who would not be another David or Saul.

"How else can he ascend the throne of David," observed the insurrectionary Abbas-bar-Hedekiah, "if he does not earn that distinction against the enemy?"

The boy had smiled. "You see, even one who only speaks of the Prophets has no honor here."

They indulged him because he was young and because of the air of remoteness which gave him a strange sort of dignity. With their little games they tested his knowledge and at the same time kept alive an awareness of their Jewishness.

Mary had watched, bemused, as they flung their questions at him.

"Tell us," said another scholar, "what you know of the twelve tribes of Israel?"

Jesus' blue eyes stared out at him ingenuously.

"That which you know, sir, or that which you don't know?"

"Name for me, sir," the scholar mimicked, "the twelve sons of Jacob for whom the twelve tribes are named."

"They are named," the boy replied, "not for the twelve sons, but for the ten sons, and the two grandsons, Ephraim and Manasseh, who were the sons of Joseph, who was sold off by his brothers into slavery but became great in the land of Egypt."

The scholar's eyebrows arched in pleasurable surprise.

"And the ten others?"

"Reuben, Simeon, Judah"—looking at his mother, who was of the Judean tribe of David—"Zebulon, Issachar, Dan, Gad, Asher, Naphtali, and Benjamin."

"And what of Levi, the twelfth son, what tribe did he give birth to?"

"His was the thirteenth tribe of Israel," came the prompt reply, "but since all the land had been allotted, and the Levites had no portion of their own, certain cities supported their religious functions, and later they became Temple servants."

All, save the dour Abbas-bar-Hedekiah, clapped their hands in pleasure.

He looked at the boy askance. "Ask this prodigy what he knows about the division of Israel, and when it will be one again."

The boy turned the thrust with a smile.

"In the days of Rehoboam, the son of Solomon, ten tribes broke away and formed the Northern Kingdom, which was called Israel. And the Southern Kingdom, Benjamin and Judah, with Jerusalem as its capital, became known as Judah."

Bar-Hedekiah scowled. "Any schoolboy would know that. But tell me, my young genius, when God will smile once again on a united land, free of tyranny and taxation?"

The boy rose from the floor, where he had been sitting with his legs crossed. "When that people, sir, is united with its God."

The discussion invariably got on to the Messiah, for nearly all agreed this was Israel's sole hope.

"When," asked bar-Hedekiah, "can we look for the Messiah?"

"When God wills it," came the prompt reply.

"And when may that be, O enlightened one?"

"Look into your own heart and that of your neighbors."

"Mere platitudes. For the Prophets have given us many signs to look for."

"We have no need to look outside ourselves."

Bar-Hedekiah was no mean adversary.

"Isaiah," he said, "provides a time for the glorious coming of the Lord: 'Then the eyes of the blind shall be opened, and the ears of the deaf shall be unstopped.'"

"True," said the boy, "but this is not why he comes, only a sign of his coming."

Occasionally, there were visitors. Joseph of Arimathea came, as did Simeon, and they spent virtually all their free time with the parents and the boy. Joseph, who had business in Alexandria, tarried for weeks and would take the boy on tours of the city, into the native quarters, and even to the palace of a Roman tribune, an official he had bribed many times in a business way.

The tribune, L. Pontius Aquilinus, was well thought of in Rome for leading a legion successfully against the Germans.

Aquilinus was much bemused by the boy.

"I have a son but a few years older," he said with a sigh, "but my service for the Empire, alas, keeps me apart from my family."

"What is the boy named?" asked Joseph out of politeness.

"Pontius Pilate," said the tribune. "An ambitious boy, he hopefully will follow in my footsteps."

The name had meant nothing at the time. But that friendship out of the past may well have accounted for Joseph of Arimathea's ready access to the son.

Joseph of Arimathea held many conversations with the mother. "I will send word," said he, "when it is safe to return."

He had been as good as his word, promptly notifying them when Archelaus, Herod's son, who shared his father's fear of the prophesied successor, no longer ruled the tetrarchate. And so in the declining years of Caesar Augustus they returned quietly to their homeland, settling again in Galilee rather than Judah, where the boy's precocity might not stir unwanted attention.

They lived simply in a one-story limestone house with a thatched roof, shaded by cypress trees, where the boy would sit and read. He did not mingle with the children, choosing rather to converse with adults.

As we looked now, following her eye, she pointed out a window to a tree-shaded bench.

"He would sit there for hours," she said, "reading and rereading the holy books, until the law held no secrets for him."

I was startled for the moment. "You mean this was the house he grew up in?"

She nodded. "Until he departed for Bethabara."

Looking around at the simple chairs and tables, I thrilled at the realization that they had been fashioned by him. They were solid and well put together.

"Could I see his room?" I asked.

Quietly she led us down a dark hall to a corner room. The room was small but bright, and a pitcher stood on a slight wooden table next to the narrow bed. There were three water-colors, unframed, on the walls. One was of Mary, another of a shepherd with his sheep. And the third, holding my eye, a nimbus of dark clouds through which shone a piercing light, appearing to expand from the parchment itself.

We looked at her inquiringly.

"Yes, he painted them."

"This light," I said, "I have never seen its like."

She sighed. "He never spoke of it, but I knew it must have been born of a vision."

"There is no angel's figure in it," I said.

An indefinable tenderness softened her face.

"It was no angel he saw."

Life had been peaceful; they lived on the outskirts of the village and had few visitors. Since there was no synagogue in Nazareth, they occasionally traveled to nearby Magdala or Capernaum for the Sabbath services, but more often they conducted their worship at home. It was not necessary to school him, since he had a greater command of the Talmud and the Torah than any scholar they knew, and was even versed in the mysteries of the Kabala, which he had studied in Alexandria.

He had an abiding curiosity about Jerusalem and the Temple, but they waited till it was time for the traditional consecration of the adolescent before they satisfied this curiosity. And so he was twelve before they traveled again, journeying with other pilgrims to Jerusalem for the Passover celebration. The city overflowed with three hundred thousand visitors. And since there were no inns available, they camped with thousands of others on the slopes of the Mount of Olives, each day descending into the Temple for the sacrifices of the sacred lambs in the Court of Priests.

It had not been an altogether reassuring experience. Jesus had not understood why his mother could not sit with him and Joseph during the services commemorating the exodus of the Jews from bondage in Egypt.

"Why is it, sir?" he asked of Joseph. "Are not women the equal of men?"

Though the boy never called him Father, they were close, and Jesus showed him all the honor decreed in the decalogue.

"They are different," Joseph answered.

"That does not make them less."

"It is a custom from Abraham's time." Joseph shrugged, taking recourse in tradition.

"Men and women should not be kept from one another," said the boy, "in this communion with their God."

They later moved into the Court of Priests, where with terrified cries the sacrificial lambs were led to the slaughter, the blood splashing over the basins onto the Levites and the multitude. He was grateful then that his mother was not permitted in this court as well.

Joseph saw then that the boy was troubled. "What is wrong, Joshua?"

"Does it please God that these animals be butchered in his name?"

Joseph threw up his hands. "This is the religion of Abraham, Isaac, and Jacob, all of whom sacrificed living animals in their devotion to Jehovah. It is not for us to change these things."

Mary had been more sympathetic. "He thinks of God as one who loves all that he has put on this earth. Is that so strange, Joseph?"

Joseph shook his head. "I worry not so much about the world, but about him. It will be like butting his head against a wall of the Temple. I leave it to you which shall give way first."

His being different worried her, but at the same time she knew that he could not be anything but different. She watched proudly, as, months ahead of the customary time, he was consecrated into manhood. The pilgrims from Nazareth crowded about and congratulated her on his accomplishment. He was no longer a boy but a citizen of Israel, always subject to the Romans of course.

It had been an exhilarating Passover for them all. And it was with an air of satisfaction, despite their fatigue, that they rounded up their party of pilgrims for the journey back to Nazareth. But thinking he rode with friends, they were on the road for a time before they missed him. They inquired about anxiously, but none could remember seeing him after they left the Temple.

Joseph thought hard. "He must surely have gone back to camp with us."

But a precocious girl of twelve, who had eyes for the aloof young man, said she had last seen him in the Court of Gentiles with a group of rabbis and scholars.

Joseph and Mary went back together, bidding the caravan go on without them. Nearing the Temple, they overheard the people talking about a boy who was engaging the greatest scholar of Israel in a duel of wits in the Portico of Solomon. Anxiously, they threaded their way through the Court of Gentiles, and there they saw the boy and a bearded man in rich robes conversing solemnly.

The crowd stood at a respectful distance, for it was seldom that the great Gamaliel chose to mingle with the people. With wonder, not unmixed with apprehension, the parents heard the boy stand up boldly to the Nasi of Israel.

"Why, Rabbi," he asked, "should Jehovah be so wroth with the people of Israel?"

"Because they are sinners and break the commandments."

"But is he not our creator, and our Father who created us in his own image of infinite goodness?"

Gamaliel looked at him warily. "Say what you mean, young man, and lay no snares for me."

Jesus had observed Mary and Joseph at the edge of the crowd.

"Is my earthly father, Joseph, more just than God and more merciful?"

"Of course not," snapped Gamaliel. "Is this another of your tricks?"

"But my father, Joseph, is always patient with me and never scolds, not even when he is displeased with me."

"That is admirable of him," said Gamaliel, "but what has that to do with the one God?"

"He is our Heavenly Father, is that not true? Now as the creator and Father of all, understanding what he has created, with all its frailties, should he not be at least as merciful as my earthly father, who is after all only his creation as well?"

The crowd applauded enthusiastically, and even the Reb Gamaliel, who liked a worthy opponent as well as any man, clapped the boy on the shoulder. "You have made a point, but you forget one thing. God speaks through the Prophets, and none dares question what Isaiah and Ezekiel and the others say through him. Does not a wrathful God speak of his stiff-necked people? Speak you with more authority than Isaiah?"

The boy returned his gaze evenly. "My Father's business is not to punish sinners but to redeem the righteous."

It was evident from Gamaliel's manner that he was enjoying the debate.

"What more is there, pray, about your Heavenly Father?"

"He would not be pleased that a drunken Gentile was stoned to death because in his drunkenness he wandered from the Court of Gentiles into the Court of Israel."

"But that is forbidden all who are not Jews, and the warning signs are plainly posted."

"But it was evident that he was intoxicated."

"The laws must be enforced, young man, or soon there will be no laws, and no Jewish people."

The boy frowned.

"It is not even a question of mercy," he said, "for does it not follow that the God who created all the universe created the Gentiles as well?"

"But the Jews, since they worship only him, are his Chosen People. So he told Moses and the other prophets."

Jesus smiled with such radiance that the whole assembly appeared to be illuminated. "But did not Isaiah say that he would send a Messiah who would be not only a light to Israel but a light to the Gentiles as well?"

Gamaliel stepped back and looked at him with widening eyes.

"Who are you?" he finally asked. "And who are your parents?"

Mary and Joseph came forward quickly. When Joseph sought to make some apology, Mary gently interrupted. "We are of the House of David, sir, and believe in the law and the Prophets, as does our son. He is a good boy."

Gamaliel gave them a shrewd glance. "You do well not to apologize. Israel will hear more of this boy one day, of that I am sure."

Jesus regarded him calmly.

"I go now with my parents. But we shall talk again another time, in a place not far from here."

I marveled now how the paths of these two had crossed, and remembered with a start how Gamaliel had mused over the name.

"Gamaliel is no man to have for an enemy," I said.

Instantly I regretted my remark, for her eyes grew sad.

"He has no friends," she said, "but his Father."

CHAPTER EIGHT

THE DISCIPLES

ONLY I BELIEVE HE IS GOD and can do whatever he will.

Simon Zelotes protested: "But he speaks of God as his father. Is not the son less than the father?"

"The son is the father, and the father the son. Did not John, when he came down with Peter from the mountain, say they had heard in the whispering of the wind: 'Thou art my Son, this day have I begotten thee. Ask of me, and I shall give thee the heathen for thine inheritance, and the uttermost parts of the earth for thy possession.'"

Simon looked doubtful. "This is but a psalm."

"Why say 'but a psalm' when it is of the spirit, and no man knows whence it comes?"

"Only God's will is sure."

"But this is God's will, a voice heard by all when there is no human source. What matters is that Jesus believes he is being guided. For does not the psalm say: 'Thou shalt break them with a rod of iron. Thou shalt dash them in pieces like a potter's vessel'?"

Simon now seemed to waver. "He seems more a prince of peace than of action. Now the Baptist was another matter. He was indeed a Maccabean." There was a shadow of regret in his voice.

"We are God's people," I pointed out. "Since we worship him alone, we alone are his people. And so there can be no rebellion without his approval."

Simon shook his head sadly. "The Maccabean found God in a good right arm."

To be perfectly honest, I had to admit what I had not freely acknowledged before. "The Romans are not the Syrians, even with all their weaknesses. We need Jesus. For none seeing his miracles can question his God-given powers."

Simon was a soldier and could be forgiven for not following the thread of my reasoning.

"Judah," he said ruefully, "he may be a God in heaven, but on earth he is very much a man. I have seen him tired and discouraged. He even wept, I understand, when his father, Joseph, died. Why if the dead are reborn should he feel any sorrow?"

"It is like being parted from a friend, nothing more. Did you not feel bad at leaving wife and child to be with the Master?"

I had made an unfortunate analogy.

"I wonder sometimes whether it was worth it." He sighed.

"He knows what the disciples say of him. I read a psalm to him from the sacred scroll only last night, and he thought we should all read it."

He looked back silently. "Action, Judah, not words."

"Words are weapons as well, and sometimes slice deeper than a sword.

"'Be wise now therefore, O ye kings. Be instructed, ye judges of the earth. Serve the Lord with fear, and rejoice with trembling.

"'Kiss the Son, lest he be angry, and ye perish from the way, when his wrath is kindled but a little. Blessed are all they that put their trust in him.'"

Simon listened good-naturedly. "I hope you are right, it would simplify matters. But meanwhile I meet with Joshua-bar-Abbas, Cestus, and Dysmas in regard to arming the Idumeans and the Syrian Jews. I leave the disputatious sons of Israel to you. They are too much for a Galilean like myself."

"But not for our Galilean."

Whenever it became uncomfortable, as when the Baptist was arrested and flung into Herod's dungeon, we could be sure that we would soon be on the road. "My time is not yet at hand," he would say, "there are still souls to be harvested."

And so we moved from Engedi, in Baptist country, to Jerusalem, Galilee, even Samaria, camping out at night in caves or on the wooded slopes, taking our food from the fields, or purchasing what we needed from day to day, taking alms only when we stopped overnight in homes open to our prayers.

It had been raining all day outside the Holy City. Soaked to the skin as I was, surveying the motley group, I felt depressed for the moment at the thought of the tremendous obstacles that lay in the path of our undertaking.

I looked around the campfire morosely. I saw little help from the Apostles. They had been picked chiefly because they were Galileans and were trusted as familiar things are. There was a saying that Galileans loved honor more than money. But, actually, there was little temptation to riches in Galilee, and so they deserved no credit. Yet they were a rough lot. They had fought under Judah the Galilean, and, as we know, had demonstrated bravely, if blindly, against the viaduct, though it was not properly their concern.

From the start it had been necessary to stress the Master's Judean heritage. He had lived outside the mainstream of Jewish life, so that he could lose himself in the Talmud and Torah, until God gave him the word.

The Pharisees questioned his humble beginnings and Nicodemus replied: "Does our law judge any man before it hears him out, and knows what he does. I tell you he is a prophet."

They laughed as much as they dared. For Nicodemus was so rich that he could feed the entire population of Israel for ten days if he wanted. "Search all you want," they still scoffed, "for out of Galilee arises no prophet. Does not the Scripture say that the Messiah comes of the seed of David, and out of the town of Bethlehem where David was?"

Fortunately, we had records of Jesus' birth and copied them. But the doubters called the birthplace an accident. For the Pharisees, too, had researched the Nazarene's life. Indeed, they saw a plot by a simple carpenter and his obscure bride to ensnare the nation with a fairy tale. But to what purpose?

They well knew the prophet Micah. "But thou, Bethlehem Ephratah, though thou be little among the thousands of Judah, yet out of thee shall he come forth unto me that is to be ruler in Israel; whose goings forth have been from of old, from everlasting."

And whereas Bethlehem meant the house of bread, Ephratah signified rich in fruit, symbolized by the golden clusters of grapes which hung over the Temple gates as a reminder of Israel's abundant future.

The Pharisees had looked into his family but for Mary, who saw only us, and talked to Jude, James, Simon, and Joseph. They were plain working people and bore no resemblance to the Master. As I had been told, they were brethren, but not brothers, but still he inducted two into his family of disciples. They seemed very much like the Galileans in his fold, the fishermen and fish dryers, the carpenters and cabinetmakers, the boat makers.

Of the Apostles Andrew impressed me, for even Simon Zelotes was a changeable fellow, who felt at times we could overthrow Rome with arms alone. Andrew, the first chosen, was fair and slim with a ready smile. He stood as a buffer for the Master, turning aside the others' petty complaints. He had influence over all but Peter, who was a year younger but who, in his forwardness, behaved as if he were the older. They were the eldest among the disciples, only two or three years younger than the Master. Nearly all the others were of my age, twenty-eight, save for the beardless John. He represented the coming to manhood of Israel, so said the Master, who loved him because he saw himself in John's youth and innocence. The other son of Zebedee, Jacob, whom Jesus called James, was quiet and serious-minded, seeming to miss his family. The orphaned sons of Alpheus the boat maker had their names changed, from Jacob to James, called the Less because of his stature, and from Judah to Jude, to distinguish him from me. Jesus said a new baptismal name accented the individual's rebirth particularly when this name had a meaning of its own.

After Bethabara, Jesus himself was called the Messiah or the Christ, in the Greek style, more often than not. Jude meant Praised of the Lord, and Matthew, for Levi the Publican, signified a gift of the Lord, which he surely received when he was wrested from his evil ways. In renaming Philip, Jesus had smiled and said: "I like better the word loving," for this Philip signified. Nathaniel was a sign of the Lord's praise. A Syrian-Greek Jew by origin, he was sometimes referred to as bar-Tholomew, the son of Ptolemy, or Tholomew. He was an amiable sort, but undistinguished like the rest.

The Master, as always, set the example. He preferred to be called Jesus, rather than Joshua. We all were struck by this, for there was a design to everything he did. In permitting himself a Greek name, he was obviously making a declaration to the Gentiles. It was as if he were saying to all, and not to the Jews alone: "I am Jesus Christ, the Savior and Deliverer, the Anointed, the eternal Son of God." For in the Greek, this name meant all these things.

As for my own name, he added to it my ancestral home in Kerioth or Carioth, but gave it a connotation that could be misconstrued. Judas Iskerioth, or in the Greek style, Iscariot, he had called me. "A name," he said, "that will live always with mine."

I was flattered, but liked not the abbreviation SKR, almost an anagram, which stood in our language as a symbol for the betrayer.

He put me off with a smile. "You have not chosen me. But I have chosen each of you."

How else but for this would Peter have gained precedence? He was hardly the rock that his new name suggested. He seemed so gullible, so slow to grasp the obvious. Once he suggested I make an accounting to the Twelve.

"I answer only to the Master," I replied stiffly.

"But," said he, "the Master accepts whatever you tell him."

"And what am I to think from that?"

A look of embarrassment made his fisherman's face even redder than before. "There are reports," he spluttered, "of money being diverted to weapons."

We had received a number of secret benefactions from the rich, such as Nicodemus and Joseph of Arimathea.

"You are the rock," I said, "and I the treasurer. When you give me the rock, I will give you the treasury."

He did not even know what I meant.

Because of Peter's insecurity, the Master felt it necessary to keep reassuring him. I would have thought Andrew, or James, the son of Zebedee, a better adjutant, since they were well organized and practical. Peter was too easily confused. But the Master obviously saw in him some quality I didn't. It may have been Peter's humility, but how else could he be but humble? The Master did not make a move for himself. Peter fetched his food and wine, washed and mended his clothes, and constantly hovered over him. He made a good butler, if nothing else. He didn't seem to understand anything.

"Every good tree," the Master said once, "brings forth good fruit, but a corrupt tree beings forth evil fruit. Wherefore by their fruits you shall know them."

"What fruit, Master, is the good fruit?"

All of course understood the parable, all but the Rock. The Master indulged him always. He put his arm around those hulking shoulders and said: "Whoever listens to the son is a wise man, who builds his house upon this Rock. The rains and the floods and the winds will come, but the house will stand on this Rock."

Jesus never did anything without a reason. He was no gentle easygoing creature floating along with the tide. Nothing happened without his knowing about it and accepting it. His every move was intended to establish a point or to impress us with the nature of his world. He was especially concerned with directing our activities, for he counted on his Apostles and disciples to spread his word.

"Salvation lies with the Jews," he enjoined, "and as Jews you shall bring this salvation to every household. Go forth as lambs among wolves. Carry neither purse, nor scrip, nor shoes."

Some of the seventy showed their bewilderment. They had left their homes, their families, their work, and he sent them out with only a cloth on their backs to knock on strange doors.

Although I guarded the purse strings well, I felt it wise to spare these missionaries a few pennies so they would not yield too readily to the despair of rejection. He cared less for money than anybody. Yet he stayed my hand.

"The Lord will provide," said he.

"But," I remonstrated, "if the householder shuts his door on them, where will they abide?"

"The door to heaven, Judah, is surely harder to enter than the home of the haughtiest Pharisee."

"But would it not be easier, Master, if they were better equipped for their mission?"

"Like troops separated from their baggage, they have nothing to consider but the battle."

"But they are novices and have not studied at your feet as we."

"Judas, Judas," he said, half mocking, "you would lead troops against Rome, and you concern yourself with trifles."

"My soldiers would be armed," I rejoined.

"And so, too, are they armed, with the weapons of the Lord. For they shall heal wherever they go with the faith I send with them."

He paired off the two Zealots whom I had made disciples. "Cestus and Dysmas," said he with a grave face, "you shall be inseparable to the end."

He coupled dull, heavy-witted Simon-bar-Jonah with the bright new disciple John Mark, James with his brother John, Bartholomew with Philip, Jude with his brother James the Less, and careful Thomas with amiable Andrew.

"You, Judah, should feel at one with Simon the Zealot."

I could not have asked for better.

While dining, I sat at his right, Peter at his left, next to his heart. I was not blind to this honor, but then I was the only Judean, besides himself, the only aristocrat, and save for Matthew, who had learned to write in confiscating the property of the oppressed, the only one with formal education. Young John had been schooled by Jesus and, like Matthew, was forever scribbling, the Lord only knows what.

He constantly encouraged us. "You are instruments of God," he stressed, "each called for a very special purpose. You, John, and you, Matthew, shall one day send your message to the far corners of the earth. You, Peter, shall build a church that shall never die. You, James, experienced with me the transfiguration. You, Thomas, shall confirm my triumph, and you, Judah"—my heart stood still—"shall be my vehicle on the road to life everlasting."

The seventy were even more undistinguished than the Twelve. They were a scrubby-looking lot, with shaggy heads and beards, unwashed and disheveled from days on the highways. Though many were named by the Twelve, all were confirmed by him. But they appeared no more qualified for their missions after their baptisms than before. But, as I soon saw, he was sending out a fox to catch a fox.

"How," asked a bedraggled Amharetz, "does a shopkeeper like myself, a poor seller of hides, heal anybody of an illness? I am no physician."

Jesus looked reassuringly at this dreary appointee of Peter's who was so like those he would help.

"You will heal in my name, with faith in the Father. I send you in pairs, not for companionship, but because if two agree on what shall be asked, it shall be done by my Father. And where two or three are gathered in my name, there am I in the midst of them."

He bade them take heart from what he wrought. "As I do, so you all can do with love of the Father," he would say with each leper or lunatic he cured with a touch of his hand and a few simple words.

But we all knew he was of different stuff. For though we sat at his feet and ate and drank with him, there was a gulf, never quite defined, but which could be likened to that between master and servant. He was removed, not so much by virtue of his manner as by our feeling that he was so much greater than any of us. We dared only speak when he gave us to speak. None, not even Peter or John, addressed him as anything but Master. For this reason, though there was a great curiosity about him, very little was known by the multitude. For even as he performed his miracles, he had instructed us to tell no man about his origin and his mission except as it unfolded of itself.

He tried to make each of us think we were different, relating to different qualities in people even though our work was the same. "Theoretically," said he, "you represent the twelve tribes, and the twelve types represented in astrology by the zodiac."

"Do you recommend this idolatrous worship of the Babylonians?" I asked in some surprise.

"Only as it reflects God's order in the universe and its relation to people."

"But is this not a pagan belief?"

"Know you not the Psalms, Judah? Surely, even a backslid Pharisee has this knowledge." His eyes lifted reverently to the sky. "The heavens declare the glory of God, and the firmament shows his handiwork. Day after day, it speaks, and night after night, it shows knowledge. There is no speech nor language where its voice is not heard."

"Is this why we carry the sign of the fish?"

"The stars heralded the birth of the Son of Man, and they shall proclaim his death."

The other disciples now crowded about. "But, Master, you say there is no death."

"Death, Judah, is a friend well met on the way to a pasture far greener than any you have known."

While the disciples fanned out over the land, the main body of the Apostles remained with him. With the Baptist's incarceration he had become increasingly cautious. On the way north from Judea, he directed that we skirt the larger communities and proceed by side roads through Samaria, which pilgrims ordinarily avoided in journeying to and from Jerusalem.

As a Galilean, Simon-bar-Jonah knew the lot of pilgrims passing through the territory of this God-forsaken people who styled themselves Jews.

"But, Master, these evil Samaritans take pleasure in taunting and stoning the faithful bound for the Holy City. They even mock them with huge bonfires in the night so that they will think it dawn and rise and get on their way. Would it not be simpler to pass east of the Jordan through Perea and the Decapolis, and cross by the Galilean Sea into Capernaum?"

"Simpler, perhaps, but not as fruitful. When I see the Samaritan temple at Mount Geritzim, I am minded of the shallowness of these great churches which man builds for man. For God, not having man's conceit, is satisfied with his own sky and meadow. Yet the Samaritans, ejected from the Temple by the Israelites, seek to outdo them in the same fashion."

When we still hoped to bypass this benighted people, he gave us a parable with which he had confounded a quibbler of low estate, a lawyer of Philadelphia, in the Decapolis.

Some robbers, he pointed out, had attacked a man near Jericho, and left him for dead in the street. His plight had been ignored first by a

Temple priest, then by a Levite, both crossing to the other side of the road. But then a Samaritan came along and bound up the stranger's wounds, and brought him to an inn and had him cared for, even to paying the bill.

"Which of the three," the Master asked, "was a good neighbor to this hapless victim?"

As though on cue, Simon-bar-Jonah blared out, "Why, the good Samaritan of course."

Simon-bar-Jonah showed, as usual, how pious he was.

"Lord," said he, "if my brother sins against me, shall I forgive him seven times?"

"I say forgive not seven times, but seventy times seven."

Matthew had looked up at this.

"And if we do not forgive, Master?"

"It will not go well then. For if you forgive men their trespasses, your Heavenly Father will also forgive you. But if you forgive not men their trespasses, neither will your Father forgive your trespasses."

It was easier said than done.

From Jerusalem we took the hill road at night to escape the heat of May. In the afternoon we gratefully felt the soft wind by which Boaz winnowed his barley, and by evening we came to Svchar stopping by the well which the patriarch Jacob had dedicated to his son Joseph. Since we proceeded north, away from Jerusalem, the Samaritans did not molest us. Their fight actually was more with the hierarchy than the people. It was an ancient grudge. They had been barred from the Temple when their ancestors committed the sacrilege of casting two huge golden calves as the Lord Jehovah. In reprisal thereafter, they had stolen into the Temple and shamefully flung human offal into the Sanctuary. The feud persisted and no Temple-going Jew would abide in Samaria overnight, particularly at the well where Jesus had us camp. "The water of Samaria," said the rabbis, "is more unclean than the blood of swine."

But Jesus had no scruples about dealing with the Samaritans, or with anybody who expressed interest in his Kingdom of Heaven. "My Father," he said, smiling, "can cleanse even the blood of the Pharisees." And so, after we made camp by this shrine of Joseph, the Master sent us into the village for provisions and reclined by the well to meditate. On our return we saw him talking to a woman who held a waterpot in her hand. As I came close I could overhear the conversation.

"How is it that you, a Judean, ask water of me, when the Judeans have no dealings with Samaritans?"

The Master shook his head. "There is neither Israelite nor Samaritan, Galilean nor Roman. All are children of God and may drink of the living water."

She gave him a puzzled frown.

"What now is he up to?" whispered Simon Zelotes in my ear.

"It is always the same," I whispered back, "this Kingdom of Heaven in which all live happily ever after."

The Master silenced us with a glance. He gave the woman the quizzical look I knew so well. "Whosoever drinks of the water I give him shall never thirst again."

With some trepidation she offered him the waterpot, and he sipped from it slowly. She looked at him intently, hypnotized, as so many were, by his magnetism.

"Sir, give me this water that I thirst not."

I had seen women melt under his glance before. Nevertheless, I was baffled by the encounter, the reason for it not yet being clear.

His eyes moved over her and found her comely, in the impersonal way he had with women.

"Your name is Deborah," he said finally.

Her chin dropped in consternation. "How know you my name, when I have never seen you before?"

He still regarded her speculatively.

"Go fetch your husband, and bring him here."

She hesitated for a moment. "I have no husband, sir."

He nodded. "You say well, for you have had five husbands. Yet he with whom you now live is not your husband."

Her eyes almost dropped out of her head. "How do you know this?" she cried.

He seemed to be toying with her. "You have no children, and for this reason keep remarrying."

Her dull Samaritan eyes widened.

"How know you this?" she asked again, as if the Master had divulged something of importance.

He brushed aside her question. "This last, with whom you live, does not marry you because of his position in the community."

She let out a deep breath. "You are indeed a wizard."

For the life of me, I could not understand why the Master had stooped to such fortune-telling. Who cared whether this scrawny wench had married a hundred times? Of what moment was it to any but herself?

"Why do you tell me all this?" she asked.

"So you will know who I am and who sent me."

"I perceive," said she, still shaken, "that you are a prophet, sent with the living water."

"God is the living water, and who worships him must worship in spirit and truth."

It was now apparent to the Apostles for whom these words were intended.

The woman's eyes showed her wonder as she considered the miraculous stranger.

"I know that the Messiah of the Jews comes soon. And he will clear up all things, they say."

His eyes fell for a moment on the Twelve, and he said in a ringing voice: "I that speak to you am he."

She kneeled in her joy, but he raised her up with a gentle smile. "You are twice blessed, who is a Samaritan and yet believes."

She kissed his hand devoutly and hurried off, forgetting her waterpot. In the afternoon she returned with a company of Samaritans. They immediately surrounded the Master. The leader was a shepherd named Amos, an amiable giant who looked more Syrian than Jew.

"This is the headman of the village," said the woman Deborah. "I told him of your wonders."

"You still have not married him," said the Master with a smile.

As always, he picked out the relationships of people with a glance. There were no secrets from him, not of this life, in any event.

The Samaritans bowed low before the Master, their heads almost scraping his feet. They bore gifts of costly frankincense and myrrh, as if paying homage to a King. I quickly stepped forward, to accept the offerings. But the Master stayed me with a frown.

They also brought gifts of food, but he turned these away with a smile. "I have food you know nothing about, to do the will of him that sent me and to finish his work."

He spoke slowly, almost as if to himself. "The Son of Man dies for you. So be not afraid when they seek to kill him. Fear them not, for though they may be able to destroy the body, they have no more power ever after over you. Rejoice in the constant presence of the Father, who has the power to deliver you from all judgment. The sparrows cost but a few pennies, yet the Lord, who is the source of all life, marks the flight of the smallest bird. How can you fear trifles when the very hairs of your head are numbered? God watches over you, for you are of more account to him than the sparrows.

"I came into this life to reveal the Father and to lead you to him. The first I have done of my own, but the last I cannot do without your assent. The Father compels no man to enter his kingdom. But why should Jew or Gentile hesitate to accept the glad tidings that he is eternally a son of the eternal God? Tarry not in the valley of decision, but come and partake of the water of life."

These Samaritans, as though transformed, came forward and kneeled before the Lord. And, kneeling, they were baptized by the disciples, for Jesus still did not baptize, saying again that he would not take from the Baptist this distinction of being the greatest dwelling on earth to prepare the way.

"I dwell in the Father, and he dwells in me. And he who dwells in me, also dwells with the Father."

The Samaritans marveled at the intimate way he spoke of God.

"How can we best please the Lord God?" asked the giant Amos.

"By conducting yourself in such a way that you will become a worthy companion to him in heaven."

The Samaritans were much taken with this answer. "Please tarry with us," they said, "for we know that you are no ordinary man, but indeed the Christ who will save the whole world. Why else would you, a Judean, trouble with Samaritans?"

We remained for two days, the Master telling his parables to ever increasing multitudes, while I, with Simon Zelotes, sought out the temper of the people. Amos, though simple, like our Peter, seemed to reflect the mood of his people. "Our fathers fought for and against the Romans, serving as mercenaries, and then again as patriots for Palestine. But with a leader like Jesus we could muster an army of brave men to do battle for the one God against the pagan Pilate."

"Would you not be afraid," I asked, "to repeat the fate of Judah of Galilee?"

"It would not be the same," he said confidently, "for that Galilean was a false prophet. Neither did he come out of Bethlehem Ephratah, nor was he of a virgin born."

I was understandably puzzled. "Whence came your information?"

He pointed to Simon-bar-Jonah. "The big fisherman told me."

"He told you correct." For once I agreed with the bumpkin.

Jesus never stayed long in any one place, fearful that the soldiers might seize him before he was ready, as he said, to go of his own accord.

I protested his easy assumption of his own early death. "Who will lead if you go?"

He smiled sadly. "You will know about my going before any of the others, Judah. Think well of what I say this day, but remember that no man taketh my life. I die to fulfill the ancient prophecy and show the world that life is everlasting."

If all was ordained, why then did we so frantically plot and strive? "If we are merely instruments of the Lord, what matter who we are or what our ambitions?"

He smiled. "Without who and what we are, God's will would not be done."

"But who would be served, Master, by your death?"

"Humanity."

It was all very baffling.

"But you have cured many minds and bodies, and given a life of hope to many more. How better can you serve your people than by giving them the freedom you speak of?"

"This freedom, Judah, is of the soul, which is everlasting, and belongs to all. When only one nation is free, then others are less than free."

"But it is with Israel God made his covenant, and his promise of the Messiah."

"God makes his will known to his prophets at different times in different ways. There is nothing unalterable in God's world, save for God."

"What then happens to the human will, Master? Is it like a puppet, pulled by strings it does not see?"

The Master's smile widened. "By the decisions in this lifetime, Judah, by the lessons we learn, even tardily, we establish our place in the Kingdom of Heaven."

"And why is this of greater moment than our life on this earth?"

Matthew, Peter, and John had walked into the camp and squatted down about the fire, rubbing their hands together. I felt a twinge that our moment of intimacy was so rudely ended.

"It is well that you are all here," the Master said, "for I had thought to speak to you all on this subject, which is that what we do lives after us, and returns with us."

Matthew looked up inquiringly. "You speak then, Master, of being reborn. But in all of Israel none but the Pharisees believe in the angels of God and the rebirth of man. With the Sadducees the current experience is all, and yet they manage the Temple and worship of the Lord God."

"The Sadducees are completely Hellenized," I put in, "and more like Stoics and Cynics than the Hellenized Romans. As for the Pharisees, they are so lost in ritual that they cast God in their own crabbed image."

"Well said, Judah," observed the Master, as my heart sang with his praise. "But there are others in Israel besides the Sadducees and Pharisees. The Amharetzin, in their simplicity, are open to God's teachings, and the Essenes teach that life is not of this world alone. They believe with John the Baptist in the resurrection. None knows better than the Baptist that by the choices in this lifetime, by one's virtue or lack of it, one establishes the conditions of this rebirth. But one must still die to be reborn." His eyes became soft and reflective. "And this, too, the Baptist knows and must deal with."

His eyes held a haunted look I had not seen in them before. I sensed John's quick concern, but the Master's mood swiftly passed. And it was not until morning when the news came of the Baptist's execution that we had reason to recall his prophetic words.

One of the seventy disciples brought the word from Perea, where the Baptist had been imprisoned in the Machaerus dungeon. Herod's wife had demanded his execution as a price for her continuing affections, but not till the Baptist's followers stopped paying their taxes was his doom sealed. Herod was too much the fox to indulge the whim of Herodias or her nubile infant, Salome, unless it served some larger purpose.

When told how the Baptist's head was brought out on a silver platter by the dancing Salome, the Master groaned and motioned for the disciple to end his recital, saying: "He was a burning and a shining light, and the people were willing to rejoice in his light. For of men born of woman there was no greater prophet than John."

As much as he grieved for the Baptist, he stressed that the message was of more import than the messenger. "I have a greater witness than the forerunner, for the works which the Father has given me to finish bear witness who sent me."

Few of us doubted his powers, only his mission. In a world of so many inequities, who knew which injustice had a priority? Simon Zelotes and I saw clearly that with his charisma he could quickly muster legions enough to push Rome into the sea. Andrew, Peter, and James saw him as the true High Priest of Israel, superseding Annas and the rest. And the others, these simple, superstitious peasants of. Galilee, were impressed mainly that he healed the sick and gave to the indigent.

Only Matthew and John seemed to seek the meaning of his heavenly salvation, but their concern seemed that of chroniclers wishing to clarify and pass on what they witnessed.

"The Sadducees," said Matthew, "say the soul perishes with the body. There is no beyond, no place of rest or torment, no judgment, no separation of good from bad. No retribution in life or death."

"They believe in tithes, taxes, and money changers," he replied with scorn. "Why would you heed them?"

Matthew's brow puckered. "But the Pharisees believe in this afterlife you speak of, where there will be rewards and punishments as one behaves in this life. The virtuous will return, and the wicked be confined to prison. The Essenes hold that virtue shall survive after death in a model land beyond the sea."

"It is not as they say, but as God wills," said the Master. "With repentance there are no sinners, and the Kingdom of Heaven is for all who would be reborn without sin."

Saint or sinner, what mattered heaven, without recognition of the more immediate problems on earth?

Like me, Simon the Zealot was anxious that Jesus declare the extent of his leadership. Was he not the bridegroom rather than a mere guest, and the wedding long overdue?

"You speak of being a light unto the Gentiles, yet the Rabbi Eleazar, the great scholar, invokes the words of the Lord: 'Since you have recognized me as the sole God, I have recognized you as the only people.'"

Jesus smiled. "That is how it was until the present time. But with the advent of the Son, God through his Chosen People brings his light to all nations."

I could see my own impatience in Simon. "How can there be light without freedom?"

"The truth shall make you free, Simon."

"'We be of Abraham's seed, and were never in bondage to any man,' say the Pharisees. How say you, you shall be free?"

The Master smiled sadly. "Stay and see, Simon, stay and see. For you shall become free in a way you do not expect."

Not unlike ordinary mortals, his moods varied for no discernible reason. When we came to Caesarea, the capital for the Romans, he seemed more expansive than usual. We spread our robes on the sands for a midday meal overlooking the blue Mediterranean. The Master partook sparingly of a handful of grapes, some sour milk, and a flat cake of barley. I offered him a good wine from the vineyards of Galilee, but he shook his head with a smile. "I drink no wine, Judah, until the last time we sup together."

Shading his eyes, he looked off at the gleaming gold-domed palace built in the Greek style by Herod, and said in a reflective tone: "There dwells the Procurator Pontius Pilate with his wife, the fair Claudia Procula, little knowing in his overwhelming ambition that his fame shall rest through eternity on his meeting with the Son of Man."

"Would you then lead the Judeans against Rome?" I asked with quickened breath.

He gave me a pitying smile. "Judah, Judah."

"But you have said that you have come not to bring peace but to unsheath a sword."

"Ask better, Judah, whose sword it shall be. I am not of the Maccabeans, but of one whose work serves all mankind. You should all know by now who I am and who sent me, just as the lady at the well knew from our brief meeting. Is not that appointment in Samaria of more moment than all the things you have witnessed?" There was almost a railing note in his voice. "Or does one have to be a Samaritan to believe in the Son and the Father?"

He beckoned to John, who sat facing him, as was his wont, and to bar-Jonah, who seemed only dimly aware of the course of the conversation.

"Tell me, dear John, who do men say I am?"

John's gray eyes glowed with pleasure at being the first to be asked. He, of course, had heard all the stories spreading about the land, and with them the prophecy of Malachi. Had not Malachi said: "Behold, I will send you Elijah the prophet before the coming of the great and dreadful day of the Lord. And he shall turn the heart of the fathers to the children, and the heart of the children to their fathers, lest I come and smite the earth with a curse."

John stood up in his enthusiasm. "Some declare, dear Lord, that you are Elijah, the prophet of good tidings, and others, Jeremiah, come again to smite your people with the truth, or one of the other prophets, such as Isaiah or Ezekiel, whom you constantly read from." His rosy countenance clouded for a moment. "Some even say that you are John the Baptist. But how could that be, since you were baptized by him but a short time ago, and he has only recently died. Is it possible, Master, for his spirit to have merged with yours?"

The Master shook his head. "No, dear John, the spirit in man is but one, though joined with God it forms the soul eternal."

Nathaniel, who prided himself on being a student of the law, reacted with more than usual vigor. "Why then have the Scribes, as well as the Prophets, said that Elijah, who is long dead, must first come before the Messiah?"

The Master's eyes passed from Matthew to me, as though we shared this little tidbit he was about to deliver. "That is well said, Nathaniel, for in truth it was necessary for Elijah to make the way ready, which he did. But the authorities knew him not, and so they did what they would with him."

Nathaniel's normal placidity failed him. "Do you suggest, sir, that John the Baptist was indeed Elijah, and that none recognized him?"

"Those who were ready knew him."

"But he came and left without accomplishing that promised of Elijah."

"He served his Father well, then went to his heavenly reward, just as the Son of Man shall suffer of the Philistines."

That by the Philistines the Master meant the unbelievers was apparent even to Philip and Nathaniel, who were indeed birds of a feather. Had not Nathaniel said on first hearing of Jesus: "What good can come out of Nazareth?"

The disciples had formed a close circle about the Master in their anxiety to resolve the identity of the leader they followed with secret qualms. Slowly his eyes traveled till they fell on the ruddy face of Simon the fisherman.

"And who say you that I am?"

Simon-bar-Jonah's eyes fell under the sardonic glance. He wet his lips nervously, then, lifting his eyes to heaven, said, as if coming to an inspired decision:

"You are none of these, Lord. For you are the Anointed, the Promised One of Israel, the Son of the Living God."

Jesus stepped forward and rested his hands on Peter's broad shoulders in a rare demonstration of affection for any but John.

"You are blessed, Simon-bar-Jonah, for this was revealed to you not by flesh and blood but through the divine inspiration of my Father in heaven."

I saw nothing earth-shattering in the fisherman's remark. It was only what the Master had claimed on countless occasions. Yet Jesus took this opportunity, on the basis of Simon's apparent revelation, to raise him formally now to the front rank of his followers.

Until now, though he had called him the Rock, there was no distinction among the Apostles. As his deputies we were all equal unto each other and before the public.

But with his hands still on Simon's shoulders, Jesus conferred the prized accolade: "On this rock I will build my church, and the gates of hell shall not prevail against it, for I give you the keys to the Kingdom of Heaven, and whatsoever you do on earth shall be done as in heaven."

And so there it was, finally. First he had called him Peter the Rock, then he had sat him next to his heart, and now he made it clear what he had intended all along, using the flimsiest of reasons for doing so. But in truth it was only an empty honor, for other than adding to his sense of importance it served no purpose. Andrew still was his secretary, I his treasurer, and John his favorite. And so why had he done it? Perhaps Matthew, with his chronicler's eye, saw it more clearly than any of us.

"Peter," he said, "with all his human frailties, his hopes and aspirations, his good intentions gone sour, his doubts and fears, will in the end know best how to bring his message to the people. For there is a bit of everyman in him."

And so it might well be, but the subject of reincarnation plagued me more than Simon Peter. For if one lived on and on, constantly coming back to complete the unfinished task, striving, as the Master said, to reach perfection in God's image, then indeed it might be a prudent man who would mark his time against Romans, in this lifetime if not the next. But what proof was there? It was not enough to say "Have faith," for faith needed some small kernel of reality on which to grow. All the talk among the Pharisees and the Essenes of the afterlife was just talk so far as I could see. Jesus, too, spoke of the Kingdom of Heaven, and of rebirth, man's needing to die to be reborn, but again they were words.

Jesus was not entirely friendless in high places, nor among the Pharisees. For many of the Pharisees, particularly the rich and the elderly, were intrigued by the prospect of not only living on in this Kingdom of Heaven but also descending again onto earth. Therefore, I was not surprised that some communicated with him secretly, not wishing their sympathies to be known, while others watched patiently to see which way the wind blew.

To Nicodemus, one of the Pharisees intrigued by his teaching, Jesus made clear his belief in reincarnation. Nicodemus, a guiding light of the Great Sanhedrin, stole into our camp one night as I was making an accounting to the Master. He had been fretting over Jesus' references to man reborn. He looked at me askance, but the Master quickly reassured him that he could speak plainly. "The least of my disciples is as great as I."

Nicodemus seemed embarrassed that a son of his old friend Simon should witness his appeals to a dedicated foe of the Pharisees. But he soon overcame his nervousness. "We know that you are from God," he said, "for no man can perform your miracles except that God be with him."

Jesus knew what this visit must have cost the Pharisee.

"You speak well, Nicodemus. But I tell you, unless a man be born again he cannot see the Kingdom of God."

Nicodemus' reaction was the normal one. "How can a man be born when he is old? Does he enter a second time into his mother's womb?"

"Except a man be born of water and of the spirit, he cannot enter into God's kingdom. For that born of the flesh is flesh, and that born of the spirit is spirit. Only the spirit, Nicodemus, is born again, for the body is but the temple of the spirit."

Nicodemus' long face was still troubled.

"Does man return to his former estate?" he asked.

"Only if he is deserving before God, and then his estate is bound only by the sky."

Nicodemus hesitated, for he did not want to be thought greedy.

"Was it not said of old that man is like the dust?"

"That was said of the body, not the spirit. Repent and be saved, for even the rich man can find an abode in heaven if he cares for his neighbor as himself."

Nicodemus' concern was still with the earth.

"Do we have any choice as to what we become?"

I saw the flicker of a smile on the Master's lips.

"Let me say again," said the Master, "that no man, unless he has already ascended from the earth, descends from heaven. Even the Son of Man must be lifted up so that whoever believes in him shall not perish but have eternal life."

Nicodemus at length departed satisfied, having found somewhere in what the Master said a definition of eternity that suited him. But Jesus' constant allusion to his own death, however he lived on elsewhere in perpetuity, bothered all the disciples, but none more than me. For if he were to die prematurely, who would lead the insurrection?

His appeal was to all classes. Some considered him another David, the giant killer. Others were drawn by his healing powers, or by his promise of eternal life. Still others by the hypnotic spell he seemed capable of spinning at any time. Whatever it was, there was the common desire to follow him.

Nicodemus had eventually been so impressed that he impressed his son by merely telling him of the Master. Boaz came to me, and with a glad heart I took him to Jesus, for with the upper classes we recruited the flower of Jerusalem.

The Master was in a garden, caressing the flowers and speaking tenderly to them, as if they were living creatures. He rose from his knees with a smile, offered me his cheek, and then gave Boaz his hand.

Boaz affected a tone of great humility. "My father has told me of his conviction that you are truly a teacher come from God, and that you preach a doctrine of eternal life. How, Lord and Master, may I partake of this life?"

Jesus regarded him with his enigmatic smile.

"How much do you desire this life?"

"With all my heart." Boaz's brown eyes kindled with emotion, and he tossed his fair head. "I would do anything you ask."

Jesus' smile deepened. "You call me Lord and Master. Know you not there is only one Lord and Master, and that is the Lord God of Israel?"

"I meant no offense to the Holy One," said Boaz, "only honor to his messenger."

"I come from him," said Jesus, "but he exists apart from me, whereas I cannot exist without him."

"Some call you the Son of God."

"The Son is not as great as the Father, though in time some will unwisely call me God. You are ready to do anything, you say?"

"Anything." Boaz's head bobbed eagerly.

"You must keep the commandments."

"Is one more important than the other?"

"You shall worship the Lord God with all your heart. From this others will naturally follow. For then you cannot lie or steal, and it becomes easy to love your neighbor and honor your parents."

Boaz's eyes gleamed with pleasure. "I have kept all these commandments from the time I was a boy."

"Have you a wife or a maiden you fancy?"

"I am unwed, and there is none I cannot leave."

"And your occupation?"

"I have helped my father with his estates."

"And he has rewarded you well?"

"He has already given me my inheritance."

"It is considerable?"

"Yes, for I am his only son."

"Those who follow me have no family but the company of man."

Boaz nodded quickly. “I am ready.”

Jesus paused. “Are you ready to dispose of the possessions given you by your earthly father?”

Boaz hesitated.

“I do not take my property with me.”

“You cannot travel without taking all that you are with you. Give what you possess to the poor, then follow me, and you shall enter the Kingdom of Heaven.”

I saw the doubt in Boaz’s eyes. “I cannot give away that which is my birthright.”

Jesus sighed. “Your inheritance shall be of this world alone. Only he that forsakes all for my name’s sake shall inherit everlasting life.”

With a downcast face, Boaz turned and trudged slowly away.

“There is a lesson here,” said Jesus sadly, “for even those who have thrown in with me.” His eyes looked through me. “Rome was not built in a day, neither shall it fall in a day.”

I looked up eagerly. “Then it shall fall?”

“All shall come to pass as prophesied, and Rome shall be as a footstool of the Lord.”

CHAPTER NINE

COMING EVENTS . . .

NOT UNDERSTANDING MY PATRIOTISM, most of the disciples considered me an unbeliever. But Jesus himself turned aside their barbs and let me know that he held me as good as the others.

"You, Judah, have your mission like the rest, and will be remembered long after many are forgotten."

"My mission," I said, "is to free my people."

His eyebrows arched delicately. "Your people, Judah? And, pray, who are they?"

"The Jews throughout Israel and the Diaspora who would be free of Rome."

"And the other people? Are not the people of Rome, whom you despise, also the victims of this tyranny?"

He was forever complicating things.

"Is it not clearly spoken by the Prophets that the Messiah shall deliver Israel, so that it shall triumph over the seventy nations?"

"So you would replace the Roman tyranny with another?"

"I care not about the others," and then more boldly, "nor should the Messiah."

"Judah, Judah," he reproved me gently, "how often must you be told that only God's will is important. All else is vanity."

Even in his faded robe and worn sandals, he had the look of a King. And that he surely was, even though he spurned the scepter many would have given him. In the face of his indecision, the faith of the disciples, and the people, often flagged. Then he would perform some new wonder which made all realize that he was truly the Deliverer of Isaiah and the Son of Man.

On the road from Jericho we passed through the Valley of Kedron, intending to enter the Holy City by the Fountain Gate. There was a goodly company at our backs when the Master turned toward the Siloam Pool, just southeast of the city.

Normally, he avoided the shrines where the ailing gathered, for he healed publicly, with few exceptions, only to reveal his relationship to the Father. And so I had the feeling he was up to something again. Now, as he approached the pool, he was predictably mobbed by the sick waiting their turn in the water.

Hearing the excited murmur of the crowd, a blind man raised his hands imploringly, crying out in a quaking voice: "Jesus, Son of David, have mercy on this son of Israel." For so Jesus was known to many who were not sure yet that he was the Promised One but who wanted not to offend him if he did prove himself the Deliverer.

Others in the multitude, hoping themselves to be healed, called on Josiah-bar-Timaeus to hold his peace. But Jesus peered over their heads and bade Andrew bring the man forward. Josiah threw away his cup and prostrated himself before the Lord.

"Son of David," he cried, tears streaming from his sightless eyes, "my eyes would see the bright flowers and the blue skies, the beloved faces of my aging mother and father. For I have been blind from birth and have seen no man, nor in my mind can I fathom how I myself look, though my hands have gone over this countenance endless times."

Peter had his usual question.

"Who did sin, Master, this man or his parents, that he was born blind?"

This was not the first time Jesus had been asked to help somebody born blind, only the first time publicly.

The Sadducees in the crowd turned up their noses in disgust, for they believed in no life but the present. But the Master replied, without affirming or denying reincarnation: "Neither has this man sinned, nor his parents, that he should have been born thus, but that the works of God at the appointed time should be made manifest through him."

Since Josiah was now thirty years old, it seemed to me cruel that he should have gone sightless all these years just so the Master could use him as a sign.

"Josiah-bar-Timaeus," said the Master, as if divining my mind, "shall bear witness before all of the power of the Lord."

The light of the world was about to deliver light to the blind. I saw the sneers of the Sadducees and Pharisees and Scribes. They would see and still not believe, for to do so would overturn their comfortable world.

Usually Jesus healed with a word or a touch. But now he spat on the ground, made a clay of the spittle, and applied the moist mass to the eyes of the blind man. Josiah stood as still as a post.

"Do you feel," said the Master, "that you will be cured?"

"I have no doubts, Son of David."

"Good, wash then in the pool, and be healed."

Andrew and Peter helped Josiah into the pool, empty now because all the sick had crowded about Jesus, praying to be next.

Josiah kneeled and laved his eyes with the water. And then, rubbing his eyes, he let out a jubilant cry: "I see, I see." In his excitement, he began jumping up and down, until I thought he might fall and do himself damage. But Andrew and Peter got him out of the pool, and took him to the Master.

Jesus' aura was strong that day, and his eyes piercing.

"You were healed. Josiah-bar-Timaeus, because you had faith. All the clay in the world, without faith, will not heal the bite of a mosquito."

Josiah's hungry eyes drank in every sight. "I bear witness that I was blind all my years, until I was healed here today."

The Pharisee Ezra, self-styled the Truth Watcher, said coldly, out of the crowd: "And who bears witness to you?"

Josiah's face clouded. "I know not what you mean. I have sat by the pool twenty years and none questioned my blindness. Why would I lie, sir?"

"You have a devil in you, and we know well who put it there. For this healing, if it is such, has been done on the Sabbath day, when there is a ban on public activity."

Jesus' eyes flashed.

"Ezra, if your ox fell into a pit and was suffocating, would you extricate him on the Sabbath?"

"The Sabbath is God's, and it is blasphemous to work on this day."

"God is more merciful than the Pharisees. For he made the Sabbath for man, not man for the Sabbath."

The Pharisee shot out his lip, but the Master coolly turned away, followed, as usual, by the crowd.

"What shall I do now?" called Josiah, running after him.

"Enjoy your sight," said he, "and deny me to no man."

Two days later, as we camped on the Mount of Olives above the Garden of Gethsemane, word came that the Pharisees planned to put the blind man on trial and reveal Jesus as a charlatan.

Somewhat troubled, I went to the Rabbi Gamaliel's home in the afternoon. He was praying in the garden but looked up with pleasure when he saw me.

"I am glad to see you," said he, holding out his cheek, "not only for yourself but so that you can tell me more about this Galilean whom they whisper is the Messiah."

"He is the Messiah," I said. "He fits the prophecies perfectly, except that he dallies about Rome."

"He is wise there," laughed the rabbi, "or you firebrands would have him on the same cross as Judah the Galilean."

"There is no cross that can hold him. He shall reign forever, for he fits all the requirements of the King of Kings."

"We have enough Kings," said Gamaliel drily. He took me by the elbow. "But excuse me for being a negligent host. Let us go to the study, where we can sip of Persian wine and sit privately and talk." He led me from the flowered atrium to a small room with windows overlooking the splendid palace of Caiaphas and the palace of Herod.

"You have fine neighbors," I said.

He smiled. "Your father's house is but a short distance." He coughed. "Which reminds me that your mother is back. I think you should call on her."

I looked up eagerly. "Did she ask after me?"

"No, but her coming back suggests that she would mend the wounds. You are younger, Judah, swallow your pride."

"But she is my mother." My sense of grievance asserted itself.

He smiled. "Even so, does not your Master preach that to forgive is to be forgiven?"

I looked at him closely. "You have been following him?"

His head inclined slowly. "Since he was twelve, it would appear. But go to your mother, promise me that."

I promised.

We reclined comfortably, facing each other over a table laden with wines from many countries. "I would prefer a Judean wine," I said.

"Always the patriot, Judah? Well, that is one request I can readily fulfill." He looked up slowly, the decanter poised over my cup. "Is there any other request?"

"Why," I asked, "does the Sanhedrin concern itself with so slight a matter as a healing at a healing pool?"

He frowned. "It is not slight when you consider how sacred the Pharisees hold the Sabbath."

"But he saved a man's sight. It was like restoring a life."

"According to the law he had no right on the Holy Sabbath even to pick a plum from a tree."

"But it was God's work."

"The Temple decides what is God's work, and"—his eyes twinkled—"the Sanhedrin decides the Temple's work."

"Annas' family runs the Temple, and the Sanhedrin."

I had spoken too quickly, and his red face reminded me soon enough of his position. He went on quickly before I could apologize.

"The Sanhedrin is evenly divided between the Sadducees and the Pharisees, and they are not quick to do Annas' bidding in all things."

"They have convened at his request to question the blind man and his parents."

He held out a long finger. "But they have not called your Jesus."

My curiosity was piqued. "And why is that?"

"Because he has friends even in the Sanhedrin, Pharisees who have an honest curiosity about this Son of David and would know more about him before they pass judgment."

My eyes studied that shrewd, jovial face. Not for naught did they call him the Owl. "And they fear the thousands that follow him like the Messiah," I finished his thought. "Who would, if he gave the word, take over the Temple and the Fortress Antonia."

He chuckled in his beard. "He will never give the word, for he thinks too much of Israel."

I looked at him questioningly.

"From all I hear he is a very wise man, and wise men know there is a time and place for everything."

There was no point in discussing Roman arms and Roman might.

"May any but the blind attend this hearing of Josiah-bar-Timaeus?" I asked.

He did not laugh.

"With your credentials that should not be difficult."

"My credentials are my secret."

"True, so observe as Gamaliel's guest, as one whose father was an elder of the Court."

"Good. Then Jesus will not be summoned."

"Not if the healing is deemed valid. For it would be foolhardy to make an issue of the Sabbath at this time against a popular hero. He must be discredited first, and that has not happened."

I was chilled by his cold logic, so calculating it seemed evil.

"I am just looking at the situation through Annas' eyes, Judah. To achieve success, one must concern himself not so much with what people say or do, but with what they want. Now ask yourself what the old High Priest wants."

"To stay in power. Everybody knows that."

"Exactly. So ask yourself what would undermine this power?"

"A rival power."

"Precisely, and what else?"

"Trouble with the Romans?"

He gave me an embrace. "You are indeed your father's son, Judah."

I had only mentioned the obvious.

"But it is the obvious that eludes people. You should adopt the same approach to your Master. I am sure it would be illuminating. But of course you are too close to him to be dispassionate, and too influenced by wishful thinking."

He waved aside my objections.

"I shall see you in the morning. Remember," he cautioned, "you are but an observer."

As I left I realized that I had not touched my wine.

The Court of the Hewn Stone, where the Sanhedrin met, was nearly filled. Only a quorum of twenty-three was necessary in lesser trials, whereas in capital cases a majority of the seventy was usually required. Sessions were customarily held on two successive days to assure the accused the fullest opportunity to reverse the outcome of the first hearing. As always, the law was more merciful than man.

I saw many familiar faces in the chamber. Annas sat on a raised platform facing the tribunal, and slightly below sat the Nasi, the Reb Gamaliel. I took a seat in a back row of the windowless room, first showing a guard a pass signed by the Nasi. Near the prisoner's dock, I noticed Nicodemus and Joseph of Arimathea, quietly waiting for the proceedings to begin.

The charges were brought by the Rabbi Ezra, but as the accuser he could not be a witness. Caiaphas, the Prosecutor, took his place at the head of a long table. Two witnesses were necessary, and since the accused was hardly a bona fide witness against himself, I wondered who the others might be. With a start I recognized the disciple Cestus, who I remembered now had been in the company that day.

He was my responsibility, since I had named him, and Dysmas and Joshua-bar-Abbas as well, after they had shown some interest in using this cloak to cover their activities for the cause.

From time to time, I received reports of their forays and wondered whether I had done the right thing. I comforted myself with the thought that they were toiling in the vineyard of the Lord, spreading Christ's word, even as they were collecting weapons and other material for the final judgment. But now I was not so sure, seeing the recklessness in Cestus.

Two others sat across from him at the witness table, an elderly couple, obviously of the working classes, for the needles in the man's rough cloak proclaimed him a tailor. They appeared uneasy, their eyes showing their awe of Annas in his shimmering gold-and-white robes.

The charges were of the flimsiest sort: that Josiah had conspired to break the Sabbath, then perjured himself in the bargain. What kind of a charge was this? Obviously, it was nothing but a ruse to get at Jesus.

Josiah-bar-Timaeus was the first witness. He stepped forward timorously and stood on the witness stand, his hands nervously grasping the rail.

Caiaphas approached him slowly.

"Your name," he asked in a tone he would have reserved for a dung heap.

Josiah barely had time to reply.

"Your occupation?"

Josiah's face showed bewilderment. "I have none," said he, "for I have been blind from birth."

It was all I could do to restrain a chuckle.

The Prosecutor thundered. "Mind your tongue, man, and answer only the questions."

Josiah looked about helplessly, no doubt wondering how it had helped to gain his sight.

"Yes, Sir Prosecutor."

"And you live where?"

"On the road to Jericho, with my parents." He pointed his hand in his eagerness to please. "They are at the table, sir." And so that explained the elderly couple.

"Explain what you were doing at the Pool of Siloam."

"Seeking alms, sir, as is the custom of the poor and the blind."

Caiaphas looked at him contemptuously. "But why this particular place, when it would have been easier to do your begging closer to home?"

Josiah's eyes shone across the chamber.

"I hoped for a miracle, sir."

"A miracle." Caiaphas pounced on the word. "What kind of a miracle?"

"That which takes place in the healing waters."

"How long have you sat at the pool?"

"Some twenty years."

"And you have been in the waters?"

"Many times."

"And you were not healed?"

"No, sir."

"Did you know anybody that was healed?"

"Only by what they told me. For I could not see for myself."

There were some titters among the Pharisees. The Prosecutor reacted angrily. "Never mind what you couldn't see. That is what this examination is about."

Josiah smiled inanely.

"Whatever you say, Sir."

Caiaphas spoke very deliberately now, as if to give the questioning new importance.

"How did you still hope for a miracle when there had been none all these years?"

The witness's eyes glistened. They were hazel eyes, and they held a look of constant surprise, as if the owner could not get over the shock of what everything looked like.

"Because I had heard of a man, greater than John the Baptist, who was doing all manner of healing, even bringing the dead back to life."

"And who is this man?"

Josiah shrugged. "Some called him the Deliverer, others said he was the Son of David, the rod of Jesse promised by the ancient prophets."

"And how knew you of these prophecies, blind as you were from birth?" Caiaphas' eyebrows arched mockingly.

The words gushed out. "My good parents are pious Jews, of the Pharisee persuasion, who read me from the Prophets from childhood."

I could see the satisfied smiles among the Pharisees.

"Even so," said Caiaphas, "why would this Son of David, as you call him, single you out?"

"My dear parents have always told me when I despaired that I must keep faith and not question God's will."

I myself had questioned the Master's choice of this man. But I saw now he must have been chosen for the occasion.

Sooner or later, Caiaphas had to get to the reason for the hearing.

"What claims did this man make?"

"None."

"What did he call himself?"

"The others called him Master, but he claimed nothing."

"Did you not call him the Son of David?"

"Only because I overheard the others."

"Did he not say he was a prophet?"

Josiah hesitated. "When asked, he merely nodded."

"Didn't you take this for consent?"

"He must surely have been a prophet, for how else could he have healed me?"

"This cure you speak of," said Caiaphas, "tell the court how this was done."

Josiah repeated how Jesus had made the clay and placed it on his eyes. "I washed then in the pool and could see."

For a moment, Caiaphas looked like the cat that swallowed the dove.

"Had any ever been healed in this pool?" he asked again.

"As I said, Sir, I know only what I have heard."

"Then there have been some?"

"Not that I could tell with my own eyes."

I could see the Prosecutor's exasperation mounting.

"But there were healings, or you would not have heard, is that not correct?"

"I would not swear to it, Sir, for I . . ."

Caiaphas cut him off angrily.

"Were you aware of the day on which you were presumably healed?"

"You mean, when my sight was restored?"

"The day that the Son of David, as you put it, violated the law."

Josiah was now plainly confused.

"I know of no law that was broken."

"Were you not aware this was done on the Sabbath?"

"I did not think of it, Sir."

"Were you not aware that it is sinful to participate in any public function on the Sabbath, even to wash, for that matter?"

Josiah's face dropped.

"But others were in the pool."

"That does not excuse you."

Until now, the Rabbi Gamaliel had followed the proceedings silently.

"Are you questioning that this man was healed?" he asked.

Caiaphas turned to him in annoyance.

"Since it is a sin to labor on the Sabbath, then this man, Josiah, and the other must be sinners. How can a sinner perform such a miracle?"

Gamaliel's wise old eyes twinkled. "In truth, that is the crux of it. Can a sinner perform such a miracle?"

Caiaphas too late saw the trap he had set himself. I smiled at the scowl on Annas' face.

"If I may say a word"—Annas held out a well-manicured hand—"it seems to me that evidence for a miracle hinges on proof that this man was sightless from birth."

Gamaliel nodded approvingly. "For that reason, we have summoned the parents of this man."

At this point an unusual interruption occurred. A Temple guard, greatly agitated, slipped into the chamber and spoke animatedly to the High Priest. Annas listened with a solemn face, then beckoned Caiaphas. They conversed for a few moments, and the guard withdrew. There was a rustle of curiosity in the room, but the hearing continued as if there had been no interruption, save for a certain abstraction on Annas' part.

"First I would call a disciple of this Jesus of Nazareth," Caiaphas announced.

"It might have served more purpose," said Gamaliel, "to have called the Nazarene himself."

Caiaphas shot him a resentful look.

"The independent witness is always better than the one witnessed."

"Proceed with your independent witness," said the Nasi.

Cestus' eyes roamed the courthouse boldly, stopping when they came to me. He seemed startled, and gulped nervously, but still stepped firmly into Josiah's place.

Caiaphas spoke more confidently now.

"You are a disciple of this Jesus?"

Cestus nodded. "I am."

"Do you believe in him?"

"I do."

"Did you see him heal this Josiah-bar-Timaeus?"

"I did."

"Had you any way of knowing this man was blind?"

"Only that he said so."

"Hah." A gleam came to the crafty eyes. "Only that he said so. Did you have doubts of the healing?"

"None whatsoever." It was more and more confusing.

"And why was that?"

"Because I had seen miracles as great, even to healing a verminous leper before my very eyes."

"Then this Jesus is the prophet he claims to be?"

Cestus shook his head grimly. "He is more than a prophet. When I heard that he changes water to wine and walks on the sea, I knew then that he was the Anointed of Israel, the Deliverer, the Messiah we have waited for."

Caiaphas strutted before the Nasi. "You see, we deal here with a more dangerous situation that we thought."

I groaned at the foolhardiness of this overzealous Zealot. He was so misguided as to border on treachery. "You fool, you unadulterated fool," I thought.

But help came from an unexpected source.

"This testimony," said Annas severely, "is only opinion."

I could see a semblance of surprise in Caiaphas' eyes, and even a dent in Gamaliel's habitual control.

"And for this reason," Annas imperturbably went on, "it is not admissible at this time. The witness is dismissed. There are no more witnesses."

But the Rabbi Gamaliel was not to be disappointed.

"Let us not forget the parents of the accused," said he. "They should be heard before the tribunal arrives at any verdict."

Annas grudgingly acceded.

It was necessary to call only the father, since a woman's testimony could not contradict her husband's.

Timaeus was a simple tailor, a God-fearing man who subscribed to the Pharisean belief in a world hereafter.

Gamaliel, with a look to Annas, asked in a mild tone, "Would the Sadducees mind if this Pharisee asked a few questions of this devotee of the Pharisee teaching?"

"Not at all," said Annas, "the Pharisees have equal voice in the deliberations of this court."

Gamaliel's questions were gently probing.

"This Josiah," said he, "is your son?"

Overawed, Timaeus coughed nervously. "Yes, by my good wife."

"Now, was this son blind until healed by the man known as Jesus?"

"I did not see the healing," said Timaeus, "so I cannot vouch for it, except as I learned about if from my son."

"Was your son able to see at all?"

"He was totally blind."

"Did you consult physicians?"

"Even the Egyptian and Greek physicians, but to no avail. He was born without an optic nerve."

A murmur of disbelief rippled through the room.

"How could he see even now without an optic nerve? It is not possible."

Timaeus bowed his head. "So the physicians said, and so we lost hope." He looked up for a moment and his eyes gleamed. "It was a miracle. Nothing else!"

"How do you explain it?"

"I have not seen this Jesus of Nazareth. But my son tells me there is a luminescence about him that defies description."

"But how does a mere man perform such a miracle?"

"He was surely sent by God," said the old man. "God listens not to sinners, but if any man be a worshipper of God and does his will, him he listens to."

There was a dead silence in the chamber, and then a rising crescendo of wrath.

Caiaphas rose angrily to his feet. "Who are you to preach to us, old man?"

Josiah rushed to his father's aid. "My father speaks the truth. This man was surely sent by God."

Caiaphas burst into a towering rage.

"You who were born in sin," he shouted, "dare lecture the Temple Chiefs in your abysmal ignorance? Away with you, before we clap you in chains."

"Do we put this matter to a vote?" interposed Gamaliel in his most urbane style.

The High Priests exchanged covert glances, and I could see Annas barely wag his head. "These are such clods," said the Prosecutor, "that it would be absurd to consider their testimony. For this reason, I recommend no determination at this time."

Annas nodded his agreement.

It was a most surprising development. But the matter still hung over Jesus' head. That was clear. The Rabbi Gamaliel quickly joined in the dismissal. "For the sake of the community, we accept the Prosecutor's recommendation."

I chased after Cestus in the hall.

"What foolishness is this?" I demanded.

His manner was surly. "Something is needed to wake him up. If his enemies name him the Deliverer, then he must deliver, to save Israel—and himself."

"Careful," I said, "this borders on treason."

"The man is for Israel, not Israel for the man," said he, turning around what the Master had said about the Sabbath.

I looked for Joseph and Nicodemus, but they had slipped out a back door. I soon found out why. At the front door I recognized the guard who had spoken to Annas earlier.

He made us a low obeisance.

"Go out at your own risk. The people have gone mad."

I reached for the latch. "We have nothing to fear from the people."

"For," added Cestus, "we are the people."

An astounding sight greeted us. The Court of Gentiles was jammed solid with people. They stood, heads bared, without a sound. Some carried swords and spears, others had raised standards which said: "Jesus of Nazareth, the King of the Jews."

I knew now why there had been no resolution of the trial. From his dealings with the Romans, Annas had learned long ago that he who mixes discretion with valor lives to fight another day.

The throng was well-controlled and orderly. Yet it conveyed a greater threat than any undisciplined mob. In the forefront I saw Simon the Zealot. He brandished a sword in one hand and a spear in the other. Obviously, he did not believe that they who live by the sword die by the sword.

This was not a helpless mass of pilgrims. My eyes traveled to the Fortress towers. The red-cloaked Roman soldiers stood in full battle array. But there were no mocking smiles today. They were tense, quietly ready, as the legions always are. But even though their commander stood among them, his skull gleaming in the midday sun, no command came. Pilate was too much the diplomat. Rome could tolerate one massacre, but two in such rapid succession might indicate an uneasy hold on the reins of government. And this was a crowd of a different temper.

Cestus held up an arm in a victory salute.

"Jesus," he cried, "was vindicated here today."

A deafening roar, as of one man, arose from the throng. "You see," said Cestus with a wave to the grinning Simon Zelotes, "how easy it is."

A sense of disquietude came over me at this moment of apparent triumph.

I looked up again at the tower, at the tall commanding figure in the garb of Rome.

There was a smile on his face.

CHAPTER TEN

MARY OF MAGDALA

JESUS ENJOYED WOMEN, and they enjoyed him. He liked the sweet softness of their voices and the gentleness of their manner. There was a secret nature about women that appealed as well to his sense of the mystic. Perhaps because of his closeness to his saintly mother, he associated all women with her in his ideal of chastity and virtue. Contrary to custom, he held all women in the same respect in which he held men. Their needs and functions were different, but their humanity was the same, and he showed them the same consideration. "Actually, we owe them more," he said, "because they are made less before the law. They cannot sit in the synagogue with men, must lag behind in the street, and have no standing in court. They do not even have security in marriage and hence are helpless since the professions are barred to them."

He rigidly opposed moral standards which demanded more of women than men. And he abhorred the ancient practice of stoning degraded women in the public marketplace for their sins.

"Is their degradation not enough of a cross for them to bear?"

All but John had put aside loved ones to join him, so it would seem that he was making our loss appear the greater by exalting the female.

He did not disagree.

"The more you give, the more you gain."

Peter, as usual, seemed to have the most trouble understanding.

"Why, Lord, was it necessary to give up our families?"

He shook his head in mock wonder. "Peter, whom I have named the Rock, does not understand. Recall you not the word I sent to my own mother and brethren when they waited outside the door?"

"You said you had no family."

"I said my family was the world."

Thomas, always the skeptic, received this with a frown. "But then are not our wives and children of this world, too?"

"But no more so than others, when you have chosen to minister to all equally in the Kingdom of Heaven. For as I have said many times, it is not possible to serve two masters. The love of family, while a delight, must needs infringe on the love we are deputized to bring in God's name."

In my current state, the vision of Rachel's lovely face and form played tantalizingly through my mind.

"May we not cling in some way to this love for a woman and still serve the world at large?"

He considered me gravely. "You, Judah, would be a captain of men. Who would you deem the most valiant in battle, the soldier with a wife and child to consider at home, or the bachelor whose whole being is committed to a sacred cause?"

Even Peter's eyes lighted up, and I silently agreed.

But how does a man conquer the fevers that beset him as he vainly seeks sleep? I was no Essene perpetually committed to celibacy like the Baptist, nor, like the Master, totally caught up in the lives of others.

Simon the Zealot harbored similar misgivings.

"Is it natural, Master," said he, "to subdue the urge God has put in the loins of all men?"

There was a stillness, as the eyes of the Twelve flew to the Master's face.

The Master was seldom diplomatic, accounting too much tact a form of dissembling. And so, again, he made no effort to cater to our wishes. "In Moses' time, it was 'Thou shalt not commit adultery.' But I say, whoever looks on a woman to lust after her has already committed adultery in his heart."

I was quick to protest. "But adultery, Master, applies only to man and wife. How can a single man violate the commandment, unless, like King David, he consorts with a married woman?"

Peter had to show his superior knowledge.

"Bathsheba," he said with a smile, "was a widow."

"Yes," I snapped back, "and who made her a widow?"

Jesus had followed the exchange with a wisp of a smile.

"David lusted after the woman," he said, "and soon the thought became the act."

"With murder added as well."

The Master frowned, for his love of David was always apparent.

"David repented, yet he still suffered the retribution of the Lord in his declining days, when the son he loved turned against him."

I had no intention of being turned aside.

"Adultery and fornication are not the same, for the single man can fornicate as he likes without being unfaithful."

"He is unfaithful to himself, the greatest infidelity of all."

"But how," I asked, "can one then love a woman, without being married?"

"Love has many expressions, Judah, and I say again that spiritual love is tenfold that of the flesh."

I found an unexpected ally in young John.

"Master, must one remain a virgin till the wedding night?"

Jesus replied with the fond smile he reserved for the youngest of his company. "It means, dear John, that one must remain pure in one's thoughts."

He regarded us all gravely. "All here are chosen for other things, our energies expressed in other creations."

"But what, Master," said John with his guileless air, "is greater than man's love for his brethren? Have you not told us time after time to love one another?"

"You have all been chosen for a purpose greater than self. You are instruments of a grand design, of which I, too, am an instrument. As you know more of God's purpose, what you have turned your back on will seem a small price to pay for the light you bring the world."

Jesus' eyes moved from Andrew to Peter, to the sons of the Thunderer, and down the line until they fell on me. "You Twelve represent the majesty and meanness of man. No sacrifice will be too much for you, no betrayal too small. Some of you, reflecting the passion of man, will suffer in my name. Others will rejoice knowing what I tell you is true. You doubt now, as generations shall doubt until God restores his people once again and the Son of Man returns a second time with the trembling of the sky and the breaking of the earth."

I cared not about distant earthquakes but about the nagging present. Had he himself not said: "Sufficient unto the day is the evil thereof"? He was a pragmatist himself. When the disciple Dysmas asked leave to bury his father, he made it clear that he believed in the moment. "Follow me," said he, "and let the dead bury the dead."

Every day in Jerusalem we went to the Temple. He sat in a familiar place, in the shadow of the colonnades in the Portico of Solomon, where he could preach to Jew and Gentile alike. He seemed to enjoy most his encounters with his adversaries, and more than once I caught a mischievous gleam in his eye when he was hoisting some petty Pharisee on a spear designed for himself. His logic was unassailable, and this nettled them greatly. For before his ministry they monopolized the field of learning and shared the adulation of the audience with no man.

He called them nit-pickers and invoked the name of the Baptist in attacking their hypocrisy. "John the Baptist came neither eating bread nor drinking wine, and you said: 'He has a devil in him.' Then came the Son of Man eating and drinking, and you say: 'Behold a gluttonous man, and a winebibber, a friend of publicans and sinners . . .'"

He used them as a sounding board, while they tried to indict him out of his own mouth. It was absurd to think they could contend with him. But they kept trying. Joel of Hebron, a rich landholder and a Pharisee, had invited the Master to sup with him. Only I of the Twelve went along, since Joel had little regard for Galileans. We entered by way of a flowered atrium and walked through a marble arch into a vast dining room teeming with servants. It almost seemed as if the wealthy Pharisee were seeking to make the Master aware of the beauty and comforts available through worldly abundance. I was surprised, as we sat down, reclining Roman style on huge pillows, that there were only the three of us. For I had half suspected a jury of some sort, of carping, caviling Pharisees. The dinner was sumptuous. Fruits and cheeses, and fish and fowl of every kind, and a roast of lamb, browned to a succulent richness. We could have fed the Twelve for a month on this fare.

The Master ate sparingly and merely touched his lips to a rare Greek wine served in golden cups. He looked past the Pharisee to the door from time to time, as if expecting somebody to come through it. I addressed myself wholeheartedly to the meal, for seldom, since I had left my own home, was I able to enjoy so elegant a repast.

Absorbed as I was, I was unaware of another presence until I felt a breath of air as a dancing form breezed lightly past me. I looked up, startled, to see the Master gazing at a scantily clad young woman gyrating seductively before our eyes. I stole a look at the Pharisee, and in, his crafty eyes there was a gleam of satisfaction.

The woman was well formed, but her features were undistinctive, marred by a slight cast in one eye, an affliction which is commonly called a *yetzahara*. She danced with a certain animal-like vehemence, but it was obvious at a glance that dancing was not her true profession.

As she finished her dance, she swept low before the Master, and in a swift curtsy, before he could stop her, kissed his sandaled feet.

As she crouched on the floor, as if suspended, he leaned forward with a look of compassion and said gently: "God bless you, daughter, for you have been more sinned against than sinning."

She held up her head, and her dark eyes were moist.

"Master, I have heard you speak in the street, and in my unworthiness I have found myself drawn to you."

By now I was sure it was some trap. "How is this woman here?" I asked sharply.

Before the Pharisee could answer, the Master had waved my protest aside. "What matter why she is here, so long as she is here?"

She now stood up and fetched an alabaster box filled with a costly spikenard of the finest moss and laid it on the floor by his side. "This is for your comfort, Master."

I could only speculate how she had gained the money to buy it; it was plainly a slight to the Master that he should be contaminated in this way.

I looked angrily at the Pharisee, who appeared to be enjoying himself, and sought to divert the gift to the treasury.

"I will take this expensive unguent and sell it and give the money to the poor."

The Master shook his head. "Do not trouble this woman because she would do something for me. Do you not know, Judah, that the poor you shall always have with you, but me for only a short time?"

She began to weep, the tears streaming down her face. He sought to comfort her, but the sobbing only increased. Suddenly she kneeled, and with a graceful gesture removed his sandals and began to wash his feet with her tears. And, with the long tresses of her hair, she wiped his feet dry and commenced to anoint them with the ointment.

The Master had closed his eyes and seemed oblivious to everything but the woman's bounty.

"You speak like a Galilean," he said when she had risen once more to her feet and was gazing at him spellbound.

"I am from that part," said she, "and when I was a little girl I heard stories of one like you who would deliver the people of Israel from their sins. Later I listened as you spoke of salvation from sins through penitence, and I wept for what I am."

"And what are you," he said gently, "but a child of God?"

Joel the Pharisee obviously felt that the Master had been found wanting. Behind his hand he leaned over and whispered in my ear: "If this Jesus of yours was a true prophet, he would surely have known that this woman whom he allowed to touch him, and whom he has touched, is a confirmed sinner."

The Master, overhearing, turned to him with the same smile he had for the woman.

"I have something for you to think about, Joel of Hebron. So listen closely."

"That I will," said Joel good-naturedly.

"There was a certain creditor who had two debtors. The one owed this man, whom we shall call Joel, five hundred pence, the other owed him but fifty pence. Neither could pay him and so, having no other course, he forgave each their debt. Now tell me Joel"—the Master's voice sank confidingly—"which of these two shall cherish him most?"

Joel's brow knit in concentration. "I suppose he to whom most was forgiven."

"Exactly Joel. You have considered well."

As the Pharisee preened himself, the Master's face grew dark. "See this woman, Joel. Mark her well, for she stands as a judgment on you. I entered your house, and though you served a fine supper, you gave me no water for my feet, as is our custom. But she washed my feet with her tears and wiped them with the hairs of her head. You gave me no kiss, as is common with friends, but this woman since the time she came in has not ceased to kiss my feet. You did not anoint my head with oil, but this woman did so with the costliest ointment."

Joel seemed flustered, knowing that, in his desire to belittle his guest, he had neglected the simple amenities of a host.

"You have shamed yourself with this woman," he blustered, "and now you accuse me.".

"You are your own accuser, Joel. And for this reason I say unto you that her sins, which are many, are forgiven. For she loved much. But to whom little is forgiven, the same loves little. You, Joel, are forgiven little."

Joel, in his discomfiture, averted his face and turned his back on the woman he had hired for the occasion.

Without a glance for the Pharisee, she approached the Master and reverently kissed his hand.

"Go in peace," said he. "We shall meet soon."

"I hope so, Master, for you fill my heart with song. And it has been empty these many years."

"I will take the devil out of you, and you shall be as an angel of the Lord."

Before my very eyes, the woman's face assumed the tranquillity of a saint.

I looked at her in astonishment. "Master, how did you this?"

"Judah, Judah," he cried, "how many miracles must there be before you know that the Son of Man performs only what you and the others can do with faith in the Father?"

In truth, I had discovered in myself an ability to heal and to tranquillize the sick and troubled that I would not have suspected. I had noticed, without comprehending, that whatever healing powers I had dwindled when my mind was not completely on the person to be healed and there was no feeling of accord with nature. It was almost as if the healing gift functioned through a special channel which became stopped up when I felt no flow of energy from the surrounding atmosphere.

"Think of the living breath from the Father," Jesus said, "and with this breath comes the living force from God's universe."

"Is there not a healing vibration in the atmosphere which the healer captures and then transmits to the subject?"

"You speak of mechanics, not the source, Judah. It is like treating the symptoms rather than the disease."

The woman had listened carefully to all this, but it was obvious it was beyond her comprehension.

In her simpleness, she related only to the magnetism of the Master.

"May I follow you?" she cried, again kissing his feet.

Again he raised her.

"The time will come," he promised, "when none will follow with a greater faith to a greater place."

He watched her depart with a sorrowful face.

"We shall meet again soon," he said, "never fear."

We had pitched our camp on the Mount of Olives, far from any others, and went into the city only to pray or purchase the few provisions we required.

I normally supervised the buying, for I held the purse strings, but I did not like shopping in the Temple stalls. The prices were exorbitant, for the pilgrims would pay anything to say they had made their purchase in the seat of God's worship. Since I held the money closely, the others conformed to my wishes as well. One day I had gone for provisions in the Street of the Cheesemakers, as it again gave me the opportunity to converse with the Amharetzin and sound out volunteers for the time of the rising. I had purchased some goat cheese, which stood up well in the warm weather, and a quantity of dried figs and dates, the Master's favorite fare. The other disciples had meanwhile fanned out in the poor quarter of the city for additional supplies.

As I headed for the Temple, where the Master had been holding court earlier, I noticed a disheveled, distraught-looking woman of forty or so who stopped me in the cobblestoned lane.

"Sir," said she, "know you anything of a teacher they call Joshua, who they say can accomplish all kinds of wonders?"

"I know of such a man," I said noncommittally.

She gave me a harried look and pushed back the hair from her eyes.

"Is it true what they say of him?"

The Master had enjoined us to be cautious. For all I knew, though it didn't seem likely, she could be a Roman spy. They had their people everywhere.

"What do they say?" I shortened my steps to her pace.

"That he can heal the sick and turn water to wine." She gave me a sharp, probing glance. "Some even whisper that he is the Promised One of Israel, sent to deliver us from the pagan invader."

The thought again struck me that she might be an agent of Pilate's, for it was rare in Israel for a woman to accost a stranger in public so boldly.

"You are a Galilean," I said, sparring a little.

"Why say you that?"

"I have friends who are Galileans," I said with a secret smile, "and you speak with the same curious sibilance as they."

"I have been in Jerusalem since I was widowed and prided myself I had no accent."

She had been distracted for the moment, but the worried frown soon reappeared.

"I look for my daughter, and I thought this man of miracles might be able to help me. They say he can even help the dying."

"How long is she missing?" I inquired as we moved along at a snail's pace toward the Temple.

"Some seven years." She then proceeded to enlighten me with a garrulousness that caused me to reconsider my earlier judgment. No spy could prattle so much about so little.

"My husband and I sought to wed our daughter to a young man not of her choosing. She fled on the eve of the wedding, and we have not seen her since."

Why was it that anybody would so afflict their own flesh and blood?

She hesitated for a moment, then said with a frankness that some oddly reserve for strangers:

"She was precocious beyond her years, and we feared for her chastity. For she was attractive to men much older, though she suffered from a minor affliction."

How strange a coincidence, that both this woman and the Master were so deeply concerned with woman's virtue.

"How old was your daughter?"

"Fourteen, old enough to be wed."

Her story recalled the young woman healed by Jesus only a few nights before. She, too, was a Galilean, and would have been of the daughter's age. But of course this was straining coincidence. Yet, just as he helped the one, he could help others. I was sure he could do anything. And now that my suspicions had subsided with her jabbering, I wondered how the woman came to speak of the Messiah.

"Years ago I had a dream," said she with a faraway look that almost made her attractive. "In that dream, I saw the Anointed One of Israel, the Deliverer for whom my people have so long prayed."

"But you are a Galilean."

"And so was he, a stalwart young Galilean, with bronze hair and blue eyes, and the lean, supple strength of ten."

I started in spite of myself, but said with a smile: "What do Galileans have to do with Israel's fondest hope?"

"I am Judean, from my mother's side, and so was he."

"Judean on both sides." I spoke under my breath.

How incongruous that the rough land of Galilee, so blemished in its blood and aspirations, should figure so prominently in the advent of the Messiah. Jesus said life's mysteries were hidden from the wise and prudent and revealed to the simple and the uninitiated, and he may well have been right in choosing the Galileans on this ground. What better reason was there?

This woman was of Galilee, but, still, she could dream, a dream I had seen in the eyes of many women as they gazed on this man apart. Perhaps it was he that she had seen. We were in strange times, when coming events cast long shadows before them. Who knew but that it was a portent given the uninstructed and denied the cynical and sophisticated?

"And this dream you had?" I said with mounting interest.

"It was the strangest thing. I saw him bending over and blessing a young woman. And this woman, from what I could see of her face, was my own daughter."

"Why should your daughter be with the Messiah?"

"I don't know. That has always puzzled me. But the dream was so vivid that I never doubted it. Alas, it never materialized."

It was obviously nothing, a silly woman's mirage, born of Israel's abiding desire for her savior.

And yet I felt drawn to ask: "And what happened to this man of your dreams? Did he ever materialize?"

"I thought I saw him once, in a synagogue in Magdala. He came from Nazareth, and he preached while I stood next to his mother in the loft upstairs. She looked barely old enough to be his sister."

"And her name?"

"It was Miriam or Mary, Hebrew or Aramaic, as you will." She sighed. "I must have been mistaken. For that was ten years ago, when he could have been little more than twenty, and I have not seen or heard of him since. Surely, had he been the Messiah he would now be known throughout the land."

Conversing easily, we had passed a number of decrepit buildings, holding our noses against the gagging stench of offal. Then from the Street of the Winemakers and the Street of the Goat Herders, we attained a slight rise where we could see the Temple plainly.

Stopping a moment, we could make out a crowd milling about noisily in front of the Temple gates. There the Master was sure to be, for all crowds gravitated to him. From where we stood, it was clearly an angry crowd. Shrill voices vibrated in the thin air.

"Kill," they shouted. "Kill, kill, kill."

For a moment I had a sickening feeling and started to run on ahead, beckoning the older woman to follow as she could. She half lurched after me, stumbling a little. Panting breathlessly, she caught up with me at the fringe of the crowd. I could see now that it was a raging mob, dominated by the Scribes and Pharisees. The object of their wrath was a slim woman of twenty-one or so, who was defiantly tossing her long black curls. There was not a hint of fear in the flashing eyes or the lissome body crouched as if ready to spring.

With a start, I recognized her. How fragile the flesh, how weak human resolve. She had been healed and saved, and had so soon sinned again.

The Master was in the center of things, of course. He had planted himself firmly by her side, his hand raised and a glint of fire in his eye.

A stone flew past him, and with a thud struck the young woman on the head, knocking her to the pavement.

The Master moved quickly between the crowd and the prostrate figure.

A second stone, hurled from the rear of the crowd, thumped against his chest.

His piercing eyes jumped out at the throng, and his face clouded over like a thunderhead.

"Stop," he cried in a voice that shattered the crisp autumn air.

"He who throws another stone shall die in sin, without hope of salvation."

I could see the hesitation in the crowd. They looked to the Pharisees and Scribes, and these worthies, shamed by his wrath, cast their eyes sheepishly away. Still, a mob, once aroused, does not easily give up. And I was looking around warily at these cowards, when I was startled by the agonized cries of a woman hurtling past me.

"My daughter, my daughter," cried the woman with the dream, "they have killed my daughter."

She would have thrown herself protectively onto the prone body but was stayed by the strong hand of Jesus. Swiftly he kneeled and tenderly examined the young woman, breathing into her mouth and touching her on the temple, where a welt now showed. "Rise and be well, Mary Magdalen," he said quickly.

She sat up, rubbing her eyes.

The Pharisees and Scribes stood sullenly at bay, and the mob which they had directed, awed by the apparent miracle, nervously backed off, allowing the stones to slip from their hands.

Our old friend, the Rabbi Ezra, and the Master faced each other across the expanse of a few feet.

"This woman," said Ezra coldly, "was taken in the very act of adultery, and under the law of Moses sentenced to be stoned."

Jesus returned his look with a benign smile. "And what sentence," he asked, "was given the man with whom she was caught?"

A shock wave went through the crowd. "But the law makes no reference to the man."

The Master's eyes moved mildly over the crowd. "How does one sin alone in adultery?"

I laughed inwardly at the Rabbi Ezra's discomfiture.

"Do you set yourself up as greater than the law?" he shouted.

With all eyes on him, the Master stooped and wrote on the ground, his finger tracing easily through the loose soil.

Then raising himself, he peered over the rabbi's head into the crowd and repeated what he had written:

"He that is without sin among you, let him first cast a stone at this woman."

Under his gaze, many in the crowd began to melt away, avoiding the glance of the Pharisee leader, who was beside himself with wrath. "Cowards," he cried, "shameful cowards."

There was a shadow of a smile on the Master's lips. Again he stooped and traced some words with his finger. And to those still lingering uneasily, he read again what he had written:

"Let him who has not lain with this woman or any other, let him cast the first stone."

By the time he looked up, all had departed, even the Rabbi Ezra, who had shaken his fist and then shambled away after the others.

Save for the weeping mother, we were alone with the fallen woman. She had eyes for only the Master, but he spoke to her sharply, saying: "Comfort your mother, whom you have found here today. Mother, comfort your daughter."

They embraced, but the one called Mary Magdalen quickly returned her gaze to him.

"How do I repay you for twice forgiving me?" she said.

He regarded her gravely. "You will always be remembered for your devotion to the Son of Man."

The mother had recovered sufficiently to be aware of her surroundings. She, too, seemed fascinated by the Master and could not take her eyes from him. It was almost as if the long-lost daughter had not existed, at least in that moment.

"Sir," said she in a tremulous voice, "come you from Galilee?"

"So men would say."

"Have you a mother named Mary?"

"I have no family but in the Kingdom of Heaven."

Her eyes widened now and she slipped reverently to her knees.

"You are the Savior of my dreams," she cried, "the Anointed One of Israel."

The tears streamed from her eyes. "Thank God that before I die I have witnessed the glory of his Son."

I could see that Jesus was strangely moved.

"For your faith you shall ascend and be born again."

The mother had seemed in distress from the beginning. And now the shock of her reunion with both her daughter and her dream was too much for her. Her face had taken on an unnatural pallor, and her eyes glistened as if she were reliving the fantasy of her dream. "Thank you, dear God," she breathed, "for letting me see the Deliverer." And with these words, before our very eyes, she uttered a low moan and gave up the ghost.

I reached quickly for her pulse. There was no throb of life. "She is dead," I cried, aghast.

The Master peered into her face. "Have you ever seen features more tranquil?"

And, in truth, she had a look of peace.

"She is with God," he said.

I did not understand why he was so philosophical about her death when he grieved about others.

He looked at me in surprise. "Can you not see, Judah, that her mission on this earth is accomplished? And now, because of her faith, she is with God in a kingdom far more rewarding than this."

The daughter was dry-eyed and unmoved.

"I have no family," she said, "any more than the Master."

"It is different," said he, "for my family is of God and yours is of this world."

"I would be a hypocrite to manifest grief after all these years. Were it not for my parents, I would not be the object of men's contempt today. They forced me into the streets."

He looked into her eyes.

"Do you have a sister?"

"Yes." Her voice was sullen.

"And did her path turn as yours?"

"She was loved more than I."

"Mary, Mary," he said sadly, "if you love those who love you, what reward have you in that? Do not even the Romans and the taxpayers do the same. But bless them that curse you, and do good to them that do you evil, and you shall be perfect, even as your Father in heaven is perfect."

She looked down at her body, the flesh gleaming like ivory through the tattered garments, and began to sob. "How can I ever be clean?"

He gazed at her with compassion.

"Your penitence cleanses you before God, and no others count before him. Your accusers are sinners as well and fade before the judgment of the Lord. There is none to accuse you but your own conscience."

He put his arm around her shoulders. "Look well, woman, where are your accusers?"

Her eyes shone gratefully.

"You have driven them off, Master."

"What man now condemns you?"

She bowed low. "No man, Lord."

"Neither do I nor the Father condemn you." He patted her head as she looked at him in silent adoration. "Go and sin no more. With the baptism of the heart, you are purified and reborn."

Jesus looked now to the dead woman. "For the family's sake, Judah," he directed, "I would have you take charge of the remains and see that she is buried in sight of God."

Mary Magdalen sighed. "Help me take her to the home of Martha and Lazarus in Bethany. They were her children as well."

Jesus looked at her closely. "Are they not also your brother and sister?"

Her mouth tightened, and she said severely: "Their door is closed in my face."

"Not for long, Mary Magdalen, for Martha and Lazarus, too, must forgive if they would be forgiven."

Her eyes snapped. "I do not want their forgiveness."

"That is not for you to say, but to receive gladly without their claiming special merit from it. As you are forgiven, forgive them their forgiving you."

At his piercing look, she bowed her head. "Your will be done, Master."

"Not my will, but God's will."

How often I heard him say this, and yet who knew God's will?

CHAPTER ELEVEN

THE DIE IS CAST

"WHAT IS THIS DAY?" Jesus asked with a twinkle in his eye.

"Why, the twenty-fifth day of Kislev."

"And is this day, Judah, not especially dear to you and Simon Zelotes?"

The disciples looked up from their frugal fare of goat's milk and honey and a handful of grain.

"It is the last week of the Roman year," said Matthew, still thinking in terms of the calendar he once set his taxes by.

"It is a day," said I, "that fills me with sadness."

"And why is that?" Jesus spoke softly.

"It is a reminder not so much of the Maccabean's glory, but of our continued submission to Rome. How can we celebrate the day Judah Maccabee liberated the Jews when our own deliverance is so slow in coming?"

"Our deliverance is not that distant, Judah."

He scanned the sky with a practiced eye. "It is a good day for the High Priest's procession into the Temple, honoring old Mattathias and his five heroic sons."

"It is the only day," I observed sourly, "that the High Priests remember the Maccabeans."

"But we shall give them new cause to remember this day, Judah. We shall have our own parade. It shall be a people's parade. It shall be a day sacred to all who know the Prophets, and this knowledge, Judah, you must confess to as a proper Judean."

Rarely did he mention our common heritage, preferring to think of himself, like the others, as a Galilean. And so it had significance, for he rarely wasted words.

"Yes," said he, "this will be a day that even the Prophets will remember." He had a way of speaking of Isaiah, Elijah, Ezekiel, David, and the rest as if they still lived in the bosom of the Lord.

I felt a growing excitement, sensing that he had come to some critical decision.

His manner had become crisp and businesslike.

"You, Judah, and you, Simon Zelotes, will be my special missionaries on this day. Now listen carefully, and do as I tell you."

To the envy of the others, we stood by his elbow, eagerly awaiting his instructions.

"Go into the village of Bethany," said he, "and as you enter by the main street, you will find a donkey and its foal, which has never been broken. They will be tied to a door. Loosen them, and bring them here. Now, if anyone questions your actions, tell that man the Lord has need of him, and he will help you dispatch the animals."

Neither Simon nor I doubted for a moment that we would find the donkeys, for he had just come from Bethany where he had visited with Mary, Martha, and Lazarus and could easily have arranged this. Nevertheless, we felt a letdown at being assigned so trivial an errand.

He saw our disappointment.

"It will be a day you will not soon forget, Judah. That I promise you."

In a street such as he had described we saw the two donkeys tethered to the door of a small cottage. Several men stood and glumly watched at our approach. And as we untied the animals one of them protested: "What are you doing with the donkeys? They are not yours."

"It is for the Lord we do this," I said.

Instantly he drew back, as though I had given the password. "Take them," he said, "and may God ride with you."

My natural curiosity stirred. "Has this foal never been ridden?"

The man eyed me strangely. "He is your Master and you do not know?"

"Know what?" said Simon, tiring of the obscure conversation.

"That you do what you do so that the Lord's prophecy may be fulfilled."

With a thrill, I remembered the words of Zechariah:

"Rejoice greatly, O daughter of Zion; shout, O daughter of Jerusalem; behold, thy King cometh unto thee. He is just, and having salvation; lowly, and riding upon an ass, and upon a colt the foal of an ass."

Simon shook his head dolefully.

"What kind of a King is it that rides into Jerusalem on a donkey?"

"Don't you see, he is finally declaring himself as the King of the Jews: Is that not enough for you?"

"Not when it is his own hand that fulfills the prophecy."

"What difference how it is fulfilled? All that matters is that he has taken a step forward this day."

He sighed. "Judah, you and the rest are deceiving yourselves. He is not of our temper. He keeps telling us: 'They who live by the sword shall die by the sword.'"

"But don't you remember his saying that he didn't come to bring peace but a sword?"

"But," said Simon, "he did not say the sword would be his."

I looked at him over the donkey's swaying back.

"Then why stay, Simon? Why don't you and Joshua-bar-Abbas, Cestus and Dysmas, and the others just go off on your own?"

"I am a Galilean. Is that not enough?"

"You stay because you are loyal; there is no other reason?"

"All right," he sighed. "Perhaps one day he will find himself in a corner. There will be no way to turn, and he will confront our enemies and show them a power greater than theirs."

"And then all Israel will rally behind him."

"All the world," Simon enthused. "Don't forget all those slaves in Rome waiting to overthrow the slavemaster."

I could have kissed Simon for rousing my flagging spirits. "You see, we are not in a lost cause."

The word had somehow leaked out that the Master was up to something, and a crowd had collected in the streets on our return.

"Hosanna, hosanna," they cried, "to the Son of David. Blessed is he that comes in the name of the Lord."

Simon and I helped the Master onto the foal while Peter hopped around nervously on one leg, fearful that the Master would look ludicrous making his entrance on a jackass.

"He lends majesty," I said, "to any beast."

Knowing the Prophets as well as I did, the adoring crowds threw down their robes and shawls in his path, to proclaim him the King of the Jews. Others cut down branches and scattered their buds along the roadside, crying: "Hosanna, hosanna, to the All-Highest," all the way to the Temple gates.

As the procession moved through the Shushan Gate, into the Temple, the crowds grew thicker and more demonstrative. For it seemed all Jerusalem knew the prophesied King would enter meekly on a jackass.

All week he had meditated quietly in the Temple, in the Pharisees' favorite place, in the shadow of the Portico of Solomon. Now as the people in the Temple took up the cry, saying this is Jesus the prophet of Galilee, he motioned the Twelve to lead his donkey toward that center of Pharisean activity. A goodly number of the faithful had already gathered there and were listening to the Rabbi Ezra.

Ezra looked up with a malignant smile.

"Look," said he, "here comes our King, with not only one jackass but two."

Jesus smiled at the throng as though he had not heard.

Simon Zelotes whispered in my ear: "With all these people behind him, it is time for him to declare himself and blow that nincompoop off his perch."

Jesus dismounted gracefully, then chose a shaded spot some distance from Ezra, squatting comfortably on the stone and bidding us do likewise. Ezra, with a lordly smile, ordered his chair moved closer to the Master.

"You would not be avoiding me, Rabbi?" said he, giving him this title with an ironic smile.

"I did not know you were here," the Master replied with an innocent look.

The nature of the crowd had changed somewhat. The Temple guards had driven off many of the Amharetzin and others who trailed noisily after the Master, and the Temple birds had flocked to their place. In the throng were many who often jeered at him when he preached in the Temple and yet resented his preaching to any but Jews.

"How," said the crafty Pharisee, "do the Gentiles receive this Kingdom of Heaven you speak of when they have not been circumcised in accordance with God's covenant with Abraham?"

Jesus replied mildly: "After Abraham there was one law, and then with Moses another. And just as Moses added on and changed the existing law, with the advent of the Son of Man it becomes necessary for the Gentiles only to obey the commandments and know that salvation is with God."

Ezra's beady eyes were those of a serpent ready to strike.

"Among your disciples there is even a tax collector."

Jesus smiled. "The Pharisees should not mind, since that is one tax collector the less."

Only the few Amharetzin in the crowd dared laugh, and Ezra rewarded them with a poisonous glance.

"These are already corrupted by you," he cried.

The Amharetzin made up in noise what they lacked in numbers.

"What do you say," one shouted, "to the corruption in the Temple?"

I now saw a familiar face among these untouchables who observed none of the dietary laws and scorned clean kitchen vessels for the holidays. It was Adam the Tanner, and he was surrounded by his cutthroat friends with the high-blown names.

The guards had moved to silence them but thought better of it when they saw the ruffians were armed with swords and daggers.

Ezra gave them a look of horror. "They are worse than Samaritans," he cried. "They mingle meat and milk products at the same meal in defiance of the law, and feed on swine contrary to Moses."

This drew gales of laughter from the tanner and his band, and I assumed they were already sotted with wine.

"One plate and one pot," cried the tanner, shaking his fist in the air. "Let Jesus speak. We've heard enough of these vultures."

The Master had listened with a frown, and I could see he liked these Amharetzin no more than he did the Pharisees.

"I tell you all," said he, "worry not so much what you put in your mouth as what comes out of it. There is nothing entering into a man that can defile him. For it passes not into his heart but into his belly. It is from the heart that come evil thoughts, adultery, deceit, and murder."

The tanner's crew looked mystified by the implied rebuke, for had they not been with those who hailed him King?

"We call you King," said the tanner, "and you damn us in the same breath with your enemies."

"Why do you behold the mote in your brother's eyes but do not consider the beam in your own eyes?"

Adam the Tanner was even more bewildered than before. "But we are for you, and the Pharisees hate you."

"The means by which we do things, Adam, are as important as the ends."

"Are you not the promised King of Israel? Is this not end enough?"

"The end is not yet here."

I could well understand the tanner's confusion.

"Did you not ride on the donkey, Son of David," he cried, "so that men would know that by the word of the prophet you were King of the Jews?"

I could almost hear Jesus' sigh. "There is no kingdom," said he, "greater than God's kingdom. To this Heavenly Kingdom you make your obeisance."

Ezra listened impatiently, then proceeded with his attack.

"You set yourself up as a lawmaker and put yourself ahead of Moses."

Jesus gave him a scathing look.

"I put myself ahead of no man, Ezra. But I see clearly what is in your heart and what comes out of it. You do well to call yourself a truth watcher, for all you do is look at the truth."

Ezra flushed but went on with a new accusation. "You break the law by touching the lepers, who are forbidden the city, and thus hold all up to contamination."

Jesus arched his brows in mock wonder.

"Would you have me deny them the help of God?"

"God has made them unclean," shouted Ezra.

"Why do you object then when he makes them clean? Surely, you do not credit me with the healing."

Ezra's venom grew in his frustration, and he returned now to familiar ground.

"You have encouraged your disciples to plant and sow wheat on the Sabbath."

Self-righteousness and pettiness infuriated the Master, for they were the false badges of piety.

"Hypocrite," he cried in a voice that caused even Ezra to shrink. "You Pharisees style yourselves good Jews because on the Sabbath you will not tie a knot or eat an egg laid that day. You take pride in not wearing your false teeth or even cutting the branch of a tree, nor will you walk more than a half mile in any direction on this day. You fast, wearing a long face, trusting that all in the synagogue know of your piety. But you are hypocrites ten times over. For God asks love, and you give him rubbish. Has this generation of vipers not read what David did when he was hungry? He went into the House of God and ate the consecrated bread intended only for the priests, and the Lord favored him."

Ezra bounced right back. "It is blasphemy that you should speak for God."

Jesus' eyes were like gimlets. "Did God so speak to you? I tell you, Ezra, that God cannot enter your hardened hearts. The prophet Isaiah, whom you say you revere, has prophesied of this time: 'These people will hear you, but understand not. And see, but perceive not. For if they see with their eyes, and hear with their ears, and understand with their heart, they would convert and be healed.' Isaiah, knowing your hearts, said wearily: 'O Lord, how long?' And the Lord answered: 'Until the cities shall be wasted without inhabitants, and the houses without man, and the land be utterly desolate.'"

He looked at Ezra grimly as my heart leaped with expectation. Were the days of conciliation over? Was he now ready to be the leader the country wanted him to be?

"My Father is everywhere. He works on the Sabbath day, glorifying the flowers, the trees, and man himself. And the Son of Man does the Father's work on the Sabbath."

Ezra drew back in horror.

"You must be deranged to speak of God as you do."

"I only speak what I know," said Jesus, "and you speak of what you do not know."

Ezra sneered. "You give yourself such airs for a Nazarene, and a carpenter at that."

The Amharetzin, who had been quiet since Jesus' rebuke, now sent up a great clamor.

"What is wrong with being a carpenter?" cried the tanner. "Does he not give an honest day's work, so that he can support the Temple rogues in their luxury?"

Ezra was beside himself with fury, but the Temple guards appeared not to notice, for only the High Priests had authority in the Temple area.

"You see," he cried in his exasperation, "how you make rebels of these men?"

"I only call them to my Father's work, that they should see and do no evil."

Ezra stamped the ground in his rage. "Your Father, your Father. How dare you call him Abba, the child's fond address to his own father?

"Are you his child?"

Jesus shrugged. "You have said."

In his impotence Ezra took a threatening step forward, but a restraining hand was laid on his shoulder and a silken voice whispered in his ear. I would have known that face anywhere, and that twisted little body, no better than its mind.

Sadoc approached the Master with a smile.

"Some think that you teach the way of God, and the truth, as you see the truth, and that you have no ambitions of your own."

Jesus smiled. "Speak your mind, friend of God."

Because of Jesus' popularity with the people, some Sadducees thought it politic to shift the jurisdiction of his guilt to the temporal authority. Pilate well knew how to quash dissension.

And so it came as no surprise when Sadoc inquired: "Is it lawful, Rabbi, to give tribute to Caesar or not?"

"Show me the tribute you speak of," said Jesus, holding out his hand.

One of Sadoc's company brought him a Roman copper.

Taking it, without looking at it, Jesus asked quietly: "Now whose image is on this coin?"

"Why, Caesar Augustus," said Sadoc. "His name and legend are on the older coins, and Tiberius' on the new."

"You are well versed in Roman coinage," Jesus observed ironically.

Sadoc persisted. "You have not answered the question, Rabbi."

"But I shall." He held the coin up in the light, turning it over in his fingers. "It has two sides, and both signify the power of Caesar where he has established that power. Therefore, I say to all here in God's house, render unto Caesar the things which are Caesar's, and unto God the things that are God's."

I could have embraced him on the spot. With this deft stroke he had not only turned aside the malice of Sadoc but manifested his independence of Rome. For all knew that the Roman coinage was worthless in the Temple, having value only when traded with the money changers for Jewish silver or copper.

Sadoc was quick to see that the trap he had sprung had closed instead on him. But he only moved his crooked shoulders slightly and became even more ingratiating than before. He now sat himself down comfortably before the Master.

"I have only a few more questions," said he in a wheedling tone.

"I have received your questions before," Jesus replied with his chin in his hand. "Do you not also set yourself up as the arbiter of truth in Israel?"

"I know the law and the Prophets," said Sadoc with assumed modesty.

"Then you have not the blind man's excuse for not seeing?"

Again, his guile was no match for the Master's simplicity. Sadoc's eyes became thin slits. "Let us proceed from the Prophets of old, with whom you claim special kinship."

"Proceed then."

"You tell the people to give up what they have and follow you. If all do so, who will be left to maintain the community and contribute the services by which all survive?"

"It is in the spirit I bid them follow me, for in work there is also salvation if it is of the spirit."

"You speak of things," said Sadoc with exaggerated respect, "that not even Moses dwelt upon."

The Master gave him a mocking smile. "If you do not heed Moses, why would you listen to me? But I tell you again, so that your blindness will no longer excuse you, that the law and the Prophets prevailed until John the Baptist, and since that time the Kingdom of Heaven is preached."

Now rejoining the fray, Ezra appealed to the Temple birds.

"This carpenter from Galilee, with no learning that we know of, would put himself above the law."

Jesus gave him a withering glance. "I come not to change the law," he said with a majesty that made me proud, "but to add to it."

Ezra sneered. "And are you the King of the Jews? We have no King."

This was more than I could brook.

"Who then are Tiberius, and Sejanus, and Pilate even, but Kings of the Jews?"

"Hear, hear," cried the Amharetzin, but the Master silenced them with a gesture.

"If you continue in my word, then you shall know the truth, and the truth shall make you free."

The people looked at one another, bewildered. For the truth was ephemeral, and like the wind.

Sadoc answered for the doubtful faces.

"Abraham's seed, as even you know, is not in bondage to any man. So why do you say: 'You shall be free'?"

Jesus gave him a disdainful smile. "I know you are Abraham's seed, but you still seek to kill me because I have told the truth, which I have from my Father."

Sadoc hid his wrath with a smile.

"And what is this great truth, Nazarene, that you have had from your Father? Was he not the carpenter Joseph, and did he not die when you were still a young man?"

"I repeat, if a man finds the Father through me, he shall overcome wickedness and never see death."

Sadoc's derision was reflected in the faces of the others.

"Abraham, our father, is dead, and the Prophets are dead. And so how do you, Galilean bred, say there is no death?"

Jesus' blue eyes flared.

"You say that we have the same God, but I would be as false as you to say that you know him as I do. Even Abraham rejoiced in the knowledge of my coming."

The Pharisees and Scribes laughed till their sides split, and even the Amharetzin showed their puzzled faces.

"You are not thirty-five years old," mocked Sadoc, "and you have seen Abraham, dead some hundreds of years?"

Jesus gazed at his adversaries scornfully.

"I tell you," said he, "that before Abraham was, I am. This you do not understand. For you do not truly worship the Father but only your skins."

On being told they were not good Jews, the Pharisees and Scribes picked up stones and ran at Jesus menacingly. Simon Zelotes and I came between them, but he sternly brushed us aside.

"Let them be," said he, "they have a devil."

They stopped in their tracks, for they regarded him as a magician who might cast a spell on them. And indeed, his eyes held that hypnotic stare that had transfixed crowds before.

The Amharetzin, to their credit, had taken out their swords and formed a phalanx to safeguard him from violence. But Jesus only shook them off.

"It has been said, an eye for an eye, and a tooth for a tooth. But I say unto you, here and now, love your enemies, bless them that curse you, do good to them that hate you, and pray for them which despitefully use and persecute you."

Adam the Tanner and his rogues looked at him in disbelief.

"You say yourself they would kill you."

"Let it be on their heads then, not on yours."

As they stood, arms poised, he turned on his heel and stalked off.

I was stunned that he should withdraw before such contemptible adversaries and then saw indeed that he was advancing with purpose on the religious procession then turning into the courtyard from the Probatic Gate. Side by side, holding aloft the torch of light, and proudly enshrined in their sacred vestments, the High Priests Annas and Caiaphas walked slowly as if relishing each step. As the sun had not yet set ushering in the holiday, the bazaars and money tables were doing a frantic last-minute business. Annas smiled amiably as he saw the crowds wrangling in the narrow stalls and trading their shekels at the money changers' tables.

Their route took the priests directly between a shop hawking whiskey and wines and a wooden table where a money changer was berating the throng for not stepping up fast enough. With a tolerant glance, Annas was about to pass when his path was suddenly blocked by a lean but muscular stranger. He smiled tentatively, then put out a hand as if to remove the trespasser from his path. But something in the stranger's eye stopped him. Caiaphas' eyes flew to the Temple guards. But these worthies were hemmed in by the Amharetzin who had followed after the Master.

I looked to Simon Zelotes, for like me he carried a flat sword under his robe. He was already standing over the Master's shoulder.

I will say for Annas that he never lost his composure. His haughty eyes moved over the assembly, held mine for a moment, without a glint of recognition, then returned to the man so boldly confronting him. In that instant, as the heavy lids drooped over those crafty eyes, I saw that he knew who this interloper must be.

"By what right, sir, do you halt this sacred procession?"

Jesus pointed disdainfully to the money changers and merchants, who had only now ceased their commotion and were gaping with dropped jaws.

"You call this sacred? What is good comes out of good, and evil comes only out of evil. And so how say you this procession is sacred, when this evil prevails in God's place of worship?"

My heart swelled with pride, for with all his splendor the High Priest of Israel looked like a jackal next to this Lion of Judah.

Caiaphas' eyes snapped, and he was about to raise his hand when Annas waved him off.

"Let us hear what this good man has to say," he said in the bland voice that all Israel mistrusted. "I have been waiting a long time to hear the Nazarene."

Only then did Caiaphas realize who stood before him. But even as his eye searched about for the guards, the wily Annas shook his head. Folding his hands with a show of patience, he said mildly: "Give us a reason, Jesus of Nazareth, that you deter us from God's sanctuary?"

I had never seen the Master so angry. "Sanctuary," he cried. "Do the Sadducees know that God warned of this day through the prophet Jeremiah? 'Go and proclaim these words toward the north, and say, Return, thou backsliding Israel; and I will not cause my anger to fall upon you. Only acknowledge your iniquity, that you have transgressed against the Lord thy God, and have scattered thy ways to the strangers under every green tree, and have not obeyed my voice. Turn, O backsliding children, and I will give you pastors according to my heart, who shall feed you with knowledge and understanding.'"

Caiaphas could submit no longer.

"Out of our way, scoundrel, before I have you lashed to within an inch of your life."

Annas' voice cut in. "Let the man speak." For he hoped that by his own words he would destroy himself.

Jesus' voice carried Jeremiah's message to the far corners of the vast courtyard, and not a soul stirred in the great assembly.

"In vain, as the prophet said, is salvation hoped for from the hills, and from the multitude of mountains. In the Lord our God is the salvation of Israel. For shame hath devoured the labor of our fathers from our youth. We lie down in our shame, and our confusion covers us. For we have sinned against our God, from our youth even to this day, and have not obeyed his voice."

"Now," said the High Priest Annas in his silkiest tones, "may we pass?"

Jesus' eyes traveled down the long procession to the vessels and urns of incense and wine and costly sacrifices borne into the Temple for the ceremonies at the sacred altars.

"I have come to finish Jeremiah's work, and John the Baptist's, whose life you claimed."

At the angry stirring in the crowd, Annas gave a signal for the parade to move on.

"We shall meet again, Nazarene," said he with a smile.

"You see me now in this mockery of God's house."

Annas led him on. "Would you tear down this Temple?"

"This Temple I can restore in three days once it is destroyed."

"What rubbish this man speaks," said Caiaphas. "Out of our way, knave."

"In this place," rejoined Jesus, "there is one greater than the Temple, and he has been mocked long enough."

He turned from the priests and with an incredible fury began dashing the vessels from the hands and shoulders of the bearers.

The Amharetzin began to cheer lustily. "Hosanna, hosanna, for the King of the Jews."

At this salute, Jesus' frown grew deeper than before.

But nothing would deter him. With his supporters surging around him, he approached the nearest table and quickly overturned it, scattering coins over the marketplace. Adam the Tanner and his crew joyously entered into the occasion, smashing one table after another. They followed him into the shops, where he stormed at the shopkeepers, and joined in flinging out their wares. They were the vultures at the holy feast.

"No man," he cried, "can serve two masters. For either he will hate the one and love the other, or else he will hold to the one and despise the other. You cannot serve God and Mammon."

Under the auspices of holiness, the Amharetzin began to break things for the pleasure it gave them.

"Down with the High Priests," shouted a drunken Adam the Tanner, and his small legion of Solomons, Isaacs, and Jacobs added their ribald voices to the chorus.

Jesus pointed an accusing finger at the tanner. "Sin not with the others. I do what I have to do because it is written. God's house is a house of prayer, but the priests have made it a den of thieves. Be not as they."

Annas, with a face the color of parchment, confronted the Master.

"Is this the law you preach, Nazarene?"

Jesus faced him calmly. "Do you not read in Scripture that the stone which the builders rejected, the same is become the cornerstone? Therefore I say unto you that the Kingdom of God shall be taken from you, and given to a nation bringing forth the fruits thereof. And whoever shall fall on this stone shall be broken, but on whomever it shall fall, it will grind him to powder."

Without understanding, the crowd took up the adoring chant "Hosanna to the Son of David," and would have laid hands on the High Priests had Jesus not restrained them with a glance.

I had never seen Annas so moved.

"Beware, Rabbi," said he in a voice of suppressed fury, "lest you be ground into bits."

Jesus gave him a pitying look. "My Father has already made that decision. You do nothing with me that is not of his will."

At the prospect of violence I had nervously watched the terrace above the Portico of Solomon, where the Roman soldiers customarily stood guard during the holy feasts. They were looking on cheerfully, enjoying the smashing of the shops and the turning over of the tables. And like their master, Pilate, laughing uproariously at the antics of these strange Jews.

Annas was loath to precipitate a confrontation which could only result in Roman intervention. He whispered to Caiaphas, and I could see the change immediately in the son-in-law, in the slight shrug of the shoulders and the cool mask that fell over his face. There was always another day.

After this some feared for Jesus' life, for he had made it clear there was no room in the land for both him and the priests. I would have preferred that he picked a better time. But still, he had shown a fire that could set all Israel aflame.

"In another six months we will be ready to seize every garrison in Palestine," Simon Zelotes exulted. "All we need is his blessing."

"He still scowls," said I, "when the people proclaim him King of the Jews."

Simon shook his head ruefully. "If he is the Deliverer, then he must deliver us. Otherwise we take this chance for naught."

"He can do anything he wants."

Simon flexed his brawny arms. "So you say, Judah."

"If God is all-powerful, which we all grant, and Jesus is as one with God, then he is equally powerful."

Simon shook his fist under my nose. "Words, words, and more words, Judah, while the Romans speak with steel."

CHAPTER TWELVE

THE MAN WHO WOULDN'T BE KING

IT BECAME COMMONPLACE for the sick to follow Jesus like sheep. They moved in companies, prostrating themselves in the highway, moaning and groaning so that he could not ignore them. He had said his healings were but for a sign, which was to bring closer communion with God and show that life was everlasting.

"I heal," said he, "only so people will believe in the Father who sent me."

But how could he so love all people, particularly the oppressed, and not stir a finger in their behalf when that was all that was required?

At dusk Jesus had already healed a number of people, delivering his little homilies about God and life eternal, in this vague kingdom of his. He was weary and planned no more miracles that day. And so he drew back as the leper stumbled forward, the stench from his sores clearing a path through the crowd. As Jesus shook his head a murmur of disappointment ran through the crowd. John, standing by the master's side, whispered in his ear.

"Blessed are the merciful"—he used Jesus' own words—"for they shall obtain mercy."

And had he not also said: "Blessed are they that mourn, for they shall be comforted"?

He gave a deep sigh. "The Son of Man has no place to hide his head. His days are numbered, and yet this generation comprehends not why he came. The sick you will always have with you, but me for a short time."

Andrew and Peter looked with pity at the misshapen leper, now on his knees, holding out his arms in his wretched helplessness.

I could see the indecision in the Master's face.

"The sick become sick," he told John, "because they have not lived properly, but in the eternity which I offer, they shall dwell happily in the Father's kingdom."

He turned now to the leper and again shook his head.

"Rejoice in God and be gone. For great will be your reward in heaven."

There was an angry rustling in the crowd.

"If you be the Son of God," they cried, "then do what God would do."

"How say any of you what God would do, when you speak to him sent of God?"

He faced them fearlessly, his blue eyes flashing fire. "You have no faith, you generation of vipers, for you will not heed the truth unless it be wrapped in a package you know."

I moved closer to the Master not liking the look of the crowd.

"Show this leper mercy, Lord, for have you not said that the poor and the meek shall inherit the earth?"

He gave me a peculiar look. "You speak out of your time, Judah."

Mary Magdalen had taken to following him of late, and she too gave him a look of entreaty.

His eyes turned from her to the leper, who was groveling in his misery, and his face quickened with decision.

"Come forward," he said gently.

The leper crawled forward on his stomach, making hideous guttural noises. "If I but touch you," he cried, "I will be saved."

Jesus regarded him compassionately. "You show more faith than my disciples, and for this you shall be made whole."

He touched him lightly and said a little prayer.

Before our very eyes the sores fell off in clusters and the skin resumed its normal texture.

The fickle crowd set up a clamor, and many rushed forward to kiss his hand.

"Hail to the Son of David," they cried. And this time there was a more insistent cry: "Hail to the King of Israel, hail to the King of the Jews."

He stood quietly with his arms folded, and the look on his face stilled their cries. "There is but one King and one kingdom. And this King has anointed me to preach to the poor, to heal the oppressed, and to set at liberty whoever is captive."

He had altered his course, for the first time healing for the sake of healing. The inflexible man might be more flexible than he thought. For what was it to liberate a captive but to free Israel, since the entire land lay captive to Rome?

Even as the leper ran off, shouting Jesus' praises, the Master saw that many of us were rightly confused. "I have only widened the path to heaven," he said. "Since God made the physical man as well as the spiritual, it becomes proper when necessary to reach one through the other."

Thomas had been eyeing him skeptically.

"Now, Thomas there has a limpid eye, which casts back a reflection of everything as it is, shape and color, even texture. And his ear warns him of the approaching storm, and of the footpad, or the preying animal."

His eye had a merry twinkle. "Now what man could fashion such an eye or ear? And if any says he can father a child with these attributes, I say he is only an instrument. The creative power is God's and still remains a mystery to man, though man applies the principle of creativity in this elemental function because of the instinct planted in him by God."

Not understanding the creative force, the disciples were dismayed that they could not heal as effectively as he.

"You have no faith in God and so no faith in the God in each of you. The body is a living temple created by God, as is everything else, from the boundless energy of the universe. And so is subject to God's laws."

"But so many people who are helped," said doubting Thomas, "only become ill again."

"It would be strange if it were otherwise, for the body is sensitive to the attitudes which produce illness, hate, resentment, rancor. To heal and stay healed, body and mind must be attuned to the God force that created this temple."

"And how," said Thomas, "is this done?"

"God is love."

He made no effort now to limit his healings. The multitudes besieged him even on his pallet of straw. The lame, blind, dumb, and demented threw themselves at his feet, and he raised them whole. When the crowd saw his power, they glorified the God from whom this power came.

Matthew scrambled about in the crowds to record the people's reactions. As long as he satisfied their desires, they worshipped him.

"He can be the undisputed ruler of Israel any time he gives the word," Matthew observed.

"And would they revolt against Rome because of him?"

"In their present mood, Judah, they would jump off a cliff for him. But who knows about tomorrow?"

"You have influence with him, Matthew. Would you urge him to commit himself to the cause? Even Nicodemus and Joseph of Arimathea look on the Zealots favorably, and this may influence him."

Matthew looked at me in surprise. "You do not know him if you think he can be diverted by anybody short of God."

"We have just seen him heal whoever asks, instead of using this power only as a sign."

Matthew shook his head. "He merely redoubled his efforts when he saw that the people readily accepted this sign as proof of God's power."

I looked at him doubtfully. "Was this his explanation?"

Matthew laughed. "Believe me, he has not changed his view in the least. He told me clearly: 'The man who has faith in him who sent me possesses eternal life.' It is only more of the same."

Matthew spoke truly, for Jesus in his healings made no distinction between Gentile and Jew. Indeed, he chose not only to heal the servant of a Roman centurion, but used the occasion to praise this pagan for his faith. Andrew had come to him, saying that a centurion, Cornelius by name, had helped the Jewish community in Capernaum by building them a synagogue because he was entranced of the one God. And now his body servant, who had once saved his life in battle, was gravely ill and none could help.

Jesus listened for a moment, and said: "Send this Cornelius to me, for surely he is a goodly man."

"He comes after me," said Andrew, and we could see the thick figure of the Roman officer coming up the road.

He kneeled before Jesus, and the Master raised him, saying: "Rise, for in many ways I am a man like yourself."

The centurion looked at Jesus as if he were a god.

"Master," he said, "my servant lies at home, sick of the palsy, and is terribly tormented. I fear for his life."

Jesus' eyes went from disciple to disciple, noting the disapproval by some, then he said quickly: "I will go to your house at once and heal him."

Cornelius bowed low, and with that look of awe still in his eye, said: "I am not so worthy that Your Lordship should honor me by coming under my roof. And indeed it is not necessary; only that you should speak the word, and my servant shall be healed."

I saw a smile come to Jesus' eye.

"You are a Roman, and you speak thus?"

"I have seen your works," said the Roman, "and heard you speak, even at the wedding of Ephraim's daughter in Cana."

Of course, the dull Roman had become persuaded of the Master's magic by his turning the water into wine. He saw him as a magician, nothing more.

"What makes you so sure of my power?" asked Jesus.

"I have many soldiers under me," said the centurion, whose company numbered a hundred or more, "and when I tell them to come and go, they do as I tell them, for they recognize my authority."

"And whose authority am I under?" Jesus pursued.

"I have seen the light from you as you speak, and I know that you come as a light to the world."

Jesus' eyes fell almost mockingly on his disciples.

"You hear this man, surely I have not found such great faith in Israel."

"The Roman flatters you," I said.

"How does one flatter God? For when he speaks of my power, he speaks not of me but who sent me, or he would not have helped the Jews to build a synagogue to the one God."

The centurion looked at Jesus gratefully. "You speak with God's tongue, Lordship."

"And you speak with such faith that your faith shall not only make you free, but shall free your faithful servant whom you love. Go your way, and as you have believed, so will it be done unto you and yours."

Some time after the centurion had departed a great number of people came unto the Master and sang his praises, for the servant had been healed in that selfsame hour. After them came the centurion and a younger Roman.

"This is he," said this Cornelius, "whom you made well."

Jesus, contrary to custom, leaned forward and kissed the Gentile.

"One day," said he, "you shall be baptized and enter the Kingdom of God. For I tell you that many shall come from the east and the west, the north and the south, and shall sit down in this kingdom with the fathers of Israel. But many that traditionally belong in this kingdom shall be cast out because they had not your faith."

My own faith had become suspect because I had made no considerable bequest to the cause. But I only bided my time to accommodate my mother's needs and to ascertain what I could safely divert from my estates into the coffers of the Zealots for the arms buildup now going on. Just because I was in charge of the funds was no reason for my giving any more than any other. But I begrudged the Master nothing and gave generously for alms to the poor, knowing how he felt about those with much giving much.

My own interest in the poor had provided me with a useful platform for discussing diverse matters with the Master, and since I was confused by his even treatment of Gentile and Jew at this time, I sought a private meeting, with the excuse that I would like to discuss alms for the poor. We had a gift from Joseph of Arimathea for the Master's comfort alone, but the Master wanted it returned unless Joseph removed this restriction.

He never questioned me about money, for once he delegated authority it seemed to pass from his mind. He looked up at my approach but appeared preoccupied, staring into the fire.

I mentioned that Arimathea had withdrawn his stipulation.

"Give it to the neediest," he said, the flickering flames giving his face a ghostly look. "I know you care not where the money goes except to achieve your fondest hope."

His remark gave me pause. "And what, Master, is this hope?"

"You know as well as I, Judah. You will not rest until you subdue Rome single-handed."

"Not of myself, Master, but with your help."

"That chestnut will not roast any longer. In the family of man there is no difference between Roman and Jew."

Never before had he been so precise about what it meant to be a light to the Gentiles.

"But they are our captors. You came, you said yourself, to release those who are captive."

"And so I have."

"But how can this be accomplished without force when it is force alone that imposes this captivity?"

He shook his head sadly. "Do not think I have come to impose peace by force, Judah. I have come neither to impose peace nor yet to declare war."

He smiled at my bewilderment.

"Someday you will understand."

"Must you not take a stand? The Essenes say that John the Baptist would have rallied Israel long ago had you not taken the leadership from him."

"I took nothing from John, but added to him. He lives now with the Holy Spirit. And when the Son of Man returns one day, John will precede him as well, caring for the dying all over the quaking earth."

I was struck by his gloomy forebodings. "Is there any happiness for man?"

"Not till he is penitent."

"And will these dying enter the Kingdom of Heaven?"

"Only with faith in the Father, doing his work."

"But still the good perish with the wicked."

"With the holocaust God finally tells man that he permits him to sin no more."

"Then what good was it for the Baptist to die in Herod's dungeon if nothing is gained of it?"

"As God measures time, a lifetime is only a moment in infinity."

"But the injustices, the inequities, the crimes against man, how long must these continue before God intervenes?"

"He has already intervened, but his word must be repeated, for man's memory is short."

All my frustration burst forth. "If you preach his word, then you are surely the Messiah."

"I am not your Messiah, nor bar-Abbas', nor Ezra's, nor Sadoc's, but the Lord's. For it is not for any man's vanity that I am sent."

"But how long, and to what end, must we bear Daniel's iron men with the feet of clay?"

"All things right themselves, if not in this lifetime, then in another."

"If this life does not count, why should any other?"

"With death ultimately destroyed, man will become aware of the power God has given him to develop his nature with right thinking."

"You speak of Israel's suffering for its sins, but what of the Romans? Are they invulnerable because they are pagans and have no God to fear?"

"If you were a Roman, knowing the uncertainty of the times, you would not call them invulnerable."

"But at least they call their souls their own."

"They do not acknowledge the soul, but they will, and what a resurrection that will be."

How could he be as concerned about the pagan as his own?

"Freedom is the same for all," he observed.

I looked at him incredulously. "You have seen Jews hanging upside down on crosses because they offended Rome. Are they as free as their executioners?"

"Only if they know salvation through the Son of Man."

"If not born to be free, to what purpose is our life?"

"We grow through pain, and even though the circumstances are buried deep within the soul consciousness, we do remember, and in remembering, even dimly, improve on our condition, if refraining from the mistakes once made."

"May I ask when this resurrection of man shall take place?"

He regarded me with an enigmatic smile.

"You know of Jonah and the whale?"

"A fine fairy tale," I said.

"More of a parable, really, for its kernel of truth. Do you recall how long Jonah remained in the belly of the whale?"

"Three days, but of what matter?"

"And so shall the Son of Man remain three days in the belly of the earth."

He would not elaborate.

"It will all be unveiled in time. But remember that I come not for myself but to show what all men can do, with the Father's help."

His lids drooped with fatigue, but I knew no more than before.

"One thing would convince people of God's power more than any other," I hastened to say.

"And what is that?"

"If you were to show God's power greater than Rome's."

He gave me an almost pitying glance.

"But do we not already know that?"

"Not only Israel would know it then, but the Roman world. Wherever the eagle soared, it would still be no match for the legions of the Lord."

He nodded drowsily. "You paint a stirring picture, Judah. Now let us retire and cultivate peace with thoughts of God." He leaned forward to kiss my cheek. "Peace to you, Judah, who knows so little peace."

I slept fitfully and was up and about early. Of late we were nearly always on the move. For after the crowds gathered the Temple spies would come, and then the agents of Rome. I could visualize the horror in Annas' crafty face—or was it glee?—at their reports. For there was nothing better he could carry to Pilate. There could be High Priests and prophets, inquisitors, and tetrarchs, but for the Romans there was only one Deliverer in Israel, and that was Caesar, and Pilate was his emissary. I confided my misgivings to Matthew.

"As much could be made of the shadow as the substance," he said darkly.

"Annas," I said, "has never meant him well, especially since that day in the Temple. Were it not for the liberal Pharisee leadership, Gamaliel, Nicodemus, and Joseph of Arimathea, he would have been in chains long ago."

"He almost seems to court danger," said Matthew thoughtfully.

"He is not safe in Judea, and I would sound out the Holy City before he moves out of Galilee."

Matthew shook his head. "He will go where he wishes, thinking his steps guided by the Father."

I gave Matthew a quick glance. "Have you doubts?"

"How can you witness what he does and doubt him?"

"I only wondered about your beliefs."

"I have no divided allegiance."

I shrugged off the implied rebuke. "I seek what is best for Israel."

Matthew, without a word, turned and walked away. Tax collectors are a pretentious lot.

It was good to see Jesus relax. He seemed to know every mountain trail and stretch of seashore in Galilee. He particularly enjoyed his camp overlooking the Galilean Sea, where he had swum as a boy. The purple mountains, green fields, and bright flowers appeared to lighten the sad face he increasingly wore. Yet, for the sick and needy, he always had a smile and a kind word. He never failed to stop and talk to the children, saying they were closest to God because they had not yet become prisoner to the fears and ambitions that make liars and hypocrites of men.

By some strange telepathy through which they divined our movements, the multitudes were at every little crossing long before we arrived. In some cases they gave up their jobs and left their homes to follow him. This excess of popularity, ironically, was a factor in the eventual decline of his fortunes. There were always new and greater demands on him. We had camped on a hillside overlooking the sea, and he could see that many hungered, for they had followed us for three days and had no food. He seemed especially concerned about the poor, I suppose because they could not help themselves. As always, in an emergency, he turned to his treasurer. I carried a money bag hidden on my person, along with a dagger. And so it was perfectly natural for him to ask of me first: "Judah, have you money enough to buy all these bread?"

I groaned, thinking to what good use this money might be put. "But there are not enough markets nearby for such a throng."

He laughed drily. "I see I have your answer, Judah."

"And you, Philip, know you where we might buy bread, that these people might eat?"

"Even if they took whatever money we had, it would not be enough to feed all."

He turned now to his favorite. "And you, John, what would you do?"

John invariably said the right thing. "Moses brought down manna for the hungry of Israel."

"True," said Jesus, "and what say you, Andrew?"

Andrew could only shrug. "There is a boy here with five loaves of bread and two small fishes, but what is that among five thousand?"

He glanced now at Matthew and said: "I cannot send them away hungry lest they faint on the way."

I could understand his concern, for many looked pale from their fasting and the heat.

I saw the boy sitting on the grass between his parents, holding a basket with food in it. Then my eyes traveled through the crowd. It was a motley group, chiefly of the Amharetzin, in Galilee rough tillers of the fields who looked for much because they had so little. They had become restive, desiring to witness the healings which now marked his mission.

Fully half the multitude was made up of the ailing and their friends or relatives. The disciples moved among them, listening to their plaints, while the Apostles clustered about Jesus as usual. I noted with surprise the disciples Cestus and Dysmas in the throng, speaking to Joshua-bar-Abbas. They had traveled ahead of the company preaching the word, and were not to meet up with the rest until Capernaum. But now they actively mingled in the crowd, and I assumed they were comforting the people, for so they made their converts. Jesus saw them as well, but his mind was on the multitude.

Andrew, privileged to approach him at any time, said with concern: "Shall we send them away so that they may go into the villages and buy themselves some bread?"

Jesus shook his head. "Andrew, they are like sheep without a shepherd. I would bring them into my flock. For the good shepherd gives his life for the sheep. Before me have come thieves and robbers, but the sheep did not hear them, for they came quietly to steal and destroy. But I come so they may have abundant life. I am the door by which any man may enter and be saved, and where he may graze and find pasture. And there are other sheep I have as well, which are not of this fold. They also I must bring into the pasture of the Lord. They shall hear my voice, and there shall be one fold and one shepherd."

His eyes were clear and untroubled now. "Moses, with God's help, guided his flock safely through the Red Sea and into the Promised Land. The same God who helped the Israelites in the desert, providing food when there was none, still would show his people that he is their God. For there are no other gods before him, whatever their name be and whatever their cause be called."

His eyes rested on mine for a moment, and then he commanded the disciples to divide the crowd into groups of a hundred. As they sat expectantly, Andrew brought him the basket with its five loaves and two fishes, freely given by the boy and his parents.

Taking the basket, Jesus looked into the sky. "Dear Father, give us this day our daily bread, as you blessed your son Moses, invoking the same forces which caused all things in the beginning."

I had seen the sick healed, and water made wine, but I would not have believed what followed had I not seen it for myself. As Jesus broke the loaves and gave them to his disciples to distribute, new fragments kept multiplying before our eyes. There was no trick, no sleight of hand. He uttered no incantation and had nothing up the sleeve of his robe. The crowd sat as if hypnotized, barely able to believe what it saw, until it ate of the bread and the fish, which had also multiplied of itself. Some quantities still remained as Andrew returned the five loaves and two fishes to the delighted lad.

I could see Cestus and Dysmas haranguing the people, telling them that never before had there been such a leader. "He is the Messiah sent by God to deliver us from our enemies," cried Cestus.

"Let this Son of David be our King greater than David," Dysmas shouted, standing on a rise, the better to be seen and heard.

He held up a laurel wreath. "Let us crown this Son of David here and now, and all Israel shall march with him against the Pharaohs of Rome."

Joshua-bar-Abbas, a fiery speaker, capable of stirring the masses, joined Dysmas on the mound and turned an impassioned face to Christ.

"By the miracles you have performed," he cried, "you have shown yourself the Promised One of the Prophets. All Israel has waited for this moment. For with the Messiah comes an end to persecution and oppression. You have no choice but to assume the mantle of your illustrious forebear and, as King of the Jews, to carry the word of God triumphantly to the seventy nations."

Even I, knowing his design, felt the throb of his oratory. And into the tired faces of the multitude, particularly the Amharetzin, had come a gleam of forgotten pride.

I stole a look at Jesus. His face was rigid, his lips pressed tightly together. He looked like a man who had come to a sudden and shattering realization.

"Andrew," he cried almost in despair, "they don't understand. They have never understood."

"They mean well," said Andrew soothingly. "But, like all people, they accept only what they know. And all they know is a sovereign, whether he be Judean or Roman."

Jesus' eyes turned to the sky. There was a new resolve in his face, and he took a determined step forward, causing those in the forefront to step back hastily.

He spoke in a clear voice. "Have you not wondered about this bread that you have just eaten? Have you not asked how it appeared out of thin air? Have you not thought that it was not only to be eaten but to be instructed by? Your fathers also did eat manna from heaven, and they are now dead. But a man could eat of this bread and not die. This is the true bread of heaven, and for this reason God shone on you today. But you have witnessed what has been done and still believe not in the heavenly message. For I came down from heaven not to do my will but the will of him that sent me, so that everyone who sees the Son and believes in him may have everlasting life and will be raised on the last day."

The crowd, keyed for an entirely different response, did not take well to his reproach. I heard the rumblings of discontent.

"Bar-Abbas is right," cried a young militant, "for if he is the Messiah, then he should act the Messiah, and lead us like David against the Philistines of Rome."

It was incredible that the tide should turn on so slim an issue, but the passion for freedom burned brightest in the hearts of those with a tradition of freedom.

Simon Zelotes was clearly outraged by the pressure on Jesus from his own Zealots. For he had learned to love the Master and believe in him, hoping, as I was, that he would one day see the merit of our cause and take a stand out of his own conviction.

We exchanged glances, and both drew closer to the Master.

The grumbling continued, and the well-fed grumbled most.

"Who is he," complained a little man with a sly smile, "to say that he came down from the heavens? If he is God, he is not flesh, and all know that this carpenter is the son of a carpenter."

"Maybe," said another with a wink. "For the father was thoroughly surprised."

What a mockery of human nature. A moment before, excited by the miracle of the loaves, they were ready to enthrone him, and now that he would not do their bidding, they were ready to pull him down.

Only the boy with the basket spoke up for him.

"Only God could have done it," he said in a piping voice, "I put the five loaves and two fishes in the basket myself, and there was no way they could have become hundreds of loaves but for God."

Some were impressed, but others knew not what to think. Taking advantage of this uncertainty, Joshua-bar-Abbas again confronted the Master.

"We know nothing of the Kingdom of Heaven who suffer tyranny on this kingdom of earth. This is where we live, not in the clouds, and here we take the bread of life, not in heaven. If you are the Messiah, take up the challenge, or put all pretensions aside."

In the flush of his own oratory, he came bounding off the mound, and the impressionable crowd made way for him as he approached Jesus.

Jesus peered over bar-Abbas' head, as if he didn't exist.

"You ask for little who could have so much," he cried scornfully. "I give you everlasting life, for the bread I give is my flesh, and this I offer from the life of the world."

As the crowd stood chastened, bar-Abbas would have placed the wreath on the Master's head.

"Any man who touches him answers to me," I cried, drawing my dagger.

There was a startled murmur in the crowd, for these people had no stomach for violence.

Bar-Abbas gave me a murderous glance. But by this time Andrew, Peter, John, and the rest had formed a protective barrier around the Master.

"Have no fear for me," he said. "I could vanish in a moment, but it is not necessary, for my time is not come."

Bar-Abbas again challenged him. "If you are the Messiah, take up this crown. If not, sink back into the obscurity from which you came, for you only confuse the way for the true Messiah."

"Since when," said Jesus, "does God take counsel from his servants? Your mission is ended, as is that of Cestus and Dysmas, for your cause speaks more of your own natures than it does of God."

Some lingering awe of the miracle worker still clung to the crowd, but when they defied the Christ and were left unsmitten, they echoed the cries of bar-Abbas.

"If you are not our King, stand not then in the King's way."

Jesus gave them a wrathful eye. "And who is this King you speak of? Some mindless fool for whom you shall suffer disasters, which I see now you richly deserve."

If not for bar-Abbas the crowd might have fallen away. But bar-Abbas seemed intent now on thoroughly discrediting a leader he had never given more than lip service.

"Bar-Abbas, bar-Abbas," the crowd shouted, and I marveled anew at the stupidity of man.

Jesus gave them a withering look.

"There is no reason for the Son of Man to receive better of you than Moses received. Moses gave you the law, but none of you keep it. I have done one work, and you marvel. And then you ask for another work, for your hearts are closed to understanding God."

"We understand," said bar-Abbas boldly, "that you will do nothing about the Romans while our people hang from the trees because they refuse tribute to Rome. We expected a Maccabean, and we have a soothsayer."

"You see what you want to see," said Jesus, "but no man traces my course for me."

Bar-Abbas' body shook with emotion.

"You come to save Israel and yet lift not a hand in its defense."

Jesus' hands were calmly folded in front of him.

"You have your generals and your lieutenants, your bands of armed men, why ask this of me?"

"Without the Messiah, they have no faith to stand up against the myth of Roman invincibility."

Jesus gave him a mocking look. "And so you would manufacture a Messiah if you have none."

Bar-Abbas started as his half-forgotten words were flung back at him. But he soon recovered. "Pilate massacred your Galileans, and yet you have no reproach, but say render unto Caesar what is Caesar's."

"And what is Caesar's, any more than yours, or this man's or that's? It is all of God, and he is the same God for all."

Bar-Abbas flushed angrily. “You hold yourself greater than Moses, but Moses led his people against the Egyptians and others who would destroy his flock. But you say when the Romans smite us, turn the other cheek. How many battles will be won thus? How many hearts are shattered in a land once filled with hope and now cast down?”

Jesus silenced the applauding crowd with a glance. “You speak of Moses, but you forget the warning to a generation no better than this:

“‘Because you served not the Lord your God with joyousness, and with gladness of heart, therefore shall you serve your enemies which the Lord shall send against you, and he shall put a yoke of iron upon your neck, until he has destroyed you. He shall bring a nation against you from afar, as swift as the eagle flies, a nation whose tongue you shall not understand. A nation of fierce countenance, which shall not regard the person of the old, nor show favor to the young, and he shall eat the fruit of your cattle and the fruit of your land until you be destroyed.’”

He paused dramatically. “This scourge of iron you all know. It is here, sent by God.”

He cast his eyes over the assembly. “And just as this generation is paying for the sins of the other, so will future generations suffer for the transgressions here today.”

Many looked abashed. But bar-Abbas was undaunted.

“So you would have us believe that the Romans are the scourge of God and their shackles should be worn gracefully around our necks like a string of pearls. But why should God so persecute his own people?”

Jesus’ eyes flashed. “Because you are hypocrites. You honor God with your lips, but not your hearts. And in future times you and your children will pay a bitter price for closing your hearts to salvation and the promise of eternity.”

“Words, words, words,” cried bar-Abbas.

The fickle crowd had responded to bar-Abbas, for, not being for Jesus, they were now against him.

Jesus measured them with a discerning eye. “Of whom much is expected, much is resented when the expected is not to their expectations.”

Here and there a cry rose again in the crowd: “What can one expect of a Nazarene?”

Another cried: “He calls himself the Son of David, and yet where is his father?”

Zelotes and the others bristled, but Jesus restrained them with a look. “I know my Father, and my Father knows me. That is enough for now.”

The change in bar-Abbas was not altogether surprising. He had always shown his reservations about Jesus, not acknowledging any more authority for him than he was capable of seizing.

"Unless you show yourself to be the Messiah," he cried, "you are no different from other men."

How absurd, when we had all witnessed what Jesus could do. But there was a single-mindedness about bar-Abbas which, while laudable in some ways, blocked him from the truth. He was obsessed by one thought, a liberated land, or so it seemed at the time. Yet there was something about his mad frenzy that appeared almost contrived, for it should have been plain that Jesus was our only hope.

Jesus, I could see, eyed him with contempt he usually reserved for the Temple parasites.

"The seeds of your own destruction are in you, bar-Abbas," he cried.

The renegade flinched, and then his customary bravado asserted itself.

"And in you as well, for he who does not resist tyranny shall succumb to it."

"You mock the Kingdom of Heaven, and it is well. For you shall never enter it but will live in the hell of your own treachery. You are not only false to me but to God. And though you gain your ends, you shall lose salvation."

Bar-Abbas seemed like a man stunned. But shaking himself, he turned scornfully on his heel, taking Cestus and Dysmas and many others with him. "Israel," he cried, "shall remember us long after this false prophet is forgotten."

Others drifted off with the crowd until none was left but the Twelve.

Jesus looked around the grove solemnly.

"Will you also go away?"

Simon Peter spoke up plaintively: "Where shall we go and to whom? For you are the Anointed, the Son of the living God, with whose descent from heaven has been established eternal life."

Jesus' face became radiant. "Bless you, Peter, for what you said came from the living God, because it could not have come from any man. For your faith, you shall abide forever in the hearts of men. And fear not, you shall leave this earth like the Son of Man."

And Peter rejoiced, for what was better than to do what Jesus did?

CHAPTER THIRTEEN

THE DEAD LIVE

UNLIKE THE BAPTIST, Jesus was not a simple man. His behavior was never predictable. He could show the worst sinner mercy, then with the cords of his robe flog the money changers unmercifully. He had a deep sense of his own worth. "If I care not for myself," he said, "then I show no regard for him who sent me."

Not once did he accommodate his views to the multitude, and whenever I brought up the subject of Rome and its tyranny he would smile and say, mysteriously, that without Rome there could be no spreading of the gospel.

"My father sent me at a time when all roads lead to Rome, and then out of it."

Matthew, who had become quite a scrivener, pretended to understand, but to me it was all confusing. What had the Romans to do in their black paganism with the God of Israel?

He seemed resigned that the bulk of the people did not understand his mission, and, for that matter, I could not comprehend myself why it was not possible to bring salvation and at the same time throw the Romans out of the country. How did one negate the other?

In their travels, he enjoined the Twelve to endure no insults but to put an ungrateful community behind them. "Cast not holy water to the dogs, nor pearls before the swine," he said, reflecting his contempt for those who had eyes and would not see.

He enjoyed the good things of life and found pleasure when Martha and Mary Magdalen took turns in rubbing his weary frame with the soothing lotions they had acquired for this occasion. It made his visits to Lazarus' home in Bethany a gala affair.

His friendship with Lazarus intrigued me, for on the surface there was not that much to commend him to the Master. They spoke frankly, however, and Lazarus expressed the views of the business people, who were more concerned with the pacification of the land than with rebellion, for in a time of chaos and confusion they could not prosper.

"My people are content," said Lazarus, speaking of the hundreds who toiled in his many groves and wineries. "I pay them well and they work well."

He paid Lazarus the tribute of speaking to him in the third person.

"Lazarus," he said, "is a good man, for he knows that the laborer is worthy of his hire, and he allows his hirelings to share with him the profits that ensue from the sweat of their brows. He is an example for others, and he will one day find an easy road to heaven on the arms of the many he has helped."

In no way did he begrudge Lazarus his success, nor was he disappointed when this friend did not leave his business to join the disciples.

"They also serve God," said he, "who make the way easier for his servants."

We questioned him closely when he observed that it was easier for a camel to go through the eye of a needle than for a rich man to enter the Kingdom of God. Matthew was particularly concerned, for he could not understand how Jesus could love so much his dear friend Lazarus. And what of Joseph of Arimathea and Nicodemus, who believed in him and contributed to our cause without stint? How else would we have alms for the poor (or weapons for the revolution)?

He made no distinction, said he, between people of different classes and creeds, considering only that it was more difficult for the rich to qualify for the Kingdom of Heaven, since their temptations were greater than those of the poor.

"It is not because they are rich that they are proscribed, but because of how they gained these riches and what they do with them." He held out two coins, the silver shekel of Israel and the golden shekel of Rome. "See you any harm in these innocent pieces of metal? Give them to the poor, or build with them a modest home or farm or road, and they are beneficent and good." He gave me a searching glance. "Buy with them weapons, or build vast ornate temples in the name of God, and you break God's commandment that there shall be no other before him."

His eyes clouded over for a moment. "Riches can free a man or make him a slave. And no man can serve two masters."

Peter looked to Mark, his handpicked disciple, who transcribed his own observations, whatever they were, and said with a puzzled frown: "Master, would you give us an example of the deeper significance of riches and poverty, in view of what you preach?"

Jesus liked nothing better than to prove a point with one of his parables. "As you will." He squinted slightly into the fire. "There was a certain rich man, named bar-Abbas"—we all laughed, for everyone knew that Joshua-bar-Abbas was as poor as a mouse—"who was clothed in the merchant's purple cloak and fine linen, and fared sumptuously every day. On the other hand, there was a certain beggar named Lazarus"—we again laughed at what we thought a mere jest—"who, having no place to go, camped at the rich man's gate, because he was tired and hungry and full of sores. He was happy to be fed with the crumbs which fell from the rich man's table. Moreover, the merchant's dogs came and licked his sores till the pain eased. It was his only glimmer of happiness in a life of misery, but he did not once complain, for he felt that God had visited these tribulations on him for a reason. Now it came to pass that the beggar died and was carried by God's angels into Abraham's bosom. The rich man, who never thought of God in his devotion to riches, also died, and was buried in a grand sepulcher.

"But in death he found himself, unexpectedly, in the hell he had never known on earth. In this torment he raised up his eyes and there saw at a distance the patriarch Abraham, and clasped to Abraham's bosom was the miserable beggar Lazarus.

"At this, bar-Abbas lifted his voice and cried: 'Father Abraham, have mercy on me, and send Lazarus, whom I allowed my dogs to lick, that he may dip the tip of his finger in the water and cool my tongue, for I am sorely tormented by the flames of hell.'

"But Abraham only shook his head and said: 'Son of Israel, remember that in your lifetime you received many good things which you did nothing with for the people, and likewise Lazarus suffered many things, through no apparent fault of his own, but now a balance is established and he is comforted and you are tormented.'"

Jesus looked up to see how we were responding to his story. I was particularly fascinated, for, as a Pharisee-bred, I had long considered the prospect of reincarnation and the evening of scores by one's behavior from one life to another. Matthew, too, had been listening avidly, rueing the darkness that delayed his putting the Master's words on parchment.

The Master was pleased at our interest, and continued with this tale dear to his heart.

Abraham, as it were, had even sorrier tidings for the rich man who had missed his opportunities to do good with his wealth. "And beside all this torment of hell, there is a great gulf between us, so that none can pass from heaven to hell, and neither can they pass from hell to heaven."

The rich man asked a boon of the patriarch. "I plead, Father Abraham, that you send this Lazarus, who is now in heaven, to my father's earthly house, for I have five brothers, and I would have him testify unto them, so that they may be spared the torment of this blazing hell."

Abraham (whom I suspected was Jesus) shook his head vigorously. "They have Moses and the Prophets to follow from childhood. Let them listen to them while there is yet time."

But Lazarus was only the more insistent. "Nay, Father Abraham," he said, "for it would count more if one came to them from the dead and gave testimony, for then they would surely repent."

"If they hear not Moses and the Prophets," said Abraham, "neither will they be persuaded though one rose from the dead and spelled out their sins to them."

No one could have escaped the full brunt of this parable save Peter. "But, Master," he said, "why is it you made the poor man Lazarus, and the rich Joshua-bar-Abbas, when all know these roles are reversed on earth?"

"Exactly," said Jesus, "for the unfruitful rich shall suffer the pangs of the poor, and the deserving poor the consolations of the rich in this life that extends into infinity."

The disciple Mark, the son of a rich man who frequently befriended our cause, appeared to be troubled.

"What is it?" inquired Jesus softly, mindful always of the young.

Mark's blue eyes were somber. "Will the rich man linger always in hell and the beggar in paradise?"

"Not so," said Jesus, "for when the lesson is learned, when the rich man accepts the word of the Father as given by the Son, then he too shall find redemption and return to a new life."

The important thing was to know the truth. But what was truth? Jesus spoke of it often. It was not some vague philosophical concept, but an outlook which colored every act of a man's life. And yet truth for one man was not necessarily truth for another. The Romans thought theirs the true way. It showed in their smug smiles and swaggering walk. They had brought peace to the world, and they even had a name for it, the Pax Romana. But it was their peace, not ours.

Our truth lay in the Deliverer, theirs in whatever supported their Empire and way of life. They didn't scratch below the surface of their own sick society to see the creeping corruption which needed only a firm prod to push them beyond the abyss. For them, Palestine was but a passageway from Egypt to Syria for troops and supplies, and the Jews were troublesome children, to be occasionally spanked into obedience.

For the Romans, Jesus didn't exist so long as his kingdom remained a heavenly one. But he was very much aware of them.

"Someday, Judah," he chided me, "Rome shall carry God's message to the distant corners of the earth."

I thought of those hard, flintlike faces under those metal helmets, the thin-lipped contempt, the unbearable arrogance, and shook my head.

"It would be so simple," I said, "if you would raise your voice but once against the authority of Rome."

"Someday you will understand, as will the world, that the Son of Man is sent to do God's work and not to suit the whims of those who want a Messiah in their own image. Is not God's will above man's?"

He knew as well as I all the predictions of the coming which promised the delivery of the country from its adversaries. Why else had he come at this particular time, when the world was nearing the end of an age and people talked darkly of the millennium? Some said that if you walked far enough, you would fall off the earth into hell, and others said that hell was all in a man's mind, just as was the heaven he spoke of so easily. And that all these truths would become self-evident during the reign of Israel's new King. Why else had he usurped the Baptist's place unless he was this ruler? We already knew about the one God. We needed no new reminders. Why else had we borne persecution and captivity, the scorn of the Gentile all these years, unless God was to redeem our suffering in the name of his messenger? He could not have come at a better time for God's people, nor more perfectly endowed. He was not quite thirty-five, of overpowering presence, when I first met him on the banks of the Jordan, in the fifteenth year of Tiberius. There was much confusion about his birth, and some placed it in the month of Kislev, which is the Roman December. But actually it was in early Shebat, corresponding to the Roman month of March, which comes under the constellation Pisces. This was during the twenty-third year of the rule of Tiberius' predecessor and stepfather, the corrupt Octavius Augustus, who ruled so insidiously that the Roman Senate kept conferring titles on him until he contemptuously ordered them to desist.

Many had confused the prediction of the coming of a King of Kings with the unparalleled power of Octavius, sitting like a Colossus astride the three continents. But Herod the Great knew better, or he would not have ordered the Massacre of the Innocents to keep his wicked line unbroken.

Jesus was well aware of the doubts that grew out of his delayed ministry. And yet it would not have been propitious, he said, for him to have come before the public at any other time. "The world," he said, "has reached a crisis of insecurity, and this crisis brings forth the state of mind that influences the course of people and nations. It is not by chance my ministry begins with Pilate, for it shall also end with him."

It seemed incongruous that a petty Roman procurator's assignment to an obscure province (for the Romans) should have any bearing on the Messiah who had been Israel's shining hope for centuries.

"Not so, Judah," said he with a smile, "for even so you and John and Peter and Matthew and the rest have come together at this time to do in your way what Pilate does in his."

"It is all ordained then?"

"Not in the particulars, for man, with faith in God, has the opportunity to alter his direction. There are some things he can change which help him in God's kingdom, but others are God's will and not subject to change."

"How do we know which is God's and which man's?"

He smiled sadly. "That only the Son knows but remember well"—he turned to John—"you and the others, that no man shall take my life, even though many shall be persecuted down the ages for this in my name, and their persecutors shall not be lightly forgiven. For God is not as merciful with the unjust as the just, and the keys to the kingdom do not serve those who twist the teachings of the Son."

John would have stopped him from speaking in this vein, but he silenced him with the tender glance he seemed to reserve for this son of Zebedee. "Know this, that I have the power to lay down my life, and to take it up again. And for this reason my Father shall love me, because I do freely lay down what he has given me that I may take it up again, and show man his ultimate destiny."

Without his power to heal, I question whether Jesus would have continued to attract the crowds. There were few who could swallow the idea of an afterlife, or of rebirth, without evidence. And Jesus could offer none.

Only words. And so it was that when he healed a cripple or a leper with a word, many were ready to follow him and believe whatever he told them. For how else could he work these miracles but with God's help?

He never performed a miracle without attributing it to the Father's power.

After he came down from the mountain, I asked how he had gone six weeks without food. His cheeks were ruddy and his breath sweet. His teeth glistened in their whiteness.

He pointed to the sky.

"It is no task for my Father to make bread out of stones. When the children of Israel hungered in the desert, did it not rain manna? And when they thirsted, the prophet Moses knocked his staff against a rock."

I often wondered why the Pharisees questioned his miracles when they cheerfully acknowledged those of Moses and Elijah, which they knew only by repute. Even when they witnessed his healings and heard firsthand testimony as to how he made the blind see and made water into wine, they would not grant that he was sent by God. "He is of the devil," they said, disregarding the fact that he had driven the devil out of many.

I thought perhaps it was his familiarity with the times, his newness, for no man was a prophet to his neighbor or friends of family. But Matthew, who now prided himself on being historian, found a more subtle reason for the distinction. "The prophets of old," he said, "relied on nature to help them with their miracles. Moses tapped on a rock in the desert, and a hidden spring emerged. He led the people of Israel into the Red Sea, through the canal which all know they had in those times, and then a cataclysm closed the waters on the pursuing Egyptians. But Jesus does it all himself. With a word he quiets the wind and the waves, and he rids the sick of fevers and pestilence. In Moses' time these were inflicted on the Egyptians directly by the Lord, who spared the people of Israel."

I found it interesting but not conclusive. "What difference where the power comes from, as long as he commands it?"

"He is too much the sorcerer for them," said Matthew. "They would like more of the supernatural and God, and less of the man."

"Yet," I said, "the people would have made him King."

"The people, yes, but not the Pharisees. They see their Messiah as the supreme High Priest but still a humble servant of God, yet Jesus tells them what God thinks and says."

"But he speaks the truth."

"So we think."

"So they will not accept what their eyes tell them?"

"Not entirely, for they can accept a Judean born in Bethlehem of the House of David, but not a sorcerer from Nazareth who calls himself the Son of God."

"He calls us all children of God."

"It is different when he speaks of himself. Do we speak of the Father as Abba, in the same way that children speak familiarly to their parent?"

"It matters not what anybody says," I rejoined. "I have seen him do wonders in the Father's name, as you have, and I am sure he can do whatever he puts his mind to. There has never been another like him, and none can touch him, for have we not seen him vanish in crowds when the demands were too great on him?"

"True," said Matthew thoughtfully, "there has never been such a miracle worker, but who knows where his own will takes him? He knows us, but we do not know him."

At times the Master conjured up miracles no more incredible than his walking on water. For anybody who knows about women recognizes that they are the most devious and self-centered of creatures, ever scheming to manipulate a man to their secret desires. Never do they act without self-interest. Even my mother's wrath was directed at me because she desired Rachel as her daughter, and not because she was concerned with my happiness. For otherwise would she not have been satisfied with my wish to remain unmarried? But for the Master all this changed. In Mary Magdalen and Martha, Joanna, the wife of Chuza, who was Herod's steward, and even Susanna, a half Jewess who was handmaiden to Claudia Procula, the wife of Pilate, I saw a devotion nothing short of miraculous. They would forsake all else to follow after him and prepare his food, and that of the Twelve, and minister to his wants, which were not many. However, after a hard day's travel, suffering from the unhappy vibrations of the sick and the evil, he was grateful for the soothing ointments with which they lovingly eased his weariness. They lived purely for the pleasure of serving him.

"He is the Anointed of Israel," said Mary Magdalen, "so why should we not anoint him?"

Joanna had left Herod's household to trail after him. But Jesus persuaded her to return, telling her that marriage was a sacred covenant when performed with the rites of the one God. She had suffered from an issue of the blood which had weakened her so much that she could hardly crawl to the oasis in Perea where she was healed merely by touching the hem of his robe. Even reunited with her spouse, she continued her service to the Master whenever we went into Perea, or when her husband's business took her near. And when she could she kept us apprised of Herod's plans, and of Pilate's, for they were in close correspondence.

My favorite was Susanna. She was a picture of innocence, with soft blue eyes from her Macedonian father, and a shapely form that recalled Rachel's secret charms. Unbelievably, this beautiful maid, who had already attained her peak at fifteen, had been marred with a deformed hand, the four fingers grown together from birth. But the Master had only touched her and said a few words, and the fingers had detached themselves and assumed a normal shape.

She was such a delight that I longed to caress her, but I knew this would be misunderstood, for her devotion was exclusively directed to ministering to the Master, and any mark of affection from another, however innocent, might be taken amiss. The Master trusted me, for more than once he said: "I know how hard it is for you, Judah, to remain celibate, but in resisting temptation you reaffirm your faith in the Father and the Son, and my faith in you. You cannot serve two masters, and the bondage to women can be a greater tyranny than any you find in Rome."

Because of Susanna, Jesus' fame had spread into the very household of the Procurator, and Pilate's wife had become fascinated by the tales her little handmaiden brought back with her, out of this interest renewing her permission for these little interludes.

I had thought it conceivable that Susanna might artlessly do us harm by revealing our movements in Judea, but Jesus had only smiled at my nervousness. "Do you think for a moment that they know not where to take me? The time is not yet ripe, for both the enemies of man and the Son of Man. But it approaches and none shall know it before you."

Amid all this uncertainty, we traveled into Galilee, then crossed the sea at Tiberias into the Decapolis, the other side of the Jordan, and found the crowds there as enthusiastic as ever. The majority were Gentiles and so cared little whether Jesus was the Messiah or King of the Jews, as long as he healed and comforted them.

The company of women dwindled, for it was difficult for many to leave their homes in Judea for any period, but the Magdalen, as I knew her, was always with us, insisting that her sister Martha stay at home with Lazarus. There had been some dissension over this, but Mary had prevailed, and Martha had disconsolately returned to Bethany. Joanna could not come out of Herod's land, but Susanna brightened our days with her beauty, and there were others of nondescript quality, notable only in their wish to be of service.

My relationship with Mary Magdalen was never cordial. She had resented my opposition to her anointing the Master in the Pharisee's home, thinking it had something to do with the intimacy fostered by this act of devotion.

I cared little what she thought, but for the fact that she had not only the Master's ear but that of Susanna, who blushed prettily when I caught her looking at me. By Judean standards, the Magdalen, at twenty-one or so, was beyond the first flush of youth, and more shopworn than most. She had been forgiven much but could not herself forgive those who remembered her calling. And how did one forget, since her presence was a constant reminder?

She taxed me once with calling her by a vile name.

I pleaded my innocence immediately. "I do not know what you are talking about."

She gave me a scathing look. "You know well enough, Judas." She insisted on the Greek form of my name, knowing it annoyed me.

I shook my head, and would have been off, but she threw out a hand to detain me.

"You called me a prostitute."

I looked at her in pity. "If it is wrong to call a bricklayer a bricklayer and a lawyer a lawyer, then I wronged you. I was only telling somebody how the Master took the devil out of you. Should I have called you an angel the whole point would have been lost."

In her anger she bared her teeth. "I know your sly ways, and have warned the Master."

"You can do me no harm, for I love him."

"What do you know of love?" She almost snarled the words. "You stay with him for one reason, and all know it, hoping that he will lead your petty little army of ragamuffins against Rome. Let him satisfy you, just once, that he marches to a different tune, and you will run off to a new master." She pointed an accusing finger at me. "I know you, Judas, you cannot deceive me, for I have learned in a hard school to look on people as they are."

I felt myself turning cold inside.

"You can do me no damage. I am one of the Twelve, handpicked by him, and sit next to him in the fellowship of our councils. Only Peter takes precedence over me."

"You are what he made you. Without him you are nothing, or less than nothing."

I had not been so infuriated since Rachel sought to trick me into marriage.

"You would do well," I said, "to stay home with your brother and send Martha in your stead. She knows what it is to respect an Apostle."

"You command no respect from me. Think not that I am unaware of the eyes you have for that child Susanna. Have you not heard the Master say that whoever looks at a woman with lust in his eyes has already committed adultery with her in his heart?"

"She is woman enough to know her mind."

"And you are man enough to know the vows you have made."

"There was no oath taken."

She laughed with such scorn that I could cheerfully have slapped her face.

"You must be deaf. Has not Jesus said that whoever offends these simple souls who believe in him shall be worse off than if he had a millstone around his neck or drowned at sea?"

I had listened enough.

"I must speak to Andrew about your breaking into our camp whenever you please."

"I do so at the Master's invitation and care not a fig what any man says. Save for John, and perhaps Andrew, there is none good enough to kiss his feet."

I did not fret over her. For the Master never listened to gossip. He called it a coward's way of stabbing his adversary in the back. Nevertheless, I was relieved when word came from Martha that her sister was needed at home to help nurse their ailing brother.

Jesus became grave when told of the illness, for he loved Lazarus for his good nature and hospitality.

Mary was troubled more, I was sure, by leaving the Master than by her brother's malady.

"Will you come if we need you, Master?" she pleaded.

He looked at the multitude appealing to him for help.

"I cannot come now," he said, "but I promise that Lazarus will be well."

Tearfully glancing back wistfully over her shoulder, she trudged off to the south, but not without making amends for the contemptible way she had treated me.

"Forgive me," she said, "for not behaving toward you as the Master would have me behave toward all persons. The Twelve are as dear to us as our own."

And so I forgave her, for her sake and the Master's.

I saw no more of Susanna at this time, for the Master had mysteriously sent her back to Jerusalem. When I inquired after her, he only shrugged. So I asked:

"Is she not with us because they learn our movements through her?"

He gave me a sad smile, which I found even more mystifying than his silence.

"We have nothing to fear from this child, only from ourselves, Judah." He waved his hand, ending the discussion.

We moved through the cities of the Decapolis, preaching to Jew and Gentile alike. The Gentiles were becoming more numerous, and the Jews, even the Amharetzin, fewer, since the news spread that the man adored as the Messiah had spurned the throne rightfully his own. It grieved me that we were losing strength, for this dwindling of his following could only harm the Master, whose ready command of the masses kept Annas and Caiaphas at arm's length. Of that I was sure.

Toward the week's end, an unexpected messenger came from Bethany. He had flown by camel, but even so he was days tracking us down. He bore an urgent message from Martha and Mary. The Master's face turned solemn as he read: "Master, he whom you love so much is gravely ill and needs you at once."

The messenger, Jedekiah by name, asked: "What word shall I take them, sir?"

Jesus' eyes traveled from the weary animal to its rider, red-eyed from lack of sleep. "Rest yourself first, for Lazarus' sickness is not fatal but manifests itself so that the Son of Man may glorify the work of the Father."

The following morning the camel and rider left for Bethany. Jesus tarried two days, healing many and preaching the gospel, and then gathered the Twelve together, saying: "I must go to Judea, for Lazarus is sick and needs me."

Peter threw up his arms in protest. "But, Master, they have sought to stone you in Judea in their wrath at your refusing the crown of the Jews, so why would you go there at this time?"

"They would have stoned me in Galilee as well, for the same reason. So does it matter where the Son of Man lays his head? Even the fox has a hole he can crawl into, but I have nowhere to go."

He closed his eyes and sighed. "I must depart at once to awaken our friend Lazarus from his sleep."

Peter, as usual, did not comprehend. "If he sleeps, then rest will make him well."

Only Andrew seemed to grasp the Master's full meaning. And so Jesus elaborated. "It is the sleep of death that grips our friend, and it is well that it is so. For you of all people have little faith, despite what you have seen, and it is intended that you again have evidence of the Father's power."

Because of the uncertain situation in Judea, they still pleaded that he not go to Bethany but send his disciples.

He shook his head. "There is still something I must show you before I leave you."

"We shall go with you," said Andrew, "for we have pledged ourselves to the death."

"And beyond," smiled Jesus.

I had always considered Thomas the least of the Twelve, but he now said: "Let us all go with him that we may die with him."

"Worry not so much about death, it comes soon enough. Meanwhile, we go to Lazarus."

After three days, we came to the outskirts of Bethany and saw the mourners returning from the cemetery. They looked askance at Jesus, who did not notice them but went straight to Martha, who was receiving their condolences. She seemed distraught, and her eyes were red with weeping.

There was a secret pain in her eyes, and it was not all from grieving for her brother. She would not criticize, but she was plainly distressed that he had not arrived earlier.

He took her hand and squeezed it.

She looked at him mournfully. "If you had been here before," she said with just a trace of reproach, "my brother would not have died."

He looked at her in surprise. "Martha, Martha, how little you have learned. Know you not that whatever you ask of God through the Son he will grant to you?"

She blushed and impulsively kissed his hand.

"Forgive me, Master, for ever doubting."

"Fear not, your brother will rise again."

"I know that he shall rise again in the resurrection, when all men are resurrected."

"You speak well, and for this reason Lazarus was called, to prepare us for the resurrection. For in Moses and Elijah's time there was no such resurrection of man, but now through the will of God it comes through the Son of Man. For I am the resurrection and the life. He that believes in me, though he were dead, yet shall live."

His eyes scanned the crowd. "And where is Mary? Does she pine at home, not knowing that he who believes in me shall never die?"

"She knows not that you are here, for none loves you more than she."

"And know you who it is you love?"

"Yes, Master, for we believe you to be the Christ, the living Son of God, who came into the world to free it of fear."

"It is natural that you blame me for not coming sooner, for that is the human way."

"We owe you much, for you gave us a sister whom we thought lost, and made her loving through showing her how to forgive."

The people in Bethany had brought word of Jesus to Mary. Hastily she left the house and went out to greet him. At his approach, she fell at his feet, saying through her tears: "Master, if you had been here, the brother that you gave me would not have died."

I could hear Jesus groan, for Mary had shown no more faith than Martha and the rest.

"Where have you laid him?"

Mary and Martha gave him their hands and said: "Come, we will show you."

I could see that Jesus was troubled, for, after all he had said and done, they still questioned his powers. There were tears in his eyes, for even those who loved him most seemed to deny him. He looked over the crowd, and for the first time I saw despair in his eyes. But he recovered quickly, and led the way to the burial place. A stream of mourners, not knowing what Jesus intended, followed out of curiosity. Before long we reached the cemetery grounds and came to the cave where the casket had been buried and a stone laid over it.

Jesus turned to Andrew. "Take away the stone," he commanded.

Martha and Mary both recoiled in surprise. "But, Master," said Martha, "he has been dead for four days."

"Yes," said Mary, still sobbing, "his flesh will have decomposed by now in this heat. For this reason we buried him before you came."

Again Jesus wept that they who had been shown so much still would not believe.

As the stone was removed, he knelt at the mouth of the grave and raised his eyes, speaking softly in Hebrew. The only word I could catch was "Abba," the familiar word for Father he used in speaking to God.

I thought for a moment how embarrassing it would be if he failed, for it did seem beyond even his capacity to restore the flesh once it had begun to stink.

His face wore an exalted look now, and he said in a ringing voice: "Father, thank you for hearing my prayers."

The coffin was only lightly covered with earth. Andrew, at a signal from the Master, had pried open the lid with John's help. The stench was overpowering, and I shuddered at what the corpse would be like. I stole a look at Martha and Mary. Their faces were filled with revulsion, and they looked as if they were about to throw up. They ran into the fresh air, retching and coughing. And so they did not hear Jesus say that he spoke aloud so that the witnesses would know he was sent of God.

"Not my will, but your will be done," he said, using a phrase I had heard many times.

Martha and Mary, their faces ashen, had returned to the grave.

The Master, seemingly insensitive to the odor, bent over the corpse and in a loud voice commanded: "Lazarus, come forth out of the grave."

Before our very eyes an eerie figure swaddled in the white wrappings of the dead began to rise slowly in the coffin. Andrew and John moved swiftly to its assistance, and the figure, bound hand and foot in grave clothes, with a towel about its face, sat up in the coffin. They removed the towel, and we saw the clear features of Lazarus, the friend we had thought lost, and lo and behold, his flesh was as sound as when I saw him last.

With Andrew's help, he now stepped out of the coffin. His eyes lighted first on Jesus, and then on Martha and Mary and the mourners at his funeral.

"What do you all do here?" he asked, surveying the cave with wonder.

"We are here," said Jesus, "to manifest the glory of God. For that you became ill and passed through the door of death. And for that, you were made to live again."

If not for the smell, I would have thought it entirely possible that we had imagined it all. Miraculously now, the stench had disappeared, and the air was clean and pure. Lazarus embraced his sisters, then turned to the Master, and his eyes gleamed with gratitude.

"I was sick unto death, and you made me alive."

"And how did you know you were dead?"

"I remembered at first my sisters crying over me, as I lay expiring in my bed, sorrowing that you were not here. Then there was total darkness, and I seemed carried to a great height while my lifeless body lay as it was in my house in Bethany. I saw a million lights, like huge stars, flickering in the distance, and then great banks of clouds, and shadowy figures beginning to emerge. There were hazy faces and forms, and yet when I reached out, my fingers combed the empty air."

Mary and Martha, like the rest, had been listening enthralled.

"And were these fingers and faces like any you knew?" the Master asked.

Lazarus hesitated, and a look of wonder came into his eyes. "I saw my own dear mother, and my father, who had preceded her by many years, and they seemed content, saying how pleased they were the family was reconciled."

The sisters turned marveling to the Master. "Was our brother truly in heaven, as he thinks?"

Jesus looked as though he would again weep. But instead he replied in a solemn voice: "To live truly one must die and be reborn again. Poor Lazarus would have known all the blessings of heaven, but he was recalled to confirm the Lord's message and so has served God."

Many of the Apostles were astounded that Lazarus was brought back to the living.

"How was this done?" asked Thomas.

Andrew frowned. "Did not the Master explain that it was done of God?"

"Everything is God's," said Thomas with a grimace.

Philip nodded his head in assent. "This is no explanation, for we do not see God's hand at work."

For myself it was all crystal clear. "How many times must he tell you that his power comes of God? Since God has the power to create life, and end it, which none question, then Jesus can do as much, as God's channel on earth."

"Well said, Judah," Simon Zelotes boomed approvingly.

It was obvious that Jesus had deliberately allowed Lazarus to die so that he could prove his own power.

"Why else," I said, "did he not come to him at once when told he was ill? It was to show the multitude that he could triumph over any adversary, including the most unquenchable of all."

"Which," Zelotes finished for me, "is death itself."

"And if he can do it for another," I said, "then he can do it for himself as well."

CHAPTER FOURTEEN

THE PLOT

THE SUMMONS CAME FROM ANNAS, which I thought odd, since Caiaphas usually arranged the Temple audiences. The courier, a Levite, found me at Lazarus' house in Bethany, for I was on my way to smooth things over with my mother.

"Come without delay," said the courier, a young man with bushy hair, "for it is of supreme importance."

"I will be there tomorrow," I said, quickly going over my vulnerable areas and finding them well covered. I had already explained my becoming a disciple to their apparent satisfaction.

After the messenger left, Mary and Martha looked at me with concern.

"Are you in any difficulty?" Martha inquired.

"None that I know of," I replied with more assurance than I felt.

"It is about the Master," cried Mary. "They plot to kill him, I know it. I could see it in the face of the High Priest that day in the Temple."

Her voice trembled the least bit. "They hate him because the people follow him."

"As long as the people support him," I said, "we have nothing to fear."

Lazarus had walked in and, seeing the faces of the two women, quickly asked: "What is wrong? Have I stumbled onto another funeral procession?"

I made an attempt at heartiness. "You know how women are, always fretting about things that never happen."

Mary stood in the center of the room, her eyes closed as if she were praying. "Ever since he came into my life I have felt a close community with him, knowing when he suffered and when he rejoiced. I know that of late his heart has been heavy."

Lazarus' face mirrored her own concern, but his ready humor and good spirits, for which Jesus loved him, soon came to the fore.

"We stand around and moon, and for all we know they only wish to borrow money from Judah, knowing how frugal he is. Let us sit down to our supper, partake of a little wine, and chase away our errant fears."

As we broke bread, saying the "Our Father" prayer that Jesus had taught us, I couldn't help but think, looking at Lazarus, that the Master truly seemed capable of anything. Lazarus had been dead four days. And yet here he was, alive and well, a living reminder of the Master's power.

Mary did not touch her food. "I would go to him if he needs me," she said.

"He is on the road from Capernaum," I said, "but your fears are unfounded. The Temple priests would have acted long ago if they meant him harm."

"They only dare now," said she, "because the militants are not as much for him as they were."

"And how is that?" I asked, wondering how she knew.

"They do not realize that his message is essentially spiritual, and they stew about taxation, and the Romans, and his being a light to the Gentiles as well. They do not understand his liking for the heathen."

"They want a Messiah who is a Messiah," I acknowledged, "one who has come to deliver the Jews, and not be concerned about their captors."

She sighed. "I have variously known Romans and Jews, Judah, and I have seen little difference in them, except that the Romans enjoyed wholeheartedly what they did, and the Jews lowered their eyes as if committing some great sin."

Lazarus regarded her glumly. "I thought these matters were forgiven and forgotten, and not to be discussed in this house."

For a moment there was a devilish gleam in her eyes.

"Lazarus hides his head, and thinks he is not seen."

"I know now what you talk about."

"I talk about sin, which the Master forgives, but not so with hypocritical Israel, which can find no reason but tradition for God preferring it above other nations."

Martha gave her sister an affirming nod. "He is for all people, regardless of race or creed, for he has healed Syrians and Samaritans, and even the Romans and their servants."

Lazarus wiped his lips and said gruffly: "We sit around and speak loosely like women, without having the slightest idea of the problem or whether there is a problem. Let Judah go first to Jerusalem, and we will know soon enough what is astir."

Mary did not seem at all encouraged.

"In a land held captive none can feel any certainty of the morrow."

I pounced on her words. "You see the importance of our being free and independent."

"The Master says that freedom is of the spirit."

Lazarus had tired of the discussion, as could be expected of a man of affairs, an owner of many businesses, respected even by the Romans.

He turned to me. "I hear that things are seething in Rome. They say that Tiberius has hurried back from his self-imposed exile in Capri and that Sejanus' position is threatened by his own plotting."

I shrugged. "What does it matter which monster rules?"

"You forget," he said, "that Pilate is Sejanus' creature, and if the master goes, the servant may not be far behind."

"So before Pilate it was Valerius Gratus, and before that Coponius and Vitellius. Was Israel any better off?"

"At least we did not harbor an ambitious tyrant who sought preferment by indulging the anti-Jewish sentiments of his overseer in Rome."

"One Roman looks like another." I scowled. "The important thing is to get rid of them all."

He gave me a curious look. "As a disciple you are committed to the teachings of Jesus, and Jesus makes no distinction in his kingdom between Jew and Roman. You are aware of that, are you not?"

"It was not always like that," I said. "The change came over him when he went into the mountain, and the visions of Moses and Elijah faded before his eyes."

"Is not that enough for you?"

"It is a matter of interpretation. I question not what he saw, but to what purpose. Simon Zelotes argues that by their presence the visions indicate that God still smiles on the people of Moses and Elijah."

Lazarus snorted. "And if every disciple is to set himself above the Master, who then is the Master?"

I had never been overly fond of Lazarus. He gave himself airs because of the special favor shown by Jesus in stopping at his house whenever in Jerusalem. If he loved the Master, why had he not followed him like the rest? He was no more than a transplanted Galilean, and Magdala, whence the family came, was hardly a resort by the sea.

"How can you judge the Twelve," I said, "when you have not given up everything as we have?"

He looked at me with a sardonic eye. "Everything, Judah? Be frank, have not you relinquished only that which was not dear to you?"

I flushed. "Does a host quiz a guest under his roof?"

He took my hand impulsively. "We are not guest and host. We speak as friends. I could not leave my affairs, and he understood. 'You will win more converts as an outsider,' he told me. I did not know what he meant, but later I understood. One day you also shall understand that we are all in places where he wants us to be, so that the unseen skein of his life can be spun out to the end."

Mary and Martha had followed the conversation with frowns, neither quite comprehending the issues that had been unexpectedly injected. "He saved your life," said Mary accusingly. "You should go with Judah and make sure they mean the Master no harm."

"You make a river out of a brook," he cried. "There is nothing I wouldn't do for the friend who saved my life."

"He did more," she went on relentlessly. "Your life was gone, for we buried and wept over you, and he brought you back from the dead."

"This is the same," I said, "that he did with Jairus' daughter, who was only twelve when Jairus, a ruler of the synagogue on the other side of Galilee, came to him, saying his only daughter was dying. And when Jesus came to the house the family and friends were sobbing because she had expired. He told them to desist, since the maid was only sleeping. They laughed him to scorn and would have ejected him from the house had not Jairus taken him into the room where the damsel lay. He took her by the hand and said: 'Arise and be well' and straightway she rose and walked."

Martha had heard it in greater detail. "I had the story from Peter and John, and they described how Jesus told the spirit to go back into her again. And then, showing the bond between body and spirit, he commanded her parents to give her food immediately, so she would rise and shine."

It was hard to believe he could raise the dead, but then nearly everything he did was equally incredible. Although I had witnessed Lazarus' experience, I had wondered, as had others, how dead he was. Had it not been for the corruption of the flesh, I would have had more reservations, for it was not unusual for people to be in a somnolent state akin to death in its aspects. Jesus was even accused by some of putting a devil in Lazarus so that he could then, like a conjurer, remove this devil by the power of his mind, with what the Greeks called suggestion or hypnosis. Indeed, there were many who said that he had done this at Cana and again with the fishes and loaves, claiming that all he had done was hypnotize the multitude into thinking they were imbibing wine in one case, and eating manna from heaven in another. This was said to be a common occurrence in Egypt, where he had spent some years as a boy.

It seemed unlikely, since I myself was a witness on these occasions and had no feeling of being under another's influence. But some said that the hypnotized person was the last to know.

In any event, I saw no harm in questioning Lazarus about his experience after death, for that might well throw some additional light on the kingdom the Master spoke of so casually.

"Can you say again what you recalled after you were put in the tomb?" I inquired.

He gave me a shrewd glance. "So you doubt as Thomas did? One must acknowledge that the Master is surrounded by doubting Thomases."

"I do not question his powers, only their extent."

I did not like his smile. "You shall know, and Matthew shall know as well, for he is the Apostle to the Jews. But is it not ironic that our own people demand more proof than the heathen?"

He looked around as if inviting Martha and Mary to leave the room. But they appeared not to notice and settled themselves comfortably in their chairs.

I saw little change in the Magdalen, for all the noise that was made of her redemption. She was frequently brusque and offensive, for she had seen more vileness and chicanery than honesty and honor and had little regard for the most virtuous.

"He was dead all right," said she with a turned-up nose, "for he stank like a fish after three days."

She appeared oblivious to Lazarus' frown of annoyance. "The weather had turned warm, otherwise he might have kept better."

It was obvious that she enjoyed mocking her brother, for what reason I cannot venture, except that she still had the devil in her.

"I am not so much interested in the state of his corpse as in that of his spirit."

Lazarus gave me a grateful glance, and now hastened to satisfy my curiosity.

"I saw my own body, as though I were standing next to it, and then I saw a white ethereal substance leave the body, forming a luminous envelope of corresponding shape from head to toe, which eventually moved upward into space and disappeared."

"And was there any impression of what this could be?"

"I had the feeling it was the Holy Spirit, and that it lived on as an energy form after my body had succumbed to the fever."

"So you were not then dead in reality?"

"If I had not been awakened I would still be in the tomb, and you would be conversing with my ghost."

This misplaced humor of Lazarus' flared forth in disconcerting fashion, and for the life of me, I could not comprehend how the Master relished his company.

"You might only have been in a coma, in a catatonic state, in which people are often mistakenly thought to be dead, but which is in reality a state of suspended animation characterized by a trancelike absence of normal consciousness."

"He did not breathe," said Martha, "for I held a mirror against his mouth and there was no answering vapor or mist."

Actually, there was little doubt in my mind that he had been brought from the dead, but it was vital that there be no doubt at all.

"Do you believe Jesus when he says the last enemy to be destroyed is death itself?"

Lazarus smiled smugly. "What more proof do you need than myself, or Jairus' daughter for that matter?"

Martha nodded, her assent echoing my own thoughts. "If he can do it for one, then he can do it for all."

"Then why do you worry about his welfare, if he has this ultimate control over death?"

Mary gave me a scornful eye.

"They cannot do anything to him unless he permits, but lately have you not heard him talking about joining his Father in heaven? It gives me a feeling of desolation."

"But how can they take his life when he can bring life to the dead? It does not make sense."

Lazarus would have shut off the conversation, but Mary was not easily silenced.

"How often has he said that his Father sent him to show that life is everlasting, and so how else can he manifest this to Israel?"

"But then all dies with him."

Her dark eyes had taken on a tragic look.

"If it is as I fear, who knows how much he will suffer?"

My mind went back over the two years and more I had served him. "I have never seen him fail in anything. Do you not know that he once walked on water?"

"So they say." She shrugged. "But of what matter is that?"

I was incredulous. "He does what no man has done since the beginning of time, and you do not even marvel."

Into Lazarus' deep-set eyes had come a reflective look. "There is only one of him, and no man can do for him what he can do for others."

"He says the Apostles can do whatever he does with faith in the Father."

"There is not that much faith in all of Israel, for only he knows what the Father knows, and only the Father knows what he knows."

"You say yourself that he is invincible, and I have seen proof myself."

Martha was the quiet one, but there was invariably a good deal of wisdom in her words. "We all thought the Baptist protected by God, and yet Herod was able to slay this prince of the world and lay his head on a platter."

"It was his spirit that was unquenchable. I saw this for myself."

"And so also is Jesus', but more so, for he is wholly of the spirit."

It was odd that two sisters could see him so differently. Mary's face grew dark with her morose thoughts. "He is also very much a man, with a limitless capacity to love and be loved, and all close to him, whether man or woman, feel the irresistible impact of his manhood."

I looked at her in surprise, for I had not thought of Jesus like other men, with the attributes and qualities of a healthy, virile man in the prime of his being.

Occasionally a thought came to me that I knew to be the truth because it conformed with the orderly pattern of the discernible universe and so reflected the will of him who had created heaven and earth.

"Jesus," I said, "is the universal man, the first and perhaps the only one, whereas his ancestor David epitomized the worldly man, with all his faults and frailties. In this way we are reminded of Jesus' perfection as a man even as we are cognizant of the other's imperfections." My glance included both Martha and Mary. "In this perfection he expressed his love for all, undiluted by any love of family or of woman. He does not look at women like the rest, for even when we ordinary mortals have forsworn temptation, our thoughts still do battle with our wish to be as he would have us be."

Lazarus looked at me guiltily. I had heard he had many mistresses and was as hard-pressed to leave these as his wealth and comfort. I found it remarkable that Jesus did not chide him for his weaknesses, but he often made allowances for those he loved. "If not for sinners," he said with a smile when I once questioned him, "we would have no work to do. The Lord loves all alike, so long as they confess their weaknesses."

Lazarus may have read my mind.

"You have spoken well," he said now in his condescending way.

Although I had not acknowledged it, I too was concerned about the summons and thought it expedient to get my things together and take to the road.

Mary Magdalen took my hand and peered deeply into my eyes.

"Remember at all times his love for you."

"I need not be reminded of that."

"Go in peace, and know that we count on you. Only you can speak in his defense where you go."

She made me uncomfortable without my knowing why.

"You make a mountain out of nothing."

Lazarus took my hand. "You are dear to us because of him. Farewell, and call on us if there is any need. I can never repay him."

With a sense of disquiet, I set out for the Holy City, traveling by foot, as it was but a few miles. The Temple was astir as usual. Jesus' assault on the money changers had little enduring value, and they were back at their old stands, cheating the pilgrims as unconscionably as before. It was another reminder, if one was needed, of Jesus' ineffectiveness for want of a position of authority. What he could do if only he were King.

I passed through the Court of Gentiles and ascended the steps in the Court of Priests, where I had been told to come. As before, there were guards at the door, but again they quickly passed me through. I could feel my heart pounding, for no valid reason, save for a premonition of evil that suddenly seized me. I threw it off with an effort. I knew that the summons concerned Jesus. What other reason could they have? Of himself, Judas Iscariot, as I was becoming known, was of no importance.

I was quietly relieved, therefore, when the Reb Gamaliel's soulful eyes peered into mine.

He gripped my hand with surprising strength. "You come in time to help Israel," he said.

Over his shoulder I could see the pinched faces of Annas and Caiaphas.

"You have been dilatory," said Annas by way of a greeting.

"In what way?" I quickly withdrew the hand I had offered.

As I took the chair pushed forward by Gamaliel, the High Priests continued to stand.

Annas promptly took the initiative, saying accusingly: "He was offered the kingdom, and you did not let us know."

"What was there to tell you? He ran from it like a frightened hare."

I deliberately deprecated him, thinking to minimize the incident.

"Did you think that out of a crowd of five thousand none would apprise us of the insurrection he inspired?"

"He cannot help what others say or do."

Gamaliel had taken a chair next to mine, thoughtfully resting his bearded chin in his hand.

"What he says is true. Who can govern the actions of others?"

"Pilate cares not for reasons or rationale, only that there be no hint of a disturbance."

The Procurator's name was enough to make me see red. "Must we always jump when he barks?"

"Just as he jumps when Rome barks," said Annas drily.

"There was no real disturbance, just a commotion when Jesus scorned the crown that some few offered."

Caiaphas had been eyeing me maliciously.

"Julius Caesar was thrice offered the kingship of Rome and three times he refused, waiting for a more expedient time while cloaking his ambition with false modesty."

"For all we know," put in Annas, "like Caesar, he had his friends stir up this spontaneous demonstration." He turned to his son-in-law for a moment. "Was not the crowd incited by two or three of his own disciples?"

How well Jesus' activities were reported! I had not seen any of the familiar Pharisee and Sadducee faces, but in a throng that large anybody could pass unnoticed.

"I can assure you," I said boldly, "that Jesus would not for a moment consider any temporal advantage."

"I see," said Caiaphas. "His ambitions are devoted to the priesthood."

"Not at all."

"Then what is his interest? What does he want of Israel?"

"He asks nothing of Israel but that it be repentant, and he offers salvation and everlasting life."

There was a sneer on the cold, crafty face. "He offers? Is he God then that he disposes his bounty with such an open hand?"

Caiaphas' lips turned down at the corners. "No, he makes no such great claim. He is only the Son of God. He had the heavens for a father and the earth for a mother." If not said in mockery, it would have been well spoken.

"He says we are all children of God."

Annas walked over to the window and looked beyond the Court of Priests out onto the Court of Gentiles, on the grasping shopkeepers and the Amharetzin with whom they were haggling noisily. He waved a disdainful hand. "And so these are God's children."

"All have that potential."

I saw in Gamaliel an uneasiness absent at our earlier meetings. His eyes had clouded over, and he wore a pensive expression.

"It goes not easy with Israel these days, Judah," he said with a sigh.

"It will be better, the Messiah will make it better."

Caiaphas had taken a more aggressive position than before. "Your Messiah," he spluttered, "will be the ruination of Israel. We sit here, waiting for the sword to drop, and you speak of his saving the country. I had thought you many things, but never a fool."

I was mystified by the tenor of the conversation, sensing there was something unspoken that was agitating even the normally imperturbable Annas.

"I know many who will speak in the Messiah's behalf before the Council. There will be no question that it is he whom all Israel has been waiting for."

"It is a different kind of Council that he will face." Caiaphas bit off the words savagely.

Gamaliel's long face grew even longer. "The mighty arm of Rome reaches into our most sacred conclaves. Sejanus has fallen, and the capital of the world is in a turmoil. The word has gone out that every rising be nipped in the bud, every insurgent hanged from the nearest tree. In every little rebel, every street-corner orator, the frightened Tiberius now sees a Sejanus, plotting to cast him from his throne."

Sejanus was gone, incredibly. He had ruled Rome without restraint, and how he was betrayed by the very forces he had conspired with. How frail indeed was this Empire with its mantle of might and glory and its feet of clay. All that was needed was a Spartacus with a mission, a Jesus to light the spark that would inflame the Empire from Parthia to the distant islands.

And Pilate was Sejanus' man.

"This should be an end of Pilate," I said, "so there is some good news from Rome."

Caiaphas' face darkened.

"You fool, why do you think we sit here, but to do the bidding of Pilate who now has to disclaim his sponsor by loudly thundering his loyalty?"

"And how will this assassin of the innocent manage that?"

Annas gave me a reproving glance. "You have a dangerous tongue, Judah."

Caiaphas laughed disagreeably.

"He thinks he plays games with his gang of cutthroats."

"I play no games with any man's life."

"As we have said before," said Caiaphas, "the Romans are not the Syrians, Greeks, or Persians. Their God is their legions. They may lose an encounter, but they do not lose wars. Tempt them, and they will wipe out your band of idiots like the brigands they are."

"They are patriots," I said hotly.

He gave me a malevolent look. "You play a fool's game, and were it not for Gamaliel's sentimentality, you would be a likely candidate for the gibbet."

"What further use have you of me? For I would have none of you."

"You have worked into a position where you are extremely useful to Israel."

"I have done what you asked."

He gave me a hard smile. "And more. For it qualifies you eminently as a witness."

I looked at him in horrified disbelief. "For this you made me your agent?"

The Reb Gamaliel held up a hand. "Circumstances have given the project a different color."

I stood up to them boldly. "My color is the same, I have not changed."

Caiaphas gave me an ugly look. "You dare to lie to us! You have become his trusted follower, his treasurer, and none is in a better position to impeach him."

I rose to his defense.

"You have nothing to fear from him; his followers leave him and others scorn him because he did not conform to their idea of the Messiah." I saw my mistake in diminishing him the moment I spoke, and so I added quickly:

"But many people still love him, and those who have slipped away will return once they realize that he does not have to be a King like David to be their Messiah."

"No matter," said Annas, "the crown was still offered, and he could improve his position at any time by accepting what he first rejected."

"You do not know him. He cares not for earthly matters."

"If we let him alone," said Annas, "all men will believe in him, and the Romans shall take away what rule we have and throw out the priests and our religion. What would Israel be without its Temple?"

I thought it best not to make the reply that leapt to my lips.

"His is truly God's voice," I pleaded. "Listen to him, and Israel's troubles will vanish."

"Yes," growled Caiaphas, "for there will be no Israel." His eyes smoldered. "How can you so readily betray your own class? Do you not consider it expedient that one man should die for the people so that the whole nation will not perish, together with the Jews dispersed through the Empire."

My heart stood still for a moment. "You cannot mean what you say. Even so, what power have you over him who has power over death?"

Annas' eyes gleamed with hate. "Now you give us added reason for his extinction. He claims powers not even claimed for the Emperor."

"The Emperor," I said warmly, "is not our Messiah."

"And neither," said Caiaphas, "is the Nazarene."

"You promised a hearing before the Council of Five. Gladly will I be a witness to these proceedings."

"The time for that is long gone," said Annas, "had there ever been a time. The Romans will not wait. Even now Pilate is in the Antonia expecting our decision. For if we do not act, he will, and his hand is heavier than ours."

"What has Pilate to do with our Messiah?"

"He cares not what a rebel is called. They are all the same to him. Any scapegoat will do."

I looked long at Gamaliel.

"You have always stood for justice. Stand for it now, friend of my father."

Gamaliel regarded me uneasily.

"I would speak with him alone for a few moments."

Annas made a gesture of impatience. "The longer Pilate waits, the uglier he will be."

With a curt nod to the others, the Nasi of the Sanhedrin drew me into an adjacent room.

We surveyed each other silently for a few moments.

"And so," I said bitterly, "I was but a pawn."

"You were used, it is true, but for a good cause. I, for one, wanted to know more about the young man who impressed me so as a boy." His wise old eyes peered mildly into mine. "And you, Judah, were not above using us. Do you think for a moment that the Sanhedrin is not familiar with your activities?"

"There are spies everywhere," I said warmly.

His hands formed a deliberate steeple. "Sad but true, for in these times no man can be sure of anybody."

"Jesus can do nothing unworthy, nor does he countenance unworthiness in others."

"It would be well if it was otherwise, but we cannot survive without compromise, and to do anything, good or bad, we must survive."

"Unless we do good there is no survival, according to the Master."

"He speaks of another world, and we live in this. Which brings me to the point. Cooperate with the elders of Israel, and should Jesus come to trial, he will not be found guilty."

I stood aghast at the thought of Jesus on trial.

"With what would they charge this holiest of men?"

"With inciting riot for one thing, when the people clamored to make him King, and for blasphemy."

"He incited no one, and no one loves God more than he. Is this blasphemy?"

"He derides the Sabbath, and calls himself the Son of God."

I cared not about their Sabbath. "But if he is the Son of God, how then does this violate the law?"

He gave me a penetrating glance. "You believe in him, don't you?"

"I have seen him do what only God could do. He has made nothing of death, bringing Lazarus back when he already stank of maggots."

"If he does all this, why do you fear?"

I did not immediately comprehend.

"If he brings Lazarus from the dead, what man can harm him?"

I looked at him doubtfully. "But none can say what Jesus himself wants. He speaks of his own death at times as if it were already accomplished."

The Reb Gamaliel scratched his nose thoughtfully. "It will do no harm to placate Rome. They look for a scapegoat, but once he is tried and acquitted, they will find another."

"How can you be so sure of acquittal?"

"Nicodemus and Joseph of Arimathea are his friends, and they too have influence. It takes a majority of two to convict, and this they can never do, not while you speak for him."

"But why try him at all?"

"So that Pilate can show Rome that he moves quickly to root out rebellion. There will be others taken, and these will satisfy the Romans."

With all this double-dealing, I suddenly felt I couldn't trust anybody.

"It is a great burden you put on me."

"All I ask is that you testify to what you have seen."

"Are there not others?"

"As you know, two witnesses are required."

"And who is the other?"

He hesitated for a moment. "They have somebody from the Temple, when Jesus overthrew the tables."

"What great crime was this?"

"Nothing really, and for this reason he will be acquitted."

I shrank at even appearing to betray him.

"And if I refuse?"

"You will be summoned in any case. At least, as a voluntary witness, your testimony can be favorable."

"I trust neither of these High Priests. They think only of their skins."

"But do you not trust me?"

We looked each other in the eye. "You would perhaps not wittingly deceive me, but you could be deceived."

He laughed mirthlessly. "Not while I control the Pharisee faction in the Sanhedrin."

He saw that I was still uneasy.

"Why do you worry when you feel that he can conquer death itself? Not Pilate, nor Caiaphas, nor Annas, nor even the Emperor can harm him then. He clearly becomes mightier than any of them."

His words rang through my mind like a refrain: "Mightier than any of them." But, of course, all the leaders of the world paled into insignificance against him. Even the mighty Augustus feared death all his long life, and kept companions by his side at night so he would not be frightened of the shadows. Had not the Lord of Persia looked at his vast army and moaned that all would be dead in seventy-five years? But Jesus brought life eternal, and what he brought others was certainly his for the asking.

I looked up to see Gamaliel studying me with a frown.

"I will do it," I said, "for his sake, and for Israel."

CHAPTER FIFTEEN

PILATE

THIS MAN HELD THE POWER of life and death over us all, and yet all I could think of was that there was not a single, solitary hair on his gleaming yellow skull.

I watched, fascinated, as he brushed a meaty hand over his glistening head and regarded us with a mocking smile.

He was taller than I would have thought, and his broad sloping shoulders and his thick, corded neck, which merged with his chin, gave him the look of a gladiator. This impression was enhanced by the leather cuirass he still fancied, with the flat broadsword dangling arrogantly from his hip. It was easy to see he wanted none to forget that he was no mere administrator but had commanded the legions of Rome in battle.

He kept no court at the Fortress, even though his quarters, originally designed by Herod the Great for Mark Anthony's comfort, were lavish enough for an Emperor. His only courtiers were the palace guard, hulking brutes who stood immobile behind him, holding their spears upright. They were from every segment of the Empire, swarthy Nubians from the Sudan, red-freckled Picts from the far islands of Britain, giant long-armed Franks, and grotesque Germans with their blond manes flowing to their hips. It gave a graphic meaning to the word Rome, as none knew better than the man who arranged this show.

He seemed in no hurry to get to the matter, considering his visitors' anxiety not to keep him waiting. But so it was with those with the upper hand; they invariably let one know it.

It finally suited him to speak.

"You are late," he said angrily.

"We came as quickly as we could," said Annas.

"Having hatched some plot in your devious minds."

"We are sorry for what happened in Rome," said Gamaliel with mistaken diplomacy.

Pontius Pilate put his hands on his hips and gave us an insolent look.

"Nothing has transpired that you Jews need concern yourselves with," he said with a venomous smile. "Mind your own behavior, and worry not about Rome. Does the worm concern itself for the sparrow, or the sparrow fret for the hawk?"

"The Nasi," said Annas, "meant only that we deplore any inconvenience the Emperor suffered, for he has been our friend these many years."

"True enough, Tiberius has given your nation many privileges, a legacy from the days of the divine Julius, who was befriended by Herod in Egypt, but we Romans don't live in the past. Nobody, save the Emperor, is indispensable."

How easy it was for him to dismiss the friend and patron to whom he owed so much.

He held up an imposing sheet of parchment on which the Imperial insignia of Rome was clearly discernible. "This came from Rome," he said in a grating voice. "Every sign of revolt, however slight, is to be put down without mercy, every revolutionary is to be nailed to the cross. Where there is an overt act against the Roman authority, the Procurator will deal with it directly. Where the resistance is to the local authority, the Temple is qualified to handle the matter in its own courts."

Annas' eyes blinked for a moment. "But you forget that only the Procurator can impose a capital penalty."

"This was done for your own protection, so your rival factions would not engage in a bloodbath disruptive to the governing body here and in Caesarea."

"We may try the culprit," Annas persisted, "but only you can execute the verdict."

Pilate's jaw set in the hard lines so typical of his breed.

"Have you already prejudged this matter, to be so sure of the outcome?"

"It shall be promptly placed before our courts, for it is our desire that the Roman authority know that we are moving energetically to stamp out revolt."

Pilate poked a finger at Annas and laughed riotously as he saw him squirm.

"Now what game are you Jews up to?"

Annas inclined his head in a slight bow.

"I know not what the Procurator means."

"My meaning is plain. You Jews are always up to something."

"We come at your request," Annas said impassively.

Pilate laughed scornfully, showing his strong white teeth. His dark face glistened with perspiration, though the room was cool, and he mopped his brow with a red cloth.

"Let us not pretend," he snapped. "You are a quarrelsome lot and would kill one another off if I didn't keep you in line."

He laughed uproariously, as if he found the idea amusing. I hated all Romans, but some were worse than others. Pontius Pilate, in his vulgar way, epitomized the worst of Rome.

How I wished the Master were here now, not cringing like the tactful Gamaliel or temporizing like Annas, but standing up to the Roman defiantly, and breathing fire as he had done with the Sadducees and Pharisees. I could hardly wait for the moment when the proud Pilate would kneel before his superior power.

There was something in my demeanor that caught Pilate's attention at this time. He scowled fiercely as his gaze fell on me. "Who is this flaming-eyed youth who keeps clenching and unclenching his fists like an aggrieved gladiator? At least there is some fight in him."

Gamaliel stepped forward. "This is Judah-bar-Simon, whom we mentioned earlier. He comes from a family distinguished for their public service."

"All you Israelites are distinguished." He laughed harshly, "Like the Britons you have a King on every hillock."

"Not so, Excellency," put in Annas. "We have no King, though one presumes this role."

"You are wrong, Priest, for you do have a King, and his name is Tiberius. It will go ill with any who usurps his royal prerogatives."

With a mocking glance for his visitors, whom he kept standing, the deputy of Rome flung himself onto a curule chair, traditionally reserved in Rome for the highest dignitaries. It was a gift of Herod the Great, like everything else in the Fortress Antonia, from the clusters of bronze candelabra hanging from the frescoed ceiling to the marble floors adorned with rich carpeting from Persia.

His deep-set eyes, bridged by the prominent Roman nose, surveyed the small delegation with undisguised contempt. "Because of your indolence and treachery, our caravans are attacked, our arsenals looted, our soldiers ambushed on lonely roads. If you do not have the leaders soon in hand, I shall swiftly step in and handle it for you."

His eyes looked out menacingly from under their black beetle brows. "It will go badly with all of Israel if you seek to trick me with bogus arrests. The massacre of the Galileans will be like a Grecian festival, for I shall smite the whole land, from Perea to Galilee, and not excluding Judea, with the might of the Empire. The Emperor is in no mood to dally with traitors, and neither is he who speaks for him."

Annas preserved his calm.

"We already know the ringleader," he said, "and it will be a simple matter with his arrest to apprehend the others and break up the movement."

Pilate crossed his brawny arms over his chest. "And this culprit you speak of, is this the same Joshua-bar-Abbas whom my agents tell me is the firebrand of the Zealot cause?"

Annas recoiled slightly. "It is not he of whom I speak."

"Then your information is better than mine, for bar-Abbas has been seen leading these raids I speak of."

"The man I speak of is Joshua-bar-Joseph, a Galilean, whom the Gentiles call Jesus."

Pilate's missile-shaped head came up quickly, and the flaps of his big ears twitched.

"This Galilean you speak of, is he not the healer from Nazareth?"

"So he says."

Pilate gave him a scornful look. "You don't know? Your agents tell you that he is a revolutionary but don't know that he heals. What kind of agents do you employ?"

I was pleasantly surprised and encouraged by Pilate's attitude.

"Tell me more about this dangerous Galilean," he said. "Is he not the one who overturned the tables in the Temple and mocked the High Priests, earning the plaudits of the people?"

Annas flushed, while Caiaphas, strangely quiet, bit his lip, "If it were only this," said Annas, "it could be handled very quietly by the Sanhedrin, without disturbing Your Excellency. But our agents have evidence of his dangerous nature, and it would well behoove the Procurator to become acquainted with certain facts."

Pilate gave him a withering look. "Don't tell me my business, Priest."

Despite my contempt for Annas, my blood boiled, for his humiliation was Israel's as well.

"Would you not know what this man has done?"

Pilate's eyes swept over Caiaphas for the first time.

"So the Chief Prosecutor speaks. Tell me not what crime he has committed, or what conspiracy he has woven, for this is not the time or place. But in your own proceedings make sure that you have the right man before you come to me. I am no tool for your subtle plotting and intrigue. For that go to Herod. He is only a half Jew, to be sure, but the Greek half is no better, for it is full of empty talk."

He chuckled as if to himself, his thin, bloodless lips tightening over his teeth. "He still resents my slaying the Galileans without his permission. But how was I to know they were from his tetrarchate? Does not one Jew look like another?"

It was more than any man could bear. "No more," said I warmly, "than every Roman resembles another."

Gamaliel appeared stricken, and even the High Priests reacted uneasily. But the Roman only slapped his thigh and roared. "This rooster has some spirit. I like that."

"This is the man," said Caiaphas, "who is thoroughly familiar with the insurrectionary movement."

"And how could he be familiar without being one of them?"

Annas had indeed looked ahead.

"He infiltrated the movement as our agent, so you see we have not been lax."

Pilate waved a careless hand. "Please do not burden me with your loyalty. This Jesus must be a thorn in your side, or you would not be so solicitous of his movements." He gave the two priests an evil look. "Does he threaten your coffers with his preachings, or is it your very positions that are at stake? Rest assured, for Rome appoints the High Priests, and Rome prefers the devil it knows to the devil it doesn't know."

His eyes skipped over me lightly. "And so this is the man who can speak of the King of the Jews. How well do you know the Galilean?"

"I've been with him for two and a half years."

He looked at me disdainfully.

"As a spy?"

"As his disciple."

He laughed without amusement. "With a disciple like you, none needs adversaries."

"I have nothing but good to say for him."

"Then why are you here? We are not recommending him for office."

"To speak the truth." I teetered delicately on the edge of a knife. For I wanted to see Jesus challenged, so he could confront the Romans and triumph over them, and yet I had no wish to play the betrayer, even innocently.

"And what is the truth?" There was a sneer on the thin pale lips. "I am suspicious of those who speak of truth, for the truth needs no one to speak for it. It speaks for itself."

"Let it speak then. He is a good and kind man who feeds the poor, heals the sick, and worships the one God."

"Oh, yes, that God." From his smirk, Pilate seemed to be enjoying himself. "Why is it that Rome, with its many gods, rules the land which has this omnipotent wonder that nobody sees? Is it because we have many, and you only one?"

Annas spoke up with a frown. "This is no matter for a plain citizen, but a priest."

Pilate held back his head and roared with laughter. "I have heard the priests. Now I want truth. Didn't he say he stood for truth?"

He did not intimidate me. A brave man dies but once and, dying, might find that eternity Jesus spoke of.

"He is our Messiah," I said, "the Promised One of Israel, sent by our God to deliver our nation from its enemies."

Again he bellowed with laughter. "And how will he do this, with a slingshot, or perchance he will bring down this fortress with his bare arms like your Samson? You see, I know your history, and I must say the past is more impressive than the present. Now tell me more about this King of the Jews."

"He does not say he is the King of the Jews."

"What else is your Messiah? I have been in this blighted land for two and a half years, and all I hear are mutterings of this Son of the King David who is coming to lead Israel to victory over all the nations of the world, including Rome. That does not smack of humility to me, for how else can he rule unless he is King, whatever title he takes."

"They offered him the crown, but he would not take it."

At this he jumped off his chair and put his face close to mine, scowling darkly. "Who offered him this crown? Who, who, who?"

I had no desire to implicate Cestus or Dysmas and the others.

"There were so many that I could not distinguish one from the other."

From the smiles that passed between Annas and Caiaphas, I realized I had blundered. In trying to balance the truth, I had slipped off the edge of the knife. "By many, I mean only enough so that I could not pick out any two or three."

"I know well enough what you mean. And how did Jesus react to this offer?"

"He was disturbed that the multitude did not understand what kingdom he spoke of."

Again he gave me a grim look. "So he spoke of a kingdom of the Jews, did he?"

"A Kingdom of Heaven, for Jew and Gentile alike. It was no temporal power he sought."

I seemed to be involving Jesus in a way I had not thought to do.

"It might be well to examine this Jesus," Pilate said. "I hear he is a harmless man who helps people in his own way, not caring whether they are Jews or Romans. But it will do no harm to see for myself what manner of man he is." A frown ruffled the dark brow. "Rome has little patience with rebellion, or with these endless conversations. That is for decadent Greeks and Egyptians."

He waved a jeweled hand in dismissal. "You have your Temple guards, and other conscripts, use them well; I will be watching closely, and if you do not act with vigor, you can count on the Procurator of Judea to atone for your lack."

He made no move to show out the three loftiest dignitaries in all of Judea, but instead motioned for me to stay. "I would talk further with this disciple of the Galilean."

The High Priests glanced at each other uneasily, and into Gamaliel's long face there came a look of concern.

"Judah is a loyal son of Israel," he said resolutely.

Pilate grinned wickedly. "I know not whether that is an endorsement or an indictment. But fear not, for I like his face. It has all the mobility of the dissembler. He would make a splendid High Priest."

The three leaders of the highest governing body of Israel backed out of his presence as if they were common slaves. If Jesus could only have witnessed this ignominy, would he not relent in his wrath and do what he could to correct this situation?

Pilate's rough voice broke in on me, from Greek and Aramaic passing now to Latin. "I understand you have been in Rome."

"I have had that pleasure," I replied in Latin, so that he would know I was no country bumpkin.

"There is somebody," he said, "who would speak to you." He motioned curtly to one of the guards, instructing him in a low voice. My heart leaped in joy, then good sense prevailed. The Procurator of Judea was hardly a matchmaker.

In a few moments the mystery was resolved. A woman of surpassing beauty with the clean limbs and clear-cut features of the Pallas Athene, gracefully preceded a burly guard into the room. I had never seen a lovelier woman. Her soft auburn hair, blending with her delicately tinted skin, was tied back in a little knot in the Roman fashion. Her nose was finely chiseled, and her eyes, a rare violet, seemed to give off a luminous glow under perfectly arched brows of shaded gold. But it was her manner I found most captivating. She looked at me with an expression that seemed to suggest I was the most important person in the world.

I had never been with royalty before, and found it disconcerting. But the Lady Claudia Procula soon put me at my ease.

"Tell me about your Jesus," she said as Pilate stood attentively behind her. "I have had many dreams of him."

She laughed at my puzzled face.

"My handmaiden Susanna pointed him out to me once from my litter. He would be a handsome man if he were not so solemn."

I was in a quandary, not knowing what I could say that would be beneficial to him. For she was clearly well disposed. Nevertheless, it would be well to be noncommittal, for what Jew could count on a Roman for anything?

"You know of course the he cured Susanna."

She laughed, and her laugh was like a bell.

"You need not be guarded with me, sir. As my husband will tell you. I have a genuine interest in this man and thought perhaps that if I knew more of him I could better understand these dreams I have."

She smiled roguishly. "I hear he is dedicated solely to his God, so there can be none but the most virtuous explanations put upon these dreams."

"I am no interpreter of dreams. But if Her Excellency will confide her dream, perhaps I can relate it in some way to the Master."

She laughed again. "So you call him the Master? How quaint, for in Rome we have but one Master, and he is a Claudian like myself."

Pilate opened his mouth to say drily, "He is a Julian now."

"By adoption," she said carelessly, "but ceremony is not nearly as thick as blood."

Pilate seemed to weary of this badinage. "Tell the lady what she would know," he said roughly. "I like not words that add up to nothing."

She gave him a look of displeasure. "Don't frighten our young friend with your faces, for I am sure, if properly coaxed, he can clear up this mystery for me."

I understood from the centurion Cornelius that many Roman aristocrats were revolted by the corruption of the Court. But it hardly seemed possible that this beautiful lady was moved by anything more than her idle curiosity, prompted by the boredom of a life so far from Rome.

"If you but relate the dream," I said.

She frowned, as if searching her memory. "Has your Master been in Rome?"

I shook my head. "Egypt, but nothing more."

"It is curious then, for in this dream I saw him standing in the Forum, alone, amid the ruins. There was not a building that was not torn down, and he surveyed the rubble with a smile. The smile upset me, for I did not understand how he could smile in all this devastation. I spoke to him. 'Sir, why is it that you smile when the city is destroyed?'

"He looked at me kindly, saying: 'From these ruins shall come a greater empire than the world has seen, one that eclipses the kingdoms of bronze and gold and silver and iron. And it shall be as air and water, for there shall be no limit to it.'"

I was startled by the allusion to the four kingdoms, for this assuredly came out of Daniel's prophecy. Still, how did one tell a Roman that the dream signified the end of their tyranny and the advent of God's realm?

"I have heard Jesus say that through the majesty of Rome, the word of God would one day spread from one end of the Empire to the other."

Pilate had made a pretense of not listening, but now he snorted angrily. "This Jesus is either a fool or a knave to speak such nonsense. It would be treason if it were not so absurd."

Claudia Procula made no sign that she had heard him.

"Susanna has talked of this God, saying that your Master heals through him." Her lovely brow wrinkled in her perplexity. "Is he like our Jupiter or Apollo, to whom we have raised many statues in the hope they will look on us with favor?"

"He is the God of Israel, and he dwells in the heavens with his angels."

She clapped her hands in delight. "He must know Jupiter then, for there also does he reign, and there too Apollo rides his chariot through the skies."

"It is a different God that Jesus speaks of. He is not only the creator of the universe but is of the universe, ready to share our lives by virtue of our faith in him."

She had difficulty following me, and no wonder, for only from Jesus did it make sense. But how else could I explain it? It was easy to see why Jesus had to perform his healings and other good works to establish his credibility.

There was a Roman directness about her.

"Now, what relation does this Jesus have to this God you speak of?"

"He is his messenger, sent by God to redeem his people from their sins and help them find eternal salvation."

Pilate's harsh laugh broke in. "This accursed state should give me thanks, for I have helped a good many into this eternity."

Claudia Procula seemed unaware of her husband's existence.

"Do they not call him the Messiah?"

"Yes, he is the Promised One predicted by our prophets."

Pilate again interrupted. "And what does he promise, this King of the Jews?"

"The Kingdom of Heaven."

"I am sure he would make a heaven of earth if he could."

The lady threw Pilate a look of annoyance.

"I would know more of this man who heals the sick and comforts the poor and oppressed. I have heard reports that he can do anything, even to raising the dead and changing water to wine."

Pilate let out a raucous laugh. "You listen too much to your little Jewess."

The desire to defend Jesus overcame prudence. "I have seen Jesus do these things and more."

She came forward now, and her eyes peered into mine. "With your own eyes you have seen this?"

I nodded, while Pilate threw up his hands in disgust.

Her eyes glowed with new excitement. "I recall now the puzzling end to the recurring dream. Standing in the ruins, your Master looked down on the prone figures of several Emperors, and with a wave of his hand restored them to the living."

It could have signified either the restoration of the Empire or the emergence of a new way of life, just as Jesus' vision on the mountain portended a new faith.

Pilate's patience had grown thin. "At least, this dream man resurrected the Empire. Thank him for that, and let this man go back to his Master."

She sighed in resignation. "This dream I dreamed many times, so I know it must mean something."

I hesitated, wondering if I dared ask a favor.

"I have one request, if I may."

"Ask it," she said, "for much has been asked of you."

"May I give my greetings to the Lady Susanna?"

Pilate grunted. "The Lady Susanna. What airs these Jews give themselves."

She smiled, the aristocrat losing herself in the woman.

"You must be the disciple she has spoken of. But have you not taken the vow of celibacy?"

Pilate guffawed. "He looks not the part of a Vestal Virgin to me."

"We take no vows of this nature." I felt the blood rush to my face.

Pilate gave me a shrewd glance. "You stretch the truth so thin that one can see through it." He turned to his wife. "But bring the maid in. What can they do that has not been done before?"

I had thought he stood in awe of her, but it was difficult for people to share a bed and still have illusions of grandeur about each other.

His manner toward me became ironically deferential. "Claudia Procula," said he, "since this young man has now become our guest, nothing is too good for him."

As she frowned, he guided me into a spacious chamber off the Great Hall. The room was windowless, with a strangely speckled ceiling. Huge bowls of fruit sat on a large center table with goblets of red and white wine. Near a cluster of large pillows, an immense divan and couch faced each other. The light from a naphtha lamp cast its eerie shadows on the walls and gave one a feeling of contrived intimacy. It reminded me of a room in a Roman brothel.

Pilate gave me a searching glance. "I was young like yourself and know what it is to carry the vision of a maid in the mind. It does no good there, not if you have any red blood in your veins."

"I do not think of her that way."

"Then what do you think of her?"

"As one who loves the Master as I do."

His hard eyes roamed offensively over my body.

"What for are your loins, if not to establish that you are a man?"

"There are other ways of proving one's manhood."

He laughed, and clapped me on the shoulder. "Well said, Judah-bar-Simon. In the field against the enemy, is that not right?"

As I remained silent, he studied me ostentatiously.

"If you like not women, is it men then that appeal to you? To be sure, there are twelve or thirteen disciples, I am told, and no women to distract or divert them. This is not a wholesome arrangement."

My cheeks burned at the implication. "We have a company of women attached to our mission," I said defensively.

"And so your vows of celibacy are conveniently displaced."

I was tired of this Roman's gibes.

"There is no more virtuous man than Jesus Christ, and he demands the same rigid standards of his disciples. This is not Rome, where Julius Caesar was every woman's man, and every man's woman."

His dark eyes blazed for a moment, and I flinched in spite of myself. He was breathing hard, his nostrils flaring, but then, suddenly, he tossed his head back and roared with laughter.

"This bantam cock mocks the Divine Julius; that is a good one to be told in Rome." He grabbed my arm and squeezed it so that the flesh turned purple and I pressed my lips to hold back a cry of pain.

"Any time it wants," he said between his teeth, "Rome can crush you and your friends just like that. Remember that always."

And then he was gone, with his thin, mirthless smile.

How I hated these vulgar men who vaunted their far-flung military might over a small nation. O God of Israel, I prayed, let Jesus fling the gauntlet back in their faces. O Lord, let him see the light and be another Moses to the stricken people of Israel.

So caught up was I in my thoughts that I did not see Susanna enter the room. She greeted me with a flutter of the eyelids. She was so ravishingly beautiful I barely resisted the impulse to take her in my arms. A simple robe which flared at the sides revealed a fleeting glimpse of her golden thighs and set my heart pumping. Her tawny hair fell over her rosy face, and she pushed it back with a charming gesture, explaining with a blush that she had hastened at her mistress's summons.

"Forgive me for looking as I do," she breathed.

"Did you know it was for me she summoned you?"

"Not till I saw you."

We sat together on the long, low couch, designed for reclining at a feast, and I was very much aware of the sweet aroma of her body. It was like the smell of musk.

"I have missed you," I said, taking her hands. They were warm and moist.

She didn't look at me directly, but kept her head bowed, so that I saw the golden strands of hair forming on the nape of her swanlike neck.

"I have missed the whole company, especially the Master," she said softly. "But as long as he is well, I am happy."

Suddenly a cloud glazed her eyes, and she gripped the edge of my robe.

"Your being here with Pilate, has it something to do with him?"

"There is nothing to fret about. Pilate intends him no harm."

She drew back a little, and her pale blue eyes looked deeply into mine.

"What brought you here? The Procurator does not normally receive any Jews but the High Priests and the chiefs of the Sanhedrin."

I answered truthfully.

"Pilate is concerned about the revolutionaries, and it was thought I could provide him with some information of their movements."

Her eyes had now widened in alarm. "But why should you, one of Christ's chosen, have this knowledge? I do not understand."

"This is not your province," I said more harshly than I intended. "What do you know of plots and counterplots, and the intrigue that imperils empires?"

My hand fell carelessly on her thigh, and in her agitation she did not remove it. Her flesh was like silk under my hand.

"I know from Mary Magdalen," she said breathlessly, "that he is in constant danger and will do nothing to spare himself. Claudia Procula herself tells me that it is not safe for him in Jerusalem at this time. Will you not carry him this word? Or tell me where he is, and I will warn him myself."

"That is not necessary," I said. "He knows whatever you know, and he does what he has to do. He is no frail craft to be pushed this way and that by every little ripple of foreboding. He is a man for the ages who lives for his God and can do anything that God can do. I have seen him do it, and I do not doubt him."

Now she took my hands, and her eyes gazed into mine in a soulful manner. "I have done you an injustice, Judah. For little did I realize that you could express yourself with such nobility. I see now why he selected you, and gave you a seat next to him. You must love him as I do."

I had inched closer to her and could savor the warmth of her young body. She had obviously dressed in haste, as she said, for she wore no undergarments. As her bosom heaved, I could barely see the delicate pink aureole of her sweet nipples set in the soft marble of her breast. I thought of her body, taut and warm against mine, and my blood raced through my veins like wine. My hand fell casually on her bare shoulder and bent her just the least forward so that it seemed perfectly natural to brush my lips against hers. She did not resist. Indeed, her breath only came faster, and she gave a little sigh. This time I pressed my lips against her mouth, and when her arms slipped around my shoulders, I crushed her body to mine.

"Please," she whispered, "don't do anything."

"Is it wrong to love?" I said softly.

She made no answer, and my hand dropped idly now inside the robe and felt the swell of her naked breast.

She gave a low passionate cry, and with her head lowered began to sob. As my head sank to her breast, I sensed the sharp intake of her breath, and the straining of her body. "Don't, don't," she cried. "I am a virgin."

What else could she have been? For it was the sweet purity of her that incited my desire.

My lips closed on hers, the time for conversation had ended, and there was really nothing to say. She moaned and groaned and thrashed about as though in agony and then she suddenly went limp in my arms. She gave a long sigh and it was over. I found myself disappointed and strangely empty. As I looked down on this damsel who had seemed so unattainable, I felt as if I had been cheated by her appearance of virtue. I was disenchanted by her easiness. Obviously, her virginity had not been previously challenged.

"I love you," she cried. "I truly love you." She looked at me like a sick cow. "Do you love me?"

What did this silly handmaiden know of love? "Of course I love you."

"Thank God," she cried. "But there can be no marriage, for you are pledged to Jesus."

"And you also," I whispered in her ear.

I drew myself now to a sitting position, as she carefully rearranged her clothing, blushing at my gaze.

She put her fingers to my lips. "You will not say anything?"

The little idiot, who did she think I could mention this to? "Of course not. Nobody will ever know."

"Thank you, dear Judah," she cried. There was a look of exaltation in her eyes. "There is nothing, nothing I wouldn't do for you. I love you."

I looked at the heavily laden table.

"Would you pour me a glass of wine?" I had never before felt so empty inside.

She jumped up eagerly, like a child, and brought me the sparkling red grape. It was warming and restored my spirits.

I had been there perhaps an hour and was ready to leave. But as I stood up, there was a knock on the door.

I could see the alarm in her eyes and felt a sudden uneasiness myself.

The knock was repeated.

I went to the door.

Pontius Pilate stood in the doorway.

"You may go," he said to the girl.

She ran from the room like a frightened fawn, with a single imploring glance over her shoulder.

His eyes peered beyond me to the couch.

"And so, my precious disciple of God, how did it go?"

"We had a pleasant conversation."

"And you spoke of your God, and life eternal, and the nobler things of life we barbarians do not understand. Is that not correct?'

"Our conversation was private," I said grimly.

"Better you should say your intercourse."

I felt my blood run cold. "I do not understand."

His eyes moved up to the ceiling. "Look closely," he said, "you have a young man's eyes."

My eyes followed his, and I felt the blood drain out of my face. I felt faint, and barely managed to say: "Did Her Excellency . . ."

"Oh, no, I would not have disabused her, even though I am a vulgar Roman and you a cultured Jew."

Involuntarily, my eyes moved upward again, to the small speckle-like apertures that dotted the ceiling.

"Through these little peepholes," he said, "it is possible to see everything transpiring in this room."

There was no doubting that leering face.

"You deserved a little lesson," he said. "Whatever we are, we Romans are not hypocrites. We take what we want, and enjoy it. You think Rome corrupt, then what of you, my pious friend, who speaks loftily of his God and seduces innocent maidens?"

His evil face still wore that mocking look.

"You cost me my dinner tonight, but no matter, it was worth it. Now make haste to do what you have undertaken. And let nothing slip. For I will be watching, never fear."

CHAPTER SIXTEEN

THE SUPPER

"IF HE CAN FEED FIVE THOUSAND from a single basket," I told Matthew, "then he can do anything."

Like me, he did not see how it could be a hoax.

"One or two people might be so weak-minded as to imagine such a development, but not thousands."

With his healings, it was entirely different, for there was no possibility of suggestion here. The blind saw and the lame walked, the lepers became whole and the obsessed grew calm. "He has told me," said this preening historian, "of healing vibrations in the atmosphere, which with understanding one can tune in, using the vital energy of the universe to stimulate the self-healing processes in mind and body."

"But it seems to work instantly for him, and in all cases, whereas we are successful with some and not with others. Why should this be?"

"He ascribes it to a faith which brings the God within us into harmony with the God force outside."

It was all very confusing, but I had seen it time after time with my own eyes, and so had the others.

Other disciples had joined the discussion, without there being any resolution of the question, when Jesus walked into the camp. His eyes snapped angrily.

"What can we expect from the people when my own disciples have such little faith in the Father?"

"I have faith in the Lord," said Thomas, "but even so I cannot walk on the water like you, Master. Indeed, I sank even more rapidly than Peter in the Galilean Sea."

"It is not enough to say one has faith. With true faith, there comes an understanding of God's natural laws." He held out a handful of seeds. "Could one tell that these seeds, properly planted and watered, would yield a grove of pomegranate trees? Other seeds produce figs, still others dates, and fields of wheat and so on."

Thomas still had a questioning look. "But, Master, a pomegranate seed, like any other seed, grows at a certain rate, which one can predict from the soil in which it is planted, and the amount of sun and rain it receives."

"True," said Jesus, "but its growth is still part of a universal creative process which can be understood by all. What is not so well understood is that when the spiritual element is introduced, a higher creative vibration results."

Peter, as usual, related whatever the Master said to himself.

"But, Master, seeing you walk on the waves, I too felt that I could do the same. But I failed, even though I had that faith."

"But your faith was not of God; it came from watching another whose faith was greater than yours. We cannot transfer our faith but can only plant the seeds and hope they will find a place to grow."

His miracles won over many skeptics, but even so, believing only in what they saw, they seemed to comprehend little of what he was talking about.

The mother of James and John, converted through his healings, pleaded that her sons be given the positions of honor next to him in the Heavenly Kingdom he spoke of. He chided her gently, saying that the first to push themselves forward were often the last to be chosen.

"Worry not so much where you go, but how you live," he enjoined, "and you will be where God wants you."

The Passover in Jerusalem was always important to him, and this Passover even more than the others, for it might be the last, he said, that he would spend with his Twelve.

When they could not keep him from Judea, the disciples decided with some dramatics that they would die with him there. Thomas, who had less faith than the rest, took the lead in announcing his own martyrdom. Even Jesus, somber as he was at this time, was inclined to laugh at this bravado.

"Nothing will befall you, Thomas, for you still have many souls to save."

I could understand his laughter, for this band of Galileans was not distinguished for its bravery. I had made a poll of their political opinions at one point, and all but the brothers, Andrew and Peter, James and John, shared my view that Jesus should lead the rising against Rome. But at no time could I get the others to add a word to my own.

"He knows what he wants," said Matthew, "and nothing any of us say, with the possible exception of Andrew, would have the slightest impact."

"How about John? He seems to prefer him above even Andrew."

"It is not the same thing," said Matthew. "He treats him like a son or a younger brother."

"And yet," I said, "he speaks of the whole world as being equally his family."

"In the importance he attaches to their souls. Still, we all enjoy some people more than others. It is but human."

"He is not human like the rest of us."

"True, but in his earthly role he is still a man, with a man's flesh and spirit."

Ordinarily we would have entered Judea only two or three days before the Passover, but Jesus decided to visit with some friends and pick out a special place for this Passover feast.

And so, traveling only by night to avoid the usual camp followers, we came to the Holy City six days before the holiday.

As usual, when he came to Jerusalem, Jesus stopped first with Lazarus in Bethany. Mary Magdalen and Martha were overjoyed to see him but could barely hide their concern. After they made the Master comfortable, they pressed me for a report on my meeting with the High Priests.

"Have you told him of this meeting?" the Magdalen asked.

I shrugged. "I saw no point in it."

Martha's heart-shaped face wrinkled in concern.

"I like not the way he speaks of his impending death."

The Magdalen had been eyeing me closely. "You have a secret, Judah. I can tell from the way you avert your eyes."

"It is in your imagination."

"If you know of any harm they intend him and say nothing, then you are as guilty as those who would take his life."

"Who can kill him unless he wills it?" I cried. "Did he not raise your brother from the grave? How can they slay him to whom death is but a word?" I walked to a window and looked down on the street. It was already thronged with the curious who had heard that he brought Lazarus back to life and now longed for a glimpse of him.

"This crowd," I said, "stands as a testimonial to his triumph over death."

The Magdalen would not be diverted. "You avoid the issue," she said. "What transpired at the meeting to which they summoned you in such haste? These couriers are not sent out for mere sociability."

Like her or not, the Magdalen had a sixth sense that made her more perceptive than most.

"It was nothing, I tell you." I prepared to turn away, but she caught me by the edge of my robe.

"You lie," she hissed. "You betrayed him."

Martha drew back in horror. "You couldn't," she cried, her eyes widening. "Judah, tell me she is wrong."

"She is wrong," I sighed. "I could no more betray him than you could. And to what purpose?"

The Magdalen was not easily put off. "Because you have some strange idea that his betrayal would help your cause."

"Wrong," I repeated.

To my relief, the disciple Philip entered the room at this point, inquiring after Andrew.

"Some Greek pilgrims have heard of the Master's wonders, and they desire a few words with him."

The Master was in his room, a small chamber perched atop the roof, chatting with Lazarus.

He shook his head. "I have nothing for these strangers, for soon it will all be said for me. The hour draws nigh when the Son of Man will be glorified in God." He closed his eyes, and I could see his lips moving in silent prayer. And then, though there was not a cloud in the sky, there came a clap of thunder that rocked the house. There were shouts of alarm from the street. But Jesus' face was as tranquil as the sea after a summer storm.

"My Father has heard me and gives me courage. For my soul is troubled as the hour approaches, but shall I say: 'Father, save me from this hour,' when it is for this hour that I came, and for this cause?"

It troubled me that he should talk now like other men. For if he was like other men, he was then as vulnerable as they.

The Magdalen and Martha had poked their heads through the doorway. Jesus' face shone as he beckoned them forward. "It pleases me that you two ladies hear what I say as well, for I love you both dearly for all the kindness conferred by your open hearts."

They came forward and kneeled, and he said a small prayer for them.

"I have come as a light into the world that whosoever believes in me shall not abide in darkness. And if any man hears my words and believe not, I judge him not, for I came not to judge the world, but to save it."

The timbre of his voice deepened and a glow came into his eyes.

"My Father gave me a commandment, which I pass on to you. That is that life is everlasting." He looked around the room. "And there is another commandment he gave me for you, added to that given Moses on the mountain, and second only to that which I mentioned."

"And what is that, Master?" said Peter, who had just walked into the small room, straining its capacity with his bulk.

Jesus' eyes traveled around the room, stopping at the Magdalen. "That you love one another, and carry this message of everlasting life to the far corners of the world."

We sat down to an early supper, for he had been through much that day and needed his rest. With a smile, Mary served the company, saving the best portions for the Master. He ate very little, and when he finished the serving ended. Martha sat at his feet, gazing into his countenance with stars in her eyes. Mary brought out a pound of costly spikenard, with which she anointed his feet, then wiped off the residue with her flowing hair. As before, I thought of the money for which this unguent could be sold, and what could be accomplished with it.

"Why was not this cream sold, and the money given the poor?"

I caught the annoyance in the Master's eye.

"Judah, do you not learn? Have I not said that the poor you will always have with you, but me for only a little while. Let her be, for she has saved this ointment against the day of my burial. And so she will keep some by, and there will still be a substantial amount which Andrew can dispose of for the poor."

I was not sure I had heard correctly.

"Andrew? He is not the treasurer."

He smiled cryptically. "Yes, Andrew, for you will have turned to other things by that time."

I wondered, for an anxious moment, whether he had any inkling of the plan. It was on my mind to confide in him, but I had seen those eyes flash with anger and I did not relish his being wroth with me. There would be time later to explain.

Both Andrew and Peter warned it was not safe for him to appear in Jerusalem for the Passover. But he only smiled and said that he had not come to be safe but to save.

"Would you have me hide my head in my hood, and skulk through the streets like a thief?"

He already spoke of his death as though it was inevitable.

"Do you not know, Judah," he said as we set out for the Holy City, "that there is nothing any can do to blunt the will of the Father?"

"Why do you speak so," I protested, "when you have the power over death?"

He shook his head sadly. "Only by dying can the Son of Man show there is no death."

It was too much to even think about. "I do not understand."

"You will," he said, "before even the others."

We arrived in Jerusalem two days before the Passover and camped on the Mount of Olives, overlooking the Garden of Gethsemane and the Temple.

He made no attempt to conceal his presence, but moved through the throngs, unconcerned alike by the dark looks and the reverent.

As usual, he sat in the Portico of Solomon, and a large crowd assembled. I could see the malignant faces of Ezra, Sadoc, and others I knew to be agents, but they were strangely quiet at this time.

Matthew sat at his feet as if spellbound while I studied the temper of the crowd. Like his priestly adversaries, they were oddly subdued but still listened respectfully.

He was seldom in better form.

"Woe unto you Scribes and Pharisees, hypocrites, for you shut off the Kingdom of Heaven from men while not able to enter yourselves because of your wickedness. You distort and twist everything to your own evil purpose. You make much of the Temple gold, but nothing of the Temple God. You worship the sacrifices on the altar, but not the symbol of the altar itself. You insist on tithes of gold and kine, yet you dismiss the weightier matters of judgment, mercy, and faith. You are blind, though you have eyes, and so strain at a gnat and swallow a camel."

I had never realized before how deeply Jesus felt his rejection, yet he had nobody to blame but himself. For he could have had the full measure of their devotion had he but heeded their hopes and aspirations.

"O Jerusalem," he cried, "you that kill the Prophets and stone those sent unto you, how often would I have gathered your children together, even as a hen takes her brood under her wings, but you would not have it so." His voice quickened with emotion.

"Look at these buildings upon which you place such store. Look well, for because of your iniquities there shall be left not one stone upon another, for all shall be thrown down by the very enemy you mock." As the crowd murmured, he shook his head. "All your disavowals will change nothing. And your house will be left desolate, for the way of the transgressor is never easy."

Ezra's face had darkened and I could see him exhorting others to challenge the speaker. I noted Adam the Tanner sitting nearby, but the man who responded from the crowd was a Judean of the working classes, not quite an Amharetz from the look of him, but a clerk in a counting room, thin, sallow-faced, and intense in manner.

"How long do you make us doubt?" he cried. "If you are the Christ, tell us plainly, and we will follow you against this foe that would tear down our Temple."

Jesus gave him a compassionate look. "I have shown you my work, which I have done in my Father's name, but you have not believed because you would not be of my flock. But other sheep shall hear my voice, and I shall give unto them eternal life. And they shall never perish, nor shall they be taken from me, because my Father, who gave them to me, is greater than all, greater than the Temple, Rome, and the seventy nations you would triumph over."

The man still looked at him doubtfully. "You speak like a King but act not like one."

"In my kingdom, which can also be yours, my Father and I are one."

There was a stunned silence, for by now all in Judea knew whom Christ meant by his Father.

As in Galilee, the faces showed that he claimed too much, for when he called himself the equal of God they looked around apprehensively, as if fearful that they shared his blasphemy.

He understood their confusion perfectly.

"Without God I am nothing, but with him, everything."

But they did not understand. They never understood, though many, separating the man from the message, still loved him for the multitudes he had healed and would have stood with him to the death.

For this reason I was surprised by Ezra's reaction. Hoping to stir something up, he picked up a stone and hurled it at the Master. It grazed his cheek, but he faced them fearlessly, as he had that day in sheltering Mary Magdalen. Others were quick to follow Ezra, for violence begets violence. But before they could cast their stones. Jesus stormed back.

"I have fed and helped many of you and your kin and helped them with my works. For which of these works do you stone me?"

"Not for these works," cried the crowd, "but because you blaspheme God by making yourself his equal."

"Is it not written that you, too, are cast in God's image and are God's children? Shall I stone you for this reason?"

I had never felt prouder of him, for in his defiance of the multitude he now showed clearly his leadership qualities.

The crowd had become still, and though still confused, was won over for the moment. But not so Ezra.

"We question not your works, but what works in you," he shouted. "You are a magician, and the devil in you speaks, for if it were God who spoke you would give the people what they pray for."

Christ regarded him contemptuously. "If man told God, and God not man, then man would have God's authority, and this is not so."

In his frustration, Ezra dug into the stoning pile once more and launched another missile at Christ from close range. This flew with unerring aim and thudded against his chest. He fell back for a moment, then righted himself. His face grew black as night, but before he could speak, a roar of disapproval, led by Adam the Tanner, came out of the crowd. It rose into a crescendo, and I could see the stunned surprise in Ezra's eyes. He did not understand the unpredictability of crowds. By his cowardly action he had made Jesus the underdog, and the crowd had responded angrily.

Matthew, stepping in front of Jesus, took in the situation calmly.

"Ezra is so used to his own claques that he forgets there are many who still adore the Master."

Concerned as we were, we still looked expectantly for Jesus' reaction. Had he not said many times: "Whosoever shall smite you on the right cheek, turn to him the other also"?

But he was in no mood for forgiveness. His eyes were blazing. "Wide is the way that leads to hell and many will take it. Narrow is the gate that leads to salvation, and few there be who will find it, unless through me."

The crowd again stirred restlessly, and I could sense the tide of good will receding. His assumption of God-like powers made them uncomfortable, especially when he casually coupled himself with God.

Adam the Tanner stood up so that all could see him. He turned a scornful look on Ezra and his henchmen. "I care not," he said, "whether he says he is the Son of God, his brother, uncle, or God himself. Any man here that harms him will have me and my hardy band to reckon with."

His pack of rogues leered wickedly into the crowd.

"We wait for the day he will lead us against our enemies, but we know not which is the greater foe, the priests and the Pharisees, or the Romans. For it is not the Romans but the others who deny us anything but this court, as if we were Gentiles and not Jews like themselves."

At this sally the crowd laughed, and even the Amharetzin joined in.

"So throw no more stones," concluded the tanner, "or it will go badly for the thrower, if it be Annas himself."

During all of this, Jesus stood unmoved. Then, as we all waited for a message that would stir our hearts, he said only what he had said a dozen times before:

"Blessed are the peacemakers, for they shall be called the children of God."

I groaned in my disappointment, and saw the look of chagrin on the tanner's face.

All slunk away, and we disappeared as well, for what was there left to say? But that evening, around the campfire, Jesus seemed strangely introspective as he told us of the trials and tribulations which would befall the nation after his death. It seemed almost as if he was eager to go, not having succeeded in what he had come to do.

"After my return for a brief period," he said, "I shall dwell in the heavens with my father, and shall prepare a place for some of you, for after me they shall deliver you up to be afflicted, and shall kill you, and you shall be hated of all nations for my name's sake."

Matthew evinced his usual curiosity.

"And is this before or after the Temple is pulled down stone by stone?"

"Of what Temple do you speak? That which encloses the spirit of man or that of the false priests?"

"That of which you told us earlier."

He smiled sadly. "My disciples, too, are more concerned with the House of God than with God himself. But I repeat, because of the iniquity of this people, for their rejection of him sent by God, this destruction shall happen, but not before all of you have been laid to rest."

"Tell us," said Matthew, "when shall these things be? And shall there be a sign of the second coming, and of the end of the world?"

"This gospel of the kingdom shall be preached in all the world for a witness unto all nations, and then shall the end come. When you shall see the abomination of desolation, spoken of by Daniel the prophet, stand in the holy place. Then let them which live in Judea flee into the mountains. Let him on the housetop not come down to take anything out of his house. Neither let him in the field return to take his clothes. And woe unto them that are with child, and to them that give suck in those days. For then shall be great tribulation, such as was not since the beginning of the world to this time, nor ever shall be. And except those days should be shortened, there should no flesh be saved. But for the elect's sake those days shall be shortened."

Peter had listened, wide-eyed.

"And will all this destruction come of an earthquake, Master?"

Jesus shook his head. "Ask rather why this destruction comes."

"And why is that?" asked the keeper of the keys.

"For man would upset the balance of the universe if left to his own devices. His own weapons fashioned out of hate become the engines of his ruin. The very atmosphere which he pollutes shall contaminate the garments as well as the mother's milk and sicken the child."

"And how shall man know this time?"

"Wherever the carcasses are, there shall the vultures be gathered together." A shadow fell across his face. "But none asks when the Son of Man comes again, and what this will be like."

"I was just about to ask," said Peter.

"Immediately after the tribulation of those days shall the sun be darkened, and the moon shall not give her light, and the stars shall fall from heaven, and the powers of the heavens shall be shaken."

Matthew had been listening avidly. "And what then, Master?"

"And then shall appear the sign of the Son of Man in heaven. And all the tribes of the earth shall mourn, and the Son of Man shall come in the clouds of heaven with power and great glory. And he shall send his angels with a great sound of a trumpet, and they shall gather together his elect from the four winds, from one end of heaven to the other. But not until, as said before, the Chosen shall be restored a second time after the Babylonian Captivity."

"And in what year of Israel's annals will all this be?"

"No man knows that day and hour, not even the angels of heaven, but my Father only. But as in the days of Noah, so shall the coming of the Son of Man be. For in the days before the flood they were eating and drinking, marrying and carousing, and none knew the day, until the flood came and took them away. So all must keep watch, for they know not what hour he comes, lest coming suddenly, he find them sleeping."

Originally Jesus had planned to spend the Passover with Lazarus and Martha and Mary. But to avoid being taken, he had decided to have the last supper in Jerusalem, at the home of John Mark, whom we knew as Mark. This friend of Peter's was the son of Mark David, a rich Pharisee who had contributed generously to the mission.

Not only did he change the feast, but the date as well, advancing it twenty-four hours. For Moses, in commemoration of the liberation of the Jews, had fixed the fourteenth day of the first month of Nisan for the celebration, which fell this year on a Friday, the beginning of the Sabbath as well. And so we were to observe the Passover on a Thursday, while Jerusalem was only making ready for it.

"My enemies move quickly," said he with an ironic smile, "so they not violate both the Sabbath and the Passover by having my blood on their hands on these holy days."

Although arrangements had been completed for the supper, the Master still sent John and James out to show again his own powers of divination, so that we would know that he did not speak idly of the hazard to himself. "Go into the city," he told the brothers, "and there you shall meet a man bearing a pitcher of water. Follow him, and wherever he enters, say you to the head of the House: 'The Master asks where is the guest chamber, where he shall eat the Passover with his Apostles.' He will then show you a large upper room, furnished and prepared, and made ready for us."

The brothers sighted a gray-haired man with a pitcher not far from the palace of Caiaphas, and he silently guided them to the house. There, the father of Mark took them to the room, and they quickly approved the placements for thirteen.

This circuitous way of confirming the site suited the strong mystical streak in Jesus. At the same time, I suppose, it showed us the thread of inevitability that ran through his affairs. It was his way of saying that the supper and what followed thereafter was linked irrevocably with his own destiny.

Usually I sat in the second post of honor, at Jesus' right, while Peter was at his left. But, arriving late, I noticed, with a sickening in my stomach, that Peter had usurped my customary place, and John was in Peter's position, symbolically that next to the Master's heart.

Jesus quickly noted my uncertainty. "Take this place next to Zelotes," he said, pointing to a seat at the other end from him.

I felt uncomfortably warm, remarking on the stuffiness of the room.

Andrew looked at me curiously. "I find it cool, but we can open the windows if you, like."

All afternoon I had been closeted with the Sadducees, laying plans for the taking of Jesus in the night, while few were about. They felt that he still had friends enough to cause a commotion, if not to touch off a demonstration.

Gamaliel did not meet with us, as before, but Caiaphas gave me his sealed note reiterating the support of the liberal Pharisee faction, enough, he said, to preclude a conviction. Without this note I would still have done nothing, but the others I knew I could not trust.

In my uneasiness now, I looked around the Passover table to unburden myself, but I had few friends there, except perhaps for Simon Zelotes, and the Master, whom I cherished, despite what any might say.

This was the feast of the unleavened bread, commemorating Moses' flight with the children of Israel. The flat wafer-like cakes were heaped on the table along with the bitter herbs reminding the descendants of these Israelites of the hard passage from Egypt to the Promised Land. Red wine was in abundance, signifying the blood sacrifice in the quest for freedom.

Jesus said the blessing, and then, in accordance with ritual, briefly described why this night was different from all other nights. "Since we are all Jews," he said, "it has been my desire to sit down with you for a last time and celebrate this Passover with you. For, as you know, the angels in Moses' time passed over the marked houses of the Israelites and smote only the homes of the Pharaoh's Egyptian subjects, but not so shall it be with the Son of Man. For he shall not be passed over, but neither shall he be found wanting in this hour. For I promise you that I will not eat any more thereof until my own pilgrimage be fulfilled in the Kingdom of God."

He took a thin wafer, a reminder of the unleavened bread eaten in the desert, and gave thanks, then broke it in fragments with his sinewy hands and passed it around, saying: "This is symbolically my body, which is given for you and mankind. This hold sacred in remembrance of me."

He then sipped from a cup of wine, and giving thanks to God, passed it to Peter, saying: "Take this and divide it among yourselves. For I can assure you that I will not drink of the fruit of the vine until the Kingdom of God shall come. But likewise, this cup is the testament of my blood which is shed for man."

His eyes roved boldly about the table. "Drink every one of you of this blood, including he who betrays me. For he sits at this table and eats bread with me."

He shook his head at their bewilderment.

"I tell you again that one of you that eats with me shall betray me."

"Is it I?" they chorused one after another, even Peter and John putting the question.

He put the bread into the common serving dish and said again: "It is one of the twelve that dips into this dish with me."

I dared not look at him, for who knew what he had divined with his uncanny powers?

"The Son of Man must go as it is written of him," he said solemnly, "but woe to that man by whom that Son of Man is betrayed. It would be better for that man if he were never born."

The others kept looking at one another but could not see who could it be, as all were close to him.

"I know who it is," he said, "and why he does it. I chose him well, for I saw even then the seeds of betrayal in him. But with faith, it need not have been his way. Still, it had to be done so that man will know till the end of time to what purpose I was sent. For in my death, they will remember my life."

I thought all eyes were surely on me, but as I looked up I could see they were all staring at the Master. Soon some began protesting their loyalty, and then began arguing in their childishness who he preferred among them.

Jesus listened for a while, and then chided: "Darken not my final hours with such ridiculous squabbling, so like the petty satraps who surround the Gentile kings and lick their boots like dogs currying favor. Let the greatest among you be as the least, and serve those junior to him. For by your works you justify a seat in the Kingdom of Heaven."

Peter looked at him with an aggrieved expression.

"I have never wavered in my loyalty to you."

"Not to me, Peter, but to the Father in me. Satan would have had you long ago had I not prayed that your faith not fail. For I know that after my death you will be like a rock to your brethren."

Tears came to Peter's eyes. "But, Master, I am ready to go with you, into prison, or to the death."

A sorrowful smile came over Jesus' face. "My death shall be the crucible by which you find the strength demanded of you in the dark days ahead."

As I squirmed uneasily, with all this talk of death, Peter fell to his knees before the Master. "I swear by all that is holy that I shall never forsake you."

"You forget that we do not take oaths. Nevertheless, you shall deny me thrice before the cock crows."

"Never," cried Peter. "I would surrender my life first."

"Make no rash promises," said Christ, "for these are easier said."

Solemnly, he pictured the Passover, speaking of God's angels bringing death to the firstborn of Egypt, but passing over the Jewish homes, before the cowering Pharaoh let the hosts of Israel go out of the land. But not once did he see the parallel between an embattled Moses and a Jesus indifferent to the tyranny of the new Pharaoh.

"And it came to pass, that at midnight the Lord smote all the firstborn in the land of Egypt, from the firstborn of Pharaoh that sat on his throne unto the firstborn of the captive that was in the dungeon, and all the firstborn of cattle.

"And Pharaoh rose up in the night, he, and all his servants, and all the Egyptians, and there was a great cry in Egypt, for there was not a house where there was not one dead.

"And Pharaoh called for Moses and Aaron by night, and said, Rise up, and get you forth from among my people, both you and the children of Israel, and go serve the Lord, as you have said. Also take your flocks and your herds, and be gone. And bless me also. And the Egyptians were urgent upon the people, that they might send them out of the land in haste, for they said, We be all dead men."

Even in their wanderings the Lord of Moses was with his beleaguered people. "And the Lord went before them by day in a pillar of a cloud, to lead them the way, and by night in a pillar of fire, to give them light, to go by day and night."

As Jesus read from the book of Moses, I marveled that he, so much greater than Moses, would not do as much for his enslaved people. But then he had never been confronted as Moses had.

He looked up to surprise me staring at him. "Have you a question, Judah?"

I was conscious that all eyes were on me.

"Who would you say was the greater, the prophet who defied the Pharaoh and led his people out of bondage, or the prophet who saw his people slaves and moved not a finger?"

"He is greater, Judah, who better does the work for which God sent him."

His eyes now moved around the table.

"I would speak to you from the Psalms, for what troubles one man troubles all, and what mystifies one mystifies all. So listen closely, that in after years you may better understand.

"'O Lord God of my salvation, I have cried day and night before you. For my soul is full of troubles, and my life draws nigh unto the grave. I am counted with them that go down into the pit, I am as a man that has no strength. Free among the dead, like the slain that lie in the grave, whom you remember no more. Lord, I have called daily upon you. I have stretched my hands unto you. Will you show wonders to the dead? Shall the dead arise and praise you? Shall your loving-kindness be declared in the grave, or your faithfulness in destruction?

"They that seek after my life lay snares for me, so forsake me not, O Lord, O my God, be not far from me. Make haste to help me, O Lord my salvation.'"

As we pondered these words, he now stood up, called for a basin of water, and tied a towel about his waist. "Now I would show you what I mean by the highest being the lowest, and the Master subordinating to the servant, for in my kingdom there is no ruler or ruled, but all are equally companions of the Lord."

Without ceremony, he kneeled before Peter and said: "Remove your sandals."

Peter looked at him in astonishment. "Master, you will never wash my feet."

"You still do not understand, but one day those that come after you shall make a tradition of this. Still, if I do not wash your feet, then you are no part of what I represent, and so have no place with me."

Peter's jaw dropped and he looked around helplessly.

"Master, that being the case, wash not my feet only, but also my hands and my head."

"It will suffice to wash only your feet to make you clean. But there is one here, as I said, who will not be clean, if I should wash him from head to foot."

The Apostles were sorely troubled.

"Who is it?" they cried again, not noticing that I alone said nothing.

"I will give you a hint from Scripture," he said, indulging his passion for mysticism. "'Thus saith the Lord. I will send a fire upon Moab, and it shall devour the palaces of Kerioth, and Moab shall die with tumult, with shouting, and with the sound of the trumpet.'"

They still did not understand, and they looked from one to the other, shaking their heads, and I did likewise.

And so, in his sardonic way, he gave them still another clue from Scripture.

"'And I said unto them, If you think good, give me my price, and if not, forbear. So they weighed for my price thirty pieces of silver. And the Lord said unto me, Cast it unto the potter. And I took the thirty pieces of silver, and cast them to the potter in the house of the Lord.'"

From the puzzled faces, it was plain they were no more enlightened than I was. How did one understand him? Even thinking death close, he could still toy with words.

He moved around the room, commencing with John and working at random until he came to me. He looked me straight in the eye, and I quaked, for with all his reference to death I was beginning to have a presentiment of evil.

"I love you," I cried in a fierce undertone. "I only ask, like every patriot, that you stand up to our enemies and deliver us from them. That is all I have ever asked."

He sighed. "You still don't understand. Would for your sake it was some other person, but failing this, act with dispatch, so that the prophecy of old will be fulfilled."

I refused to consider his death.

"You can will what you like."

"You, too, had that choice, and what have you done with it?"

He wiped my feet diligently and replaced my sandals.

I repeated Peter's cry. "I have been loyal in my way."

"Had it been God's way, Judah, then it might have been different. But, still, the prophecy of the thirty pieces of silver must be fulfilled."

The disciples had begun to regard us curiously, baffled by the secret conversation.

"And what is this to me?" I asked.

"You will learn, as you learn many things."

He stood up now, made his towel like a sash, and returned to his seat. "What I have done for you," he said, "I now charge you to do for each other. For this reason I have given you an example. I am your Master, and the servant is not greater than his Master, nor the Master greater than he who sent him, so be happy in this thought, even as you wash the feet of the lowliest."

Peter still wore a puzzled frown.

"You speak of being betrayed, and in so speaking cast a doubt on this entire company. Name this traitor so that we can drive him out and purge ourselves of this contamination."

"You shall know soon enough."

But Peter was not satisfied, for with all his dullness he had a curious temper.

Behind the Master's back, he beckoned to John, leaning against Christ's bosom, that he put the question to him again.

John looked into Christ's eyes.

"Who is it Master? Who is this traitor?"

Christ could deny him nothing. But he answered in his own way. "Let me tell you, my brethren, that it could have been any of you. But none of you, with all your frailties, was captivated by your own desires, save one. I knew him immediately by his burning obsession. He wanted not fame, nor money, but to live in a dead tradition, and conquer another people. Even now, he does not realize that a Roman life is as dear to God as a Judean's."

I listened in horror, for he completely ignored my feelings, not understanding what I intended, in my love not only for my country but for him as well.

Now the others set up a clamor, demanding that he name the traitor. He reached for a sop of bread, which he dipped into the wine.

"He it is to whom I shall give this sop."

My heart stood still, then thumped frantically against my chest. Again, I felt an impulse to stand up and declare myself, but his eyes stopped me.

With a flip of the wrist, he tossed the sop onto the table. It fell in front of me, but also next to Philip and Thomas, who were on either side, and one could not tell whose it was.

"Let him take it whose it is," Jesus said quietly.

In the stillness, nobody moved, and then Jesus beckoned me to his side. "Do what you have to do, and do it quickly," he whispered.

I stood as if paralyzed. Then he gave me a searching glance. "After we finish here we shall take ourselves to the Garden of Gethsemane, and there in the shadow of the olive presses, I shall prepare myself for my Father."

The others were still confused, thinking from his manner that Jesus directed me to buy the necessities for the second night of the feast.

Instead of leaving right then I resumed my seat, not wanting to appear conspicuous.

"Let this be my valedictory to you all," he said. "Grieve not for me, for if you believe in God, believe also in me. We will not be separated for long, for in my Father's house are many mansions. If it were not so, I would have told you. I go to prepare a place for you. Still, I will come again and receive you unto myself, that where I am you may be also. And by now assuredly you know where I go."

Poor doubting Thomas raised his hand. "Master, we know not for sure where you go, and how can we know the way?"

The fire came into Jesus' eyes. "I am the way, the truth, and the life. No man comes to the Father, but through me."

Philip, too, appeared to be troubled.

"Master," he said, "show us the Father, and it will satisfy me."

A look of sorrow came into Jesus' eyes.

"Have I been with you so long, Philip, and yet you have not known me? For he that has seen me has surely seen the Father. So how can you say: 'Show us the Father'? Do you not believe, even now, that I am in the Father, and the Father in me? For the words that I speak unto you, I speak not of myself. But it is my Father, who dwells in me, that does the work. And if for no other reason, believe me then for the very works' sake."

How ironic it was that they should doubt him while I believed in his God power implicitly. But still he made no mention of delivering the lamb of God from the wolf cubs of Rome. And so, when none was looking, I got up and went out, knowing that we were to meet again in the valley of decision.

CHAPTER SEVENTEEN

THE CONFRONTATION

THE CONFRONTATION HAD COME at last. In a few hours, before the Passover, the world would know of Christ's power. He was not always a peaceful man. I had seen his eye flash at injustice and, risking Roman wrath, he had pulled their victims from the trees to which they had been nailed for not paying Rome its tribute or for striking a Roman soldier who trifled with their women. He would yet be a Moses to his people, that I felt, despite all his talk of dying. He who raised Lazarus could surely raise himself. Even if he did everything only with the Father's help, certainly the God that helped Moses, assailing the Egyptians with pestilence and flood, would not forsake his only begotten son.

I could see no reason for the elaborate preparations to take him. Scores of Temple guards had been mustered and Pilate's troops had been put on an alert. There was also a multitude of Levites and Temple sympathizers who were to trail along to counter any opposing opinion. But who would be there at this hour, in the lonely Garden of Gethsemane, among the abandoned olive presses, but Jesus and the Twelve? What Twelve? I winced in spite of myself.

The time had come for Jesus to take a stand. The Zealot raiders, ignored by the multitudes, were being hunted down like rats. Outside Jericho, an attack on the garrison was repulsed, and the renegades Cestus and Dysmas taken and swiftly consigned to crosses. For Rome made short work of revolutionaries, whether a noble Brutus or an evil-smelling Syrian Jew. I heard, too, that bar-Abbas was captured in the same raid, but I had no tears for him.

I approached the confrontation with some trepidation. The High Priests had commissioned the twisted dwarf of a Sadoc to go along with me, and called on the captain of their guards, one Malchus, to head the armed detail. It was an overpowering force for one man.

Caiaphas gave me my last instructions.

"Give Jesus no warning, and bring him directly to my palace."

I looked at him in astonishment. "How can he be tried here, outside the jurisdiction of the Temple?"

"The Temple," he retorted, "is wherever the High Priests are."

"But will there be a quorum at this hour?"

"We govern the trial, take care of your task, and move expeditiously or it will go hard with you."

"Has the Nasi been informed?" I asked.

Caiaphas lifted a hand as if to strike me, and my own hand came up quickly. "I am not your servant," I cried. "I do this for Israel."

"Whatever you do it for," put in Annas, "begone and get it done."

I protested the considerable company formed to seize one peaceful man.

"He has the demon in him," rejoined Caiaphas, "and who knows but he will hypnotize many into joining with him? Did he not hypnotize the multitude into thinking they were eating bread and fish, when there was but a basketful of food?"

"There is no time," said Annas impatiently. "Get on with it, man, or we will get another, and put you in chains."

"You still need me as a witness," I cried.

The guards carried lanterns and torches, and some were armed with swords and staves. I knew exactly where to take them, having been in the Garden of Gethsemane many times, and soon, walking rapidly with Malchus at my elbow, I made out the shadow of a lone figure near an ebbing fire. Even from the silhouette, I knew who it must be.

As we burst into the camp, the place immediately came alive. One person after another scrambled up from his bed of grass and rent the night with cries of alarm. The captain of the Temple guards was straining in the darkness.

"I will pick him out for you," I whispered. "Whomsoever I kiss, it shall be he. Hold him fast so that he will suffer no injury from your soldiers."

Jesus stood quietly, as though he had been waiting for me.

I leaned forward and kissed him on the cheek.

He gave me a look that made my knees wax.

"My dear friend," said he, "I have been expecting you. You see, I threw the sop rightly."

I was beside myself with grief. "Master, Master," I cried.

And this they took for a sign. But he bore no malice, this I know, for he held out his hand to me first; no disciple took Jesus' hand of himself. "Do what you have to, and do it fast," he said, for he knew that what I did was not out of spite but for what he might do.

"This is no betrayal, Master," I whispered in his ear. "Trust me. For if you but raise your voice for freedom, all will still follow you, even the Temple guards."

He turned away from me, and from the clustered lights of many torches I could see his eyes flash boldly over the multitude.

"Why do you come as though I were a thief? Have I not sat daily with you teaching in the Temple, and you made no effort to lay hold of me?"

The multitude fell back, and even the soldiers sank to their knees in their fear. Only Malchus, the chief servant of the High Priests, shook off the spell and came forward, sword outstretched. A tall, bulky figure stepped out of the light and smote Malchus. The guard clapped his hand to his ear which hung by a thread.

Jesus passed his hand over the wound, and put back the ear. Now, more than ever, witnessing this miracle, I knew he could do whatever he wished.

None dared lay a hand on him, not even Malchus, holding back in his wonderment. They might well have returned empty-handed, and what a resounding victory this would have been. But he spoke sharply to Peter, still standing between him and the soldiers. "Put up your sword, for they that take the sword shall perish by the sword. Even now I could pray to my Father, and he would give me more than twelve legions of angels. But how then shall I accomplish what I have come to do?"

While the issue appeared in doubt, Sadoc had remained discreetly in the background, but, seeing Christ's air, of resignation, he quickly took charge. "He is only a hypnotist who fools you with his tricks. Seize him and his followers. Let none escape."

Jesus called for Peter and the rest to leave. And as Peter hesitated, he gave him a push. "You will deny me," he said, "but not yet."

The disciples fled for their lives, but not before Sadoc had reached out for one fleeing figure and snatched his tunic of fine linen. Naked, the fugitive kept running until he was out of sight. It was John, the beloved disciple who so much loved the Master. That for his love.

During the march to Caiaphas' palace I pleaded with Jesus that he Still take a stand, but he just stared stonily ahead, his lips occasionally moving in silent prayer. Malchus, pressing his ear in wonder, sought to strike up a conversation with the Master, and would have done anything he asked, but he was oblivious of him as well.

Malchus came to me with tears in his eyes. "I would free him however I fared. For he is indeed the Son of God."

"Don't fret," I said, "for he can free himself."

Malchus looked at me doubtfully. "I fear it has all been arranged."

"He can do what he will," I assured him.

"You know him well. Tell me, who does he speak to, who is this Abba?"

"That is his Father in heaven. Why do you ask?"

"He keeps mentioning him, saying under his breath: 'Abba, all things are possible unto you. Take away this cup from me, if you will. Nevertheless, not what I will, Abba, but what you will.'"

I was cheered. For I took this as a sign. Whatever he was, Son of David, Son of Man, Messiah, the Deliverer, Son of God, or King of the Jews, he was as loath to die as the rest of us. How could he hope to change the world unless he was of the world? Yes, this was encouraging news Malchus brought.

Ironically, we passed the cenacle, where we had supped a short time before, just as the imposing palace of Caiaphas came dimly into view. The multitude had followed, for they were a paid claque, employed to do the priests' bidding whenever some specific public reaction desired. Some filtered into the Great Hall of the palace while others remained in the cold night until sent away.

Annas sat alone on a platform. Below him were a few familiar faces: Ezra, Eleazar, and Sadoc. But there was no Gamaliel, Nicodemus, or Joseph of Arimathea. There was not a friendly face in the whole auditorium. Jesus, his hands bound, was pushed onto a stand just below Annas, while Caiaphas stood but a few feet from Jesus and glowered.

I liked not the look of the hall; it was vast and cold, and dimly lit, so that the shadows fluttered on the marble walls and gave a somber cast to the proceedings. I quickly looked about and could see only a sprinkling of Pharisees; the majority were Sadducees, but even so, there was hardly a quorum, since at least two thirds of the seventy were required and there were less than half that number ranged in a semicircle before the priest.

As my eyes took in the bank of witnesses, I saw a familiar figure, unkempt and in rags, flung in with the others. It was Joshua-bar-Abbas; his hands were tied, and he looked about wrathfully, clamoring that his shackles be loosened. I had thought him to be on the cross by now. And yet, at a peremptory nod from Caiaphas, he was unbound and sat chafing his wrists and sneaking furtive looks around the Great Hall. Remarkably, he seemed as confident and self-assured as ever.

Ignoring bar-Abbas, I approached Caiaphas, as he finished a conversation with Annas, to protest the lack of a proper quorum.

He stood stiff and arrogant.

"Tell me not my business, knave," he shouted.

My cheeks burned. He spoke to me as Pilate spoke to him.

"All Israel will decry this injustice," I shouted back.

"We have called a meeting of the Beth Din, the lower court," he explained contemptuously, "and this requires but twenty-three members, who can act as well in an emergency."

"And what is this emergency," I said, "the improvident haste to finish with him before sunset?"

"You come as a witness, and could very well become a defendant if you do not watch your tongue."

I darted a glance at Jesus. He looked about impassively, as if unmindful of what was transpiring.

There was none to defend him, only himself. I now had some uneasiness about my own testimony. With Gamaliel not there, it was plain that the priests would press for a conviction.

I decided, with a sigh of relief, I would do nothing more to sharpen the confrontation but would testify only to that which would help him.

The trial began.

The first witness was an old man, an Amharetz, who looked like he had been browbeaten all his life. He glanced about furtively with his colorless eyes and seemed to shrink into his shoes as the Prosecutor Caiaphas pounced on him.

"You had the palsy, you say?"

"All my life, sir."

Suddenly I recalled him. It had been in Jericho, more than a year ago. It had been just another healing, and I was surprised that he should have been picked out from the multitude.

"And you say you were healed?"

"I was healed." He thrust out his hands. "You see, they no longer shake."

Annas frowned from the platform. "Answer only the question with a yes or no, as the case may be."

"Yes, Your Honor."

"And who accomplished this so-called healing?"

"Jesus of Nazareth."

"Could you point him out?"

The old man nodded toward Jesus. "His Holiness stands so close I could almost reach out and touch him."

"His Holiness?" Caiaphas' high-bridged nose sniffed at the ceiling. "Why do you call him such?"

"Well, Your Worship . . ."

"Address me as Prosecutor or Sir, you jackanapes."

The witness gulped. "He seemed to be sent of the Holy One. His power was so great that only God would have conceived it."

Annas glowered at him. "Answer the questions only, fellow."

Caiaphas spoke in silken tones. "Did this man, this Jesus of Nazareth, say he was sent by God?"

"He said only that he did God's work."

"Answer yes or no." Annas' voice was like a knife.

The witness looked bewildered. "It is neither yes nor no," said he with a helpless shrug.

"Was it not blasphemy for him to couple himself so familiarly with the Holy One?"

"Not if the healing was accomplished through God. For how else could it have come, sir?"

I could see from Caiaphas' face that he already regretted calling this witness, and as he looked down the witness bank, I could see him come to an instant decision.

"I am dismissing this witness, Your Honor, as there are other witnesses. One is Judah-bar-Simon, a disciple of this Jesus, and agent for the Sanhedrin." I gulped at this violation of a confidence, which made me seem to have betrayed Jesus for the Sanhedrin and in no way reflected my true thinking.

"The second witness," said Caiaphas, "is the professed Zealot leader, also a disciple of this Jesus, and likewise an agent for the Sanhedrin. This is Joshua bar Abbas, who was mistakenly seized by the Romans while on an undercover assignment for the Sanhedrin."

So it had been he all this time. I knew now how Jesus' movements, and those of the disciples, were known to the Temple. How even my comings and goings were noted, even to my overnight stay with Lazarus and my plans to visit my mother and Rachel.

I looked at Annas and could see it was all staged.

He nodded perfunctorily, then said to the Prosecutor:

"I would question the present witness before you proceed."

Caiaphas bowed. "As you will."

The old man looked up anxiously.

Annas' cold eyes bored into him. "Now you said that this healing came through God? Would you know this for a certainty?"

His eyes blinked nervously.

"No, sir, only what they said."

"They?" Annas leaned forward fiercely. "Who is 'they'?"

"There was another man there whom Jesus called Peter, and he said that only the Christ, the Anointed, the Son of God, could do what Jesus had done."

"And what did your Jesus say to this?"

Even the cleverest man could sometimes overreach.

"He said that he did nothing himself. It was all through the Father, and they could do as much with faith in God."

I saw Caiaphas' lip droop slightly. I suppose even he chafed under the older man's authority.

"You are free to go," he said almost pleasantly.

Bar-Abbas, twice a renegade, stepped to the witness platform. He had a scornful glance for me but he did not dare look at the Master, who still stood quietly detached, as if the proceedings had nothing to do with him.

As I looked at the rogue he seemed so transparent I could not understand how I had failed to see through him at once. The Master had trusted him as well, but then he trusted everybody, saying it was better to trust and be deceived than to be continually guarded in one's relations with people.

Bar-Abbas faced Caiaphas confidently, and well he might.

"You know this man, Jesus?"

"As well as I know you."

The Prosecutor frowned. "You were his disciple?"

"That I was, until I saw that he led the Jews to insurrection."

What a barefaced lie. I almost cried out in protest.

"Did he style himself King of the Jews?"

"He spoke often of this kingdom of his, and I suppose that was what he meant, for all know the Messiah has come to lead the nation, and he called himself the Messiah."

"Have you seen any violence come of his exhortations?"

"In Galilee the crowd was so aroused that it stampeded amid great shouting, and would have crowned him King then and there had he not drawn back when he observed some soldiers in the crowd."

How some men twist the truth to their own evil purpose.

"'Tis said that he counted himself the equal of God."

"Oh, yes, he called him by name, Abba, as is generally known, and said he and his Father were one. But then he has made no secret of this, speaking before the Pharisees in the Temple."

"He claims that, like God, he can be everywhere at once, and even walk on water and calm the waves with a word. Have you seen such evidence?"

"Only in his boasting that it was a simple thing for him, since he and God were inseparable, and God would not allow his son to fail in anything."

"His son!" Caiaphas' voice rose scornfully through the huge chamber. "And how did God beget him, did he say?"

"In a wave of clouds, for he maintained that he would never die, but would be born again and be sighted in the skies."

Caiaphas shot a look at the presiding justice. "This is blasphemy, if I ever heard it. What more remains to be said?"

Annas regarded him bleakly.

"Our law states there must be two witnesses corroborating the charges, and the prisoner himself must be heard from. We shall be judged by the way we judge him."

My eyes fell on Jesus, hoping that he would bestir himself in response to these falsehoods. But he still looked disinterested, his lips occasionally moving in silent prayer. Would that he summoned his legions of angels, and that they were the same that had exterminated the Egyptian firstborn.

"Judah-bar-Simon."

I moved forward as my name was called and saw Jesus' eyes light on me for an instant. There was no glint of recognition.

Caiaphas pointed a long finger at Jesus.

"You were one of his Twelve, were you not, of the elite from whom he had no secrets?"

"He had no secrets from anybody."

"So it would seem." His voice was heavy with sarcasm. "Did you consider him the Messiah?"

"There was no doubt in my mind."

He frowned. "In your mind the Messiah is the Deliverer of Israel, is that not so?"

"Most assuredly."

"And from whom was the nation to be delivered?"

I saw the trap, and lightly avoided it. "From its own wickedness and evil, so that it would find salvation before God in the Kingdom of Heaven he speaks of."

I smiled to myself at his show of temper.

"You know very well that the prophecy for the Messiah calls for him to make this nation triumphant over seventy others. How can this be done in heaven? Play no games with me, sir."

I shrugged. "Then if he is not the Messiah, he cannot be the Deliverer, or the King of the Jews, for that matter."

I looked up and saw a gleam of interest in Jesus' eyes.

Caiaphas' face turned purple, but at a warning glance from Annas he quickly composed himself.

"You have heard him say that he will destroy the Temple that was made with hands, and within three days would build another made without hands?"

His voice boomed across the room, and a murmur came on cue from the contemptible claque.

"Is it not blasphemy for him to speak of destroying the Temple and then building back in three days what took two generations?"

"The Temple he speaks of is not the Temple you speak of. He speaks of his body, which, our fathers remind us, is the Temple of the mind and spirit."

Caiaphas' eyebrows rose incredulously. "This is what he speaks of, and you take no offense? How does he propose to create this body in three days? Even his Father took longer to create man."

I could see the malicious smiles in the eyes of Sadoc, Ezra, and others in the tribunal.

"He speaks of rebirth, such as the Pharisees are familiar with, and the belief that man is born again after death and lives in heaven until such time as God decides he should return to earth."

Though the Sadducees had no use for reincarnation, Caiaphas was too clever to discredit the belief before the few Pharisees at this hastily drummed-up session. Yet, as usual, he twisted what was said to his own advantage. "How can he accomplish his own rebirth in so short a time then, unless he is God?"

How devious these priests were.

"He was only speaking symbolically, as he often does."

He had carefully avoided asking me about the occasion when Jesus spurned the crown offered by bar-Abbas, for this would contradict the traitor's testimony and tend to nullify it.

I looked to Annas. "May I volunteer some information?"

His beady eyes were like a reptile's. "Answer only that which is asked. That is the custom."

Though I had said nothing to incriminate Jesus, Caiaphas seemed satisfied with my testimony. I saw a glance pass from the Magistrate, and the Prosecutor's answering nod.

"You are dismissed for the present," he said. "We will now call the defendant."

My temper flared as I saw Jesus rudely shoved toward the witness stand. He made no effort to resist, nor did he seem upset by this treatment. If only he would fly into a rage and turn on his tormentors for once and for all.

Caiaphas saluted him with mock reverence.

"You are Jesus of Nazareth?"

The Master barely moved his head.

"You stand accused of blasphemy for your teachings, and this is punishable by death according to our law. Now in these teachings your disciples profess for you a wisdom and knowledge beyond any of the great teachers of Israel, including the venerated Gamaliel and Ezra. What say you of this charge?"

Jesus considered him calmly. "I have spoken openly to the world. I have taught always in the synagogue, and in the Temple, where the Jews always resort. And I have said nothing in secret."

"You are not accused of secret doctrine, but of corrupting the people, the Amharetzin, and your own disciples, who in turn have corrupted others with lies and deception concerning your greatness."

"I claim no greatness, except what the Father makes great. But why do you ask me what I say? Ask rather those who have heard me, for they know what I said and can tell you, if it is the truth you want."

Caiaphas reared back in anger. "You dare take this tone with me?"

He made a slight motion, and one of the Temple guards standing near Jesus struck him across the face. "Speak not this way to the High Priest," he cried.

I started forward angrily, but a guard halted me. "Hold still," he said, "or it will go the worse with you."

Jesus retained his composure.

"If I have spoken evil," he said mildly, "then bear witness to the evil, and let it count against me, but if well, as I believe why have you smitten me?"

"You are not here to ask questions," said Caiaphas roughly, "but to answer them. You give yourself great airs for a simple carpenter from Galilee. Now tell me who you claim to be."

"I claim nothing, except in the Father's name. Even as you could be, so am I."

Caiaphas folded his arms in his frustration, and I could clearly see that he felt Jesus was toying with him.

"Your disciples call you the Anointed, the Christ, the Son of the Blessed. How does this happen, unless this is what you call yourself?"

Jesus looked back at him silently, his eyes seeming to bore right through the Prosecutor.

Caiaphas appeared discomposed for a moment, then reacted angrily.

"I adjure you by the living God to tell us whether you be the promised Messiah and the Son of God."

"If I tell you, you will not believe me," Jesus said simply. "And if I should ask you, you would not answer me, nor would you let me go, whatever I answered."

"All who know you say you have made this claim to be the Son of God."

Jesus stood straight and proud, unflinching. "This you have said, not I. Nevertheless, you shall hereafter see the Son of Man sitting on the right hand of the power of God and coming in the clouds of heaven."

A triumphant smile came over the evil face. "This man has established his blasphemy out of his own mouth. What further need do we have of witnesses, when we have it from his own tongue?"

And then Caiaphas tore his clothes to show the traditional grief at an acknowledgment of blasphemy.

"He has no shame, but confesses to our faces."

Only one voice was raised in protest, and that a familiar one. Nicodemus had arrived tardily and was now observing the proceedings grimly.

"Our law condemns no one to death on his own confession," he cried. "You are not to condemn this innocent man, for you will tear all Israel apart with this foul act."

Annas abandoned all pretense of impartiality. "He was arrested for practicing sorcery and inciting Israel to apostasy, and as a false prophet he is subject to death as stipulated in the books of Moses. If we let him alone, all men will believe in him in time, and the Romans shall come and take away both our place and our nation."

"You think of yourselves, not the nation," Nicodemus cried, "or this trial would not be held stealthily at night as though you were a band of robbers."

They would have lain hands on him, rich as he was, but he fled from the palace, seeing he could accomplish no more.

The trial was a mockery. For not only had it been held illegally at night, but both the Judge and the Prosecutor had manifested their belief in Jesus' guilt at every instance. Bar-Abbas' evidence was tainted, and there was no rebuttal of it, and there was no public defender named for Jesus, as there should have been in a capital trial.

The vote was swift. All that was required was a majority of two to convict. As could be predicted, the vote was unanimous. No pretense was even made for the younger members to vote first, as was the custom, so as not to be influenced by the older.

They did not take the time to deliberate. "Death, death, death." It was almost a chorus. And each time the word rang out, I felt a lump in my throat. Not "guilty," but "death," they voted, though they could not execute the sentence themselves. Had this responsibility been theirs, perhaps they would have hesitated in their judgment.

The verdict did not appear to affect Jesus. As he was being blindfolded as a condemned man, to be led away to Pilate, he made no protest. My eyes searched his imploringly, but he seemed not to notice. He was letting them do what they wanted with him. But I would not have it so.

As they prepared to take Jesus off, I remembered what my father and Gamaliel had told me of Jewish justice, and I quickly stepped up to the tribunal before it could disband. They looked at me in disbelief.

"In the event of capital punishment," I cried, "the accused has the right of appeal. A second hearing must be held in twenty-four hours, when his friends may present what evidence they wish in his behalf."

Caiaphas would have had the guard on me but was restrained by a look from Annas.

"Come forward," he ordered peremptorily.

As I moved up to the platform, he reached under his desk and brought out a pouch.

"Come, take this," he cried. "It is yours."

I stretched out my hand uncertainly. It was heavy and it jangled.

"You must know what it is. You hold the purse strings for this company of beggars."

I suddenly realized what was in the bag.

I shrank back. "I want none of it."

"Take it," he commanded. "It is the price for your service, the traditional payment for information leading to the conviction of an enemy of the people."

He pulled me by the arm. "Count it well, there are thirty pieces of silver therein."

I shuddered and stole a look at Jesus. There was a faint smile on his lips, as though he remembered his words of only a few hours before.

"Make haste," bellowed Caiaphas, "the Passover will be here while you gloat over your reward."

"I do not want it," I cried. "Take it from me."

"You have no choice," said Annas, "it is the law. Put it in the bag with the money you have gathered for the Son of God and stop justifying yourself with talk of appeals."

I could have wept in my shame, for I had committed no betrayal, despite what it looked. Jesus could still save himself before Pilate, that I knew, if only he would consider the many who rested their hopes on him. I turned to him, but his eyes were covered and he saw no more.

And so we made ready for Pilate, but not before Jesus' captors had spat in his face and struck him, shouting in their perverseness: "Since you are a prophet, prophesy who it is that strikes you." He did not turn away, or wipe the spittle from his face.

As we came out of the palace, with Jesus pushed along in the lead, I saw Peter skulking in the shadows and then heard a cock crow in the gray dawn. Peter listened, too, and then a stricken look came into his face, and he ran off, tearing his hair in his despair. And so I saw for the last time the keeper of the keys, him whom they called the Rock.

The procession moved swiftly through streets just beginning to stir. In the march there were the same Levites as before, with some added to make the multitude more impressive. Jesus had no sandals, and his feet were bleeding from the rough pavements, but they would not stop, nor would they let me give him my shoes.

"He is the King of the Jews," they jeered, "let him march like a King."

He could have ended all this in a moment, calmed them as he did the waves of Galilee, and disappeared as he had one day when the crowd forced itself on him. But, still, he did nothing.

Few in Jerusalem knew Jesus' fate as yet, for as it grew lighter he was hidden from the view of the curious, and it seemed just another religious procession led by Caiaphas and Annas.

The guards had notified Pilate, and he was waiting with his retinue outside the Praetorium near the entrance of the Fortress. As always, there was a gibe in his darting eyes, and a sneer on the thin, bloodless lips. With his beaked nose, he looked like a hawk about to destroy its prey.

He looked over the crowd curiously, nodding briefly to the High Priests, giving me a mocking look, and then I saw his face harden. His eyes had fallen on the bedraggled bar-Abbas.

"Bring that man forward," he cried.

Bar-Abbas was jostled to a place between the two priests.

Pilate's face grew dark. "This man is twice a traitor. Death by crucifixion is too good for one who has betrayed a Rome that used him well."

Annas raised his hand in conciliation.

"It but seems that way," he said. "He has served us well, and if not for this man the Zealots would have done far more damage to Roman establishments. There was not a move that was made of which he did not keep us informed."

Pilate's face was still grim. "He led attacks on our men in Jericho, and elsewhere."

"Only to put a face on things. Had his zeal been less, he would have been suspect long before."

How despicable, I thought, the deceit and treachery with which he had wormed our secret plans out of us.

"Why do you fight for him?" Pilate asked.

Annas squirmed for a moment. "Because in this land of malcontents and traitors, it would go hard for us if we were to discourage men like bar-Abbas."

Pilate digested this for a moment, then, as if there were no bar-Abbas: "Now what is it you want with Jesus of Nazareth?"

"We have found him guilty of blasphemy and sentenced him to death."

"And so you come to confirm that sentence. But blasphemy against whom?"

"Against the God of Israel."

Pilate shrugged, and I again noticed how he enjoyed taunting the Jews. "How can he blaspheme the invisible? You have seen my God, the invincible Tiberius, but no one has seen yours. So how can he be sinned against?"

"He calls himself the Son of God, and as such stood ready to lead an uprising against the government."

"Now, that is different." His face grew solemn as if it were all new.

"We found him perverting the nation, forbidding the people, particularly the Amharetzin, to pay taxes to Rome, and saying himself that he is the Messiah, which is to say, the King of the Jews."

Pilate clapped his hands. "Bring the prisoner forward."

A path opened up in the crowd, and Jesus, his hands bound, was rudely pushed forward by the guards.

I was never more proud of him than in that moment.

He stood straight and strong, his eyes now revealed. Even in his simple robe he had a majesty that made others look ordinary. Pilate's sneer faded before this dignity.

"So you are the King of the Jews?" he said.

Jesus returned his gaze evenly. "You say that, sir."

"They tell me you are the son of this invisible God the Hebrews worship."

Jesus made no reply.

Pilate put the question again.

"Do others tell you this, or do you know it of your own accord?" Jesus asked mildly.

"Am I Jew to know this of myself? They bring you to me bound like a dangerous criminal, and so I must assume you have done something to merit this treatment."

"They prosecute me for reasons of their own."

Pilate smiled, his dark eyes moving like a cobra's to the two High Priests.

"And why would they do that?"

"Because I speak of the Kingdom of Heaven, and they are of this earth only."

Pilate's brow knit in a deep frown. "Now what proof have you of this Heavenly Kingdom?"

"It is everywhere, within you and every man, for it bespeaks the Father within."

Pilate's frown grew.

"You speak in riddles. Who is this Father, and what is he within? Know you not that you are on trial for your life?"

"No man can take my life unless I lay it down."

Pilate laughed in his wicked way. "We shall see about that. But now tell me about this Father of yours."

"He is also your Father and dwells in you."

Pilate regarded him uncertainly, not sure whether Jesus was making sport of him. He pointed to Annas and Caiaphas, who were standing sullenly aloof.

"These two priests who brought you before me in shackles, is this Father in them as well?"

Jesus looked at the two with scorn in his eyes. "They mock the Father with their actions, yet they may still find salvation if they repent."

Pilate made an impatient movement. "We stray from our purpose. You are accused of resisting the authority of the Emperor and plotting insurrection. What say you to that?"

Before Jesus could answer, Caiaphas spoke out. "Remember, he is charged also with blasphemy, claiming to be God himself."

"A proconsul of Rome," cried Pilate, "cares not for your silly disputes among yourselves. You Jews are always squabbling."

As Caiaphas opened his mouth to speak, he cut him off sharply.

"Let this man answer. This is no Jewish trial, where the accused is prejudged by some sniveling schemers, but a Roman trial, with justice our end." His eyes moved over the assembly proudly. "We Romans stand for justice. If this prisoner were a Roman citizen he could appeal his sentence to the Emperor himself in Rome. But even so, I stand for the Emperor, and justice shall be served."

It was a noble speech, but I had seen enough of the Romans to know how they bent the truth.

Had not Julius Caesar professed himself a lover of the Republic while plotting to become King? Augustus, while presuming to be a friend of the Senate, had subtly deprived it of all its power. And would not the devious Sejanus, patron of this Pilate, be Emperor today if the Emperor himself were not more devious? Let Pilate amuse himself. It fooled nobody, nor was it meant to fool anybody. He toyed with us as if we were puppets.

"Now tell me exactly how you sought to overthrow Rome." As Jesus remained silent he went on. "You must surely know it is as reprehensible to think treachery as it is to commit an overt act of rebellion."

By his easy attitude, which surprised us all, Pilate put off the confrontation which formed my whole design.

Not once had Jesus glanced my way, but now his eyes swept the pavement and rested on me.

"I came not for any confrontation with Rome, but for another Armageddon."

"This riddle deepens," said Pilate. "So if you confront not Rome, whom do you confront? If only the Temple, then this becomes a matter just for them."

Jesus still stood passively, his head slightly bowed.

"What is this confrontation you speak of?" Pilate repeated.

"It is between good and evil."

I took heart, for what could this mean but freedom versus tyranny?

Pilate's small eyes suddenly filled with malice. "And I suppose you are the good and we the evil?"

"I speak of the good and evil within each of us. We have jurisdiction only over ourselves. And so I bring the Father's blessing for any who will reflect the good in them, and reject the evil, which grows out of lack of faith."

"How do we know what is good and what evil, unless it is good or bad for us? Tell me that, Jesus." For the first time, he called him by name, as though elevating him from the nondescript ranks of the faceless accused.

"To this end I was born," said Jesus, "that I should bear witness unto the truth."

I remembered how Pilate had jeered at the truth.

"What is the truth?"

"The truth," said Jesus, "is God."

Pilate chomped on his teeth. "We always get back to that, don't we? The truth is God, and God is the truth. And so what does that prove?"

"In love, we find the truth. There is no greater love, nor truth, than in a man laying down his life for his friend."

"You call Caiaphas and Annas and Judas your friends? You must surely be mad. And how speak you of laying down your life? You do not die unless Rome decides you die. The Sanhedrin has no power of life and death except where Rome gives it."

"My end was decided long before by a higher power. For this also was I born."

"We all die sooner or later," said Pilate. "Why should your death be different from others? Know you not in less than fifty years everyone in this assemblage will be dead, and the world will be no different for their living or dying."

He stood undecided, not trusting Jesus, but neither wanting to give the High Priests and their adherents what they wanted. I could see the thought running through his head: If only this man would show some defiance, then I could quickly dispatch him. He pointed to the Praetorium, where pious Jews dared not go.

"I would speak to him away from the crowd," he said.

The priests looked at each other uneasily, as with a nod he beckoned me to follow.

In the hall, Jesus and I stood side by side, but he stared ahead, as if I were not there.

Pilate looked me up and down until I felt naked before him.

"Tell me, Judas Iscariot, why you have betrayed this innocent man?"

I gave up all thought of dissembling. "I only wanted him to declare himself," I cried, "that is all I ever wanted."

His expression was stern and forbidding. "Declare himself to what purpose?"

"To that purpose for which he came."

"Which was what?" He cuffed me across the face. "Don't play at cross purposes with me or it will be you on the cross."

I turned to Jesus, but he still stood immobile, as if he were alone.

"I would gladly die for him," I cried.

"You may get your wish," said Pilate grimly.

It was not too late for him to prove himself.

"All Israel knows why the Messiah came."

"All but he, is that it?" He turned his piercing eyes onto Jesus. "What say you to all this claptrap?" He had flung himself into a judgment seat, and was reflecting darkly, when one of his guards came up to him and handed him a scrap of parchment. He read it aloud in Latin, as it was written, for it came from his wife, Claudia Procula. Jesus had no trouble with this language, or with any other, for that matter.

"Have nothing to do with that just man. For I have suffered many things this day in a dream because of him."

He sat like a man bedeviled.

"What say you to that, Jesus of Nazareth?"

Jesus' face grew radiant with emotion.

"For this day she shall find a place in heaven, though she be a Gentile, for the concern she showed the Son of Man on his Judgment Day. But the Son of Man came not to be ministered to, but to minister, and to give his life as a ransom for many."

Pilate pushed his missile-shaped head next to Jesus' face. "I do not understand you. I have been a Roman soldier for thirty years and have fought with many brave men, and yet you are the first man I have met with no fear of death."

"I accept his will and go to his house."

Pilate gave me a perplexed glance.

"Let us see what kind of King he is." He ordered the guards forward with a flip of the wrist.

"This man, they say, is the King of the Jews. Will you attire him for the occasion?"

The guards looked at him narrowly, then deciding he meant it, burst into laughter.

They pulled off Jesus' plain robe of linen and put a purple robe on him, while he stood unprotesting, a resigned look on his face. Then they quickly made a crude crown of thorns and put it on his head.

Falling over one another in jubilation, they began to salute him: "Hail to the King of the Jews."

Then, as Pilate watched impassively, they struck him on the head with a reed as if they were dubbing him King and bowed their knees to the floor in mock worship of him. Some then spit on him, singing out joyfully: "See how we anoint the Anointed of God."

I could stand it no longer, and rushed forward to put myself between him and his tormentors.

They raised their spears and would have pierced me, but Pilate cried: "That is enough."

He turned to Jesus curiously, seeing the blood trickle from his mouth where a soldier had struck him.

"You see how it will go with you if you do not tell me the truth about yourself?"

"Only the truth recognizes the truth."

"I know not what to do with you," Pilate sighed. "A Jew's life means nothing to a Roman, no more than a Greek's or a German's, even less when I think of the provocation I bear, but still I am not satisfied that you mean Rome trouble. If so"—he drew his hand across his throat—"I would make short work of you."

He had been cruelly mocked, beaten, and soon he was to be scourged, and still he did not call on the God power that he vaunted to the skies.

"Jesus," I pleaded in a voice strange to me, "summon those legions of the Lord and smite the Philistines."

Pilate gazed at Jesus curiously. "Call on this Lord of yours and let him strike me dead for the way you have been treated here this day."

Jesus looked at him with tranquil eyes. "You are as near death as I, or any other, for that matter. For your days are numbered as well."

Pilate seemed startled for a moment. "You play some game with me. Think not I am one of your craven Jews who is open to the powers of a Jewish prophet's suggestion. How can you prophesy for one who holds the power of life and death over you?"

There was a trace of a smile on Jesus' lips. "Because I speak for him who holds the power of life and death over you and all men. Still, he who hears my word possesses eternal life, though he has passed from death to life."

"From death to life, what foolishness is this?"

"For that reason, I have come, and for that reason, I go, and none cause my death, only the manner of it, and for this they may repent, if it be given to them to do so."

"You are a curious one," said Pilate. "Though I put you on the cross you will not hate me for it?"

"You will hate yourself in time. Your kingdom shall not be left to other people, but it shall break in pieces, and these pieces shall then join together, until the final judgment."

Pilate looked thoughtful. "Under Roman law the questions are put three times, to give the accused time to reflect on his answers, if need be. I have asked before, and I ask again, why do you seek to die? Why?"

Jesus sighed. "I die so that I may be reborn. All Israel should know that, but, alas, they have listened to me no more than to the other prophets, or to the Father himself. But a time will come when they shall listen, with others, for the world will have no choice, other than destruction."

Pilate shook his head. "You are a dilemma that I would keep alive to know more about, and to please my wife. But I do see some danger in you to the public peace, and to the government. For you cast a strange spell over Romans as well as Jews, and I trust it not."

He scowled fiercely.

"What would you say if I let you go?"

Jesus gazed at him evenly.

"You have no intention of letting me go."

Pilate's eyebrows tilted sharply.

"How do you know that?"

"I know what must happen to the Son of Man."

The confrontation was going directly contrary to what I had conceived.

"You speak," said Pilate, "as if you were already not here."

Jesus regarded him dispassionately. "Even thinking me innocent you will not let me go."

"I can do what I like with you," said Pilate brusquely. His eyes became thoughtful. "But in Claudia Procula, the centurion Cornelius, and certain of the soldiers whom I have heard speak of you, I see a hazard to Rome. Tell me that you will stop your preaching and inciting men to dangerous thoughts."

Christ shook his head slowly, and there was a smile almost of compassion in his eyes.

"My Father's work will one day prevail."

Pilate frowned. "You give me little choice."

He turned to me. "You stand proof that I gave him his chance, and he took it not."

"I only give evidence for him," I said. "Why did you have your soldiers mock him if you would help him?"

"I test him as you do, but still"—he shrugged—"I can do no different than I do. I owe Rome too much." He turned to Christ.

"We have done all we can here. I give you back now to the High Priests, and see what they do with you."

He dearly loved to tease his Jews, as he styled them. For he again brought Jesus outside and mocked the multitude once more. "You have brought this man to me as one that perverts the people, but I have examined him and find no fault in him touching those things about which you have accused him." He paused. "He is somewhat intractable, nor appreciating the authority of Rome, but for that I would scourge him and let him go. I myself find no fault in him worthy of death."

The hypocrite, I thought, playing with the crowd over a man's life, which he seemed to hold out, and yet his decision was sure, prompted by his own regard for his standing in Rome.

The crowd played his game, for they too were well schooled.

"No, no," they cried, "crucify him, crucify him. He has sinned against God."

"Why don't you take him and crucify him?" Pilate said. "Since it is your laws he broke, and not Rome's."

There was a malevolent gleam in his eye, and I knew again he was toying with them. His wife's warning had given him pause, but soldiers of Rome paid no heed to idle dreams, though he might appear to humor her.

"We have a law," said Caiaphas, "and by our law he ought to die."

"Then stone or strangle him by your own law, and leave Roman law to Romans."

Annas spoke up.

"Of old, it has been said that he who blasphemes the name of the Lord shall be put to death, and all the congregation shall stone him."

Pilate assumed his familiar posture, his hands on his hips and a sneer on his lips.

"You have your congregation with you. They will stone him gladly at your behest. Why trouble Rome?"

"Because it would be illegal."

Pilate chuckled mirthlessly. "So you want it legal, do you? And whom do you fool?"

Annas regarded him sternly.

"He is a threat to your position here."

Pilate's eyes became narrow slits. "Speak not to me of my position, old man, but remember yours, or I shall."

He turned now to Jesus, and though his mind was clearly made up, he still seemed torn by a strange desire to justify himself in Christ's eyes.

"Tell me who you are and for what you were sent. For I have the authority to crucify you or to release you, as I will."

Jesus answered him. "You have no power at all against me except what you receive from above. It is he who delivered me unto you that has the greater sin." He meant Caiaphas, that I could tell by his glance.

Pilate laughed in his coarse way. "That is true enough. Well, I have a mind not to give them what they want, for they would use me, playing on my fear of insurrection, and think I know it not."

Annas held his ground. "If you let this man go, you are not Caesar's friend. For whoever makes himself a King stands opposed to Caesar."

Pilate's face turned the color of scarlet. "No Jew tells the Proconsul of Rome how to serve his Emperor."

Seeing the delay, but not knowing its cause, the crowd now took up his chant: "Away with him, crucify him, crucify him."

He gave them his mocking look. "Shall I crucify your King? Look how majestic he is in his robes and crown."

Annas and Caiaphas completely abased themselves. "We have no king but Caesar," they cried.

Pilate looked at them with scorn. "If it takes this man's death to prove your loyalty to Rome, then it is all done in a good cause."

He hesitated, then said in a sardonic voice: "Before I pass judgment—you have a custom that I should release one political prisoner unto you at the Passover. Would you therefore have me release unto you this King of the Jews? For verily he looks like a King." Knowing the crowd, he already knew the answer.

"No, no," the multitude cried at a look from the High Priests, "give us bar-Abbas."

Pilate's face filled with disgust. "Bar-Abbas, that brigand? You choose him over this gentle man? Very well, I will give you bar-Abbas, and you shall remember his name whenever this day is remembered."

"Bar-Abbas, bar-Abbas," they cried, as though acclaiming a hero.

"His blood be on your heads, not mine," shouted Pilate.

Then the multitude, all friends of the priests, shouted, as was the custom in Israel at an execution:

"Then his blood be on us, and on our children."

"It is your blood, not mine," cried Pilate again. He sent for a basin of water, and plunged his hands into it. "I wash my hands of the innocent blood of this just man."

He then wrote out a title, in large letters, on a crossbar which was given to him.

"This is Jesus of Nazareth, the King of the Jews."

Caiaphas regarded the inscription angrily.

"Write not the King of the Jews, but that he said he was the King of the Jews."

Pilate looked at him wrathfully. "I have written what I have written."

I saw now what he had done. For in putting this epitaph on Christ, he had justified his own crucifixion of him while putting the blame on the Jews.

"You hated him," I cried as we stood apart, "and knew all along which way it would go. Bar-Abbas was but a sham. Why?"

In his rage, I thought he would run me through with his sword.

"Why, why, for the same reason you betrayed him, fool. Because I feared him. What we cannot control we must destroy."

"But I loved him."

"Love, what do you know of love? If you loved him, you would have wanted what he wanted."

How could this Roman judge what he stood for?

"If he were indeed the King of the Jews, you could have done him no harm."

A gleam came into the fierce eyes. "But he was the King of the Jews, and you knew him not."

He muttered under his breath.

"He boded trouble for Rome. My own centurion came to me and pleaded for his life, my wife urged me to spare him. He too much affected people. In no time at all he would be overturning tables in Rome. I know not how, but all I know is that it is true. In that solitary man there are a dozen Emperors. Now, begone, and live with what you have done, as I must as well."

As he turned away, with a last look over his shoulder at the lonely figure being led down the dusty road, I heard the blare of the trumpets from the Temple signaling the noon hour before the Passover, when the priests began to slay the paschal lamb for the sacrifice to God. And I remembered, as if it were ages before, the Baptist pointing to that lone man coming over the hill. "Behold the Lamb of God, who takes away the sins of the world."

CHAPTER EIGHTEEN

THE CROSSING

THOUGH MIDAFTERNOON, the skies had darkened and the sun, shining brightly moments before, had disappeared in banks of clouds. An uneasy hush lay in the air. The chattering of the birds had ceased, and even the vultures circling overhead had vanished.

The figures dangling on each side of Jesus had been branded as thieves. But they were actually political prisoners, ironically dying next to the man they had betrayed. On one side was the renegade disciple Dysmas, and on the other, Cestus, likewise one of the seventy, but who now berated Jesus.

"Son of God, free yourself," he cried.

Jesus appeared not to hear. Beads of sweat trickled down his face and lost themselves in his beard. His blue eyes, once so full of tenderness, were now glazed with pain. Still I could not believe, even watching his strength visibly wane, that he could not free himself whenever he chose. As a drowning man recalls the high points of his life, I remembered his telling me when I doubted him: "Fear not, Judah, raise the stone and there you will find me, cleave the rock and there I will be."

Believing the Prophets, we had believed that through him our enemies would be destroyed and Israel would enthrone the one true God on the day of final judgment.

I had hardened my heart for the challenge I put him to, but as I gazed on the suffering brow I had once kissed in reverence, I felt my heart melting.

"If I have told you earthly things and you believe not, how shall you believe if I tell you of heavenly things?"

But I had believed, I of all had believed. Why else had I challenged him? For I loved him as none of the others. My love was greater, for I demanded more of him.

And now the vulgar barbarians of Rome were spitting on him and dealing him blows. They were pleased to taunt him, offering him a cup of water, then quickly withdrawing it as he lowered his head to drink.

"If this be the King of the Jews," cried one, "no wonder the Jews are the most despised of people."

He had been on the cross for three hours, the hot sun had been beating down mercilessly on his head, bare save for its crown of thorns. The cruel spikes festered his flesh and his tortured frame stretched agonizingly on the tree to which he was nailed. I prayed to God, who had deserted him, that he would soon grant him the boon of oblivion. But, still, the end was not here.

I could almost reach out and touch the bleeding feet I would have denied the comfort of the soothing oils. How narrow and small-minded I had been to have grudged him anything, I, who was at the glorious beginning and now the dreary end. The Romans had examined my Temple credentials and let me be. Joseph of Arimathea, being accounted a friend of Pilate's because he knew his father, had been allowed to pass through the city gates to Golgotha with a party including Mary, the mother of Christ, Mary Magdalen; the mother of Mark, Nicodemus, and the disciple John. There were also the Temple dignitaries and their creatures. Otherwise there would have been none but Romans to watch him die.

The others in the throng, for fear of demonstrations, had been permitted only so far as the gates. Three had been a considerable procession, many weeping as they trailed after him. For at noon Friday, on Passover Eve, all work had ceased in the Holy City, and the Amharetzin who still cared for him had joined the march as the word spread like the wind.

I saw Susanna in the crowd, and she was sobbing as if she had lost her only friend. As usual, the wailings of the women were the loudest, and Jesus, hiding his own agony, turned to quiet their lamentations.

"Daughters of Jerusalem," he said, "weep not for me, but weep for yourselves and for your children. For, behold, the days are coming, in which they shall say, Blessed are the barren, and the wombs that never bear, and the paps which never gave suck. Then shall they begin to say to the mountains, Fall on us, and to the hills, Cover us. For if they do these things in a green tree, what shall be done in the dry?"

He could be excused his obscureness, but even so, it was plain that in his heart he was bitter, and he spoke of the great calamities that his Father would visit on an unrepentant world.

He had been compelled to bear his own cross, but then an old man, who seemed to pity him as he stumbled, asked if he could carry the cross for him. The Romans had laughed uproariously at the sight of this decrepit ancient who would take this burden upon his frail shoulders, but had agreed because of the comic figure he cut for them. I moved forward to shake this man's hand, and then I saw who it was and stopped short. It was my old foreman, Simon the Cyrene, a penitent sinner, who was to walk this last mile with the Master.

But there was none to share the cross with him now. The two on either side could not lighten his burden, nor could he help them. It pained me to watch. His cross was higher than the others, his feet dangling fully three feet from the ground, causing him almost unbearable strain. And yet, save for closing his eyes from time to time, he had given no indication of his suffering.

It was well that the Romans had banned the crowds. Otherwise the Amharetzin who loved him would surely have torn him from the cross and the Roman legions would have repaid them a thousandfold, without the result being altered in the slightest.

Happily for my own emotions, the hood concealed my face. But the others who agonized with him were not similarly shielded from the stares of the profane. I could see Joseph's tears, but John and the mother Mary were dry-eyed, though their faces were pale and pinched. They appeared to be praying. I could hear John reciting under his breath from the prophet who heralded the coming.

"He was oppressed, and he was afflicted, yet he opened not his mouth. He is brought as a lamb to the slaughter, and as a sheep before her shearers is dumb, so he opens not his mouth. He was taken from prison and from judgment. And who shall declare his generation? For he was cut off out of the land of the living. For the transgression of my people was he stricken."

The others joined in the prayer. It may have been the lowering skies, or the solemnity of the moment, but the Roman soldiers stopped their taunting of him and leaned uneasily on their spears.

"I like not that sky," said one, and in truth it had become almost like the night, as a deep purplish aura cast its ominous shadow on the earth.

"Could it really be that his God is wroth at what we do here today?"

The idea was so absurd that in their relief they fell to laughing and scuffling once more. He turned at the sound, and a groan escaped his lips. To my surprise, I saw a centurion, sternly quiet till now, approach the cross and bring a sop of wine to his mouth. I had noticed this Roman before, for all Romans looked alike to me in their helmets and cuirasses. But now with a start I saw that it was the centurion Cornelius, whose servant the Master had healed over my objections. His lips were drawn together, and he seemed paler than before but otherwise his features were set with the stony expression of the legionnaire.

He had eyes for only the one man on the cross. The others did not exist for him. They were only Jewish brigands, caught in the act of stealing. But of course it wasn't mentioned that they were captured while looting the Roman arsenals of weapons, for this would have given them distinction as patriots. The Romans made an art of degrading their enemies before destroying them.

The Syrian Cestus, who had dreamed with me of another Maccabean, railed deliriously at the Master. I forgave him, for I knew in his final throes he knew not what he was saying. "How can you save us, Jesus of Nazareth, when you cannot save yourself?"

But the other, the Idumean, Dysmas, rebuked his fellow, saying weakly: "Do you not see that he suffers for us? We should ask forgiveness for misjudging him, for he was never of our thinking. But through him we may still find salvation. Look how he faces death with a smile."

Some say the dying are given a glimmer of the truth in their last extremity. Had Dysmas been so favored on the cross? His eyes rested on the sign above Jesus' head, which said: "Jesus of Nazareth, the King of the Jews."

"Yours was a greater kingdom, and we knew it not. Lord, prepare me when you come into your kingdom."

Out of the timeless depths of his soul came an encouraging smile.

"Verily, I say unto you, that you shall dwell with me in paradise. For your faith has set you free."

Those were their last words together.

The two Zealots lapsed into a coma. They had been hanging for hours before he came to the cross. It was a major concern of the Temple authorities that all die before the sunset, so there would be no breach of the Sabbath and the Passover as well. What hypocrites they were.

As was customary, the soldiers took up cudgels to smash their legs and ribs so there would be no question of death. Cestus and Dysmas no longer showed any life. Their eyes looked out vacantly. Their jaws hung slackly, showing their parched tongues.

I thought for a moment that he had expired. But he stirred slightly at the sickening crunch of their breaking bones. No sound came from their lips. The Romans took down the bodies and prepared them for an unknown grave. They looked inquiringly at the lone figure on the uprights, but Milo, the centurion in charge, after a glance from Cornelius, shook his head.

He had languished quickly, but still hung on. It was a merciful sign that a victim should collapse on the cross in so few hours. But the High Priests, standing by, taunted him nonetheless.

"If he be the King of Israel," cried Annas, "let him now come down, and we will do him honor."

Even with the mongrels snapping at his feet, as the psalmist foretold, I had hoped that he would save himself. He had healed the sick and returned the dead to life. I had seen him feed the thousands and vanish in a crowd. Peter had watched him calm the waves and walk on water. He was a man of miracles. Was there anything he could not do? He had said that with faith in the Father we could all move mountains. And Rome certainly was no mountain. I still had thought, even as he was flogged, even as the sharp nails cut into his flesh, that he could be free with a word, a thought, a prayer. I saw his cracked lips moving, and I strained to hear him. He was reciting a psalm of David which began: "My God, my God, why has thou forsaken me?"

He seemed at an end. But even so his gaze was unwavering, dimly searching. His eyes fell finally on his mother and John. His lips forced a painful smile and, as his eyes moved on, I saw that he recognized me even with the hood over my face.

I held his gaze, beseeching him to save himself and show himself mightier than Rome. But his eyes were lifted upward now, and he continued from the psalm, not in Aramaic or Greek or Latin, but in the Hebrew of his fathers.

"I am poured out like water, and all my bones are out of joint. My heart is like wax; it is melted in the midst of my bowels.

"My strength is dried up like a potsherd, and my tongue cleaveth to my jaws, and thou hast brought me into the dust of death.

"For dogs have compassed me, the assembly of the wicked have enclosed me, they pierced my hands and feet."

The Romans clapped their thighs and laughed uproariously, pointing to "the King of the Jews" scrawled on the crossbar overhead.

Milo held up the robe given Jesus in mockery. "What am I offered for this royal cloak?"

There was more merriment in the scramble for the simple tunic he wore under the robe, and the scrubby sandals tied with a single thong. The little pastime continued with the casting of lots for the tattered garments. He must have heard them, for he murmured as though from far away:

"They part my garments among them, and cast lots upon my vesture.

"But be not thou far from me, O lord. O my strength, haste thee to help me."

His head slumped forward and he gave a great sigh. A sublime expression came over his face, as it had after the transfiguration on the mountain. There was an angelic look in his eyes, and I knew with a sad, sinking feeling that he was leaving us. His taut fingers loosened and his whole body appeared to relax. A scrap of parchment fell unnoticed from his hand.

I scooped it up, unseen, then slipped it inside my tunic.

But Caiaphas and Annas had not finished with him and were still venting their hate, for this is what motivated them.

"He saved others," cried Caiaphas, "but himself he cannot save. If he be the King of Israel, let him come down and we will believe him."

I cared not whether they knew me. "It matters not what you think, but what he is," I said in my passion.

Their noses raised in the air, and they took no notice of me.

"He called God his Father," sneered Annas, "so now let his Father deliver him. Did he not say: 'I am the Son of God'?"

I could see the defeat in the sagging shoulders and the bowed head. I saw the slight pulse in his throat. His eyes gazed out again where his mother stood with John, and he spoke in a faltering voice. "Woman, behold your son."

His eyes turned for a moment to the young disciple. "Dearly beloved, behold your mother."

The disciple took Mary's hand and nodded. She dropped to her knees before the cross and said softly: "O Lord, how I dreaded this day when my soul should be pierced, but let it be your will and not mine."

A smile came to his eyes, such a smile as I saw after he came down from the mountain and spoke of meeting the Lord.

His lips parted slightly, and he said: "Father, I thirst."

We who were with him at the well knew what he meant.

Not understanding, Joseph of Arimathea held up a beaker of wine with hyssop.

He drew his head back and sighed. "It is finished. Father, forgive them, for they know not what they do."

His head fell forward, and unbelievably, incredibly, it was over. I fought back a desire to pull him down and take him in my arms. But I could not move.

Finally, Cornelius broke the silence.

"Certainly," he said, "this was a righteous man."

Joseph of Arimathea looked into the sky, and his eyes gleamed in the murky light. His face was pale, and he spoke in awed tones:

"The star is the same that I saw at his birth."

I looked and could see but one star in the heavens. It was a fiery red, almost the color of blood, and it was set in a giant white cloud in the shape of a cross.

I saw Joseph of Arimathea cross himself, and I knew then that my eyes had not deceived me. He had seen the same sign.

It was now almost totally dark, and the very skies seemed to be dropping on our heads. The Romans held up their hands, as if shielding themselves from the heavens, then cowered on their knees, all but Cornelius, praying fervidly to Jupiter and Apollo.

Cornelius' eyes gleamed in the darkness. He seemed transfixed, as if he had seen a vision.

"He lives," he cried. "I see him in his Father's arms, and there is a smile in his eyes. I tell you, he lives."

The soldiers looked at him as if he were mad. And then the one who called himself Crito, a Syrian mercenary who had laughed loudest at Jesus, picked up a spear and quickly thrust the point into the Master's left side before any could stop him.

"Now you are dead," he shouted, "you King of Satan."

I watched the blood dribble out, and then came a flow of water, as if from a fount. In my anguish, I saw Jesus, as I had first seen him, standing quietly before the Baptist, as the water splattered over him.

A cold wind blew against my face. The trees trembled and bent low before the heavy gusts stirring the air.

Cornelius pushed aside the mercenary and tenderly cut down the body while Joseph of Arimathea came forward to claim it in the name of Jesus' friends.

My brain was in turmoil, but dimly I still saw Caiaphas and Annas, laughing together as if the world had not ended. I remembered Jesus saying to turn the other cheek. But, oh, how I hated them at that moment, and desired their destruction.

The heavens were rumbling now, and daggers of lightning rent the darkness. Cornelius and John, with Nicodemus, were helping Joseph with the Master's body.

I had moved off to a side of the mound, away from Joseph and Nicodemus, and paid little attention to the discussion over the burial. What difference did it make, now that he was dead? He was gone and with him the dream of a victorious Israel. Rome had won as always, and Pilate would be praised.

I found myself alone. The bodies had been removed, and the executioners had hurried off before the threatening storm. The remains of Dysmas and Cestus were bound for criminal pits. I no longer had any heart for the insurrection. For who else would the people follow?

I had to keep moving. I needed to talk to somebody, to anybody who knew him as I had, who would understand that I meant him no harm.

I took the path to the city by the Gennath Gate and soon overtook the mourners. Mary Magdalen had been weeping, and his mother had her arms about her, consoling her. The other Mary, the mother of Mark, walked silently between John and Nicodemus. Joseph had hurried off to prepare the sacred ground.

At my footsteps, John's soft eyes turned in my direction. I had the impulse to speak to him. Of all the disciples he was the gentlest, the most imbued with the word of Christ.

He stared for a moment, then fell back as if stung by a serpent.

"Judas," he cried between his teeth, "traitor, thief, apostate, murderer. How do you live when he whom you slew with a kiss lies cold and still?"

"He told us he would live forever in his Father's house. I knew not what he meant He would know this and forgive me if he were here."

"There is no forgiveness for him by whose offense he left this earth. Woe unto you by whom this offense came."

He pulled up the hem of his robe with an expression of loathing.

The mother laid her hand on the disciple's arm. "He said that no man took his life. It was prophesied of old. From his birth, I feared this day."

John's face was rigid. "Let those forgive who can."

"Think of how he would have you be." She gave a little sigh. "Though my heart is heavy, I feel him about me now."

John took her arm. "Let the traitor live, but let him take himself out of our sight."

Mary Magdalen eyed me bitterly. "I forgive Caiaphas and Annas, even Pilate and the rest. They hated him because he held the love of the people, and they knew not what he might do with it. But you, Judas, he trusted as his own." Her gaze held mine without compassion.

"From him to whom much is given, much should be received." How often had I heard him say this.

"What," she asked, "did he receive from you?"

A moan escaped my lips. "He forgave your sins, Mary Magdalen. Can you not forgive mine?"

"Not while the memory of that body stretched on the cross is still fresh in my mind."

She had learned nothing from him.

Nicodemus and the mother of Mark were too overcome to do more than listen.

"Let him be," said Nicodemus finally, "he is not the only sinner among us."

The Master's mother touched me lightly on the forehead. "Had it not been you," she whispered, "it would have been another. He knew this."

It had all been prophesied, the spear stabbed deep info his side, and his bones left unbroken, even the thirty pieces of silver, but would that it had been another. Had they not prophesied forgiveness as well? But first one must repent, and how did one repent what was only a mistake?

My thoughts were in turmoil. If he was not what we thought, then what was he? Perhaps another Simon the Magician, who, they say, had flown like a bird? What kind of Messiah was it to whom Jew and Gentile were alike? His beloved John had called him the only begotten Son of God. But when the Sadducees tried to trap him with their story of the widow wed to seven brothers, he said that in heaven all were equally children of God.

I had committed no betrayal. Anybody could see that if they only knew how it had all begun. But to whom was I to turn? My mother was always sympathetic until Rachel spoiled what had been. If only I could speak to her. And why not? She would not have returned to the house if she still resented me.

It was not a long way. And from the Gennath Gate, I ran headlong all the way, until, winded, I came to the house. It felt strange to knock on the door of my own home, but I was uneasy now about my reception, for everybody seemed to misunderstand. I was no bar-Abbas, or Cestus or Dysmas. They had not cared as I had.

A servant responded to my knock.

"Your mother will be pleased," he said, trying not to show his surprise. "She is in her room."

I was not prepared for the changes that little more than two and a half years had wrought. Her face was faded and worn, her eyes tired and distant, her step slow and unsure. "I am glad you have come," she said. "I know not how long it will be before I join your father. It is all I ask now."

I moved forward to kiss her cheek, and she stepped back. "Let me look at you first." She seemed satisfied by what she saw. "It has not been easy for you, has it?"

I wanted to fling my arms about her, and bury my head in her lap, and weep as I had when I was a child and hurt. But there was something about her manner that restrained me. Rachel had come irrevocably between us.

I saw the table set for the Passover feast.

"Will you not take your place at the head of the table?"

I could only think of that other Passover feast, twenty-four hours earlier.

"I must go on," I said.

"Where do you go on this Passover night? You look distraught, stay and rest."

I could contain myself no longer. "They killed him, Mother. The Romans killed him, and he did not resist."

"Who? Who do you speak of?"

Her voice was oddly listless.

"Jesus of Nazareth, the Messiah, the Lamb of God."

She nodded vaguely. "Gamaliel has told me of him. He says he was a good and Godly man. It is too bad." She sighed. "But then these are troubled times, and many good people perish. It is well, Judah, that we Pharisees believe in the life hereafter. It is surely sweeter than this vale of tears."

I liked not the detachment I saw in her, it was like speaking to the door. Something seemed to have died in her since I saw her last.

I looked around the room.

"And Rachel, where is she?"

I had dreaded the thought of seeing her, but now that she was not cloying over me or giving me a sad-eyed gaze of reproach, I was content to see her.

"Rachel?" she said dimly. "I have not seen her for two years."

"Where could she have gone?" I wondered, for she had no friends besides us.

She looked at me with glazed eyes. "She is dead."

"Dead?" My heart skipped a beat.

"She killed herself."

"Killed herself, but why?" I was stunned to silence, and then my mind became like a roaring maelstrom, torn apart by its very activity. In my frenzy, I felt like pounding the walls. "Why should this beautiful young girl end her life? She had everything to live for."

Her eyes stared at me vacantly. "She died of her shame."

"It was not that great a scandal," I cried. "None knew of it but us."

"And, hopefully, the God above, who will give her the pity she could not find on earth."

"It was not my fault, Mother."

"Nobody has blamed you."

"Your eyes find me guilty."

"You convict yourself, Judah."

"But what was so shameful?" I thought of Mary Magdalen. "Others have experienced as much and gone on with their lives."

She looked at me as if I were a stranger.

"She carried your child. How many others have had this experience?"

I looked at her incredulously, and I felt my hair rise on end. "My child? Impossible."

"Think back and you will not find it that impossible."

"Why did you not send for me?" I pleaded with her now.

"Why should she be twice rejected?"

"I would have come back, I would have married her, I would have done anything."

She looked at me with a pitying expression. "And broken your sacred vows? Did you not make it plain what was important?" She shook her head. "No, she stood all that she could stand. Let us pray that God is more merciful than man."

I hesitated, but I had to know.

"And how did she die?"

I saw now a tear in her eye. "Does it matter?"

"I know not why, but it does, very much."

Her small voice trembled. "She hanged herself."

I fell back as if I had been hit by a pole.

"May God have mercy on her soul."

She did not appear to have heard me.

"Stay for the Passover," she said, "and go in the morning, if you like. This night is not fit for any man."

I could hear the rumble of thunder overhead, and the house shook. The night matched my mood. I felt wounded and stricken, as though my heart had been rent from my body. Where could I find the peace I sought? If only I could reach out and touch his hand. Only he could understand, and he, unbelievably, was gone.

I got to my feet, dazed, and passed my hand over my throbbing brow. "I must go, I cannot stay in this house, it is full of her."

The tears now filled her eyes. "And he who was sent to the cross. Where can you go to forget him?"

"You knew something more about him?"

"All Israel knew about him, and many cared, but they did not care enough." She shook her head. "Poor Rachel, some cared for her, but not enough."

I turned on my heel and fled, I could stand no more. Never would I see my mother again, that I knew, nor could I think of Rachel, even in sorrow, for another face, sometimes gentle, sometimes stern, but always understanding, crowded everything else from my mind.

The streets were deserted, the inhabitants taking shelter from the storm and marking the holiday. In every home they were preparing the paschal feast, doubly sacred because it was joined with the Sabbath. In a hundred windows I saw the candlelights. I had meant to bear right, along the western wall, but instead turned for no reason by the Joppa Gate in an easterly direction. The sky was almost pitch black now, the thunder so close and ominous. I ran through the dark streets, stumbling in my confusion, until the Temple ramparts loomed dimly in front of me. It was so dark I could barely see the towers. There were no guards on the walls, for they, like the others, were observing the Holy Day. I raced through the Court of Gentiles, empty now of worshippers and priests alike. Even the shopkeepers had locked up and left. But the place was still alive with memories: the stones on which he trod, the tables he overturned, and in the Portico of Solomon the shady area where he had sat and meditated.

I stood alone in that vast concourse and felt the urge to cry out against those who had sent him to be slaughtered. They would be judged as they judged him, cursed till the day of the final judgment.

"Anna, Caiaphas," I shouted to the rooftops, "this Temple shall be pulled down over your heads. You shall wander homeless until the days of retribution, for you have slain him by whom there was salvation. May God pity you and yours for the generations to come. For no others shall."

My voice rang out in the silence, and the echo came back hauntingly in the words of the prophet Isaiah, in a voice like that I had heard long before on the banks of the river Kedron.

"He is despised and rejected of men, a man of sorrows, and acquainted with grief. And we hid, as it were, our faces from him. The chastisement of our peace was upon him, and with his stripes we are healed."

There was a tremor under my feet. The stones shook, and the Temple, revealed in a brilliant flash of lightning, rocked a moment, then settled back with a groan. I drew closer to the great wall, thinking to be buried under its ruins. But the trembling of the earth stopped, the heavens opened up, and the rain fell as if the skies themselves were weeping.

There was still no life. It was almost as if the Temple priests and the soldiers cowered in their corners, to escape a just retribution. But there must be something there, for it was the custom for certain favored priests and Levites to take the Passover feast at the Temple. From the Court of Gentiles, passing the sign which forbade any but Israelites to proceed further, I passed into the Court of Israel, and then the Court of Priests, and there, looking up, saw a feeble light flickering in a window. I bounded up the steps, past the room where I had sat with the High Priests, and stopped before a door guarded by two soldiers. I showed my credentials. "I am expected," I said haughtily.

They looked at me doubtfully, taking in my wet and bedraggled appearance. "It will go badly with you if you do not admit me. I bear an urgent message."

Boldness won out.

I saw first the surprised countenance of the crafty Annas. He sat at the head of the table and was flanked by Caiaphas and, of all people, my great benefactor, Gamaliel. By this time I was incapable of surprise, though Gamaliel had the grace to blush. I could see they had not yet begun the feast. I looked around the table, thinking of another supper, and counted thirteen. It seemed a fit number for such an occasion.

Gamaliel stood up, and I thought for a sickening moment he was about to apologize. Instead, he said, with a quiet dignity which I found misplaced: "He had to die to save the nation, of that I became convinced."

"How readily you change partners," I cried. "My father would not know this double-dealer."

Annas moved angrily to summon the guards but was stopped by an authoritative wave of Gamaliel's hand.

"If the Sanhedrin had never raised a finger, he would still have died, because Rome willed it."

"Rome," I cried, "did not try him on trumped-up charges."

"There is no room in Israel for two Gods, or two Kings. Pilate knew what he must do from the beginning."

I tired of their duplicity. "The Roman wavered and looked for some pretext to free an innocent man, but the High Priests and their lackeys would not have it so."

"Do you think the Pilate that massacred the guileless Galileans in the sacred precincts of the Temple cared for a moment what the Sanhedrin did about a single Jew?"

"I saw him look for another way."

"It was but a show he put on, as you well know."

"For whose benefit, if he cares not what we think?"

A shadow darkened Gamaliel's long face. "For the benefit of those who come after him." He paid no heed to the growing murmur of impatience around the table. "He knew the Nazarene was no ordinary man and came for no ordinary reason."

"And how did this insensitive Roman know that?"

"They do not rule, Judah, because they are insensitive. Somehow they get to the heart of a matter quicker than we." It was almost a reprimand. "In the captive eyes of his own people, he could see the future, if he let live this light to the Gentiles."

As Gamaliel spoke, I had become calmer. "You mean," I spoke scornfully, "if he came but for the Jews, Pilate would not have intervened?"

"Most likely not, even though it gives him pleasure to frustrate and torment us whenever he can."

So it had seemed at the time, but just now I could not accept any of this, not with the Master gone, and they pleasantly celebrating the deliverance of an Israel now forever in chains.

My hand reached into my tunic, slid over the parchment that had slipped out of his fingers, and then found the pouch with the thirty pieces of silver.

"How dare you give me this blood money? I have sinned only in my own innocence. I will have no part of this filthy lucre." I flung the pouch across the table to where Caiaphas sat scowling blackly. "Give it to him who deserves it," I cried.

Some of the silver pieces flew out of the bag and rattled across the floor.

"Out with you," shouted Caiaphas in a fury. "What is it to us how innocent you proclaim yourself? We all know what you have done, and your reasons matter not, for actions speak more than words. But this money shall never go back to the treasury. For it is blood money, and it is not lawful to keep this reminder of your perfidy."

"My perfidy," I shouted. "I am innocent, I swear it to the world. He wanted to die, to fulfill the prophecies of old. He said so himself."

The guards now came and took me by the arms to drag me off. In my desperation, breaking away, I stood and cursed the priests and elders with a passion.

"May what you have done stick in your throats, not only on this feast night, but until the end of time."

I fled down the stairs, thinking terrible thoughts. My mind was so restless that my body compulsively kept pace with it. I started running, and kept running until I came to the Golden Gate, which enters onto the Garden of Gethsemane.

The trees creaked and groaned in the wind, but otherwise nothing broke the grave-like stillness. I moved toward the abandoned warehouse where Joshua-bar-Abbas and the others had so valiantly described their plans to bedevil Rome to the death. I was irrepressibly drawn to the place where I had made my first impassioned cry for freedom. The weathered door creaked as I opened it, and the sound startled me. I strained my eyes in the darkness and saw a shadow near the front of the room. It moved ever so slightly, and I found myself jumping nervously as though at a ghost. Drawing closer, I heard a rasping noise, as if from heavy breathing, and the shadow seemed to bob up and down. It was the muffled sobbing of a man. I let out a cry: "Who sits there in this accursed spot? Rise and show yourself." I was afraid of no man, shadow or substance, for of what import was my life now? The figure stood up and in a burst of lightning through the gaping holes in the roof, I recognized the last man I expected to see in this forlorn place. His back was bowed, the shoulders slumped, and the strength appeared to have gone out of him.

His head was sunk in his hands, and he appeared not to care that any had arrived.

I shook him roughly.

"What brings you here, traitor?" I cried.

He looked up and even in the gloom I could see the defeat in every line of the churlish countenance.

Joshua-bar-Abbas gave me a blank stare.

"Nobody came," he said apathetically. "They were to have met me here, but they are all gone. Cestus and Dysmas, on the cross, the others trapped and cut down like rats. You are the only Zealot to show up, even Simon Zelotes is not here as promised."

I shrank from him in horror. "Idiot, I came not for any meeting. The insurrection died with Christ, and you helped to kill it with your treachery."

"Whatever else," he said with a glimmering spark, "I resisted the Romans at every turn."

"You betrayed all, the perfect traitor."

"Who are you to call me traitor?" he cried. "You believed in him and still betrayed him. To me he was never more than a magician who could hypnotize the gullible with this alien gift of his. Had he been the Messiah, he would not have left us when we wanted him for our King."

I looked at him, stunned. So that was how the world would see me, unless I corrected this misconception before the others condemned me out of their envy because of the place I held with him. Before I left this place I had to make sure that all those who came after me would know of my love for him.

"Listen closely, bar-Abbas, for one day you may be called upon to testify for Judah-bar-Simon. This is my final testament, so again I say, heed me well.

"From my first memory I dreamed of a Messiah. I stood in the Holy Temple and implored God that these eyes of mine might behold his Promised. My heart was uplifted before I became a man at the age of thirteen, for in my soul I heard his assurance that I would see his Son.

"I encountered Joshua-bar-Joseph in a little town on the Jordan when I was searching for the Messiah. I had dreamt that I saw him, all glorious and beautiful, radiant with holiness and the Godhead, and when I saw him in truth I believed it was he.

"I left my house and my mother and my estates for him. I followed him and exulted in him, and his words were as sweet as the juice of a pomegranate, and as living as honey and as fulfilling as milk and manna, and as tender as the flesh of the date. I saw his miracles, and heard the resonance of his great voice, and all who saw him were amazed, even those who hated him. Yet he carried no golden rod of authority and power, no carved ivory staff, and there was no crown on his head. But my heart leapt at the sight of him, my soul rejoiced, and I said in my heart: 'He has come!' A poor carpenter, they said of him, a man of no consequence, a barefoot rabbi, a peasant, a humble creature. But how grand he was. How could a member of the poorest and the meanest, the despised, a Nazarene, possess such a presence? I doubted at first, for was it not promised that on his appearance Israel would be delivered, and Zion would be illuminated like the sun and the world would prostrate itself before him and cry 'Hosanna!'

"None loved him as I loved him. None who followed him was as I, a Pharisee of a noble family, a man of wealth and gold, honored in the holy places. The others were miserable people of no learning and family. I suffered agonies of impatience when they could not understand his words, which, though apparently simple, were profound and strange and oblique. But I understood. There were times when the others bent their foolish heads and silently mouthed his words, and shook their ragged locks, but he looked at me and faintly smiled and knew that I understood what he had said. Then my soul would burn with joy at the meeting of our eyes, and I was exalted and we exchanged smile for smile, though his smile was shadowed with sadness. He would then avert his head, and a peculiar coldness would paralyze me and I wondered. What had I done to offend him, he the fiery core of my heart, the life of my soul? The glory of his face proclaimed in its radiance that here was in truth the Messiah, and he was no mere man of the street rabble, of the dusty places of Nazareth. Here, I said to myself, was the priest of all priests, the God of the universe, the King of Kings, clad in might and honor, divine and elevated to the throne.

"How dared the rabble touch him, speak with him, walk in his footsteps, importune him, follow him, hold up their miserable children for his blessing, put their hands on his garments? How dared they ask him to cure their sick? Among them were the very Roman centurions and their officers, and even the judges and the Scribes, and often, to my amazement, my fellow Pharisees. How dared the humble offer him wine and fruit and dates and bread and fish and meat? It was an offense that cried to God for punishment for the sacrilege. Why did he condescend to walk into the houses of the tax gatherers, the oppressors hired by the Romans to afflict starving Israel, those who took the very bread from the mouths of the Jews? They were criminals, these tax gatherers, who, for a few shekels, drove their fellow Jews to penury and despair. Yet he suffered them and had compassion for these jackals, these most accursed of God—these whores of the Romans!

"Would God have pity on those who afflicted his people? Once I spoke of this, and he said: 'The righteous have their own reward in their souls, but the evil must be lifted from darkness and delivered to the light.' Then he gazed at me, and there was great sorrow in his beautiful eyes.

"When he was arrested by the Romans and the Temple guards, I rejoiced, for I said in my heart: 'Now he will repulse them. Now he will reveal himself; Now he will expand in his majesty and all will know him! I have forced his hand! If they touch him they will die! Angelic hosts will descend to guard him and bear him away! God will not permit his Son to be befouled by the hands of men!"

"But he went with them meekly. I saw his degradation, his whipping, heard the revilements of the mob, heard the laughter of the rabble. I also saw the aristocratic sneer of Pilate, his lifted lip, his shrug. I pondered Pilate's obscure remarks before he turned away."

All this now poured out of my love for him, and my sorrow, and it was comforting that at last I found someone who would listen, even if he was but a traitor.

I looked up finally and saw that bar-Abbas had not moved. His head was bowed, and he seemed to be staring at the floor. He had not heard a word.

"Do you hear me?" I cried.

He barely shrugged. "But who hears me?"

"You cared not for him, nor even for Israel, or you would not have traded his life for your own."

He groaned. "He did not die for me. If not I, it would have been another."

I started at his words, for this his mother had said, and this I had been telling myself. It was small comfort when I heard it from the lips of a knave himself.

"He looked farther than Rome, bar-Abbas, beyond this speck our minds had made a mountain. We were preoccupied with petty principles, and he would have none. In this way, I suppose, he betrayed us. For when we asked him to kill Romans and deliver us from them, he said: 'I go to deliver them who through fear of death are all their lifetime subject to bondage.'

"He promised he would come again, to show there was no death, but if he is as powerless as before, what more can he do in a cruel, spiteful world? You were there, bar-Abbas, when I questioned him about his coming back. Don't you remember what he said? 'And it shall come to pass in that day, that the Lord shall set his hand again the second time to recover the remnant of his people. And he shall set up an ensign for the nations, and shall assemble the outcasts of Israel, and gather together the dispersed of Judah from the four corners of the earth.'"

Bar-Abbas gave me a dull stare.

"You look for forgiveness, Judah, but you will find none. For the one man that would have forgiven you is he whom you killed."

How dare this traitor speak like this, for if I erred it was only in good faith.

"Will you manufacture yourself another Messiah?" I said, stung into recalling the words spoken at this very spot.

With a cry like a wounded animal, bar-Abbas leaped to his feet, and without a word flung himself out of the building. I chased after him, but it was to no avail. He had disappeared into the night, having done his evil and too late repented. The Garden of Gethsemane seemed to hem me in. I could barely breathe. I found myself in the very olive grove, under a gnarled old tree, where I had last kissed him. I looked up at the strong branches. Was it on such a tree, I wondered, that Rachel had hanged herself? It was all over with me as well, that I knew. What can a man do but die when an encompassing dream is destroyed in one moment? When a man has devoted his life to that dream, and there is none other, not wife or children, not parents or kin, not joy in life, not celebration of living, not even the miserable reality of the world and its dark wisdom, and that dream dissolved in the ashes of nothingness, is there aught for him but oblivion and endless unbeing? How can a man endure when his life has lost its meaning and there is nothing but a trackless desert remaining all of the years of his life?

But, as I stand here below the tree under which I will die, I cannot help but wonder. Is he indeed the Messiah? Is he indeed the hope of man, the Promise of God? Have I deceived myself, or is he the Truth?

In death only is the answer. My question may be answered. It may not. In any event, I will be at peace.

As I moved, my hand rubbed against my tunic, and I recalled the scrap of parchment that had dropped out of his hand at Calvary. In the light of a candle, by which I had been feverishly writing, I saw, with a feeling of disappointment, that it was but one of the psalms. I would have wanted more to remember him by. Even as I looked up again at the tree, and tied my tunic into a knot, I wondered why he had carried these words to the cross with him.

"The Lord is my shepherd," I read, "I shall not want.

"He maketh me to lie down in green pastures, he leadeth me beside the still waters. He restoreth my soul, he leadeth me in the paths of righteousness for his name's sake.

"Yea, though I walk through the valley of the shadow of death, I will fear no evil, for thou art with me. Thy rod and thy staff they comfort me.

"Thou prepareth a table before me in the presence of mine enemies.

"Thou anointest my head with oil, my cup runneth over.

"Surely, goodness and mercy shall follow me all the days of my life, and I will dwell in the house of the Lord forever."

And so perished he whom the prophet called Wonderful, the Counselor, the mighty God, the everlasting Father, the Prince of Peace. But let no man put his death on my head. And let he who calls me traitor first search his own heart well, for each time a man sins he puts another nail into that cross on the hill of Golgotha, known by the Romans as Calvary.

I go forward hopefully, for the prophet said that of the increase of Christ's kingdom there would be no end. And so, hoping to join him, I wait for that time when the earth shall shake and the very mountains fall into the sea, and we shall see his sign once more in the sky.

Then we shall know that he is with us, and all mankind will rejoice, even amid the desolation, for the last battle will be fought at a place called Armageddon, and the last enemy destroyed shall be death itself. For all men will know then that he ascended the cross for the salvation of us all, and to show life everlasting. This is my last testament, and if any man take away from any part of it, so shall as much be taken from his own life. I come quickly, dear God, as even so came Jesus. Accept me, Lord, for I sinned in my pride, and in that pride, I knew not what I did. May Jesus Christ be with all, as he was with me. Amen.

EPILOGUE

The Testimony of a Certain Disciple by His Own Eyes and As Given to Him by Mary of Magdala, Sister of Lazarus and Martha, and One Who Knew Jesus of Nazareth As the Lord and Loved Him More Than Life Itself.

MARY OF MAGDALA had not slept since the execution two days before. Her grief and desolation were complete; she was numbed by sorrow. Clouds of thoughts and anguish blew through her mind like dust; she could never gather them into order and coherence. She would sit on her bed gnawing her knuckles, her head bent; her hair falling about her face like a burnished curtain, her features as blank as a desert stone which had been scoured by harsh winds and sand through the centuries. She had not, since that terrible day before the Passover, eaten or drunk. Her soul was in abeyance, dulled and empty. The sun came, the sun departed; there were voices outside her little house, the querulous complaints of camels, the skittering of donkeys' hoofs, the call of a distant trumpet, men's laughter, children's insistent demandings, women's scuffling on the stones. A few times there were knocks on her door; she did not heed anything at all. The lantern beside her bed flickered, then went out, and darkness crept into the chamber. She sat in the gloom and did not notice. The sun returned glittering through the coarse curtain across the window. It struck her wringing hands and she did not see or feel it. The apathy of despair had brought her a living death. There were hours when she was aware of nothing, not even of herself, as if in a swoon.

Then, as if she had heard an imperative and beloved voice, she awakened from her stupor and looked about her. It was becoming dark again; the lantern was cold and dead. She stood up, throwing back her tangled hair. She still had no thoughts, no purpose. She saw her soiled hands and felt the grit of sand between her teeth. She washed without thought in the warm and stagnant water in the bowl near her bed. She was like a wooden-jointed figure on a tiny stage, the amusement of the Romans which she had seen in the bazaars, a figure moved by a will not her own and without volition. She lit the lantern; it was as if they were dreaming. But the echoes of the imperative voice moved in her hollow mind, and she obeyed without thought. The lantern gave off a foul and smoky odor, and its wan light roved restlessly about the little chamber, as if seeking it knew not what. There was a knocking on her door and her heavy legs moved to answer. But there was no one outside, only the darkness and the distant red flickering of torches and the endless movements of lanterns through the streets. A woman, or a child, was wailing nearby.

Still moving heavily, she picked up her lantern and left the house. The darkness was becoming deeper, the torch and lantern light more vivid. She glanced up at the sky, blinking; the moon was declining in the west. In a very few hours it would be morning. Morning, she thought, sluggishly. What is morning to me, who am dead? How much time had passed? Was this the second or the third day since her Life had died, when the universe had become only a skull, uninhabited? Her feet moved without her will, in a direction she had not consciously taken. The houses about her were lightless and closed, and now there were no voices, no running feet. She dimly heard the trumpets of the Romans sounding on the walls of Jerusalem, counting the hour. There was a drumming, like thunder, from the Roman garrisons.

Her head bowed, her feet moving wearily, she went on. She did not know how long this was; there were only shadows about her, capering with the torches in their apertures along the walls. Even her bones were like lead, and it exhausted her to stir her body. The lantern wavered in her hand; her cloak fell about her like the garments of the dead, the hood hiding her expressionless face, which seemed carved of unsentient marble. For a long time she walked, like a shade without substance and without life. Then, abruptly, she came alive and the world rushed in on her, huge with sound and being, and faintly she cried aloud in pain. She almost dropped her lantern.

She was standing in the wild and dark and lonely garden, not far from the tomb where her Life had been laid in cloths pungent with oils and spices. How long ago had that occurred? Eras ago, ages ago? The Roman soldiers, jesting and sweating, had rolled that enormous stone before the aperture of the somber tomb, and she had watched despairingly with the others, and at length had turned away with them, weeping but without speaking; and in silence, they had dispersed, one by one.

She stood still, staring about her with new agony and awareness. The bloated moon, which had turned to a bright yellow over the western hills, jaundiced the black cypresses, the leafing sycamores, the karobs, the scattered and half-wild silvery olive trees, the broken walls, the myrtles with their purple flowers, the faint gravel paths, the wind-struck palms, and sent long dense shadows over the tangled high grass. Here all was desolation and loneliness; not even a night bird cried. It was very still, as if the world had caught a deep breath and was holding it in fear. She could see the saffron walls of the city, winding and ancient, and the far pillars of the Temple, all citron-tinted under the moon.

Terror seized her, but she could not compel her body to retreat. She stared into the distance toward the tomb. Was it only her imagination in that haunted place that she saw a shifting white illumination through the trees? She knew that Roman soldiers were guarding the tomb lest the followers of her Lord steal away the body and then proclaim that he had risen. But only she knew, in her suffering, that not even his disciples and Apostles believed truly in his divinity. Had they not slept when he had pleaded for their comfort and company in the Garden of Gethsemane? Had they not, in weariness or sloth, deserted him? On what frail earth had he raised his altar? She shivered and whispered to herself: "Do I believe?" She had no answer. She continued to stare at the distant illumination which seemed to gather strength and breadth. It was not red or fluttering, therefore it was not the fires and the torches of the soldiers, and it was not the light of the lemonish moon.

She found herself helplessly moving toward it. The scent of disturbed grass rose, but the trees remained rigid, like groups of guardians, watching. Now the light became more intense; trunks of trees seemed to ripple in it. She could hear her own heartbeat in her throat and her ears; her flesh trembled. Now she was not so fearful of the light. It drew her, impelled her. She reached the edge of the clearing in the wild garden—which was without the gates of the city—and what she saw stupefied her and filled her with both awe and dread.

For the tomb glowed with white radiance while all about it lay uncertain and shifting darkness. Every pebble and stone in the clearing was struck with light, and treetops and trunks reflected the brilliance which lay on the tomb, almost as bright as the sun. She took several steps toward it, fascinated and quivering, until her foot struck against something and she fell back in terror. She saw now that the soldiers lay in the grass, fallen as if struck by lightning, the brilliance catching an iron-shod boot here, a wristlet there, a helmet flung aside, a shield on the earth, the hilt of a sword, the side of an unconscious cheek, a glimmer of breastplate. She had touched a soldier with her foot in the darkness, but he had not awakened. Her first confused thought was that they lay sleeping from drunkenness, but a young profile just before her was that of a man deep in a trance, scarcely breathing.

She lifted her dazed eyes and saw, for the first time, the black aperture of the blazing tomb, and she saw, disbelieving, that the stone had been rolled away from it. She gasped, putting her cold hand to her mouth.

She suddenly found herself running, fleet and random as a rabbit, away from the tomb and into the darkness, her arms flung out to keep herself from falling, her hood on her shoulders, her hair tumbling behind her, her eyes distended and glittering. Without consciously directing herself, she ran wildly, seeking the house of Simon Peter, where he sat in mourning with the disciple who was beloved of the Lord and the youngest of them all. Stones and pebbles bruised her feet; broken thorn branches clutched at her cloak. Now only the yellow light of the moon illuminated her way. Cold drops ran down her cheeks; she was weeping and moaning.

She came upon the rambling little street where Simon Peter stopped in a miserable house. A ragged curtain almost concealed the window; she saw lamplight around its edges. Frantically she beat her fists on the splintered door, calling out: "Simon Peter, Simon Peter! Open!"

There was muttering within, frightened muttering, then the door was cautiously opened to show the strained face of Simon Peter with its coarse black beard, and his rough tunic and leather belt. Beyond him she saw the slight and youthful John sitting on the bed in an attitude of absolute dejection, his handsome boy's face scoured with grief and tears. He lifted his head to stare at her in the dim lamplight and half rose.

"Mary!" said Simon Peter, and rubbed his dry lips. "What is this? Why are you here?"

She cried out: "They have taken away the Lord out of the sepulcher, and we know not where they have laid him!"

Simon's hand dropped from his lips. He gazed at her as at a madwoman. "How do you know this?" he demanded.

"I was there, in the garden, and I saw the tomb—" Her breath choked. She wrung her hands. "There was a great light on it—I could see! The soldiers—they were asleep, or drunk, or dead—! And the stone—the stone—had been pushed aside—It was not at the mouth of the sepulcher—they had moved it!"

"Who had moved it?" said Peter. His browned cheeks had become pale.

She wrung her hands again, frenziedly. "I do not know!" she exclaimed. "But they have done this thing. They have taken away the Lord—!"

Confused and silent now, Simon turned to look at the young disciple, who had risen and was coming toward them. Then they both looked at the distraught young woman and her agonized white face and her tears.

"Surely," said John in a voice roughened by sobbing, "this cannot be." He looked about him as if searching for something in a dream. "He is dead. What use could they have for his body? A jest—an evil jest." His hand reached for a lantern and he lit it from the lamp. Its feeble gleam illuminated their distracted and benumbed faces. "Let us go to the sepulcher," he muttered.

The three ran together through the dark and hilly streets, past closed shutters and hidden windows. There was a sudden howling of pariah dogs and jackals from the steep banks beneath the walls of the city. A Roman trumpet sounded the hour. An aromatic wind was rising, filled with warm dust. John, younger than Peter, soon outstripped him. Simon's sandals pounded heavily on the stones, which glistened under the moon. She, disheveled and panting, stumbled behind them, her sandals flapping on her feet.

They ran together through the garden, so overwhelmed by the news that they scarcely noticed the fallen soldiers illuminated now only by the swollen yellow moon. For the tomb was no longer afire as if lit by the sun itself. They stood a moment, and the men saw that the huge stone had indeed been rolled aside, and the black mouth of the aperture gaped at them. John held his lantern aloft. He crept fearfully to the opening and looked within while Simon and Mary stood by, shaking like reeds in a wind. Stooping, thrusting forward the lantern the better to see, John stared at the empty stone shelf on which the Lord had been laid. He could not believe his eyes. Slowly he shifted the lantern about, searching, then returned its dim light to the shelf. No body lay there. What remained were only the acrid burial cloths and the white linen napkin which had covered his head. The warmth within flowed out to John, laden with the scent of burial oils, aromatics, and spices.

Simon came forward, pushed John aside roughly, and entered the sepulcher to see what John had seen at the doorway. “It is true,” he murmured in bewildered sorrow. “He is not here.”

The two men, stricken anew, stood and looked at each other, forgetful of Mary, unaware of her. Then Simon and John, blinded by fresh grief, left her and moved toward the encompassing trees, the lantern light following them like a ghost. Soon the sounds of their passing and the lantern light were lost and she was alone and filled with dread. A deeper hush surrounded her. Walking with trepidation, she approached the mouth of the tomb, then halted, overcome with a terror she had never known before. She forced herself to bend, and she looked within.

She saw what neither Simon nor John had seen. She saw the great white figures before her, one sitting at the head of the shelf, the other at the foot, the grave cloths between them. They were the figures of men, clothed in shimmering light, but they were larger than men and their faces were beautiful and lofty, far removed from mankind and as still as alabaster. They regarded her in a long silence, while she, paralyzed, could only stare whitely at them.

Then one spoke, and his voice was like distant thunder. “Woman, why do you weep?” His words were compassionate, but his was not a human voice and it evoked unfamiliar echoes.

She stammered, holding to the side of the aperture, “Because they have taken away my Lord, and I know not where they have laid him.” Her terror increased, for she sensed that she was not dealing with anything human, and the remote faces affrighted her.

It was this fright which gave her strength, and she ran from the tomb and the clearing, stumbling over the bodies of the sleeping Roman soldiers, crying deep in her throat, sometimes falling, then rising to stagger on again in her frantic terror.

Finally she could not go on. She had fallen once more and could rise only to her knees, her throat burning, her hands torn by sharp pebbles. She covered her eyes briefly, to shut out the light of the terrible moon, and struggled to breathe. Then, cowering, she heard the rustle of a bush and the slightest sound of footsteps. She dropped the corner of her cloak from her eyes and looked with fresh fear over her shoulder. A tall dark shadow stood near her, and she shrank back, whimpering in her throat.

She heard the voice of a man speaking gently. "Woman, why do you weep? Whom do you seek?"

The voice was full of pity and kindness, but distant, and she thought that he must be one of the gardeners. She tried to control herself but could not speak for a moment or two. At last she could whisper: "Sir, if you have borne him hence, tell me where you have laid him, and I will take him away."

There was a little silence. Mary, without thinking, leaned imploringly toward the shadow, no longer so affrighted.

Then he said: "Mary!"

She could not believe what she had heard, she could not believe who had spoken. She tried to rise but fell back on her knees, her face alight with vivid rapture, her hands clasped, her head thrown back, her mouth shaking.

"Rabbi!" she cried. She stretched out her hands to him, to seize his robe. Now she saw his aspect, palpitating and trembling with light. But he retreated from her reaching hands, from her ecstatic face.

He said: "Touch me not, for I am not yet ascended to my Father. But go to my brethren and say to them that I ascend unto my Father, and to my God and your God."

Then Mary came and told the disciples that she had seen the Lord, and that he had spoken these things to her. Then the same day, at evening, being the first day of the week, when the doors were shut where the disciples were assembled for fear of their enemies, came Jesus and stood in their midst. He showed them his hands and his side. Then were the disciples glad, when they saw the Lord, even though they could not touch him.

But not all were sure he was of the flesh. Thomas, who was not with the disciples at this time, later expressed his usual skepticism. "Except I shall see in his hands the print of the nails, and put my finger into the print of the nails, and thrust my hand into his side where he was pierced by the spear, I will not believe."

Eight days later, he stood again in their midst, and as though he had heard Thomas, he said: "Reach your finger here, and touch my hands. Now thrust your hand into my side, and be not faithless, but believing."

Thomas kneeled then, and said: "Forgive me, my Lord and my God, for ever doubting."

Jesus' face was like a wraith. "Thomas, because you have seen me, you now believe. But blessed are they that have not seen, and yet have believed."

The others also fell to their knees, and he raised them with a smile. Yet, even seeing him, it was difficult for them to believe, for they were encumbered by the limitations of their minds. And so he spoke to them once more. "I have told you that all things must be fulfilled which were written in the law of Moses and in the Prophets and in the Psalms concerning me. So that men would understand the truth of the Scriptures and God's word, it behooved Christ to suffer, and to rise from the dead the third day. And now repentance and remission of sins should be preached in his name among all nations, beginning at Jerusalem."

And he led them then to Bethany, to the home of Martha and Lazarus, and of Mary as well, and then he lifted up his hands and blessed them. "I tarry not, but leave the work with you."

"When shall we see you again" Peter asked.

"When your hands shall be stretched out, and you shall be bound and carried where you would not go."

And then they knew what he foresaw for Peter.

Peter cried: "I would gladly die to be with you."

"By believing," said Jesus, "you may have life forever through my name."

And then she who loved him so well asked: "And how long will you abide with us, dear Lord?"

"I come now only so that they who believed not would go into the world and preach the gospel to every creature. But I shall again make myself known, when the hearts of men have hardened against God, and a tyranny of the mind again darkens the world. Then, amid the destruction and the chaos, you shall find me. But not till all shall submit to the Father, knowing that he sent the Promised One for a salvation not of their world but of his. And so when it grows darkest and most confused, when men's arms are raised against one another, and the whole earth trembles, then will the world know that he is near."

And so many wait, knowing that he will come, just as he came before, but this time to a world eager for his word. She who stood ready to anoint him on this earth looks forward to this day, however distant it may seem. She knows, too late, that she sorely misjudged the one who kissed him in the garden. For he had more faith than the rest, since he believed in him unto the death. Would that he had waited but a few more days.

TAYLOR CALDWELL was one of the most prolific and widely read authors of the twentieth century. Born Janet Miriam Holland Taylor Caldwell in Manchester, England, she moved with her family to Buffalo, New York, in 1907. She started writing stories when she was eight years old and completed her first novel when she was twelve. Married at age eighteen, Caldwell worked as a stenographer and court reporter to help support her family and took college courses at night, earning a bachelor of arts degree from the University of Buffalo in 1931. She adopted the pen name Taylor Caldwell because legendary editor Maxwell Perkins thought her debut novel, *Dynasty of Death* (1938), would be better received if readers assumed it were written by a man. In a career that spanned five decades, Caldwell published forty novels, many of which were *New York Times* bestsellers. Her best-known works include the historical sagas *The Sound of Thunder* (1957), *Testimony of Two Men* (1968), *Captains and the Kings* (1972), and *Ceremony of the Innocent* (1976), and the spiritually themed novels *The Listener* (1960) and *No One Hears But Him* (1966). *Dear and Glorious Physician* (1958), a portrayal of the life of St. Luke, and *Great Lion of God* (1970), about the life of St. Paul, are among the best-selling religious novels of all time. Caldwell's last novel, *Answer as a Man* (1981), hit the *New York Times* bestseller list before its official publication date. She died at her home in Greenwich, Connecticut, in 1985.

JESS STEARN has been something of a pioneer in the nonfiction field, treating with frankness the once-taboo subjects of homosexuality (*The Sixth Man*), and drugs (*The Seekers*). His book on yoga (*Yoga, Youth and Reincarnation*) helped to start a vogue in this country. And his *Door to the Future* opened the possibility of psychic phenomena to a previously unconvinced public.

TAYLOR CALDWELL

FROM OPEN ROAD MEDIA

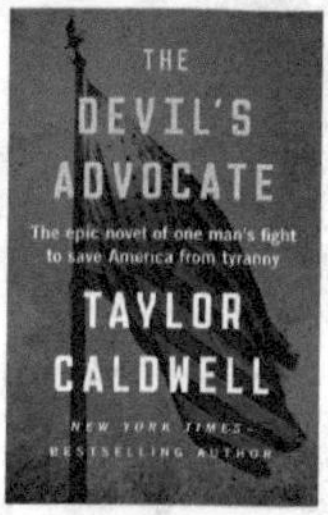